B

Briarwood Publications, Incorporated

The Eyes of Horus

by
George & Debra Kamajian

First Published 2004

Briarwood Publications & Sassy Cat Books, Inc.

150 West College Street

Rocky Mount, Virginia 24151

George and Debra Kamajian

The Eyes of Horus

ISBN 1-892614-47-2

Manufactured in the United States of America.

Printed by Briarwood Publications, Inc.

Hymn to Osiris
The Book of the Dead
3500 BC

Homage to thee, Osiris, Lord of eternity, King of the Gods, whose names are manifold,

whose forms are holy.... Thy name is established in the mouths of men.... The stars in the celestial heights are obedient unto thee, and the great doors of the sky open themselves before thee.

Thou art the Soul of Ra....

Prologue

In 3500 BC, Narmer the Great unified the kingdoms of Upper and lower Khmet, modern day Egypt, establishing the longest lived empire the earth has ever witnessed. The symbol of his power was the double crown, a fusion of the old white and red crowns of his predecessors. In the center of the new crown was the Uraeus, a rearing cobra head, offering the gods' power and protection, with the falcon-headed sky god, Horus, flanking the royal cobra on each side. It has been said that in ancient times, the eyes of Horus were gems the size of a man's fist, dug from the same secret mines later used by King Solomon of biblical fame. This kingdom of the ancient Egyptians lasted four thousand years. Every royal tomb found to date has a depiction of this double crown, passed on to each Pharaoh in a continuous line of succession.

The crown jewels of Britain, France and Russia lay in museums in London, Versailles and St Petersburg, respectively. The sum of their combined ages is still less then half that of the double crown of the ancient Egyptians. The crown has never been found, until....

Florida – the present

"Unfuckin' believable! You kept a picture?"

"Actually, it was a video. Digital, to be exact."

"What were you thinking? If any of this comes out, it could bring an end to everything."

"Christ, you worry too much. I was getting bored with the old tapes. Besides, since when did you become so self-righteous? I've seen some of your souvenirs."

"Some of us have matured since our youth."

"Save it for your priest or whoever you towel heads use to confess your sins."

"Some day I'm going to kill you for talking to me like that."

"Take your best shot!"

"So, tell me...."

"Shit! Look at you; nothings changed. I knew you were gonna' ask. Quite entertaining, really. I put the 18 gauge in his left antecubital vein and slowly bled him into the sand. He was conscious almost to the end. You should have seen him squirm and squeal like the fat pig he was. His own blood dripping out of his arm right in front of him. Blabbed out everything within a matter of minutes."

"What did you do with the body this time?"

"A small church on the outskirts of Ocala. Baptist, I think. Front row center pew. Closest he'll ever come to God. Must be driving the local sheriff crazy just about now. A corpse with no blood, no head and no fingertips to ID. They must be thinkin' the vampires are out."

"Your calling card, again. Fucker deserved it, though. It will serve as a warning to the others. Still, sometimes I think there is something seriously wrong with you."

"And your point is...?"

Boston, Massachusetts – the present
September 10th

The man was dead. That was never going to change. She tried to convince herself that it wasn't her fault and the course of events was inevitable. Still, a lingering doubt remained. That was the disadvantage of a good Catholic upbringing. She had overheard the plans that lead to the murder and did nothing to warn either the police or the unpleasant little twerp whose memory she kept trying to shake. Not that she was sorry; it was just that she knew too much about the whole sordid affair. That was dangerous. Goose bumps formed on her arms as she remembered the way the man struggled for his last breath.

Was she repulsed or excited at some primitive level of her conscience? Guilt was forever. Hanging with the wrong people was her Achilles tendon. She had a history of making poor choices when it came to love. And shit always ran downhill, didn't it? The good life had to eventually come to an end and now the ride was over.

She tried to lose herself with the view from the 24th floor of the Westin but shuttered with the recurring images of the man's last breath. Shame was more difficult to resolve as she grew older. She looked out the window again and closed her eyes. Only the real world was out there when she opened them.

The panorama was stunning. It was just as spectacular as she had imagined and as the Foundation promised. Copley Place was only an architect's dream the last time she had seen Boston. The years had been very kind to the city. To the left lay the Christian Science Center with it's magnificent dome and reflecting pool. Beyond that Mass Avenue snaked its way through the city from Harvard to Roxbury. The competing towers of the Prudential Center and Hancock building split Boylston Street. The Mall with layers of upscale shops was behind her. For a few moments she lost herself in memories of the Back Bay, Freedom Trail, Harvard Yard and Faneuil Hall, steamed clams and beer. The music of Passim's, the brilliant performances at the IMPROV, browsing through the books of the Coop, a magical kiss on the banks of the Charles when a kiss really meant something other then a prelude to sex, all these and more weaved through her mind. Still, the image of the dead man would not go away - just like Marley's ghost.

She turned from the window and sat down on the queen bed giving it a gentle bounce. It was a no smoking room. Was it a matter of honor or did the hotel have special smoke detectors that would notify the management? She toyed with the joint in her hand rolling it back and forth between her fingertips. To smoke or not to smoke, that was the question. The invitation for the interview was an unambiguous 10:00 a.m. sharp. That left about a half an hour before it was time to go. She hadn't smoked anything in 24 hours and her nerves screamed in protest. New Englanders had the reputation of being pretty tight assed and politically correct. She didn't want to blow her chances for a fellowship by offending some old biddy on the executive board with her marijuana breath. The joint returned to her purse. For rescue purposes only, she promised.

The wall mirror in the suite couldn't compete with the wonderful magnifying mirror in the bathroom. She loved staring at herself, shifting her head repeatedly to catch the best light. She was pretty and she knew it. The bruises on her right cheek and below her left eye were almost imperceptible under the layers of foundation and pressed powder. The past was dead and she knew that as well. The events of the past week just accelerated her decision to leave the hedonistic life of the Florida Keys for something more sensible and safer.

It was at least twenty degrees colder in Boston than in Florida this time of year. She had to dress appropriately – not so casually as to suggest Parrot Head indifference or so formally as to be overwhelmingly preppy. The suede skirt and angora sweater with mid calf boots would do perfectly. She tied her shoulder length brown hair into a mischievous ponytail. The mysterious invitation, airline tickets and hotel confirmation had arrived at her condo only twenty-four hours before. She had precious little time to arrange coverage at the shop. Thank God, Pat was able to dog-sit Cricket on such short notice. Opportunities like this came only once in a lifetime and she wasn't going to let this pass by without giving it her best shot. An old manuscript, lost in the passage of time, somehow caught the attention of the Foundation. The surprising offer to come up north was enough to rekindle a long sublimated dream. It might even be time to settle down.

At quarter to ten she turned off "Imus in the Morning" and left the room. The arrival of the elevator was almost instantaneous and she was the only one on it for the first ten floors down. On the 14th floor an obnoxious pair of Japanese businessmen joined her, starring at her chest and chattering on their cell phones the entire ride down to the lobby. Helpless, she surrendered in frustrated silence, starring at her shoes.

The elevator reached the main floor after what seemed forever. Her tormentors dissolved into a hotel restaurant diagonally across the lobby. As she exited the elevator, a flying elbow and teetering stroller, belonging to a harried mother with two screaming and kicking toddlers, bumped into her. The two women briefly exchanged glances, both jealous of each other's station in life, then went their separate ways.

The reception area was empty this time of day. Check-in wasn't until three pm and checkout wasn't until noon. Behind the front desk two management interns with 'May I help you' buttons on their lapels stood frozen in time, savaged by their supervisor for some unknown infraction. The senior staff man seemed oblivious to the volume he used in his discipline.

Outside the air was refreshing, the doorman polite but distant as she waited for her pickup. The sky was cloudless and a magnificent powder puff blue. For a moment she had to shield her eyes against the intensity of the morning sun. It was a perfect fall day with brisk temperatures and air saturated with the fragrance of fallen leaves and ripe apples. Who knows, she thought, maybe she'd learn how to pick apples all over again.

At exactly 10:00 am a limo pulled curbside with her name in the window. Impeccable timing, she thought. She entered the cave- like darkness of the vehicle with a new optimism for her future. The limo doors locked automatically. It took a second before she realized she wasn't alone in the back seat.

"You!" she exclaimed.

"Relax and enjoy the ride suga' pie."

From Akenaten's Hymn to Aten
1350 BC - 850 BC

When thou settest in the western horizon...
Every lion cometh forth from his den...
Bright is the earth when thou riseth...
The birds flutter in their marshes...
They sing among thebranches...
Thou suppliest his necessities
That thou may give them food in due
season.

Old Testament Psalm 104

Thou makest darkness, and it is night...
The young lions roar after their prey...
The Sun riseth...
By them the birds of the heavens have
Their wings uplifted in adoration

Valley of the Kings
329 BC

Tanis, robber of graves and lowly servant to the outcast god Seth, hated scorpions more then any other threat from this barren land. They were creatures uniformly without honor. This one was the size of his thumb. He had disturbed its nest in the cool shade of a rock ledge when he had blindly pushed his tools ahead of him on this climb. Now this thing, cursed of the gods, scurried around with both pincers and tail raised in the posture of attack. The poison in its tail was formidable for almost any living thing. Tanis watched as it darted about the sand in anger looking for a defendable position. The scorpion had never seen a human before and hesitated fatally while dancing its dance of death. Tanis had only one choice and he did not waver. He took a stone the size of his fist and sent the creature into the next life. Praise Re. Praise Horus. Praise Osiris. As it was, it shall always be.

Taking a small swig from his sheepskin water bag, he held the precious liquid in his mouth for a few moments then swallowed. A few droplets of water leaked down his stubble-bearded chin. The nearest wells were three days march to the east. This was no time to waste water or energy. Carefully he replaced the stopper and surveyed the view from his perch. In the distance he could see the outline of the Appis Mountains. The peaks glowed red from Atum-Re, the sun. To the south, barely perceptible, shimmered the reflection of the great mother Nile. He had no idea how much longer his climb would be tonight. Success was always a matter of chance. The tombs rumored to be in this canyon had never been revealed, at least not to anyone who lived to talk about it. Each step up was a mystery. It was only the vague images of last night's dream that lead him to this particular rock face today. Tanis hoped the dream was an omen from the gods.

Wiping his mouth on his tunic sleeve he began to climb. The ascent up the limestone walls was steep and treacherous. His muscles strained with every reach above his head. Eons of ancient dust disturbed from his efforts mixed with sweat, forming a pale paste on his reddish brown skin. Just like the spirits of the dead, he thought. Just like the spirits if they existed, indeed. Tanis kept one eye open for more scorpions while scanning for the tell tale pink granite chips amongst the limestone debris. That would indicate the work of the Carvers, the men who labored these rock faces for the Pharaohs centuries before. Those colored pieces of stone would lead him to success. They were the key.

A find of any kind meant wealth forever. Many of his clan had gone before him but few returned from their treks into the desert. Those who lived were always silent about their experiences, enveloped in the aura of mystery forever. Village wags would keep the fire of their discoveries alive with each piece of gold the grave robbers brought to market. Tales of magic and treasure followed them into their own humble graves until the next generation sought their own paths into tombs of the ancient ones.

God King Alexander claimed the throne of the Sun only five years before. His new capital, Alexandria, was, even now, being carved out of the Delta while Alexander marched to the east. The Nile still flooded and faithfully blessed the land, but farmers did not plant their grain. Foreigners, who had no respect for the old ways, ruled the children of the Sun. Ancient temples at Thebes and Luxor were in disrepair and all but abandoned. Old prayers and old ways were forgotten by all but a few. The new rulers made no effort to learn the language of their people, so even the scribes languished.

For generations Tanis' kinsmen had prided themselves on their ability to find the old tombs and retrieve their treasures. Now it was his turn. He shifted his tool bag and searched for a promising ledge, his gnarled hands reaching for a crevice in the cliff face, slowly pulling himself up to this new footing. There was barely room for a man to stand, even of his short stature. The glare of the sun baked his face as he broke out into a smile. In front of him were a series of carvings. The Eye of Horus, the falcon, the river gods all marched east to west, the large stella teasing him with ancient secrets. If only he could read, he thought, but that sacred duty belonged to the priest and scribes. His hands traced the rock face and looked for evidence of prior visits by those of his profession, but he could find nothing that suggested anyone had been to this tomb for a thousand years. The door of the tomb was still sealed. Tanis reached for his tools and smiled.

Fall River, Massachusetts
September 11th

She opened her eyes, slowly, cautiously. Nothing changed. Everything was black. Her head was still covered and it was the only thing she could move. How long was she out this time? Minutes? Hours? She wanted to yell for help but knew her screams would make them hurt her more. She took in a deep breath. That meant she was still alive. Now she was really afraid. Pain came back in shooting searing waves that gripped every fabric of her being. In spite of the darkness she could sense she wasn't alone. Somewhere, near by, they were waiting.

A hood was tied tightly over her head and face. There was a noise to her right. "Please don't do this," she pleaded in short halting gasps. She felt paralyzed, her arms and legs tied spread eagle to a table, its decrepit legs rocking dangerously with each wild shift in her weight. She knew her clothes were gone and she couldn't move. The room was cold and smelled of old urine and stale cigarettes. Fighting against her tormenters, her breaths came rapidly, the ropes cutting deeper into her skin. Every moment in the darkness brought death closer and she knew that as surely as God was absent from this room.

The men who surrounded the table saw her futile struggle. They relished in the torment; each with their fantasies. Even in near darkness they could see the suck of burlap against their victim's open mouth. The dim candlelight reflected their shadows moving around the woman in near choreographed patterns. The men's voices came in hushed tones and whispers, all playing homage to the demons within. Time, for this woman, was near an end. When you die, the whole world dies.

Disembodied voices moved around the room increasing her disorientation. Now the drugs forced on her began to take effect. Even raising her head was an effort beyond her strength. "Please listen to me," she slurred. "Just let me go. I promise never to tell anyone. I swear I won't say a word."

"It's too late for begging, suga' pie. Just go to sleep and let the boys have their fun."

Fall River, Massachusetts
October 1st

He inched forward on his stomach underneath the wreckage. Twisted pieces of metal and broken glass littered the pavement. He had to reach his wife. The cacophony of sirens and screams of the wounded swirled all around him; but he was oblivious to everything. Nothing mattered except her. There, one last push and he could just about hold her hand. Rose's face was just out of reach. Her face that guided him through all the insanity of the years looked past him, through him. Just keep looking in my eyes; just keep looking at me and everything will be all right. They're going to get you out soon, honey. The baby, our baby, she mouthed silently, her eyes slowly emptying of life with every heartbeat. Her hands were ice cold, colder then anything alive should be.

The pungent smell of gasoline, smoke and blood filled the air. Come on! Someone do something before it's too late! His hands, massive compared to her delicate fingers, were sticky with blood. How could someone so delicate hold so much blood? It just kept coming and coming. Oh God. Someone help me! Anyone!

He awoke drenched in sweat groping for the cell phone at his bedside. The alarm clock crashed to the floor flashing 12:00. Damn power must have gone out again. No telling what time it was. "Ekizian," he answered. Flashes of the reoccurring nightmare dissolved like soap bubbles, yielding comfort in amnesia.

"Hey, bud! It's Sherman. You awake?"

He leaned over to pick up his watch from the crumpled pile of clothes on the floor. "Yeah, sure," he grunted. The auto illuminator was on the blink. He still couldn't tell what time it was.

"Come on, Derek. Get your ass out of bed. There's work to do. Are you listening?" asked Sherman, Lieutenant and watch commander for the third shift.

"With both ears," Derek mumbled, barely awake. He began to scribble details on a bedside note pad but the damn pen was running dry. He should have tossed it weeks ago. One of the last souvenirs from a Caribbean cruise back in his old life, he didn't have the heart to get rid of it. The last few lines ended up as indents in the paper. A pencil rub would retrieve the information later. A coughing spell racked his chest as he blew green into the last of his Kleenex. "Whadda' we know?"

"More then one and less than a hundred. How the hell do I know? Peterson and Lefevre have the call," Sherman snorted. He gave Derek an address in the city's Flint district. "By the way, you sound awful. How long have you been blowin' snots?"

"Just a few days now. I'm fine," Derek said, snorting in a wad of mucous. He wheezed and coughed some more. This time he covered the receiver to mute the sounds. Murders were infrequent in Fall River. Multiple homicides were almost unheard of. He didn't want to give his boss any excuse to turf this case to someone else.

"You sure, Derek? I wouldn't want your mommy mad at me because I sent you out into the cold." Sherman mocked.

"I said I'm fine," Derek replied, annoyed with his friend and boss' torment.

"Whatever. Now move your ass before I change my mind and call the Moose." Sherman commanded. "He's second call tonight."

Derek snorted at the image of Dave Camara, a.k.a. the Moose. He was a nice enough guy but dumber then a stone. The thought of a man that size maneuvering his massive frame around a crime scene was comical. "Screw Camara. Besides he couldn't find his way to the 7-11 without a map and a GPS unit. The door is closin' on my butt now," Derek said. He hung up on his boss without giving him a chance to respond.

Derek staggered to the bathroom in the dark, his left hand groping for the light switch while his right hand scratched his crotch. He turned on the shower and stepped inside without the customary wait. The water pressure was intense, blistering icy needles pounding his skin into wakefulness. Thirty seconds later he exited the shower shivering but alert. The face that greeted him in the mirror was less then majestic. It had been a bad couple of years. His wavy black hair was too long. His mustache was thick and untrimmed. Dark circles accentuated his hazel eyes, bloodshot from drinking late into the evening. He worked the Dollar Store comb futilely to rein in his mane, finally giving up and ran his fingers through his hair. Listerine and a few tic-tacs would masquerade the evening's sins. Spitting out the last of the mouthwash he wiped his mouth on the back of his hand. It was time to go.

Valley of the Kings, 329 BC

Tanis lit his last torch. The shadows of the hieroglyphs on the walls seemed to dance as he moved about the room. It was clear he had reached the final chamber, the actual burial room of someone who had once been very important. The sarcophagus before him was massive; it's silver surface shimmering in the light. Complex designs he recognized as the Books of the Dead, the secret incantations that permitted passage from this world into the next, covered the tomb.

He maneuvered his tools with expert precision. Patience and preparation was the key. That, which may have taken five men to set in the ancient times, yielded to levers and wedges developed by his family from years of experience in entering tombs uninvited. The top of the sarcophagus slid off to the side supported by the base at three points. Tanis waved his torch up and down its entire length. The mummy of the last truly Egyptian Pharaoh lay before him but he was ignorant of this fact. He had been in many burial chambers in search of treasure and even a few of these were of royalty. The space, the complexity and the quantity of objects left for the afterlife suggested the true origins of this site. The wooden coffin easily separated into two halves with a twist of his blade. The mummy was expertly wrapped in fancy linens but Tanis's attention was riveted to the death mask. It gleamed with the reflection of solid gold. There was no doubt in his mind he was in the presence of a great king from his people's past. His first impulse to keep this object ended in disappointment when he went to place it in his bag. The weight was massive. He never would have made it down the cliff face carrying this burden. A march in the desert would have been fatal.

Three hours were left to explore, extract those items he desired and to return to his camp at the base of the cliff. To spend the night was unthinkable. Tanis searched the sarcophagus for more kingly treasures. A renewed inspection of the burial chamber revealed a trove of chariots, boats, and personal belongings suitable for the next life. His foot struck an object that crashed to the floor. A wave of the torch revealed a skeleton, probably that of a personal slave who had been entombed alive with his master. Tanis returned to his search.

He needed objects he could easily carry away. Too many of his kinsmen had been conquered by greed in the desert on their return.

A spectacular gold dagger lay at the mummy's waist along side the royal crook and flail. The dagger he would keep. The crook and flail were too long and bulky. If he were successful in returning home it would have brought him too much attention. Tanis searched the sarcophagus one last time. His eyes settled on an object at the foot of the mummy. He was surprised to have missed it the first time. It was a crown. He had seen depictions of something similar to this on temple walls when pilgrimages to the holy sites were still in fashion. The precious stones imbedded in it seemed to dance with color and life in the flickering light of his torch. His pulse quickened, his fingers resonating from the touch of the ancient object. This was something he had to have. Tanis recognized multiple royal symbols and emblems. Centered on top was a cobra head and Horus, the falcon god. Jewels the size of apricots gleamed from the eyes of both gods. Many other characters flanked the main carvings on the crown. Most were familiar to him only as amulets worn by his fellow villagers, their real names lost forever in the passage of time. The royal priests had done their job well. The last thing they would have expected was for the crown to become the property of one lowly servant to Seth, the outcast god, Tanis of Thebes.

Rings, medallions, broaches, goblets and more were scooped inside his sheepskin satchel then secured for the climb down. Levers and wedges were expertly applied again to return the lid of the sarcophagus back to its original position. Few priests remained to spread the words of the ancient teaching. Still Tanis knew enough about the Books of the Dead to observe certain rituals. He was a practical man and, though not a true believer of the old ways and the old gods, he didn't want to take any chances.

Tanis did his best to seal the tomb in the manner before his violation. He exited backwards, saying fragments of the ancient prayers the best he could. He never paid that much attention to the village elders in his days of learning and now he regretted the omission. Slowly he retraced his steps down the limestone cliffs. The ancient burial chambers were cool compared to the desert sun at his back. A few hours more and he would be shivering in the cold when the sun plunged below the horizon. The weight of his treasure was already causing him to stumble. Tanis shifted the bag to his opposite shoulder and then shifted once more trying to find a comfortable and stable position. This was going to be a long trip home.

Flint District, Fall River
October 1st

The indigo nightglow was broken, again. He should have thrown the damn thing away months ago. Derek looked at his watch and shook it in disgust. It had to be almost four o'clock in the morning, a decent time only for hookers and cats. According to the shrinks, the transfer from vice to homicide was meant to help his sleep, not ruin it. Detective Sergeant Derek Ekizian, Homicide Division, Fall Rive Police Department was definitely pissed. It was cold – colder then it should have been for this time of year. He drew his parka hood tight around his head. Why couldn't people be found dead at a more convenient hour?

Yellow police tape blocked his entrance to the front door of the building. He made quick work of the plastic barrier, waved on by a rookie cop who recognized him from last week's lecture at the Academy. "Second floor, Sir."

"Thanks. It's Marty, right?" Derek said stumbling on a dismantled water heater.

The man nodded. "Pretty messy, I hear," the patrolman said.

Derek mumbled something less then witty in response and headed to the side entrance. All the doors of the tenement were missing, probably resting in the warehouse of one of Boston's finer restoration companies. Most of Fall River was being dismantled day by day. The first few steps swayed and creaked with every move, betraying the age of the structure. All six feet 225 pounds of him leaned forward to counter the angle of the dilapidated stairwell. He had forgotten his flashlight in the rush to get to the crime scene. Now there was only the moonlight to guide his steps into the depths of the old building.

Green and yellow mucous seeped out of his tender nose, clinging to his mustache. His cold was getting worse instead of better. Unfortunately his last Kleenex littered the front seat of his car a half-mile back. Sick was bad, but dead was worse. It was damn inconsiderate to force total strangers to get up at four a.m. to claim your body - or bodies in this instance.

The reported details of the homicide swirled with the stress of yesterday's margin call on Intel. Was it the decongestants, the booze or the hour that made everything so jumbled? A few thousand here and a few thousand there and pretty soon only bankruptcy would satisfy the leeches at Merrill Lynch. They encouraged his aggressive play and, when things went to hell, they couldn't even remember his name except to send him call notices.

His mind raced through police procedure manuals. Everything had to be by the proverbial book. What did his first series of notes have to include in order to satisfy the Captain for the morning report? The rickety steps groaned with his weight as he plodded up the stairs huffing and puffing with each third or fourth step of the climb. The prospect of refinancing his house again made him cringe. Worse, the remote possibility of screwing up his first homicide report this calendar year could only contribute to his sluggish march up the career ladder. This investigation had to be perfect.

Derek pulled at the railing for support and quickly recognized his mistake. It had more gaps then balusters, almost pitching him over the side. Risking his neck to do his job was part of the game, but this was ridiculous. He rested on the second floor landing to catch his breath and focus on the job ahead. The building reeked of death even through his diseased sinuses. It was impossible to miss the smell – no rocket science. The maggots must have gotten to this scene at least a week before. Maggots, flies, and death: all part of nature's grand scheme. And he was on his way to sort everything out, God willing.

Amara, Egypt
329 BC

"Tell us again, Grandfather," the child begged. A dozen children formed an imperfect circle at his feet. The majority disciplined the few who chattered or quarreled above the gravel like voice of their grandfather. Moments later the circle settled in anticipation.

Hek-Anun sighed and put down his knife and the new comb he was carving for his wife's name day. He sat cross-legged on the bare dirt floor, staring into the distance as he recalled the stories of the ancient ones. His grandchildren deserved his full attention, for this was their heritage. Someday they would take his place and repeat this cycle to their children as his own father had done for him. He began, "In the beginning was the Nun, the great nothing. The Gods of Space and Darkness guarded a Great Egg in the waters of the Forever."

"How big was the egg, Grandfather?" the smallest child asked. She had beautiful curly hair but at the moment her name eluded him. He had so many grandchildren from his bloodline, that he could forget their names without being chastised by his wife.

"Oh, bigger then an ostrich egg, I'm quite sure," he answered gently, patting her on the head. "Soon the egg hatched. Now, from the Egg arose a single blue Lotus. Within its petals appeared the Creator God, Amen-Re, who brought order to the chaos with the Word and the Light. From his thoughts alone, he created Thoth and by his side he placed the great Maat, Goddess of Justice and Truth, and many others after them."

"Was he like my daddy?" the same little girl asked.

"Yes. Big and strong just like your daddy," Hek-Anun replied with infinite patience. "Our gods loved and fought like men, but not like men. Sometimes they were good and sometimes they followed the path of darkness. Now, out of the forbidden union of Nut, Goddess of the Heavens and Geb, God of Earth, came Osiris, the Lord of Creation, Horus, whose right eye is the sun and the left eye the moon, Seth, the Lord of Warfare and Chaos, and Isis, Goddess of Love, Magic and Wisdom. Last of all, he created Men and a land in which they might dwell, the kingdom of Khmet, Egypt."

"Are there other lands besides Khmet?" the eldest asked, a

short, fat boy of thirteen years.

"Yes, but they are not blessed by the gods. Men there live like beasts and wear clothes made out of the skins of animals. Now can I finish please?"

The children all nodded their heads in assent.

"And it came to pass that Seth became jealous of Osiris and caused him to be killed. Horus entered into a great war with Seth to avenge the death of his father. In this war, Horus lost his left eye, the moon, when Seth tore it to pieces. Thoth discovered the eye and, using magic, reassembled the pieces. Horus then gave the eye to Osiris, who was reborn in the underworld. See, children," he said pointing to the amulet worn about his neck. "This is why we wear the Eye of Horus to protect us, this and the blue beads and my Ank. Some day you, too, will wear these talismans.

"Can I give my eye to Osiris?" the littlest girl asked.

"No, child, it is only by magic and power of the gods that this can be. It is not for men to try and imitate the gods." Hek-Anun looked towards the door with surprise. He was so engrossed with his story telling that he had not seen his eldest son, Tanis, enter the room.

The younger man leaned against the door of the mud brick hut and smiled. He nodded in acknowledgement and raised the sack by his side just high enough to catch his father's eye.

Hek-Anun realized that his son's trek into the desert had been a success. Story time was over. "Go, children. Go. It is time for your dinners. Come visit later," he said, shooing the little ones out of his home.

Tanis approached his father and kissed his hand in respect. "I see you are still telling the same old tales."

"We would all do well to remember the old stories and live our lives in the old ways." Hek-Anun said, returning his son's greeting with a hug. He focused his eyes on the bag by Tanis's side. "Was your trip profitable?"

Tanis came nearer to his father and whispered, "More then your dreams." Slowly he opened the bag. One by one he removed the kingly treasures and placed them in front of Hek-Anun, deliberately teasing the old man.

Each revelation was intoxicating. Hek-Anun's gaze on the objects was unbroken by the buzz of flies, barking village dogs or the playful cries of children. The stains in his white beard were matched only by the poverty of the linen that hung loosely around his frail body. Now he saw that all this was about to change. Nothing mattered now except for treasure. Both men knew the items before them represented royalty. Finally Tanis pulled on the bottom of the hemp and sheepskin revealing the ultimate prize. His father looked in awe. Never before had anything so beautiful or more frightening been brought into his home.

Reverently Hek-Anun held the object in his hands moving it closer to the window to examine the details of this masterpiece. The setting sun cascaded across the metal, its light dancing between the cut facets of the magnificent jewel stones that ran almost uninterrupted around the base. He shifted the crown from side to side, rotating it in his rough hands, savoring the moment. Finally he looked back up at his son and frowned. "You must return it," he said after a few moments of contemplation. "It is cursed by the priests."

Tanis laughed. "The priests are all dead. Now tell me, what is it?"

"It is the crown of upper and lower Khmet, Egypt. It is older then the stars. The hieroglyphs speak of it on every temple wall in the valley."

"These markings around the top?" Tanis asked.

"It tells the story of creation, just as you heard me tell the children a few moments ago." Heck-Anun's knarled fingers traced the carvings in the metal with frightened reverence. "Here is Nun, and there Amon-Re. On top are Horus and Uraeus. By all the gods, I have never beheld anything as wondrous as this. The stones alone are worth a kings ransom."

"And?"

"And it is cursed to have among us. It is not for mortal man. You must return it."

"What makes this any different then those treasures our fathers have taken from the ancient kings for generation upon generation?" Tanis scoffed.

Hek-Anun shook his head. "There is only one double crown in all our people's time. Only one! Do you hear me?" He paced the small room agitated in voice and motions of his hands. "Believe in the gods! Believe in the priests! They have been with us forever. Ignore them at your own peril!"

Tanis laughed at his father's fear. "Never," he said placing the crown on his own head mocking his father. "See, it is nothing more then metal and shiny stones. Besides, someone may follow me if I return to the mountains so soon and I would surely be killed. Is that what you want? Remember, once into the desert, once out. It was you who taught me that."

Hek-Anun reached over and unceremoniously removed the crown from his son's head. "But no one of our people has ever returned with anything such as this," his father quaked, nervously stroking his long beard. "Here, put this away. If the priests do not discover our secret then surely the soldiers of the Greeks will follow you here and destroy us all."

Tanis laughed and refused again. "Relax, ancient one. The Greeks are fools. Only a true Egyptian could find the path to the tombs and even fewer could work their way up the cliff face. Besides, I doubt the Greeks would even recognize what I placed in your hands."

Hek-Anun shook his head in disagreement. Fear was gnawing him. "Still, you cannot remain. Someone will wag their tongue and we will all lose our heads. You must go. Tell no one, not even your dear old father, where. Just go."

"I have told no one except you, Father," Tanis lied. Only Nefertari had seen his treasure, but she was his wife. She would never say a word to anyone. "But I will do as you ask and remove this treasure from our poor village. I wouldn't want you to get any more gray in your beard," Tanis teased exiting his ancestral home.

"May the gods keep you safe on your journey!" his father called out behind him.

Tanis turned away and strode confidently from his father's side with slow deliberate steps. At the far end of the village was the communal well. He needed its gift from the earth before he could continue on his journey. It took several minutes to turn the crank before the bucket returned with its liquid treasure. He lingered long enough to fill his water bags and then wearily began the trek into the hills once again. Tanis doubled back on his trail several times to avoid being followed. By sunset, he felt confident that he was alone with just the stars for his companion in the desert, but he was deadly wrong.

Flint District, Fall River
October 1st

"Keep on comin'. You're almost here, you old fart!" a familiar voice taunted.

Derek recognized Wayne Peterson's New England twang immediately. Peterson had two speeds – serious and goofy. If Peterson was joking then things were secure at the crime scene. No rookie cop blunders to clean up. No sleep, a lingering bronchitis and an over all grumpy disdain for his life left Derek winded and even more cynical then usual. It was a dangerous combination. Turning thirty-nine made it harder to recuperate from an evening's excess. The thought of the big 'four-o' made him wince. He needed more gym time and to cut back on the booze. This resolution faded into the night air before he stepped through the threshold of the apartment. Promises without consequence always did. Tonight he needed Kleenex and a little codeine for his cough. And sleep – lots of sleep.

Peterson greeted him at the entrance of the apartment. The man was a fireplug in stature and temperament, his face like a tattered baseball. "Pretty messy, boss. Prepare yourself."

"Thanks for the warning. Have you guys scoped out the place yet?"

"We were kind of waiting for you," Peterson replied sheepishly. He shifted nervously from foot to foot. "No screw ups, right?"

"Right!" Both men winced privately. The past summer an easy murder conviction had been thrown out of court because of a rookie-league procedural error. The officer in charge was forced to take an early retirement. Reverberations from the D.A.'s office made it look like the entire Fall River Police department were idiots. Talk from the street was that Fall River was the best place in the country to get away with murder.

Derek's eyes adjusted to the room. The night shadows camouflaged little. He knew this place like the back of his hand. Fall River, one of the first mill towns in New England, was full of tenements long abandoned to pigeons and graffiti. Peeling layers of linoleum magically animated to trip him as he explored the rooms. Broken glass from windows long used for target practice by local street punks crunched under his feet. In the past, these walls were defended by squat, tired immigrant women hiding behind their doors waiting for the "poletsia" to leave their delinquent sons alone. Now, even their ghosts had abandoned the buildings, surrendering to the local rats.

Derek braced himself against the doorframe to catch his breath and caught his mistake too late. "Shit!" He rubbed his fingers together in disgust. The stickiness on his hand was human in origin. Moonlight pierced the shredded walls and windows revealing red smears everywhere. This was going to be a messy one, the investigation complex and invariably referred to the Massachusetts State Police Detective Unit. Fall River deserved its reputation as a den of iniquity, but murders were extraordinary. Just when something nice and juicy came along he had to share jurisdiction with a bunch of idiots who were nothing more then glorified registry cops. "Gloves, folks," he called out. He gave his thick black mustache a nervous twist with his clean hand.

"We're way ahead of you." The accent was Woonsocket French. Armand Lefevre, Wayne's partner of fifteen years, stepped forward from behind the glare of a halogen light. Armand was average and nondescript in everything but his police talents. Behind his mime- like demeanor was a student of human nature. Most importantly he had instinct, without which every cop would be dead in the water. Derek knew his job was easier tonight with both Peterson and Lefevre on duty.

A string of wind chimes and beads hung like a wad of cobwebs in the front hall. Great, another coke or crack head hangout. The city had an abundance of this kind of real estate. This was just a crack house, plain and simple. He moved deeper into the room. The darkness became oppressive with the odor of decaying human flesh. That fact was remarkable considering windows in this apartment were nonexistent. His mind wandered to his rookie days. The first time he had seen a dead bod, maggots and small animals had dined for weeks on the corpse before it was discovered. It was pretty disgusting then. He didn't expect anything different now. Depending on the outside temperature, maggots hatched in five to seven days. He wondered who had alerted the police. "Anyone have an extra torch?"

"Got you covered." A woman's voice, soft but business like, came from the right.

He smiled. It was Kelly. "Dr Gill. It's a pleasure to have you on board tonight." A full time emergency physician and part time medical examiner, she handed Derek a halogen lamp and took out a small pocket flashlight for herself. So even the medical examiner had beaten him to the scene. Everyone was pretty excited about the city's first homicide of the year.

"You were expecting Dr Livingston, maybe?" she asked tongue in cheek.

"Hi," he said reaching over to give her a friendly kiss. All he caught was air and a wisp of Alliage perfume as Kelly retreated from his familiar gesture. Professional or pissed, that was a question that suddenly bothered him more then the work he was about to do. Even at four a.m. she was beautiful - legs that began at her neck, strawberry blond hair, and piercing blue eyes that made him buckle at the knees. She was thirty-two and professional to a fault on the job. Their off-the-job relationship was an enigmatic tease to both.

"Hey, what was that about?" he whispered. There was no need to give Peterson any more ammunition to taunt their quasi-relationship.

"You know damn well," Kelly replied curtly. Shielding their conversation from the front bedroom with her back, she applied a streak of Vicks VapoRub, the autopsy standard room deodorizer, to the front of her mask. "Here. You'd better put this on," she said, handing him a mask. She coarsely smeared the contents of the bottle on his mustache. "You deserve that," Kelly said, poking him in the middle of his chest. "I can smell your breath right through the maggots. I guarantee you haven't heard the last of it from me. Quit drinking when you're on the job!" she demanded.

One look from her squashed his instinct to protest and deny. It was not the first time she had brought this up. "Hey, it was just a couple of beers," he sputtered.

"Bull-crap!" Kelly said, wagging her finger in his face. "You spill more in a day then most people drink in a month. It's got to stop." The wounded puppy dog look on her friend's face tempered her anger. "Please, Derek. Please," she entreated turning away, embarrassed with her aggressiveness.

Everyone drank, didn't they? Not in Kelly's universe, it seemed. Did he really violate the line between private behavior and professional responsibility? If he hung around her long enough, he might even start to think that way himself. "Thanks for the warning. Sorry. It won't happen again," he replied quietly, humiliated his evening's indiscretions were so obvious. His head hurt. His throat was sore. If he weren't afraid of contaminating a crime scene, he probably would have coughed up his own lung tonight. This was going to be a long night.

Amara Valley, Egypt
329 BC

Ay watched his prey carefully from the top of the ridge. Below, his wife's brother, Tanis, worked his way along the valley floor, keeping to the shadows. The man's pace suggested he was only seeking shade and not attempting to evade pursuit. Ay smiled. This was going to be easier then he thought. He rubbed his back on a sharp outcrop of rocks while keeping his eyes fixed on the man below. Ay had followed many of the tomb robbers from his village after successful expeditions. All sought to hide their plunder removed from the earth back into it. Each trove from his oblivious victims was lightened just enough to enrich his own horde; not enough to bring suspicion upon him. Others did the work and risk their necks while he shared in their good fortune.. Nefertari, his mistress and wife of the man he stalked, had taken him into her confidence.. Tanis had obtained something magnificent from a royal tomb. Tonight only one of them would come out of the desert. With Tanis out of the way, he could have wealth beyond his dreams. That was Nefertari's promise.

The man, whose life he sought to end, rested in the shade of a large boulder. Ay silently worked his way down the trail and now stood less then half an arrow's shot away. He watched greedily as Tanis took a long swallow from his water bag then used it as a headrest for a quick nap out of the sun's reach. Within minutes Tanis was stretched out asleep.

The shot was so simple that a child could make it. Ay selected the arrow from his harness, stretched out the bow, drew the leather bowstring taught, then let fly. The arrow was true to its mark striking the man in the chest. His poor victim sat bolt upright with the blow then just as quickly crumpled collapsing on the ground in one violent spasm. Ay scrambled down the hill and stood over his brother-in-law's body.

Tanis was still alive, but barely. The arrow had pierced his chest on the right side, blood filling his lungs with every heartbeat. Tanis looked at Ay first with a pathetic surprise then hatred for his assassin. Blood foamed in the corner of his mouth and dribbled down his cheek. His legs thrashed in violent spasms in a futile attempt to stand. Death would not come quietly. Replete in the knowledge of his total defeat, Tanis' struggle ceased.

Ay moved closer and squatted next to his victim, rocking on his heels as he watched the man's final moments. He was fascinated with death, particularly if brought by his own hand. This was as close as he would ever get to being a god. He roughly removed the water pouch that had been Tanis' headrest and drank freely of it. "I'm quite thirsty after all this." He waited for a response but found none. "You can thank your wife. She is a wonderful lover, by the way." He enjoyed this part of the torture most of all. "You've probably been too busy to notice but has anyone ever commented on how little your daughter looks like you?"

Tanis attempted to rise but fell back again. Even hatred could not give him the strength for one last blow against his tormentor.

The bag of treasure lay at Tanis's feet. Ay took his knife and split the seam. The cache from the recent raid on the royal tomb lay exposed. He raised the largest object on the point of his blade. "Ah, what have we here?" Colors of the universe radiated from the gold encrusted jewels. It held no meaning for him except as a means to secure the woman. He placed everything in his own bag and turned his attention back to Tanis. The sun was slowly beginning its descent. It was time to move on. "Sorry my friend." Ay put one foot against the dying man's chest and crudely pulled the arrow out returning it to his quiver. The agony would have been unimaginable, but Tanis was now dead. "Nothing gets wasted in the desert, Eh?"

Flint District, Fall River
October 1st

"The first one is to your right," Kelly said. She waved her gloved hand toward an indistinct figure in the kitchen.

A body sat crumpled in a kitchen chair leaning precariously against a wall. Derek shined his halogen lamp on a bloated corpse. The figure of a black male, mid twenties, appeared to have a low caliber gunshot wound to the front of his head. He circled the victim's head with his lamp. There was no apparent exit wound. Derek anticipated a round could be retrieved for potential identification. The remains of a cigarette stub was clenched in the victim's hand. Half tied sneaker laces spilled on to the floor. A menagerie of homemade tattoos, baggy pants and pierced eyebrows completed the picture.

"Looks like he was sitting here having a smoke," Derek noted. He searched his memory for any similarities between the tattoos on the kid and those in the weekly updates from the gang unit. "Might have known his shooter. Next?"

"Over here," Peterson called from the dining room. He maneuvered his Neanderthal figure through the debris of the abandoned rooms with the grace of a figure skater. Nothing touched the crime scene except for his feet.

How does he do that, Derek wondered shaking his head. Peterson overcame both gravity and God's practical jokes when dispensing body parts to be one of the department's toughest street cops. "Hey, how did you guys get the call?" Derek asked. He weaved his way in and out of scraps of furniture and ceiling debris with significantly less success then his friend.

"The usual," Peterson replied. "Anonymous tip from a phone booth around the corner. Not enough neighbors living within a hundred feet to see or hear anything."

Lefevre snuck up behind Peterson, making shadow puppets on the wall above his friend's head. He stopped only when threatened with a kick. "Hey," Armand said, "I hear the state legislature just passed the military buy-back bill."

"About time." Peterson pivoted just in time to see another image of a rabbit dancing on his patrol cap. "Will you get the fuck away from me!"

"I'm not touching you," Lefevre said defensively, dropping his hands back to his sides.

"Ten percent of your first year base salary is all you need to add to your pension time," Derek added, ignoring the rabbit. "You guys have been on the force so long that ten percent of your first year's salary would be about a hundred dollars. Isn't that what they paid you back in the horse and buggy days?"

"Very funny, Sarge," Wayne said. "But you need to be on the job for at least fifteen years before you can even consider the buy-back and I know you don't qualify."

"I'm not going to let those four years in the Marines go to waste," Derek answered.

"*Semper fi*, bro." Lefevre replied. "Looks like it's already gone to your waist, if you know what I mean."

"Screw you! I can still fit into my uniform...."

"Come on boys, let's pay attention here." Kelly interrupted. She stopped the male banter with a series of low whistles. "Jesus," she muttered. "This is unbelievable."

"What you got?" Derek could see her scribbling more notes. He watched the arch of her hand as she gripped the pen, the length of her fingers, the way they tapered to a delicate tip. He caught himself just in time as she looked up.

Three halogen lamps focused on the dining room table. The headless torso of a naked female lay on the table. All four limbs were tied spread-eagle to the table legs. Puddles of candle wax, congealed blood and cigarette stubs surrounded the body. Derek was jealous of his more experienced colleagues. He imagined that for Peterson and Lefevre, this was routine. They had years on the beat and stomachs of iron. Waves of nausea were beginning to percolate in spite of the mask and the Vicks. He wondered how Kelly was faring.

"White female, slim build, one obvious tattoo of a rose on the right ankle, strong bikini tans," Derek dictated, forcing the words into his mini tape recorder. He swallowed hard to fight back the urge to vomit.

"Of course you'd document that," Kelly observed, sarcastically.

"Just doin' my job. Not too many places to get a tan around here this late in the fall."

"Look there," Kelly replied, tracing the body with her pocket penlight. "They did a little additional cardiac surgery, too. Looks like they cut out her heart."

"Her what?" Peterson asked, moving closer to the table.

"Her heart, you asshole," Lefevre said. "Get your eyes off her pussy and look at her chest." He caught his verbal indelicacies too late. "Sorry Kell. Didn't mean to get crude."

"No offense taken. I just wish you'd use the correct term. It's called the mons pubis and vagina," Kelly mumbled through the mask. She grabbed Derek's hand and moved his lamp closer to the victim's chest. "This is amazing!"

"What now?" Derek asked, afraid to show his ignorance.

"Look, they really did cut out her heart." Kelly traced the open chest wound with a gloved finger.

"So, people have been doing that for thousands of years." Derek said, confidently. "Besides grossing us out, what's the big deal?"

Kelly bobbed her head up and down to get the best perspective in the glare of the lamps. "Aztecs and Mayans removed their victims hearts in ritualistic sacrifice; but it's sloppy work. You can reach under here, sub xyphoid and cut here, below the sternum; but, you can't get to the heart without making quite a mess unless you do this kind of stuff for a living. Whoever did this was a professional. They used a rib cutter, see the marks here, and a rib spreader. That's hospital grade equipment. God, I hope she was dead before they cut her." Kelly said, her voice trailing off.

Even at four a.m. Derek grasped the significance of the scene before him. "Hey guys, doesn't this remind you of something? Young girls, decapitation, mutilation, candles?"

"You're right," Lefevre said. "Carl Furtado. Freetown State Park in the early 80's. Series of cult murders involving mutilation and decapitation. We nailed him and he got life."

"Carl Furtado," Peterson mulled, inflecting his voice to pontificate. "Convicted for the one homicide and suspected of at least three more satanic rite specials. The state prosecutors ended their search for truth and justice with the ubiquitous plea bargain. He's still in jail."

Lefevre snorted in disgust. "You know somethin', you're like a clock. You're right at least twice a day whether you have to be or not. He got life imprisonment in the People's Republic of Massachusetts. You know what that means."

"He's out?" Derek asked.

"Hey, you're supposed to read the memos. That's what you

get paid the big bucks for," Lefevre replied. "You get paid twenty percent more then me for that extra duty."

"I get twenty percent more then you because you can't read. Besides, you get to pull as much detail work as you want at $25 per hour with a four-hour minimum. I can't do that."

"Freeze my ass off for $25 lousy bucks an hour. Big fuckin' deal."

Kelly interrupted again. "Come to think about it, I remember reading something about Furtado in the *Herald News* a few months back, but I wasn't in town when he was famous." She looked at Derek exclusively. Something connected between them besides work, she knew it instinctively. "In a half way house, I recall. The DA and the victim's families both objected, but the parole board let him back into society because he was a model prisoner and, as they say, fully rehabilitated."

"Is he still in town?" Derek asked. "Maybe we should be looking for him."

"Don't bother," Lefevre called from the front bedroom. "Looky, looky what I see."

All four investigators moved to a bare mattress in the middle of the floor, lamps focused on an inert figure lying peacefully on a pillow.

"Looks like Fall River lost its last bogeyman," Wayne said smiling confidently.

Derek immediately recognized the face of the city's worst sadist on record, Carl Furtado. Their halogen lights revealed maggots crawling in and out of the man's open mouth. A syringe dangled from a well-worn vein in his forearm. The handle of a 22-caliber pistol reflected from his belt.

"Maybe there is a god after all," Peterson said. "What goes around, comes around."

"Looks like it," Lefevre concurred. "What do you think, Detective?"

"I'll need ballistics to match the bullet in the head of the first victim with Carl's gun. Pretty clear that the cause of death was gunshot wound to victim one, dismemberment to victim two and self inflicted overdose to victim three, in that order. My problem is with the State. Sometimes what we think doesn't matter worth shit. Autopsies are tough to get in this environment with the budget cuts and all. Probably have to get the FBI to assist with identifying the girl."

"Hey, what am I, chopped liver?" Kelly asked indignantly.

"Come on, Kell. I didn't forget about you. Of course you're department is important."

Peterson rubbed his nose. He was the only one not wearing a mask. "No head means no dental records. What about a finger print search?"

"Look again, shit head," Lefevre called out from the doorway leading to the dining room. "It appears Carl and company didn't want us to do that either - no finger tips and no toes."

"All right, folks, let in the photographers. Everyone take a room or a dumpster and get me some of this young lady's body parts. Find something, anything Kelly can use. I've got things I wanna do and places I wanna go before I'm old enough to retire."

Everyone fanned out. Derek heard the voices of departmental photographers making their way up the stairs. "No screw ups," he warned grabbing the arms of both patrolmen.

"Right, boss," they replied in unison.

Alexandria, Egypt
329 BC

The Nile flowed shallow and clear before the season of inundation. Ay and Nefertari stepped off the dahabiya, the timeless watercraft of the ancients, looking around in wonder. What had once been a marshy plain, home only to Oryx and gazelles at the mouth of the Nile, was a bustling center of construction. God King, Alexander, had declared this to be his new capital. Free men, slaves, and captives from the recent wars worked with bee- like intensity to obey the king's architects, unloading large pieces of granite and limestone from barge after barge. It was clear this was a city that belonged to conquerors. Nothing Egyptian remained except for those who labored in the hot sun.

Ay looked at Nefertari's beauty with the loyalty of a faithful dog, staring at her almond shaped eyes. It was her idea to take their treasures to the Greeks. She had no interest in her people's ancient secrets, only those luxuries that she could smell or touch. With judicious barter, the earthly pleasures she had always dreamt about were now within reach. Ay sought information from a line of men offloading wheat and other grains from the river barges. The workers were all Egyptian. The guards and tax collectors were Greek. He learned the Greeks took a percentage of everything - from the farmers who grew the crops to the merchants who plied the Nile, now a Greek river. They even collected a charge for loading and unloading the cargo along route. The ancient Egyptians had invented this system of fees and taxes. The Greeks had fine-tuned it to perfection.

Ay also learned of the name, Ptolemy, one of Alexander's generals who ruled Egypt in Alexander's name. Nefertari prodded him on, but he refused. They needed to find someone in authority in order to exchange the items from the tomb for real wealth. Ay wanted to return to the comfort and safety of Amara. He needed the security of the desert lands. She saw wonder where he saw confusion.

"If you can't do it, then I will," she said forcefully. Nefertari removed a ring from the treasure bag and placed it on the third finger of her right hand, flexing it briefly in the light. She had to be careful. Their lives could easily be forfeit if knowledge of their possessions fell into the wrong hands. Nothing of the magnitude she envisioned should be done in the open. She worked her way along the rows of tents and crude structures ignoring those where foreigners dominated in number or food or animals were being bartered. She finally found one that met her satisfaction. The building was at the center of the new city, sitting at the foot of the palace of the sun king. It stood nearly complete with walls of stone as well as mud brick. Ay walked anxiously behind her, timid in every step.

Nefertari entered the threshold cautiously turning her head from side to side exploring the darkness. Within, a man of Egyptian coloring worked on parchment, oblivious to their presence. His head was shaved in the manner of priests but without the requisite tattoos. His long robes stood in sharp contrast to their poor village linens. Still, he was the closest thing Egyptian who appeared to have some level of importance in this new world of the Greeks.

"Excuse me, sir," she said, humbly, attracting his attention with a bow.

The man at the desk looked up from his work and was immediately struck by the woman's beauty. The face of her companion, silent and nervous in the presence of his betters, was shrouded in the shadow of the corner. "Yes?"

Nefertari invoked the usual salutations and ancient greetings of her people. Approaching the desk, she watched the man across from her stand up to better see her face. She smiled at him bashfully. "I have some special things to sell," she began, cautiously. "I was wondering how I might go about bringing them to the attention of one of the Greeks in charge." She evoked the name, Ptolemy, out of ignorance. It was the name Ay had obtained from the docks. That one name raised the eyebrow of the man with the shaven head.

"What do you know of Ptolemy?" the man asked, returning to his seat and his work.

"Only that he is the royal visor to our new king, Alexander," she replied humbly.

"And what makes you think the Greek would talk to a village woman like you?" he asked, refusing to look up. "Take your trinkets and sell them at the bazaar on feast day." A servant entered the room and presented a roll of parchments for his inspection and approval. The man unfolded the scroll, looked at the writings and nodded in approval.

Nefertari and Ay stood silently until the servant left. Now they were being ignored. This was not going as well as she had envisioned. Nefertari hesitated briefly then walked across the room to within arms length of the man at the table. She extended her right hand placing it on the table and covered the parchment he was reading.

The Egyptian's eyes scoured in anger at this brazen interruption. Then he noticed the ring on the woman's hand and focused on the gold. He was a man who could read and write in the ways of the ancient ones. The origins of the ring were clear to him. "Where did you get this!"

Nefertari grew more confident. "That is not important. What I offer is this and more, but to the Greek only."

The Egyptian sat back at his table and pondered. He finally addressed them slowly and deliberately. "The tallest building in the center of all you see is that of the Greeks. Approach the door that faces Anon-Re in the evening. I will meet you within and take you to my master." He removed a ring from his own finger and extended it. "Here. Take this. It will grant you entrance into the new palace."

Nefertari greedily received the small ring and placed it on her opposite hand.

The Egyptian smiled. "Now you must give me your ring." He anticipated her reluctance. "Come now, if we are to do business, we must trust one another."

Nefertari hesitated, then, reluctantly, yielded her treasure into the hands of her superior. Ay was happy that their business was successful and wanted to retreat quickly before anyone changed their mind. Nefertari held her suspicions. Withdrawing in silence they disappeared into the throngs of people who labored on the new city, walking along the banks of the Nile arm in arm, each dreaming their own dream. Neither dream was compatible with the other.

Somerset, Massachusetts
October 2nd

The .357 Magnum revolver rested in his open palm. Derek sat in his favorite Adirondack chair and rocked gently back and forth. Empty bottles of beer and whisky surrounded him, each a dead soldier, his memory the war. It was four o'clock in the afternoon but his living room was pitch black, curtains and shades drawn tight against the world. The outline of his gun was barely perceptible in the dark. It didn't matter. He knew the weapon by heart. At a bit under two pounds the gun was heavier then his carry piece, the .45 automatic, or the .32 he used for backup when on duty. It was his favorite.

The four-inch barrel was refreshingly cool to the touch in comparison to the neutral temperature of the wooden handle. He let his fingers run back and fourth along its length. It had just the proper feel of oil as he rubbed his fingertips together. He touched the cylinder latch and flipped the cylinder open. Six empty chambers awaited his decision - something that was now a daily ritual.

The gun was double action. He could pull back the hammer or just squeeze the trigger. Both would accomplish the job equally well. He spun the cylinder and pushed the ejector rod repeatedly. The sounds of the moving metal gave him little comfort. It just made the empty afternoon pass quicker.

The magnum was a powerful weapon. The bullets discharged at supersonic speeds and would go right through a human being. There were both advantages and disadvantages to this. If a round struck a bone, the entire length of the bone would shatter. Energy equals mass times velocity squared and it was velocity that guaranteed surgical penetration on human flesh. Maybe he needed something slower, he wondered. A .45 automatic with its subsonic round would tumble and do more damage. What if he missed or did a sloppy job of it? The thought of pain raised the specter of cowardice. Only his parents would be left behind.

The arguments were old. God, he missed Rose. He reached down to the floor and raised a bottle of Jameson Whiskey to his mouth, taking a long swig. As he did, a box of ammunition spilled from his lap onto the wooden floor and rolled in different directions. He held the alcohol in his mouth as long as possible before choking it down. The taste was awful, but the mind numbing results of the alcohol was certainly faster then wine or beer.

Someday, someone would invent chocolate whiskey.

Repeated pounding on his front door interrupted his self-pity. He pushed himself out of the chair, staggered off balance to the door and opened it to the limits of the security chain. It was his worst nightmare and best dream rolled into one.

Kelly stood bathed surreally in the fall sunlight like a Renoir painting. "Hey, Derek. I hope I'm not interrupting anything," she said, cheerfully. She moved her head closer to the crack in the door looking past him. "I was driving by the neighborhood and recognized your car. I rang the doorbell but I think it's broken. Sorry if I pounded too hard," she babbled, her speech pressured. "God, I hope you weren't sleeping."

Derek looked at her in a haze of alcohol and surprise. He hadn't had a female visitor in the two years since Rose's death. Quickly he found his voice. "Ah, I'm sorry. No bother at all. Come on in. Come on in," he said, remembering his manners. He released the chain and opened the door fully, blinking from the bright sunlight like a newly woken vampire. The outer screen door hung precariously on one hinge and rocked. "Don't mind the screen door. The damn thing has been broken for years. Just haven't gotten around to fixing it yet."

Kelly cautiously accepted the invitation and entered. She noticed the gun in his hand and looked at him with sudden apprehension. A small town girl by heart, firearms was not her forte. She hated weapons that weren't holstered or disabled. She stood frozen to a spot in the foyer, her fear palpable.

"The gun?" Derek asked looking at her terrified face. "Hey, not a problem. Just cleaning it. I'll put it away right now," he offered.

"Cleaning it in the dark?" Her eyes darted between the darkened room and the weapon.

Derek focused on the Magnum and starred for a moment, lost in his own nightmares. He quickly returned to the present. "Marines. You know, dismantling and cleaning a weapon blindfolded. It was part of our training. Sometimes I do it just to keep my skills up."

Kelly's eyes reflected her doubts. "If you don't mind, I'd appreciate it if you put it away for now," she said, crossing her arms. Only when he took the gun to another room did she relax. "I'm just uncomfortable around guns, to say the least," she called out.

"To say the least." Derek made a dash to raise the blinds in the living room. Each motion brought piercing shafts of light and dust, penetrating the room and making them both blink. "I'm not a card carrying member of the NRA. Its just part of my job. But you got to remember that these things are nothing more then a piece of machined metal. Without bullets the worst thing you can do is hit someone over the head with it or throw it and break a window."

"And with bullets?"

He hesitated. "Depends on whose hand is on the trigger." Derek's voice drifted. The silence became uncomfortable for both of them. He caught himself before making things worse. "Hey, what can I do for you?"

Kelly flushed. "I just wanted my halogen light back. I was in the neighborhood and. ..." Her voice trailed off surveying the surrounding neglect. "Wow, when is the last time you had anyone clean up around here?" Debris lay strewn everywhere.

Derek stood embarrassed. "It's been awhile. But I'm livin' the bachelor's life. What you see is good enough for the boys when we play poker on Mondays." There was more awkward silence as he stared at her.

"I'm sure," Kelly said. "Here, let me give you a hand with a few of these bottles." She nervously reached down to the floor grabbing a couple of empty bottles. Jameson and Jack Daniel labels clinked in her hands as she bent down simultaneously with her host. Standing up in tandem, they clunked heads and both laughed awkwardly.

"I am honored. I won't wash my head for years," Derek teased, rubbing a tender spot on his scalp. He looked at the bottles in Kelly's hands and the disapproval in her eyes. "These? Hey, had a party here a couple of days ago," he said defensively, taking the bottles from her hands. "Can I offer you anything? Juice? Coffee?" His voice disappeared in the kitchen, the sound of broken glass and empty bottles echoing from the trash.

Kelly pivoted towards the threadbare sofa nervously. She wasn't sure why she had made such a bold move in the first place. "I'm fine. I'll just help you tidy up a bit and then be on my way." She reached down to pick up a pile of frames and photos from the cushion.

Entering the living room, Derek saw it coming. "Don't touch that!" he demanded rushing over to the sofa. He took the photos from her hand and grasped them tightly by his side.

Kelly glimpsed the images of Derek and another woman in the

pictures as they were taken from her hands. It had to be Rose. Everyone knew about her. "Derek, I'm sorry. I didn't mean to...."

"Not a problem." Derek interrupted. "I'm just kind of use to things being in the same place. Didn't mean to scare you." He looked at her beautiful blue eyes and momentarily lost himself. His agitation settled with the silence. Neither said a word as they both searched for some common ground.

The detective's stare was obvious. Self conscious with the sudden flush of sexuality, she averted her eyes. What seemed to be a good idea at the time now was in doubt. "I've got to be going," Kelly blurted out nervously. "My halogen lamp, please." There was an anxious smile glued to her words.

Even in his own home he brought an edge to the way most people reacted to him. "Of course." Derek returned from the bedroom in the small ranch house and handed over her flashlight. "I was planning on returning it to the hospital later this week," he said sheepishly.

Kelly took it from his hand and hesitated. The detective didn't let go. "If there is anything...."

"Sure," Derek agreed, nodding his head. His fingers brushed against Kelly's hands. The sensation was electrifying. He released the flashlight and stared at the floor.

The man's touch was a tease. Kelly wondered what it would be like and flushed. Maybe some day, she thought, kissing him on the cheek and leaving.

Hatfield Memorial Hospital, Fall River
October 3rd

Dr. Rick Nunez looked at the rhythm strip and handed it back to the paramedic. "SVT. It was a good call. You gave the Adenosine and it broke. No sweat, guys." He signed off on the ambulance run sheet with his usual scribble and handed the papers back to the paramedics. "Cardiologists are a jealous bunch. You cured their patient without their permission. Too bad for them." He leaned far back into his chair at the nurse's station in the ER and waited for the next supplicant. Years of experience in counteracting the forces of gravity, he precariously rocked back and forth in time to the snores from the patient across the desk, not spilling a drop of his mocha cappuccino.

Derek scanned the insanity of the ER and waited patiently behind his friend. He needed some TLC or an antibiotic or both. Rick was especially dependable at times of personal health care crisis. He hoped Kelly would be on duty as well but she was off tonight.

The emergency room was in its usual state of chaos. He admired the way Rick could perform in this environment of lunacy. Nunez was a transplanted Californian, beanpole lean with brown, perpetually crumpled bed-head hair, and a temperament that reflected the best and worst of his profession. Deliberate and articulate, he could quote page and line from every major medical journal, both in and out of his specialty. Sick, not sick, or gonna' die soon were the only three categories that existed in his world of emergency medicine.

A combination of smells from leaking bodily fluids and antiseptic deodorizers overwhelmed Derek's diseased sinuses. Vomit and diarrhea odors mixed with the unmistakable stench of gastrointestinal bleeds. The ER's massive commercial air filtration scrubbers were futile against the onslaught of such poisonous vapors. Stretchers supporting the wounded and dying lined the hallways like planes taxiing on a runway. Patients and their families glared at the nurse's central station from all sides, waiting for someone to fix whatever it was broken or decaying within their bodies. The passage of time was perceived differently for the staff and patients. The speed of the medical machine never matched the expectations of patients.

The faster the staff worked, the slower they appeared to the patient or family members at the bedside, ratcheting up the tension another notch.

Derek readily took advantage of his friend's status as the ER attending on duty. He didn't give this short-cut a second's worth of hesitation. Sometimes there was an advantage in being a cop that went beyond free donuts and coffee. He coughed twice to remind Nunez that he was waiting patiently. It wasn't being sick that was the worst indignity; it was that wait that aggravated everyone. Stereo moaning of demented nursing home patients and screaming babies echoed against the walls, their sirens' song like fingernails on a chalkboard. In the ER, however, it was just another day.

An adrenaline junkie, Nunez thrived on the chaos. Pivoting in his chair he looked up at his friend. "Come on, jerk," he said, motioning with his pocket flashlight and a tongue depressor. "Open wide. Let's see what all that whining is about." He swabbed the back of Derek's throat with a culturette ignoring the gag reflex he just precipitated. "Gawd, this looks awful. You might even be right. I think this time you do need antibiotics."

The men were ambushed by the ER's resident sex kitten. "Hey, Derek. What you doin' tonight?" Paula purred, sauntering up next to Derek. She deliberately brushed her hip against his side, then leaned forward over the desk. Her surgically augmented breasts were barely covered by the loose scrubs she always wore two sizes too big. What was the use of spending all that money on surgery if no one got to see it, she maintained. "Hey, is that a gun in your pocket or are you happy to see me?"

"It's a gun. Now go away before I spread my germs," Derek replied, filling another tissue.

A thirty something blond joined the party. "Eww!" Terry said. The two women were inseparable particularly when trying to pick up wayward police officers or rescue personnel for an evening's entertainment. "You don't look too good, you big hairy Armenian."

Nunez looked at the play before him and shook his head in disgust. "Great. All the man needs is someone else telling him how sick he looks. Quit bein' a baby, Ekizian. Suck it up and tough it out," Nunez commanded, getting up to escape the temptation of Paula's dangling breasts. Any closer and it would have been a lap dance.

"Did you say 'suck it and stick it out'?" Terry joked. "Ohhhh, who's your daddy, who's your daddy?" She gave her own ample rear end a playful slap.

A small crowd of nurses and techs gathered to enjoy the show, chuckling and smiling with each wiggle. Anywhere else things would be considered out of control. In the ER it was just another mechanism to ease the surrounding tensions. "Quiet before I call administration. This is sexual harassment," Nunez said. "Now come on, the rest of you. Break it up and get back to work. We don't need anymore complaints from our customers."

"What ever happened to 'patients'?" Paula mumbled to no one in particular.

"Go ahead, call administration," Terry challenged. "I'm working a double anyway. They can't fire me until after the shift is over. Can't get anyone else to work in this hellhole anyway. What can they do to punish me? Make me work a triple?"

"Hey does anyone care about me?" Derek interrupted. "You gotta' do something for me soon so these ladies can take me home and play," he said, grabbing Paula and Terry around the waist. "Rick, your reputation is at stake. Can't you see I've got a threesome going here?"

Paula broke away from Derek and moved within whisper distance of Rick's ear. "Well, I was really hoping for a foursome." Nunez was the passion of her existence this week. Everyone knew it. The two would play with each other until the tension was unbearable; then consummate a brief relationship and move on. She leaned back towards Derek and pulled his cell phone off his pants belt. Punching in her number, she handed it back. "Now you've got no reason not to call. I'm electronically connected to you forever," she declared proudly. She looked Rick in the eyes invitingly. Jealously might accomplish that which she had so far been unable to do on her own.

"Thanks," Derek said. He readjusted the phone to its harness. "Someday I might take you up on that offer."

"I'm hopin'!" Paula smiled. She looked back at Rick suggestively.

Nunez scribbled something indecipherable on a script pad and handed it to Derek. Simultaneously he scanned a new ER chart and dismissed a phone call from a frustrated unit nurse regarding the appropriateness of his latest CCU admission. "Some good old fashion Penicillin and chicken soup should make you as good as new. Maybe even let you go eat sushi tomorrow with the big boys, "he assured his friend.

"Oki's?" Derek asked.

"You bet."

Derek smiled. Sushi was one of his only remaining connections to the world of sensuality. The texture of the fish and the ceremony of preparation reached almost religious significance in his life.

Nunez made no effort to get up and return to the fray in the ER. Paula made no effort to leave the desk either. Something special was incubating between the nurse and physician.

Derek began to leave. "Who else is coming tomorrow?"

"The usual suspects: Sherman, Desrosiers and maybe Pasternack, if his wife lets him."

"Can I come?" Paula asked, flirting with both men.

"We eat sushi naked," Derek teased. "Are you up for that?"

Paula moved in for the kill. "The question is, are you up for that?" She let her fingers weave through his long hair.

Derek blushed and retreated. Paula smiled with her victory and returned to the bedside of an elderly asthmatic. Terry picked up her laptop computer and moved on to register a new patient.

Nunez grinned from ear to ear. "You deserved that." He got up to see his next patient. A stack of charts waited for his talents. There was no beginning and no end. Why rush? Nothing he did would ever change the volume of patients. There was no catching up.

"See ya later, bud," Derek said. He waved goodbye to Rick, but the man had suddenly disappeared into the trauma room to work on a heroin overdose. He walked out of the cacophony of the ER and was glad of it. More emergency vehicles poured in as he stood outside in the night air of the ambulance bay.

Alexandria, Egypt
329 BC

It was the second time they made love that day. Nefertari was the first to rise and quickly dressed. Voices approached their small camp on the banks of the river. The workday was complete and laborers were returning to their homes. The workmen considered their camp just south of the marshes isolated and undesirable. She turned and looked at Ay. He was a barely satisfying lover but he served her needs. "Come, it's time," she ordered.

Ay slowly sat up and stretched. "We eat first?" His body was thin and lean. His chest, hairless. He slithered when he moved.

"Later, my love. We must not be late." Nefertari handed him his robe while she tied her tunic around her neck and shoulders.

Ay reached behind her and put his arms around her waist pushing her shapely buttocks into his own loins. His fingers moved over her body as if playing a lyre. Her breast were wonderfully firm. Her stomach flat as that of a teenage girl. Nefertari pushed his hands away and gave him a look that left no doubt in her lack of interest. He grumbled his dissatisfaction but did as he was told. Ay returned his attention to the preparation for their journey into the city of the Greeks. Three pieces of ancient treasure were hidden, stuffed in the bottom of a water bag he carried on his shoulder. The evening before he tied the remainder of the ancient objects to a partially submerged tree near their campsite, leaving the items protected by both the river and an occasional crocodile. Few of the beasts were found this far north, but the constant threat was enough to keep all but the most confident out of the water.

It was near dusk, their appointed hour for their rendezvous. The work frenzy at the base of the new city ceased, as if by magic. Soldiers retreated to their tents for the evening. Nearby the outline of the royal palace was clearly taking shape. It was already the height of five men. Ay and Nefertari walked the perimeter of the building in wonder. The stones of their own village, Amara, had once touched the sky in the days of the ancients; but they had been dismantled a thousand years before, leaving only the mud brick behind. What lay before them was beyond their experience. Massive blocks of granite and limestone the size of horses and oxen sat on top of each other in perfect symmetry surrounded by the tools of the masons and laborers. The building was taking form with columns and ramps in the style of the Greeks. The Nile itself had been diverted to assist with the construction. Barges with their stone burdens lined up almost to the front gate of the palace.

Cautiously they approached the gate of the palace as instructed. The lone sentry acknowledged the ring on Nefertari's hand and waved them in without a word. They were most certainly expected. Unlike Egyptian fortresses built with columns and few enclosures, the palace of the Greeks had ceilings closed with wood timbers and great stone works. Moving inside their feet echoed on the polished marble floor. Even their voices were amplified in the massive chamber that first greeted them on entry.

Torches and oil lamps illuminated the corridor, revealing the presence of a lone man who anxiously paced the floor. Recognizing them, he smiled. "Ah, right on time."

"Lord, we...." Nefertari began.

"Please. I am called Im-Tep. You are safe here with me. There is no need for formality," he replied. "Come." He led his two guests down a labyrinth of twists and turns until they reached a chamber deep inside the palace. The room held food and drink on a small table. He sat on one side of the table, watching Ay devour the meal while Nefertari sat impatiently.

"Lord Im-Tep, what of the Greek, the general Ptolemy?" Nefertari asked.

Im-Tep smiled. "Soon." He moved to pour himself a cup of wine then sipped it slowly. "You must understand, the Greek is all powerful now. My own reputation is at stake. I must show him more before I can hope to gain you an audience."

Ay stood up and silently removed the water pouch slung on his shoulder. The wine from the meal he had just consumed made him glow with confidence. Without flourish he removed a small knife from his belt and slashed the side of the sheepskin. A small quantity of water spilled onto the floor. He reached into the pouch and removed three items, each more splendid then the next.

Im-Tep focused on the largest, a dagger of magnificent proportions and workmanship. "And the rest?" he inquired casually, spinning the ceremonial weapon slowly in the palm of his hand.

"Safely hidden, Lord," Nefertari said. "Now can we see the Greek?"

"Certainly." Im-Tep smiled, clapping his hands once. The room suddenly filled with men bearing swords and spears. None wore the armor or helmets of the Greeks.

"Betrayal!" Nefertari screamed; but, it was too late.

Fall River, Massachusetts
October 3rd

The red neon glow of Hatfield Memorial's emergency department sign stood out ghostlike in the coastal mist. The first letter of the sign, E, quivered and silently sparked with an electronic short. Fog blanketed the coast of Southeastern Massachusetts from the Cape to neighboring Rhode Island. Derek opened the door of his beloved Mitsubishi Galant VR-4 and fumbled with the ignition key. The car, like everything else in his life, had been out of production for years. The hospital receded in his rear view mirror as he pulled out of the 'ambulance only' parking lot. A minute later he entered the 24-hour CVS, walked to the back of the store and handed his prescription to 'Doc' Carter, the pharmacist.

One of the few black professionals in town, Carter's coke bottle glasses accentuated the formal white coat of a pharmacist. He greeted Derek with a toothy smile that was as genuine as the hand he extended. "Hey man, how ya doin'?"

Derek reached over the counter to shake but thought better of it. He looked at the wad of crumpled Kleenex in his hand and showed them to Carter sheepishly. "Could be better," he said handing Carter the prescription.

"You sound terrible." Carter took the prescription, weaved his head up and down as he tried to decipher the medical hieroglyphics with his trifocals, and then nodded in agreement. "Yep, this will do it for you. Just be a minute."

"Your about the tenth person tonight to tell me how sick I am. Enough!" Derek said looking at the parade of customers surround him even at this hour. He sat down in a chair adjacent to the automatic blood pressure cuff and waited for the prescription to get filled, aimlessly pressing the start button on the machine and watched it cycle repeatedly in mechanical frustration. What he wanted was sleep. A few minutes later and he was out the door, prescription in hand.

There was one more task to finish before the evening was over. Norm's Bouquet, the city's only floral shop, was next door and the lights were still on. Derek pressed his face against the window and could see his friend working past official closing hours. Clutching his cell phone in a death grip, Derek wavered. He had promised to give Kelly a call tonight but still hadn't done so. The thought of rejection terrified him. Sometimes the girl acted as if she really looked forward to seeing him. He blamed his hesitation on his sore throat and cough, pressing 'clear' instead, putting his cell phone away.

Norm was there in all his splendid effeminacy. Tall as he was round, he was a full ten years older then Derek. He didn't hide his sexual persuasion but usually neither did he flaunt it. His hair was shaved almost to the scalp, a scraggily goatee gracing his baby smooth chin. Derek tapped lightly on the door and waited.

Norm looked up from his work and immediately recognized the detective. He came out from behind the counter and opened the door. "Derek!" he exclaimed, vigorously pumping his friend's hand.

Derek looked around the shop and tried to breathe in the fragrance of flowers squeezed in every corner. This was the worst part of being sick, he thought, not being able to enjoy the simple pleasures of life. Being gay was good for no other reason then to live and work in this beautiful environment. You would never find a straight man working in a shop like this. The only time he ever expected to be in the company of so many flowers would be at his funeral. "Hey, bud," He took a seat in front of the cash register and played with the petals of a withered carnation his friend had just discarded.

"What's up?" Norm asked, taking a seat next to his friend.

"Got a favor to ask," Derek said sheepishly. He explained what he wanted and for whom it was intended. It was Kelly's birthday and he needed to make a statement.

"Good for you," Norm said, smiling. "About time you get back into the swing of things." He played with his right earring. No, he hadn't any record of anyone in the city sending Kelly flowers and as he quickly pointed out, he was the only show in town, so he should know. "What kind of flowers are you looking for?"

Derek couldn't believe he was making this move. His hands were shaking. He put them back into his jacket pocket, shuffling his keys and change. He knew Kelly wasn't seeing anyone steadily. He just wanted to make sure no one else was interested. Even if Kelly thought he was a jerk, she'd never reject flowers. "I'm really not sure," he began. "I want something special, but not too special. I don't want her thinking I'm a nut case and scare her off. At the same time I don't want it to be something too casual so she doesn't think I'm really just playing with her," he added cautiously. "Oh, and the money. I don't want to make it too expensive so she thinks I'm trying to buy her. And it can't be too cheap otherwise she'll think I'm, well, cheap." Derek scrunched up his face and looked pleadingly into his friend's eyes. Things were getting beyond hopeless and both men recognized the comedy of the situation.

Norm pondered. "Let me make sure I have this right. Special but not too special, not too casual, nice but not too expensive and nothing that reeks of bad taste and being a cheap skate." He looked at Derek with the amusement of someone who has been through the scene a hundred times before. "I just happen to have a special on roses tonight."

"Roses?" Derek asked hopefully. His eyes lit up for the first time that evening.

"A dozen pink with one white one in the center." Norm reached inside the glass refrigerator and brought out the prizes. The buds had just barely started to open. "When are you comin' fishin' with us?" Norm asked, adding baby's breath to the boxed roses.

"Great. That's all I need. Alone in the deep woods of Maine with a bunch of fudge packers. That'll add miles to my reputation with the girls."

"Oh, you're such a tease!" Norm replied deliberately over accentuating the stereotypical speech and hand motions that made him the darling of the Body Shop, the only gay club in town. "You never can tell, you might even learn a thing or two." Norm knew how embarrassed Derek would be if anyone else was around, but for now it was just banter between friends. He finished the brief note that Derek requested, using a spectacular calligraphy. Something that would impress Kelly for sure, he added.

Derek looked at the box and the lavender ribbon he had specifically stipulated. His hands became acutely sweaty as he paid for the arrangement. His fingers drummed nervously on the counter. The thought of looking into her eyes while she unwrapped the arrangement was more then he could handle right now. "On second thought, just deliver them," he said, pivoting to leave the shop. "You know her address." His shoulders slumped in defeat.

"Sure. Whatever," Norm said, sharing his friend's pain. Both men's smile evaporated simultaneously. Fall River was a small town. He knew Kelly. He had known Rose as well. For a few minutes the man before him had returned to the realm of the living. Now he watched a dead man walking. He stood silently as Derek left the shop without a word of goodbye.

Alexandria, Egypt
329 BC

He had to admit the woman was beautiful. Even in the dimly lit dungeon, surrounded by river muck and the occasional marsh rat, she held herself like a royal captive instead of the simple peasant woman she was. Her skin recoiled in pain with every blow from the guard but she never made a sound. Her companion, on the other hand, was pathetic. He cried and whimpered with each threat of torture or pain. The location of the treasure sack spilled from his lips like a child. Unfortunately, the information proved to be false. That only increased his agitation, as he swore by all the gods he revealed the true location of the ancient gold. It was clear that the woman held the key. Im-Tep closed the viewing slit especially built into his private chambers. It had served as a source of much amusement in the brief history of his new residence. He sighed in frustration. It was time to get his hands dirty. He called for the captain of his personal guard and gave orders.

By the time he returned to the dungeon, the work was almost complete. Both bodies, which had hung naked for hours from ropes in the ceiling, now lay wrapped in embalming linens from head to toe. It took a special talent to prepare the living in this manner. Only their eyes, nose and mouths remained opened. Their arms were bound tightly to their side. The man screamed and begged incessantly. The woman remained quiet. Im-Tep dismissed the guards with a wave. They left reluctantly, disappointed in missing the unfolding performance. Only the three of them remained in the room.

"It seems I must make a decision. I am no nearer to the treasure then when we first began. I am not a patient man," he added, pacing the squalor of the dungeon floor.

"But, Lord Im-Tep, I told you where to find the jewels," Ay pleaded. "If they are gone, then it is the will of the gods. It is not my fault."

"So you said, so you said," Im-Tep nodded in agreement. "Unfortunately, nothing was found." He looked unwaveringly at the eyes of the female. She revealed no surprise at this turn of events. His suspicions were confirmed. Clearly she knew.

Im-Tep pushed the man's immobile form into the shallow water flowing through the dungeon. Ay's body barely made a depression in the mud and slime on the banks of the subterranean river. The further into the water Im-Tep pushed the bound form, the louder the man screamed. The level of the water was shallow and just covered Ay's back. It was no direct danger to him yet, but he knew what the future foretold. Im-Tep slowly walked to the opposite side of the cell, reached over to an iron grate at the edge and lifted the latch. Splashing and thrashing sounds grew impatiently on the opposite side of the grate. "I think you go first," he said, pushing the inert form of the man deeper into the water and through the narrow opening of the grate. "Unless your woman has something she wants to say to me." Im-Tep fixed his gaze on the female. She looked right past him in silence. If she had knowledge she revealed nothing and made no attempt to save her companion's life. Ay's struggle increased the deeper he was pushed into the water, but it was futile. Im-Tep watched the show until the body had drifted out of sight. Quickly he closed the door and latched it firmly again.

The water beyond became agitated with dark forms that fought for the meal. Screams were followed by total silence. "Praise Osiris," Im-Tep said, bowing repeatedly as he backed away from the grate. He smiled and turned his attention to the woman. "My private collection. I always keep them hungry. It makes them that much more attentive to my commands."

The woman stared at him in silence and made no effort to fight her bonds. Im-Tep returned her gaze and made another decision. His thoughts returned to the hours staring at her body as his guards worked their best to bend the woman's will. He reached over to her face and touched her skin. She did not recoil. Slowly he unwrapped the linens that bound her. The woman was spectacularly beautiful and her nakedness only accentuated that fact. She stepped out of the last of the restraints and kneeled at his feet, only her long black hair covering her back. Im-Tep removed his own cape and covered her. "Come," he said, taking her hand and raising her to her feet. "We have something to discuss."

She followed him past the surprised guards waiting in the corridor and into his private chambers. Nefertari smiled. "Yes, lord Im-Tep."

Medical Examiner's Office, Fall River
October 3rd

Kelly drew the last samples of blood from the female victim, attached the label and signed off on the release slip. Chain of evidence was paramount in her profession. Technicians should have performed this part of the job, but budget cuts made that impossible. Now the real work began. She strapped on the head microphone, tested the unit with a couple of 'one, two, threes', and proceeded to the autopsy. Anatomical dissection was not her forte, but she was learning rapidly. Gross descriptions and external physical exams came first. Then came the bone cutter with its whining rotary blade and the distinct smell of burning bone against steel. She split the chest cavity neatly down the sternum then, using rib spreaders, removed the internal organs one by one. Each organ was examined for gross pathology, weighed and serial sections obtained for microscopic evaluation. Suspicious areas were usually biopsied; but, in a victim this young, she was unlikely to find anything of concern. She duly recorded her earlier observations that the heart was absent. The absence of blood in the chest cavity indicated that the victim was dead before the heart was removed. Kelly reflected on this, shaking her head in sympathetic pity, grateful that the poor girl was dead before she was torn apart. She noted the missing head, fingertips and toes in her report as well.

Two hours later she finished. The death toll had to be raised to four. This victim had a gravid uterus and was at least two months pregnant. She replaced those organs removed and closed the thoracic cavity with a staple gun. The body was returned to the industry standard stainless steel morgue shelves. Kelly changed out of her scrubs, showered and dressed back in her civilian clothes. It was time to talk to her boss.

Joe Rafferty sat at his desk surrounded by piles of paperwork. Bespectacled, plump and balding he was past his prime physically and professionally. The office technicians and secretaries joked that the bodies in his charge had personalities more alive then the man who directed their dissection. The smell of formaline and decomposing flesh overpowered the air conditioning and ozone air filters that surrounded his workspace. Rafferty knew little about the cases that overwhelmed his constantly diminishing staff. His sole professional focus was on those investigations that had piqued the governor's interest hoping someday to extricate himself from his professional exile. He looked up from his desk wearily and acknowledged Kelly's presence. "Yes?" he asked, returning his attention to the book on his lap.

The man was the bane of her existence. How she ended up in a subservient position working for this fool was a constant mystery. The state hierarchy had its dues and she was just beginning her career. "Just finished the labs on the Jane Doe. I wanted to know how quickly you want to proceed with the other autopsies from the Furtado murders?" she inquired, readjusting the lavender scarf on her hair. The man had not looked her in the face all day. She hated being ignored more then any other indignity.

"Keep it simple," Rafferty replied without looking up again. "Finish all three by the end of your shift. I can't afford to waste any more time with this; we're already over budget."

Three bodies by the end of the afternoon was ridiculous. Kelly leaned forward across the desk and moved her face closer to that of her boss. "If you read my preliminary report, you'll notice that there are a few discrepancies I discovered at the scene. A couple of hours for three autopsies isn't enough time to do a proper job."

Rafferty looked up and glared over his narrow bifocals. "I don't recall asking you for an opinion." He reveled in Kelly's momentary defensive posture. "Look, Fall River PD is working closely with the FBI and checking out missing persons reports from around the country to identify our Jane Doe. The state police have all but closed out their investigations on the other two losers. It is time for all of us to move on."

"But my findings..."

"I don't give a shit about your findings now, yesterday or in the future. We work for the tax payers of the state and not for our own pleasures."

Kelly composed herself. "I think you're being a bit premature. I mean, I was at the crime scene that first night. When something looks that perfect, it makes me suspicious."

Rafferty returned to reading a magazine. "That's the job for the police. We just give them the facts and they're supposed to put everything all together. Death with a syringe of heroin still in your arm is cardiac arrest secondary to pulmonary edema from a heroin overdose. A gunshot to the head is death by a gunshot to the head.

The young lady was the unfortunate victim of a murder in which she was decapitated and surgically mutilated. When you hear hoof beats, think horses, not zebras. Don't let yourself get carried away."

Kelly glared at the top of the man's balding head. He was insufferable. "I'd like to do a little bit more on my own then, if you don't mind. I've got a couple of ideas I'd like to work on."

Rafferty slammed his hand on the desk. "How many ways of me saying 'no' don't you understand? You fall under my budget and I can't afford to waste any more time or taxpayer dollars on this case. These folks aren't the Kennedys. Move on. That's an order."

Kelly choked on her reply, pivoted and left. It was not the first time her life was controlled by men of pseudo-power and pseudo-intellect. Her only response to this idiot was the echo of the man's office door slamming in her wake.

Nile River, Egypt
325 BC

Alexander the Macedonian, son of Philip, was dead. Disease, not battle, claimed the conqueror of the civilized world. His last words when asked who would inherit his new empire, "to the strongest", set the stage for bloody conflict and chaos. Factions of the Greeks were in deadly competition for the wealth of Egypt. Those who ruled in Alexander's name fought for their own glory. Armed men of all ethnic and religious persuasions exchanged loyalties for the price of a gold coin that held the profile of their dead king.

It was not a good time for Egyptians of the true bloodline to remain amongst the Greeks. Everyone not of Hellas was under suspicion by those who ruled. Im-Tep needed little encouragement to move south with his possessions, keeping in front of the fluctuating battle lines. His barge, displaying the royal standard of the Ptolemy's, plied the Nile with the power of a dozen oarsmen. Circling them, dahabiya, crisscrossed in their wake oblivious to the unique treasure the royal barge held. Im-Tep stood on the foredeck with his wife, Nefertari, feeling the breeze of desert and the motion of boat beneath his feet. He stared pensively into the distant hills, his thoughts burdened by the approaching civil war that had abruptly changed his station in life forever. He was an important man in the new order of the past few years, but he was an Egyptian, never the less. He had knowledge but no army to protect him. Now he was on his own.

Nefertari, long robes fluttering in the breeze, leaned against her husband and held his arm. Her thoughts were to the luxuries left behind. "Lord Im-Tep, the decision was made," she said gently. "You must only stay the course. The gods will take care of the rest."

Im-Tep turned, kissed her on the forehead, reaching down to hold both her hands. Along the shore local fishermen were preparing their nets for the next day. The tantalizing smell of cooking pots from shoreline villages wafted in the air. Old memories of simpler times permeated his thoughts. "All the years of planning, all that work," he said dejectedly, "gone."

"You can't be sure," Nefertari said. "After the generals and armies wage their wars, someone will return to the palace. Your services will be needed once again."

"Perhaps," Im-Tep replied. He breathed deeply and stretched. The captain and oar master were at the opposite end of the barge and could not hear their conversation. The spotters for submerged hippopotamus and crocodiles were Persian captives and did not understand the tongue of the Egyptians. They could talk freely. "I know with certainty we would have forfeited our lives had we remained. Only when the fighting stops may we return. Until then this is our only safe course of action. Your gold, our gold has bought our comfort and paved my way into the inner sanctum of power. If the source of this wealth were to be discovered, then it would mean our end."

"Still, it seems such a shame to leave all our comforts behind," Nefertari said. The future was now a murky one. She had spent the past five years learning the intricacies of court life, exploring palace intrigues and converting her peasant behavior to that of a lady in waiting to her husband. She had spent the past five years making sure that no child lasted more then a few weeks in her womb. She would never be a slave to her breasts again. Now this. The thought of beginning again was too depressing. She changed the subject. "We travel to Luxor?"

"Yes. I know the ancient temples there well. My bloodline is long with those who called themselves priests. I will find a place to hide the treasures you brought to me so many years ago. It cannot remain with us. When the time is right, when the wars are over, we can return and keep them by our side. Until then we will retreat into the desert. That is our safety."

"And afterwards?"

"We shall see, we shall see."

Hatfield Memorial Hospital
October 4th

The woman on the stretcher was in status epilepticus, fifteen minutes of multiple drug therapy unsuccessful in terminating the seizure activity. Kelly ground her teeth in frustration. She was bloated, premenstrual and wired with caffeine. The night shift was less then an hour old and she was already up to her butt in alligators. "Is the Dilantin up?"

"Ten more minutes before the loading dose is in," the charge nurse replied.

"She's getting really tight," respiratory therapist interrupted. "I'm having a hard time bagging her. And we've got pink froth in the tube."

Shit! The patient was twenty-eight, two weeks post partum, and having her first seizure. "O.K. people, let's paralyze and intubate. I've got to secure the airway before she drowns in her own secretions. Succinylcholine and Versaid. Let's go," Kelly ordered, confidence waning. She removed a number 7.5 cm tube from the intubation tray. "I need a straight blade. Can't anyone remember that after all these years?"

The chief tech looked up from his station. "Sorry, doc. My fault. I'll get on it right away."

Moments later the drugs were in and the patient paralyzed. The seizures only appeared to stop if you looked from the outside. Inside the young woman's brain the short circuit was continuing unabated. Kelly grabbed the tools of her trade and went to work. The laryngoscope fit in her left hand like a well-worn glove. She gently spread the young woman's lips, tilted the head backward and inserted the blade. Simultaneously she lifted the tongue and posterior pharynx, exposing the vocal cords. Her right hand held both suction and the endotracheal tube. She cleared the last of the patient's secretions with the hose like catheter. The sound of the suction reminded her of slurping the bottom of an ice cream soda as a kid. Confidently she slid the endotracheal tube into the patient's trachea.

The respiratory therapist inflated the balloon cuff with 8 cc of air, switched adaptors and began bagging the patient. The CO2 monitor turned a reassuring pink.

"There, at least we have control of her airway," Kelly said a bit more relaxed. Vent settings: tital volume of 650, rate of 14 and O2 at 100%. Gases in 5 minutes, please." She listened to the woman's chest again. Rales were now present throughout the lung fields. Why would a twenty eight year old be in congestive heart failure? "I want a CAT scan of her head yesterday. Put a call out to her obstetrician and cardiology as well. Lasix 80 mg IV now!"

Dawn tapped her on the shoulder. "Pressure is up to 240 systolic. We're already up to one hundred and twenty mics of Nitro."

Double shit. "What were the vitals on the rescue run sheet, again?"

The original paramedics were still downloading their rhythm strips into the main computer and heard Kellly's question. "Systolic of 130. Everything was fine at the house and that was just thirty minutes ago. Her only complaint was a headache on and off since she delivered the baby," the paramedic said, not looking up. "I took that blood pressure myself."

Could the patient have an aneurysm? Kelly was flustered. "I don't care how high you have to go. Just keep the systolic below 170," she ordered. Blood pressure skyrocketing in a matter of 30 minutes, constant seizure activity, congestive heart failure all rolled up into one. She was missing something critical, but she couldn't put her finger on it.

The door to the trauma room opened. "They're ready for her in CAT scan;" a disembodied voice called out.

The stretcher disappeared leaving only house cleaning personnel to keep her company. Looking up Kelly saw the detective, Derek Ekizian standing in the doorway. Kelly's surgical mask hid her smile. Another tech entered the room just behind him. "Excuse me doc, we've got a chest pain in room three. Would you mind looking at her EKG?"

Kelly looked up at the tracing and felt nauseated. There was clear evidence of an acute myocardial infarction. Someone was having a heart attack while she had been working in the trauma room and she was the only doctor on duty after 11 pm. "Hey Detective." She warmed at the thought of the flowers from Norm's. "What brings you out tonight? Isn't it past your bedtime?" she smiled heading towards him. The man backed shyly away to give her egress.

"I was just in the neighborhood and...."

The tech interrupted again. "Doc, the patient in room three, please."

She hadn't acknowledged the flowers. "Just a moment, Derek. I'll be right back."

"Sure, no problem," he said getting out of her way.

Kelly hurried into room three and introduced herself to the eighty-year-old woman sitting stoically on the stretcher. The nurses had already initiated a nitro and heparin protocol. Suddenly the code alarm went off. CPR was in process in the x-ray department. Kelly raced down the hall and saw it was her 28-year-old seizure patient.

"What happened?" she asked breathlessly. She searched for a carotid pulse.

"Don't know doc. She's been on the monitor the entire time and doing fine except for her blood pressure. We just pulled her out of the CAT scan machine and she straight lined."

Kelly watched the team compress the young woman's chest in rhythmic count of 80 a minute. Two electrical counter shocks later, the patient had a spontaneous pulse but was still unresponsive. "Nice job, people. Come on, let's get her back to the trauma room before she decides to do this again." Kelly stayed behind to look at the CAT scan results. The brain showed no gross evidence of any blood. Another theory out the window.

"Dr Lambert's here from cardiology," someone interrupted. "The woman in three is his. Do you want to ask him about this seizure patient as well?"

Even the staff knew she needed a respite. "Sure, whatever," Kelly said.

Lambert scanned the ER record. His youthful appearance masqueraded the genius of a Mass General trained invasive cardiologist. "Sounds like a case of postpartum eclampsia and cardiomyopathy," he mumbled biting into a red McGowan apple. "Good thing you didn't administer the usual Magnesium Sulfate to stop her seizures. It has a significant suppressant effect on the myocardium. Probably would have killed her."

Magnesium. She should have thought about post partum eclampsia. She had never even heard of a case post partum eclampsia, never mind seen one. Kelly nodded her head in false recognition. "Good thing," she echoed, looking blankly at her feet.

Lambert called for a bedside echo machine. Moments later he exited the curtained room. "Ejection fraction of 10%. You need to get her to a major transplant center. If she doesn't get a heart transplant, she'll be dead by the morning," he said, disappearing into room three to address his 80-year-old heart attack patient.

Kelly was exhausted. "Let's get the helicopter in, folks." The requisite calls were made. For the moment she could kick back and take a breath of fresh air. She looked up from her desk. Derek was nowhere to be found.

Fall River, Central Police Station
October 5th

"Hey, just go away." Kelly's open palm pushed Derek back into his chair and then struck him with a bony elbow. "You're supposed to be comparing my report to yours." Her eyes, twinkling in the filtered sunlight from the office window, flirted with appreciation and embarrassment at the detective's attention.

Derek leaned over his cluttered desk and handed her another cartoon caricature. It had taken him less then a minute to create. His drawings were a safe way to break the ice and ease tension. He could make someone laugh and express himself both at the same time. This last one showed Kelly riding a stethoscope like a bronco. The stethoscope had his mustache.

"Come on, Kell. I was just having some fun."

Kelly turned and gazed out the window in silence. This territory wasn't new. "Are you afraid of me?" she whispered, separating several slats of the Venetian blinds with her fingers.

Derek's smile evaporated. "What?"

"You heard me. Are you afraid of me?" Kelly squeezed her eyes shut as if making a wish just before blowing out a birthday candle. When she opened her eyes nothing had changed. It was times like this she wished she had inherited her mother's demur personality. She could feel her ability to self-censor slip away. "The flowers were nice, but I'd much rather have had you come over for a while, even if only for a cup of coffee. It was my birthday, you know."

Derek froze. The line between girlfriend and girl friend blurred only around this one human being. "I really think you are one incredible lady," he said, retreating behind his desk. "I just didn't want to push. You know, I kind of...."

"Right!" Kelly's speech became pressured. "Am I that scary? For a smart man, you act like a real jerk. All I'm suggesting is we get a chance to know each other better."

Derek hunkered down in his chair and focused on his report. This wasn't the first time the topic was raised. Since the accident there was a threshold of intimacy he just wasn't prepared to cross with anyone. And yet.... He looked up just in time to see Kelly staring at him. They averted their glances simultaneously. Her eyes, everything always returned to her eyes. He wanted to reach up and take her hand in his own. It would be a natural act. Even that small step seemed beyond his ability. "Soon, Kell. I just need a little more time to work things out." The top of his pencil broke. She extended her lower lip and blew a stream of air against her face to push out an errant strand of hair.

"I'm not asking you to marry me. Hello!" she said, tapping her fist against his head. "Is anybody there? Anyone home?"

Kelly saw Derek's glazed look. She had been talking to the wind for God knows how long. She was doing it again. When would she ever learn? She reached over and kissed him gently on the forehead, returning to the filing cabinet, aimlessly shuffling some folders. The silence incubated little momentum on either side.

Derek watched her withdraw in silence. The further back she pulled, the closer he came to real time and space "OK, fine. I'm going to call you for a real honest to goodness date!" he blurted out to her back. "One on one. You and me. No going out with a bunch of cops."

Only this man could make an invitation into an insult. Kelly turned and looked him square in the eye. 'You still don't get it, you crazy Armenian.' The idea isn't to make me happy. It's for you. This is something you have to do on your own."

He knew she was right. She always was. He watched Kelly sit down next to his desk again, crossing her arms defiantly. He took his latest cartoon, crumpled it up and banked a rim shot into the trash can. "Hey let me tell you about the Furtado case," he said, changing the subject.

Kelly picked up on the invitation to switch topics. She needed a change of venue. Everyone had baggage, even herself. She would keep the door open, but the detective had issues to resolve. She took a deep breath. "Sounds pretty exciting even by big city standards. Although we seem to be the only ones to care," she added.

"The girl's name was Carol Boerner. From Dorchester. Made it big by Southie standards. Went to Boston University on a Merit scholarship. No known living relatives. Left Boston after college and headed for the sun and fun of Florida and Jimmy Buffett. Last known address was Jacksonville."

"Jax? Hum." Kelly scribbled notes in her case file.

"No need to do that. I'll give you a copy," Derek said. "Anyway, straight shooter as far as we can tell. No arrest records.

No outstanding warrants. Worked in some kind of shop on the beach. Store manager or something."

"Florida. I wonder what she was doing up here from Jacksonville this time of year. Too late for the beaches and too early to be a leaf peeper."

"Beats the hell out of me." Derek closed the folder. Everything was memorized. "Never married. No family. No boyfriend, just a dog. A pillar of respectability. For all we know she was a victim of an Internet predator. You know, lonely heart club kind of thing."

Kelly scoffed. "Maybe just at the wrong place at the wrong time." She took a copy of the floppy disc offered by the detective and placed it in her folder.

"We made the ID just by luck. Initially we focused on the rose tattoo on her ankle. The local tattoo parlors identified the work as something from the Navy. The Naval War College in Newport referred us to the Mayport Naval Base in Jacksonville, Florida. Then we found her monogramed skirt with a receipt for a bagel and cream cheese tucked away in the waistband in a vacant lot near the murder scene. Without that receipt, we'd still be searching. We traced the two-dollar bagel back to the Westin in Boston."

"Anything interesting there?" Kelly asked staring at her data sheet.

"One ticket to the IMPROV for the night of her death suggests she was alone up here. She was a simple girl traveling on a short trip to the big city. Her airline tickets were paid for in cash. The doorman doesn't even remember her leaving the day of her murder."

"Do you think Carl would really troll for his victims in Boston? It's a 50 mile ride from Fall River," Kelly said. "I don't think so."

Derek took a sip from his tea mug swirling the cinnamon stick a few times. Her point was well taken. "Hey, didn't you go to school in Florida?"

"I did my residency there, in fact. In Jacksonville. Emergency Medicine. 'Triage-me- away-from- U-H-J'," Kelly said aimlessly. She stood up to go.

"What?"

"'Say what', partner. You're supposed to slur the words. It means something to the effect of 'I beg your pardon, could you please repeat yourself' in southern-ese."

"Come on Kelly, I'm asking about the first thing you said. Triage something or other."

"Oh, that. It's a tee shirt I had made up for our senior resident's graduation party. UHJ is the University Hospital of Jacksonville where I did my emergency medicine residency. It was a standing joke with us."

"Who?"

"The senior residents, we called ourselves the seven dwarfs. It was our motto. Our secret handshake, so to speak. Triage me away from our hospital. Get us out of here," Kelly said animated with laughter. "The teaching supervision was often so terrible, our time there was more like a bad job. We learned medicine on the backs of the poor black folks who thought we were real doctors." She noticed Derek's eyes wandering out the window, lost in distant memory. Was he thinking about his wife's accident again? His return to reality was slow. "Hey, are you listening?" she asked giving him a gentle nudge. She noticed Derek's stare at her skirt, slit to the knee.

He turned his head away embarrassed, but comforted with the knowledge looking at a beautiful woman was certainly not a felony, just a misdemeanor. "Anyway, I'm still trying to clean up a multitude of loose ends. Remember the old adage: 'When a crime takes place, something is always left behind, and something is always taken away.' Maybe something interesting will show up. Otherwise the state police consider the case a slam-dunk."

"You know, I've been wondering about that," Kelly said.

"About what?" Derek asked, drawing another cartoon. This one was of Kelly. It was more of a portrait then a caricature. He might even keep it himself.

"Just how neat and tidy it all appeared that night. I mean, don't you wonder just how perfect everything was? The bodies all lined up in a row. Everyone killing everyone else. Who called the cops? Just too perfect, if you ask me. Even the maggots crawling in and out of various body parts; just like the movies."

Kelly's suspicions took Derek by surprise. They mirrored his doubts about the crime scene before the department brass made it clear the case was over. Pressure from above, they said. Keep it simple, they said. "Yeh, I know what you mean," he said cautiously. "Still, the state police have closed their books on this. They just want Carl Furtado out of their lives for good," Derek said, handing Kelly his drawing.

The detective was talented, at least with his artwork. She wondered if his professional skills matched those of his hobby. Kelly carefully rolled up the art, slipping a rubber band on to the tube then placed it in her briefcase. "Here's my contribution to your dilemma."

She handed him a copy of her report. "The body count is now up to four."

Derek leaned forward visibly agitated. "Four?"

"Your simple girl from Florida was pregnant. There's another party out there who has something to contribute to our little passion play. Happy reading."

Derek scowled. "A new player might possibly put a different spin on the murder scene. This might change everything. Maybe I can get the boys at the top to reopen the case. Everyone assumed it was all over."

"Remember my motto," said Kelly, kissing him goodbye on the cheek. She turned and headed out the door. "Never assume anything," she called back. "because it makes an *ass* out of *u* and *me*."

Luxor, Egypt
325 BC

Their entourage remained with the royal barge while Im-Tep and Nefertari worked their way through two thousand years of their ancestral legacy. Almost every pharaoh left his mark in the maze of temples, walls, columns, and obelisks. Fractured megalithic statues of Ramses the Great guarded the outside walls. Hieroglyphs recorded real and imagined deeds marking the greatness of kingdoms and battles long gone. Im-Tep confidently navigated the rubble-strewn paths slowly approaching the inner sanctum of the high priests. He insisted Nefertari bring along a large palm frond. Several times along the way he assisted his wife across fallen columns or stones deposited by earthquakes or looters; but he never released his grasp on the treasure bag that once belonged to her late husband, Tanis.

They were alone. He was sure of it. Desert sands encroached on the entire temple works. Light penetrated the interior labyrinth through cracks between the stone blocks. They were invisible from both the land and the river and, therefore, safe. Only the gods knew of their presence and even that conclusion was suspect.

Im-Tep halted in one corner of the innermost sanctuary. The chamber was replete with statues and images carved on every surface. He searched the walls on the temple's north face. Nefertari stood by silently and observed her husband in amazement. In all their years together they never left the comfort of Alexandria. This was her first pilgrimage this far up the Nile and her first entrance into the great temples of the ancients. She felt as a child in her wonderment. There was much to see in the world and she was impatient. She was no longer a simple village girl. Privately she disagreed with Im-Tep's fears and his need to retreat into the desert lands. The wealth that facilitated his rise in power with the Greeks had been hers. She was a reluctant participant to this current plan.

"The knife," he commanded waving her closer while leaning on a block of ragged granite. A large fragment of limestone relief crunched under his foot.

Nefertari removed a blade of iron from beneath her robe and handed it to her husband. She watched transfixed as he maneuvered the blade in one corner of the stone touching one specific hieroglyph when, to her amazement, the whole piece suddenly moved. He pushed again and the stone pivoted on an unknown base revealing an opening large enough for a crawling man to enter.

"How?" Nefertari asked in amazement.

"At one time our people were great engineers," Im-Tep said, moving forward on his belly. He disappeared into the darkness beyond. "The priests of the ancients needed a means to enter and exit these holy sanctums as if by magic. These temples are riddled with paths such as this." Only his arm protruded from the vault. He waved it motioning her closer. "The bag," commanded his disembodied voice. "This will keep our secret safe."

She dutifully obeyed, sliding the heavy satchel forward until it touched his hands. He pulled the treasure after him and disappeared once again into the vault. A moment later Im-Tep reappeared. His hands reached inside the vault and leaned on an unseen mechanism. The stone sealed itself as if by magic, no evidence remaining of their intrusion.

"The gods had nothing to do with this?" Nefertari asked staring at the stone.

"No, my love," Im-Tep said wiping the dust off his hands and clothes. "It is a simple matter of weights and counterweights the ancient ones discovered long ago. Touch here and here," he directed with the knifepoint, "and the stone moves. There is a lever on the inside that returns the stone to its original point of rest. See, reach here and pull like so."

Nefertari watched in amazement as he repeated the motion several times both within the sanctuary and the hidden tunnel. Until this moment her thoughts had been not so much on the stone as they were on the comforts and luxuries she had been forced to abandon in such haste. Now the stone focused her attention. "May I try, my lord?"

Im-Tep smiled and patted her on her head as if she were a small child. "Of course, my wife. Here." He handed her the knife kneeling by the secret stone.

The blade seemed to dance in her delicate fingers as she touched the proper place. The stone opened once again. "And to close?"

"You only need to press here." Im-Tep said, lying on his back within the tunnel. He readjusted the treasure bags inside the tunnel.

Nefertari seized the opportunity she had long awaited. The blade came down three times into her husband's unprotected chest before he realized his fatal error of judgment. She watched him try to raise himself up on his elbows but failed, never forming any words after the first blow. When he stopped moving she reached inside the tunnel, removing several smaller items from the treasure bag. She then pulled on the lever Im-tep so proudly but foolishly revealed. The stone closed sealing her deed for all eternity.

Now, the secret is safe, she thought confidently. Her return alone to the royal barge was not questioned. Lord Im-Tep's reputation for desert intrigue was well known.

The captain bowed as she stepped on deck. "Are we sailing now or are we to wait for lord Im-Tep?"

"Lord Im-Tep is delayed. He will meet us further up the Nile. He tells me there is much wonder to see along the river. You may proceed."

"Yes, Lady Nefertari."

Peoples Bank, Fall River
October 6th

The seating area in the bank lobby was full. Derek leaned against the wall, holding onto number seventeen. The electronic monitors above his head repeatedly flashed number six. Waiting gave him time to review the circumstances of his financial demise. The margin call on Intel had come though. He needed money quickly or his home might be in jeopardy. Cash flow was never the issue until this sudden demand from his broker for a lump sum payment. His lids grew heavy from inertia and fatigue. It had been another sleepless night. The dreams were getting worse.

A tap on his shoulder woke him from a semi-comatose state. "Hey, mista', I think you're next," a gruff but polite voice said in a thick Portuguese accent. The man that stirred him into consciousness was thick in size, speech and mannerisms, a several-day-old stubble sprouting from his face.

Probably from the island of St Michael's in the Azores, Derek thought envious of the man's mustache with its fine pointed waxed tips. "*Obrigado*, thanks," Derek said in Portuguese. The man nodded. Derek turned and followed the hand signal from the next service representative into an open booth. Privacy was limited to a knee wall.

"Now, Mr., ah, Ekizian, I hope I'm pronouncing your name properly. How can we help you today?" asked the sixty-ish dour-face woman, clearly bored with her job.

"Well, I'm sort of in a bind. I need to pull out equity in my house as soon as possible," Derek said. He came prepared with his supporting documents. This was not his first time. He piled the past three years of income and bank statements and copies of the latest house appraisal on the woman's desk.

The customer service representative looked at the package and smiled. She inspected the documents briefly. "Oh, yes. This will do quite nicely. I'll just complete this form for you and we will have an answer within seven business days," she said, her smile plastic.

"That's great," Derek acknowledged with a slight shake of his head, "but you don't understand. I need the money very soon. It's for my ah, my sick mother. Doctor bills and all," he said anxiously.

"Yes, yes," the woman said, oblivious to the urgency in his voice. "Your sick mother. I understand. I promise we will have an answer within seven business days."

His frustration level was rising. "You've already said that," Derek replied. "I need the money before then. Isn't there someone else I could speak with?"

The demand for a supervisor insulted her authority. "Mr. Ekizian, we are governed by a strict set of rules set forth by the Federal Reserve Bank of the United States. Even God, himself, would have to wait the seven business days. We all have to obey the government. I would suggest you accept that which is beyond your control and be patient."

Derek knew things might come to this. His last refinance with People's bank was six months ago and that, only after schmoozing the appraiser. His debt to income ratio already exceeded federal guidelines. The real estate market was tight now and home sales slowing as the economy cooled. Leveraged to the hilt his mortgage payments were stretched to the thirty-year maximum. He took a deep breath. "Well, I do know Bill Kasson, the vice president here. Do you think I can speak to him?"

"He's a very busy man." The woman looked up from her desk and saw the look in Derek's eyes. She hesitated then picked up her phone and dialed an intra-office extension. Her initial air of contempt turned to one of surprise. "He'll see you right now, Mr. Ekizian." She rose from her desk to show him the way.

"That's quite all right," Derek said with a smile. "Been there a few times," he said entering the corridor. Two knocks later and he crossed the threshold to Kasson's office.

Bill Kasson was an old poker buddy. A fortuitous marriage propelled him into his position of power and authority. His office, cavernous with paneled walls of oak and cherry stretching from floor to the top of the twelve-foot ceilings, was the epitome of 19th century luxury. Kasson sat behind a massive lawyer's desk, centered on a red and blue oriental carpet that, alone, was probably worth more then Derek's home.

"Hey, Derek," Kasson said shuffling a stack of documents into a drawer. "Have a seat." He motioned to the larger chair that sat directly in front of his desk. The size of his office furniture only served to accentuate his diminutive stature. A nose several sizes too large for his face dangled down to his trademark bow tie. Deep-set eyes danced nervously behind thick spectacles. An exquisitely hand tailored suit almost masked the hump in his back. Almost. Nature had not been kind.

"Hey, Bill. Thanks for seeing me on short notice," Derek said, reaching over the desk to shake hands.

"No problem. What's this crap about your sick mother? Alice is in perfect health. She was with my mother yesterday, playing bingo at the parish hall. What's up?" Kasson asked, giving his full attention. He leaned backwards into his chair listening to his supplicant.

"Sort of in a bind. Stock market and all. Got to refinance and pull whatever equity I can out of the house by Friday, before the margin call is due."

Kasson scanned the supporting financial documents that Derek had brought earlier. "Jesus, you really are stretched out to the max. It's going to be tight if we use the federal guidelines, but I have some leeway as one of the bosses around here. I have some discretion with certain special customers. The interest rate is a bit higher, though," Kasson said, scribbling down a number and pushing it across the desk.

Derek looked at the figure and tried not to blanch. The rate quoted bordered on usury. A loan shark could have done better. Both men knew that he had no choice. "That'll do fine," Derek said. "Where do I sign?"

Kasson smiled. "No need for formalities. I'll take care of everything."

"By Friday?"

"Done deal." Both men stood and shook hands. "See you Monday night?" Kasson asked. Poker was the only vice he openly acknowledged.

"Of course," Derek said, waving goodbye. He exited through the bank's massive doors onto South Main Street. The wind was picking up from the northeast. He pulled his coat collar tight around his neck and slowly walked to police headquarters.

Luxor, Egypt
1830 AD

The boys played in small gangs of four and five running in and out of the pillars like the desert sand that half buried most of the long abandoned structures. Luxor was a small village, it's peak glory years three millennia in the past. It survived passively in cadence with the rise and fall of the Nile. Silence ruled the temples where pharaohs once stood and the people of Egypt prayed by the millions. Imaginary forts, built with fallen debris from the ancient temples, separated the children by age and authority.

"*Sibni khalini amchi*, let me go," Aristod demanded in Arabic. The weight of his brothers and cousins had him pinned in the sand. Not yet into puberty his opponents grossly outclassed him. Today they made him eat sand. Tomorrow they would pray at the mosque together and attend religious school as if nothing were the matter.

"How many times have we warned you?" Omar said. He was the eldest and their leader. "Stay home with the girls. You are too little to play with us." At fourteen, Omar towered above everyone. He taunted his baby brother by releasing a handful of sand in his face.

"But I don't want to stay with them. I want to play with you," Aristod spurted, spitting out a mouthful of sand in between the words.

"We warned you. Now it's too late."

The boys began to chant. "Lock him in the prison. Lock him in the prison."

Aristod eyes widened with fear. He had heard of the 'prison' but had never been permitted entry. Now the secret would be forced on him.

Omar's small army carried the boy into the recesses of the temple. Aristod fought and struggled futily with every step. As they entered the inner sanctum, the brilliant desert sunlight all but disappeared. Aristod was thrown unceremoniously to the ground.

"This will teach you a lesson," Omar said.

"Why, what are you going to do to me?" Aristod cried. He stepped backwards away from the crowd of boys until he felt a wall at his back.

"It's not us that will be doing anything to you. It will be the will of Allah," Omar laughed retreating with his friends. "You're going to spend the night here." Their collective strength moved a large granite block, sealing the entrance. Aristod was going nowhere for the night.

"What am I to do if the devil dogs come?" Aristod said, fighting back the tears. The packs ran wild at night. He had heard tales of them devouring children and small pets.

Omar hesitated. Everyone knew about the devil dogs. He had not seen one himself, but at night, when the moon was full, you could hear their cries in the desert hills. It would not go well for him with his parents if his brother was eaten. Still, the boy had to be taught a lesson. Besides, he thought, he did have eight brothers. What was one more or less in Allah's grand scheme? "Here, take my knife," he said reluctantly. He pushed the blade through the narrow opening. "Good bye, little sheep dung."

"Wait! Wait!" Aristod called out. But it was too late. He was alone. He pushed against the rock the older boys had used to block the entrance with all his might, but it was immobile. He searched the walls with his fingers and eyes all to no avail. He pounded the walls and screamed at the top of his lungs, but no one acknowledged his presence. Giving up he sat down in a corner and began to cry. It was going to be a long night.

Aristod sat in one corner of the room and began his wait. Occasionally he manipulated the knife in his hand against one of the rocks. He traced the tip of his blade into the ill-defined limestone carvings poking at the eyes of the various animals that made up the pictures. This motion was repeated over and over again for minutes. Suddenly, with one pass of his blade, the block of stone at his back began to move. He jumped back in surprise. It did move, he was sure of it. He pushed again. This time the block of stone swung open revealing a narrow passageway. It was dark, but anything was better then staying where he was.

The tunnel was narrow and filled with debris. A torch would have revealed skeletal remains at his feet. But there is comfort in ignorance. Slowly he worked his way through the underground labyrinth. At one point he pushed against an object that rattled with the sound of metal against metal. This he would keep. Minutes later the ground below him became wet and muddy; ahead, evidence of a faint light. He pushed forward with renewed determination. A wall of soft wet mud blocked his egress. A final shove with his feet knocked aside two thousand years of abandonment. He emerged into the sun light on a shallow cliff above the bank of the Nile. Aristod smiled. He had escaped. Now he had a secret, a new place to play and, as an additional bonus, a bag of souvenirs from within the temple.

Omar came home in time for his supper. His mouth fell open with surprise when he saw his little brother, Aristod, waiting for him at the table.

His father looked sternly. "Omar Abdel-Rassoul, is it true what your brother said?"

Omar looked at his brother and then back to his parents. He had some explaining to do.

St Christopher's Hospital, Fall River
October 7th

St Christopher's, the oldest and southern most anchor of the Caritas network in Massachusetts, inspired mixed confidence in the citizens of Fall River. Its physical plant was archaic and, more often then not, below current Joint Hospital Accreditation guidelines. It survived due to the largess of the Diocese and the allegiance of the Catholic population in Fall River. Derek paced nervously outside the second floor corridor of the Education Center, intermittently peering through the door's glass window. Kelly was giving a series of lectures inside. It was his intention to ask her for a date. His efforts two days before were thwarted by Kelly's catastrophe in the ER. Now there would be no excuses on either of their parts.

Inside he heard Kelly's voice lecturing to the paramedics and nurses. The class of twelve sat restlessly, shifting their bodies in the small desks better suited for parochial school adolescents then for mature adults. She ran through several scenarios on trauma resuscitation to capture the student's interest, all to no avail. Derek had similar experiences lecturing at the police academy, so he sympathized. Most of the participants were here because their professional contracts mandated they be recertified in ACLS, Advanced Cardiac Life Support, once every two years. Several had street skills well in excess of their instructors. Others were administrators at the opposite end of the scale who hadn't seen the sharp end of an IV needle in years. It was Kelly's job to meld both ends of the class spectrum into a cohesive unit all equally skilled with the material from the American Heart Association.

Kelly glanced up to see Derek's face in the window and smiled. Her students noticed the distraction, many recognizing the familiar detective. Fall River was an everyone-knows-everyone kind of town to begin with. "OK, let's take a break. Get up and stretch for a minute," she said twirling her trademark lavender scarf around her ponytail. The man made her nervous in a nice kind of way.

"Hey, Kelly," Derek nodded with a smile as Kelly greeted him at the door.

"What brings you out here, Detective?" Kelly asked cautiously. It was better to play shy with this man. She flustered at the memory of their last contact.

"I was just wondering if you had plans for dinner tonight," Derek asked timidly. "I mean dinner and maybe a movie. Or just dinner if you're too busy. Either one or both. I don't mind. I mean actually, I'd like to do both," he blundered his palms sweating. "Oh, hell, Kelly. You know what I'm asking."

"Relax, Detective. I'm not going to bite. I've got nothing planned for the evening. In fact I'd love to join you."

Derek raised his eyebrows in surprise. "You would? Why that's just great."

"One thing though," Kelly said. "You're on my turf now. If you give me a hand, maybe I can finish up class sooner."

"Sure, anything," Derek agreed, relieved that the hardest part of the evening was over. "What do you want me to do?"

Kelly smiled like a shark. "Class, we have a volunteer. Detective, please assume the supine position on the table next to the defibrillator."

Next to Kelly's podium was a portable exam table with minimal padding and fragile aluminum legs. Derek hesitated briefly then did as instructed. Several of the older staff wisecracked watching him maneuver onto the small table. He rode out the humor with a couple of quick barbs of his own and began to count the ceiling tiles.

Kelly began her scenario "Detective Ekizian, here, was trying to ask a beautiful woman for a date. He became so flustered he experiences chest pains. Clutching his chest he collapses in front of you. Betty, you're first up. What do you do?"

The young nurse giggled and cautiously approached the 'victim'. Hesitating for a moment she shook Derek's shoulder. "Are you all right? If he doesn't answer, I'd call 911 and treat this as a witnessed arrest algorithm per the ACLS manual."

"Great," Kelly said. "But the first thing you should have done is check his insurance."

Laughter broke out in several rows. Tension eased as they got into the swing of things. Kelly reviewed the algorithm mantras: alternating electrical shocks and drugs. Derek patiently played the role of various victims, each scenario specifically tailored to a different chapter in the ACLS manual. He watched in awe while Kelly effortless and expertly moved around various pieces of equipment, charging defibrillators in synchronized and unsynchronized modes, demonstrating series of rhythms on the cardiac simulator.

At five o'clock the last of the students had left. Derek helped

Kelly pack up the mannequins and the electronic gear in their appropriate storage containers until the next class a few months from now. He was fascinated with the electronics and the theories behind the teaching monitors, in particular. His department had just received funding for automatic defibrillator placement in every squad car. Between his friendships with Nunez and Kelly, he had more exposure to emergency medicine then most of the instructors his department had recruited. That experience would encourage a promotion somewhere down the line.

Their work was done. "Is it my turn now?" Derek asked.

There was something about the man's smile that made her feel safe. "You're the boss. Let's go," Kelly replied taking his arm. She knew immediately that gesture was a mistake. Derek took two steps and suddenly became stiff and awkward. This wasn't the first time he had the reflex of a startled turtle when she became even remotely intimate. He retreated into his shell with every step forward. Widower's guilt, again, thought Kelly. She wanted this evening to happen but not at any cost. The man's eyes looked like a deer caught in headlights.

Kelly's cell phone rang. She disengaged her arm and removed the phone from her shoulder bag. It was Rick Nunez asking about a schedule switch for the ER at the end of the month. She knew Derek couldn't hear the other end of the conversation. "Sure, Rick, I'll come in now." She cleared the call from her phone and turned to Derek. "Sorry, duty calls. They need another body in the ER tonight," she lied. "Maybe we can do this again some other time."

Derek looked at her and shook his head in acknowledgment. He gave her a kiss on the cheek and slinked away, his thoughts impenetrable.

Valley of the Kings, Egypt
1914

Blair looked at the photograph in his hand. It was a nice shot of himself, the budding Egyptologist of his generation, preparing to climb the scaffolding of tomb KV56. KV was the abbreviation for Kings Valley. '56' referred to the 56th tomb of the ancient Egyptians identified by modern day explorers in these bleak desert mountains. Gardner Wilkinson, his 19th century predecessor, was the first to discover this resting place of 4000 years of Egyptian royalty. With any luck the hard work of the past year would soon come to fruition. The fame of his team might surpass those who wrote the textbooks. Wilkinson and Blair might someday be mentioned in the same breath. Wiping the sweat from his balding head, he tucked the handkerchief into his vest pocket and replaced the photograph into the binder.

Other stellas discovered by his men last dig season confirmed the tombs of this area to be late kingdom, probably about the time of the Nubian or Greek conquest. It was a frustrating year for Blair's team. They knew burial chambers were near by, but thousands of years of debris and earthquakes made any discovery more accidental then academic. Funding was always a problem as well. Although his patrons in England were richer then any mortal beings could justify, they were impatient as most inbred royalty. Few understood archeology was a slow and meticulous science requiring great patience. In their eyes it was better to be lucky then good. They demanded results. With word of success his masters would leave their country estates to safari in these primitive lands for a single photograph; then retreat back home in time for fox hunting.

Blair's aid, Maloof, interrupted his private musings. He lifted the side of Blair's personal tent and entered. "*Allah ma-ak*, may Allah be with you, effendi. It is as you foretold," Maloof said bowing with respect as he touched his hands to his forehead, lips and chest in one continuous motion. His clothes and turban projected a man of the desert. "The men have uncovered a new stella," he said, his movements animated.

The labor gangs toiling on the cliffs accelerated their usual languid work pace the closer the smell of fortune and fame. Most were good, simple men who needed the work even though it was hard and tedious. Many were hundreds of miles from their native villages or towns, separated from their wives and children for months during the peak of the dig season. The discovery of a piece of their own history made them dream of a more glorious time in their collective history. Each shovel or trowel full took them a hundred years further into the past.

"Let us go and take a look." Blair shook out his pipe onto the bare floor of his tent and placed it in his pocket. His shirt was saturated with sweat and clung to him like a second skin. Friends back at Cambridge would laugh if they saw him now. It was a far cry from the cocktail parties and formal occasions of their youth. There were no servants to press and starch his clothes in these mountains; no linen or china on the dinner table. He began the long climb up the hemp and wood ladder, Maloof following closely behind. Each step brought him closer to knowledge. He would leave the treasure to others. Reaching the top rung, he gratefully accepted the assistance of an unknown arm, then stretched out his weary back.

The workers at the top ledge parted as he made his way to the carvings that was the focus of so much excitement. The stella, a large stone carved with a message from the days of the ancient Egyptians, stood five feet high and twice as long. The upper right corner was missing but otherwise the stone appeared to be intact. The beauty of its design alone was worth the months of this current dig.

"Can you read the stella?" Maloof called out from below, scurrying up the final rungs of the ladder like a monkey. Youth had its advantages.

Blair removed his brush and cleaned the stella with the care such a national heirloom deserved. Slowly the carvings came to life. Behind him the sun was beginning to set. The stone glowed red with the desert glare. This was the real thing. This was why he had come to Egypt in the first place. From left to right, he traced the hieroglyphs.

"What does it say, Effendi?" Maloof asked again, this time by the Englishman's side.

Blair's eyes roved over the stone as he explored the carvings. "It's a royal stella, all right. I suspect there is a royal tomb within meters of this cliff face. Looks to be late dynasty. Hmm, let's see. It is the tenth year of his reign. Alexander has defeated the armies of the Nile. The Pharaoh has been killed in battle. The Greeks have graciously returned his body for burial, as is the tradition of the great ones. The priests of Karnack have prepared pharaoh as they have his fathers before him." Blair hesitated, deliberately calculating the impact of his next words. "Within the tomb lies the future for the next real pharaoh of the people of Egypt."

"What does it mean by "future", Effendi?"

Blair looked around at his excited crew. His last words had been translated into Arabic and Copt even before he had finished each sentence. It would be better if the stella's true meaning remained mysterious to these men. "I guess we'll have to just go in and find out for ourselves," Blair said, shaking out his pipe. It was time to send a message to his patrons in England. Maybe to the whole world if his suspicions were correct.

Fall River, Massachusetts
October 8th

The health club closed in another hour. A dedicated fitness buff, Kelly might still be there tonight. Her eyes, that's all he could think about. A touch of liquid courage eased his angst. It was only one glass of port. She shouldn't raise a stink about one lousy glass. He had to give this dating thing another shot. Derek mustered up his courage, crossed the double entry way of the Fall River Health and Racket Club and greeted the clerk at the front desk.

The woman, tall with short brown hair and a bashful demeanor, smiled politely. "Can I help you?" She asked.

"Sure, Janae, is it?" Derek asked, looking at her nametag. He flashed his detective's badge. "I was wondering if one of your members was here tonight, Kelly Gill?"

The woman touched her computer screen twice. "Yes, she is," she answered hesitantly. "Came in about an hour ago. She should still be at the fencing clinic. Is there a problem?"

"Fencing?" Derek asked ignoring her question. "Like the three musketeers?"

"Yes, we're the only place in Fall River that specializes in all three weapons. Saber, Foil and Epee," she said proudly. She noticed Derek's air of distraction. "If you care to have a seat, I'll page her for you."

Derek's mind raced through the possible scenarios. He didn't want to appear to be obsessed nor did he want Kelly feeling stalked. "That's OK. I think I'd like to surprise her."

The receptionist hesitated then buzzed him in. "To the end of the corridor and turn right. You can probably hear the sounds of the dueling," she added, her voice fading further as Derek turned the corner.

The sound of metal against metal echoed through the hallway. Derek's disorientation to the club's layout resolved the closer he came to the sound of archaic combat. The dueling room measured at least 20 by 40 feet, the size of two racket ball courts side by side. Mirrors spread floor to ceiling around the entire perimeter. The floor was wooden except for matted runways outlined in yellow fluorescent tape. In front of him two helmeted duelers were alternately exchanging parries, thrusts and lunges under the watchful eye of a wizened referee following their every move with comments and instructions that reeked of a vocabulary from a more romantic era.

"Come on, my lovely. Where is your courage? You must attack, attack, attack," the coach said with his heavy Slavic accent. The elder man's hands were locked behind his back except for those moments he would gesticulate to emphasize a point. "I have seen better leg work on a piano bench. Use your brain, your brain. Look at what he has done to you. You fight like a little girl, not a woman," he chastised one of the combatants.

The woman's dejected behavior and occasional wild sweep of her sword showed she was clearly getting the worst of it. Words 'attack', '*alle*', 'parry', and '*flash*' echoed in the room. Finally the match was over. Both fencers saluted each other and removed their helmets. Kelly was indeed the woman behind the mask. Derek was annoyed that the other fencer was John Brady, a surgeon and one of the most eligible bachelors on the hospital staff.

Kelly almost walked right past him. She looked up and smiled. "Hey, Derek."

"Hi, Kelly." He noticed Brady was only a few feet away and closing in on them quickly.

"To what do I owe this honor?" she asked pleasantly.

"I thought we might get together for coffee or something. If it's not too late of course."

Brady, oozing confidence, came up from behind Kelly placing his hand on her shoulder.

Kelly hesitated, looking at both men. She had never been the focus of two men simultaneously and the feeling was tantalizing. "I'd love to, Derek, but I've already made plans. John was kind enough to ask me out for a quick bite. Maybe tomorrow?"

"Sure, maybe tomorrow," Derek replied, watching Kelly disappear into the locker room.

"She is hot, hot, hot," Brady said staring at Kelly's pivot and the tightness of her fencing pants. "I don't believe we've met. I'm Doctor John Brady and you are...."

"Derek Ekizian. Pleased to meet you."

Both men sized each other up with equally vise like handshakes and eyeball-to- eyeball stares. "Ever do any fencing?" Brady asked, flexing the blade of his weapon.

"Can't say that I have," Derek replied, distracted, planning his next move.

"She'll be a few minutes. Women, you know, they can take their time. Would you care to take a quick lesson? I've got a few minutes."

Derek was pissed. It had taken a mountain of courage to get this far with Kelly and now a guy who reeked of money was bumping him into tomorrow. Who introduced himself with a title in this day and age? What a pompass asshole. The reality of economics made him intrinsically non competitive. Shit, the man probably drove a Porsche. He was feeling suddenly very self-conscious. Dejected, he looked up from the floor. "Sure, why not."

Brady helped Derek strap on a canvas fencing jacket and adjusted a wire mesh helmet on his head. The rules were simple. The Saber was a slashing weapon. Points were made only by hitting the target of the head and thorax with the upper third of the blade or the tip of the weapon. Brady gently bounced his sword on the target areas for demonstration. No hand, leg or arm cuts would do. They had to stay on the fencing runway otherwise it would be a foul. The one who attacked first had the 'right of way'. The defender had to parry the attack before scoring any points of his own. Five points to a set with a three set match.

"I really appreciate you taking time out to do this," Derek said, adjusting his speech to the restrictions of the chin guard. "I would think you should be in the shower by now."

"No problem," Brady replied suddenly slashing Derek on top of the facemask. "Point!"

The pain was vicious. Derek dropped his sword and clawed off his helmet with his gloved hand. "Shit!" The word must have echoed throughout the entire health club. He rubbed the top of his head fully expecting a geyser of blood. There wasn't any.

"Come on, old man. No pain no gain." Brady scored the next four points in rapid succession using his clueless opponent for target practice. The steel blade whipped around his back with the same intensity as if he had no protective gear on whatsoever. "Set!"

Derek was pissed. "That first one was just for practice, wasn't it?" he asked boldly.

"Got to keep your guard up. Here like this," Brady demonstrated, turning his wrist outward in a three quarter angle. "Keep your point at my chest. That way, an attack will slide off your blade outward and not score any points."

"Now you tell me," Derek grumbled through the mask.

"What's that?" Brady asked practicing a series of lunges.

"Nothing. I'm ready to go." Derek assumed the on guard position and waited.

"So you say." Brady attacked three more times and scored three points in a matter of a few seconds. "I'm disappointed. I thought you'd give me more of a challenge," Brady said returning to the middle of the runway. "I'll bring this down a bit to your level. Think of it as a kind of date. You attack. She parries. You thrust home and score."

"Thrust home, my ass," Derek said imperceptibly. He extended his right arm in a sudden thrust, attacking Brady's mask with a quick chop. "Point for the Fall River cop, I believe."

"Cop? So you're the police officer I've heard so much about. Not bad for your first point," Brady said, focusing on his opponent. "Beginners luck."

"How's that for beginners luck," Derek replied, sweeping his weapon into an attack arc and scoring another successful point on Brady's chest. He noted that his style and weapon swings were so unorthodox that Brady had difficulty defending against his attacks. As long as he attacked first, he kept Brady off guard and off balance. Several more passes and Derek had taken the set. All their noise, the yells, screams and clashing of metal on metal had now attracted quite a crowd of onlookers.

Brady now took the offensive. Metal slid on metal. Attack and defense alternated as the two men slid into the ways of human combat since the dawn of civilization. The 'lesson' had clearly deteriorated into something much more personal. Derek's response was often too little too late. Brady scored three more quick points and grew in confidence and boldness. "Skill and intellect will prevail," he said scoring a fourth point. One more and the set was over and the match as well.

For an athletic event that seemed less then demanding, Derek was sweating up a storm. He was down four to zero. There was little to lose at this point. Think different. Think. What could he do to upset Brady's tempo? Images of Cossacks and cavalry men floated through his memory. What the hell, he thought. He took his weapon and swung the saber several times around his head in a circle while simultaneously screaming a guttural sound. Brady froze long enough for Derek to bring his blade down sharply on the doctor's shoulder. Three more wild swings and the set was tied four all.

The crowd intensified. Sides were chosen based on friendship and professional affiliations. Derek clearly had the momentum and allegiance of most of the crowd. One point would settle the match. Brady had clearly lost confidence and control. It was a no win proposition for him. If he defeated this policeman, then everyone would say it was expected. If he lost, his reputation was at stake. Derek had nothing to lose. The men ran at each other simultaneously. No points could be scored. The ring of blades, parries and thrusts reverberated with the chants of their audience.

Derek had one last TV show to imitate, Zorro. He stamped his foot three times on the runway, flashed a 'Z' for Zorro in the air and lunged forward.

Brady, meanwhile, made his own move. He lunged forward as well.

Derek made a perfect hit on his opponent's chest. His forward momentum brought him precariously close to Brady. The blade on his saber bent like a bow and snapped. Meanwhile Brady parried downward and brought the broken steel past his protective vest and down his bare leg. Blood poured out of a twelve-inch gash down the surgeon's thigh. Brady collapsed on the ground as onlookers rushed to his aid. Derek turned away and dropped his mask and gear on the runway where he stood victorious just a moment before, just in time to see Kelly enter the exercise room.

Kelly looked at Derek and smiled, nervously aware that something was not quite right in the room. Then she turned towards the commotion on the fencing runway several feet away. "What?" she asked, the words fading as she alternated her gaze between the two men, one standing in front of her, the other fallen.

"I think John needs your services. He probably won't be able to make it tonight," Derek said walking past her, defeated in victory.

Valley of the Kings
1914

Blair turned on the diesel generators with a flourish, his right hand weaving in the air like a magician. The machine spewed out black smoke, coughed and sputtered until the engine caught. Photographer's flash bulbs popped like firecrackers capturing the moment. For months his team toiled in abject poverty. Even replacing worn out shovels was an expense beyond his means. Now money flowed to him like wine at a bacchanalia because of his discoveries. Unfortunately most of his benefactors and hanger-on politicians saw this as a carnival, an opportunity to make money or to advance their careers and personal agendas.

Deep inside tomb KV57 the workmen prepared to enter the final burial chamber. Arabic, English and French swirled in melodic harmony as work progressed. The native Egyptians were the only ones who worked in silence. They knew they were in the presence of royalty. The ancient Egyptians were resurrectionists. Their descendents, the men who worked on Blair's team, shared this belief in an afterlife. A mummy's mutilation or destruction would impact the afterlife forever, so it was their duty to ensure respect for any find.

The Minister of Antiquities broke the final seal of the burial chamber with a smack of a hammer. The potbellied politician pushed ahead squeezing through the ancient corridors and bumping his fez covered head against the door jams. His entourage hurried after him blindly kicking aside the debris of a thousand years and as many earthquakes.

"*Moustaeed teftah el makbara*, we are ready to open the tomb," the director of the Cairo museum said, lighting up a cigar. Everyone inside the chamber had a pecking order. This man was near the top.

The air in the burial chamber was stale enough from three thousand years of inactivity. Blair forced back a wave of nausea from the odor of the cigar. Diesel fumes, cigar smoke, and the breath of a dozen men made Blair long for England. He reluctantly joined the others in the burial chamber.

The room was cavernous in contrast to the narrow pathways

Blair endured to this point. His men scurried to establish more lighting in the chamber, dragging wires, kerosene lamps and torches to better illuminate the interior. The chamber was stunning in design and contents. The walls were decorated ceiling to floor with hieroglyphs. Jars, the size of men, were stacked with provisions for the afterlife. In one corner an entire river barge had apparently been dismantled, carried into the mountainside and then reassembled for the benefit of Pharaoh for his new journey. A chariot lay dismembered. The mummies of the royal horses were clearly visible. Treasures of gold and silver worthy of a royal household were piled high on top of each other.

Blair breathed a sigh of relief. It appeared that this tomb had been left undisturbed by the ubiquitous tomb robbers. He so desperately wanted the entire scene to be meticulously photographed, diagramed and catalogued. The dignitaries and invited guest were already filling their pockets with souvenirs. Blair knew to save his breath and did not protest.

The attention of his patrons and the Minister turned to the sarcophagus in the center of the burial chamber. The obese politician waddled closer to the long structure, blocking out the light like an eclipse, then moved on to the opposite side. Blair approached and let his hand rest on the metal. It was silver, typical of the New Kingdom, measuring ten feet long by five feet in height. The lid of the sarcophagus was slowly pried open by the clawing hands of the Minister as he directed his own personal attendants with a crowbar. It took five men to lift the top and then they promptly dropped it on the floor. Blair cringed. How much damage did they do this time, he wondered.

Now the photographers pushed their way past Blair. The Minister was the first to peer into the sarcophagus, smiled and waved Blair to his side. The Englishman was held in a bear hug as more flash bulbs popped around him. He smiled politely desperately impatient to see the fruit of his months of toil. It was all he could do to share a glimpse into the silver casket as others repeatedly jostled him aside. Finally it was his turn.

The mummy was exquisitely adorned in silver and gold wrap. A crook and flail crossed the mummy's chest and gold jewelry lay piled on the body. Blair searched the interior of the silver casket and its magnificent treasures with his eyes and then repeated the motion gently with his hands. The look of disappointment was noticeable only to his foreman.

"Fantastic, Dr Blair, eh? *Mabrouk*, congratulations," the Minister stated, beaming for the photographers. He slapped the Englishman soundly on the back.

Blair nodded his head meekly in agreement. Handshakes were exchanged and champagne ordered all around. Bottles overflowed on the floor desecrating ancient treasures. More photographs were taken. Blair politely excused himself and exited the tomb. He slowly descended the ladder to the base of the cliff and worked his way back to his private tent. The implications of what he didn't find were unquestionable. He had a passionate need to be alone at this time. He took refuge on his cot starring up at the canvas ceiling.

Maloof entered without announcing his presence or requesting permission. "Effendi, there is sadness in your eyes. What is the matter?" He had to know what the Englishman knew.

Blair looked at his friend and feigned a polite smile. He rubbed the back of his neck with one hand. His neck muscles were in spasm from the tension. "We were not the first here."

"But we were the first to enter. The tomb was sealed," Maloof observed.

Blair shook his head in the negative. "Probably resealed by the ancients or even tomb robbers." He sat quietly for a moment then stood up and went to his collection of maps and tracings. Reaching underneath the pile he removed his original tracing of the stella from tomb KV57, slipped the seal off the roll and spread it on the table. Several pieces of broken limestone fragments anchored its corners. "This is why," he said simply.

"I do not understand your concern," Maloof said, scanning the tracings. He had a good sense of the hieroglyphs. "It tells of the last Pharaoh, his death in battle at the hands of the Greeks and his burial. Nothing more."

Blair shook his head in disagreement. "It is more then that, my friend. It prophesizes the resurrection of the people of Egypt. It foretells a new dynasty and a sacred object that was buried with the last pharaoh that must be given to the new." Blair's hands moved across the paper. "This hieroglyph, here, represents the double crown of the upper and lower kingdoms. See the cobra and falcon joined on the top? The crown has never been found in any royal tomb because it was always passed down to the next pharaoh. When the Greeks conquered Egypt it was the one thing they did not have. The Ptolemy's had to create a facsimile. I believe that the original was buried here in KV 57 with the last real pharaoh of Egypt."

"But the sarcophagus appeared to be in tact. I thought we were the first to enter in 2500 years," Ali replied.

"Everything in the desert is deceiving. I suspect it was several thousand years ago, but still this tomb was violated, your people's heritage either buried or broken apart for the jewels."

Both men sat in silence reflecting on the impact this revelation held for their respective futures. Blair finally stood up and invited his long time coworker to join him in a toast. This cross-cultural gesture was rare under any circumstance and the significance was not lost upon the two men. He poured Cognac in small shot glasses for his guest. "To the lost double crown of upper and lower Egypt," he toasted. They clinked their glasses in unison and drained them. "Come, let us join the others. There is much work still to be done."

Hatfield Memorial Hospital
October 9th

"You're hovering. You know I don't like it when you hover."

John Brady stood at the ER station in his usual state of perfection, hair slicked back and perfectly groomed, tie perfectly knotted, teeth perfectly white. "I'm not hovering. You called me, remember?"

"I called you because you're the surgeon on call tonight. Remember stretcher number four, the triple A? You're still blocking my light. I can't concentrate with you this close," Kelly replied in frustration.

"My charming presence driving you to distraction?" Brady moved a bit closer.

"More like your cologne," Amy, the unit coordinator, mumbled.

"What?" Brady said disarmingly. The thought that anyone could be less then 100% enamored with his presence was inconceivable. "How did you find this again?"

"A fluke, really," Kelly answered, looking up from her charts. "Just another eighty year old male with chronic constipation. Blamed it on eating too many sun flower seeds. When I did the rectal exam, I felt a mass. Called Sandfort and he did his usual dance. Wanted a CT of the Abdomen and Pelvis. I bugged radiology to do the procedure while the old guy was here. You know the type - laborer his entire life and too proud to ever complain about anything. They came back with the diagnosis of leaking triple A. No connection to whatever I was feeling in the rectum."

"Sometimes better to be lucky then good," Brady said condescendingly.

Kelly turned and smiled at the trauma surgeon doing her best to control her temper. "Amy, please get Dr Brady a progress note and show him the new dictation area."

"Certainly, Dr Gill. Follow me, Dr Brady," Amy said, leading the way.

Brady leaned forward towards Kelly. "What time is your shift over? Maybe I can make up for last night," he whispered. It would not do to make everyone aware of his interest.

"Are you recovered?" Kelly asked staring at Brady's wounded leg.

"Your friend almost assassinated me. Took twelve stitches to patch me up."

"From what I hear, you got what you deserved," Kelly replied turning back to her work.

"Hmm!" The response was Neanderthal.

Kelly smiled. For the first time in recent memory John Brady looked flustered. She had never seen the man's feathers ruffled. "John, I'd love to; but I've got some lab checks for the medical examiner's office still to do. I'm afraid tonight is going to be all work."

"Fine. But I will not be dissuaded. Maybe I'll meet you there and give you a hand." Brady gave her a wave goodbye and retreated towards the dictation station.

"Anytime," Kelly mumbled considering the possibilities. The remainder of the ER shift was uneventful for anything dramatic. By seven o'clock at night her shift was over.

Rick Nunez was on duty. The man already had a phone glued to his ear working some side venture. "Hey, Kelly. What you got?" He took a sip from his mocha cappuccino.

"Sixty-five year old woman with chest pain in number three. This is her third visit in the past week. She's had a negative stress test last week but wants a cardiac catheterization and she wants it tonight, you know the type. Enzymes should be back in about an hour."

Nunez flicked on his AOL e-mail while listening to her. "One catheterization coming right up with burgers and fries. Next?"

"Usual drunken bookends in the isolation room. Both have alcohol levels above three hundred just a couple of hours ago."

"I'm jealous," Rick said. He drained his coffee and crushed the cup, blindly tossing it over his shoulder and hit the trash can five feet away perfectly. "Anyone else?"

"That's all she wrote," Kelly said. She picked up her briefcase and purse. "If anyone is looking for me, I'll be in the lab for a bit."

"Sure," Nunez said, distracted by an EKG thrust in his face from one of the roving techs. "The lab." It was time to dig in to the pile of charts.

Kelly excused herself and headed to the lab. The elevator was crowded with the usual staff and families all trying to complete their obligations and rounds before visitor hours were over. The original structure of Hatfield Memorial was too old to retrofit to the new HICFA guidelines and converted instead to labs and private offices.

She walked down the empty hallway and entered the remains of the old micro lab knowing she would be left undisturbed. No one came into this wing of the hospital until the morning. Inside the lights were fluorescent and took a few seconds to catch, the air stale with the odor of formaldehyde.

She removed her lab notebook and went directly to the incubator. Today was day fourteen since the maggot larvae were removed from stasis and placed in the growing chamber. Something was not right with the Furtado murder scene but she couldn't put her finger on it. She was doing her best to sort out the devil's work and find some kind of truth buried beneath the drama of death. Her boss, Rafferty, was of no help and neither was her favorite Fall River detective, at least to this point. Donning latex gloves she held up each plate to the light. Each container held the maggot larvae from only one victim. All the larvae had hatched. So much for her theory that the murders were done on different days and the bodies all lumped together at one place. She would have to look elsewhere.

Her concentration was broken by the sound of a door closing loudly behind her. The noise took her by surprise almost making her drop the last container. This end of the hospital should have been empty until the morning shift. She was the only one who had any legitimate business here. "Who's there?" she demanded. She turned her back to the lab bench and picked up a heavy beaker to throw at any intruder.

"Whoa there, little lady. Take it easy. It's me, John," the surgeon said reassuringly. He was still in his surgical greens, his hands raised in the sign of universal surrender.

Kelly leaned back against the lab bench with relief. "Oh, John. I'm sorry. I wasn't expecting anyone at this time of the night."

"I can see," Brady said, walking up to her and gently prying the glass beaker from her white knuckled fingers. "I think you need to take a break before you hurt yourself. Or someone else for that matter."

Kelly shook her head in acknowledgment. "You might be right. I've probably been burning the candle at both ends. Between the ER and the medical examiner's office, sometimes I don't know whether I'm coming or going."

Brady leaned over the lab bench dropping his glasses below his nose. Bifocals were a pain. "What do you have here? Growing bugs for entertainment purposes or do you have something else in mind."

"Oh, these. Just seeing if the larval pupating days match." Kelly moved the containers to the side of the counter and began to write in her notebook.

"They all look to be about the same," Brady said, concentrating on the middle container. "Who's going to do the speciation?"

"What do you mean?" Kelly asked.

"Well, they all pupated on the same day. But the ones in the middle look to be different then the other two. Maggots may look the same, little white bastards that they are, but the flies that hatch can be different. Like these. Look," Brady directed, oblivious to the significance of his revelation.

Kelly looked at the ID on the container in Brady's hand. Container number three belonged to Carl Furtado. She smiled. Now maybe someone would listen to her.

Alexandria, Egypt
1917

"Did you bring it?"

Three brothers and their sister sat at a corner table in the rear of the café. The musicians and belly dancers had gone home for the evening. A triad of ceiling fans droned somewhere out of sight. Water pipes and pillows lay scattered on the floor. The air was thick with the smell of tobacco and hashish. The siblings were surrounded by stucco walls decorated with scenes of deserts, camels and pyramids for the benefit of any straggling tourist. The only illumination came from a few scattered wall sconces and table candles.

"Keep your voice down," Mohamed, the oldest, reprimanded. He adjusted the lapels of his white linen suit taken from the body of a tourist who was reluctant to part with his wallet years before. "The police have spies everywhere."

"Did you bring it?" Sayed, the middle brother, whispered again, thick hands constantly spinning the coffee cup in front of him. There was always urgency in his voice, even when the situation did not call for it.

"Of course not. What do you take me for, a fool?" Mohamed said, twisting his mustache. He was just as proud of the big droopy wad of hair over his upper lip as much as anything else in his life. "I have it hidden in a safe place, as it has been for a hundred years."

"And how do I know you haven't sold it or broken it apart?" Houri asked fearlessly. She was the youngest in the family. "As a woman I have the right to know," she blurted out in frustration. Her words were ignored as always, and, for that, she hated them all even more. A scar across her right cheek, a gift from her father for a perceived insolence, was the only mar to her classic beauty. Her obsidian eyes burned with a femininity that had yet to be quenched.

Mohamed patted her on the head like a puppy. The act was clearly patronizing and not lost on his sister. "A woman, now, are you? Ha!"

Houri recoiled at his touch. "Don't do that. You know I don't like to be touched," she growled pulling away from his outstretched arm.

All three brothers glared at her in disapproval. To question the eldest cast dishonor on them all. For a challenge to come from a woman was unthinkable. Mohamed ignored her protest, as always. Their secret had been passed down through generations. Blood ties and honor kept most of the treasure untouched by the outside world for a hundred years.

In the front of the café two drunken patrons sang patriotic songs off key, no bother to anyone but themselves. Behind the bar the familiar face of the owner repeatedly ducked below the counter placing bottles and glasses away for the night. Outside the occasional stench of garbage rotting in the summer heat wafted through open doors. Rats and an occasional stray dog foraged for their dinner at this late hour, nosing around the piles of refuse unchallenged.

Mohamed continued. "My oldest son has now reached his sixteenth year. As a man he must take his place at my side. Since father's death I have always sought your counsel when decisions affect the family. It is his turn to guard our family's treasure. I wish to reveal the secret of the desert we hold so dear. I call upon your blessings now."

Only Houri scowled at the tradition of the first-born son of the first-born son. She knew the youth in question. In her opinion he was an idiot at best. If Mohamed were to reveal the secret of their family treasure, she feared it would turn up in the bazaar within a month. Of this she was sure. One look at her brother's eyes squelched any protest she was about to voice. All, except for Houri, nodded their heads in assent. Her silence was ignored. Mohamed's son, Girgis, would now be privy to the secret that bound them more surely than blood. With time he would take physical possession of the ancient artifact.

Hassan, the youngest brother, raised his glass in toast. As a male his voice carried authority with the others. "May he guard the secret with his life."

Mohamed waved the bartender over. He brought a bottle of Raki to the table along with a plate of meza, olives, cheese and bread. Sayed poured three shot glasses. As the only woman Houri had to be satisfied with her Turkish coffee.

"A hundred years," their voices echoed in unison, clinking their Raki glasses together.

The pair of drunken singers, their voices getting louder and more intrusive with every passing moment, interrupted the celebration. The two men staggered backwards against their table, knocking over a few chairs weaving arm in arm in alcoholic revelry. Sayed stood up to encourage their departure. He was a mountain of a man and his sheer presence should have discouraged any drunken madness. The closest drunk kept on coming. He bumped Sayed with his shoulder, suddenly pivoted and threw his Bedouin robes on top of Sayed's head, blinding him momentarily. Simultaneously the other revealer pulled out a gun from underneath his robes and pistol wiped Sayed repeatedly about the head. Sayed fell to the floor in a bloody daze.

Two guns were leveled at the table. "Abdel-Rassoul brothers, you are all under arrest. Keep your hands out where we can see them." The café was suddenly filled with police all wearing the red Fez and bandoliers of the Interior ministry. All entrances and exits were covered. Any attempt at escape was futile. The brothers all leaned backwards in their chairs. No one wasted energy in the desert.

Houri drew her chador tight around her face as one of the policemen pressed her shoulder firmly into the back of the chair.

The captain in charge looked at her in contempt waving off the policeman to another area. "A woman? What do we want with a woman? We only have papers for the arrest of the Abdel-Rassoul brothers. You can go," the Prefect of Police said with an air of indifference.

"May I at least kiss my friends before you take them?" Houri asked in feigned shyness.

"It is no matter. But make it quick," the officer answered with disdain.

Houri leaned over the table and kissed her seated brothers twice on each cheek. She kissed only as a friend would kiss a friend. She needed to allay any suspicions from the police. Now was not the time for foolishness.

"Find Girgis. He can lead you to it," Mohamed whispered in her ear as his wrists were shackled behind him.

The realization that her brother had already betrayed the family secret was insignificant compared to the threat they all now faced. "A hundred years!" she called out to her brothers as they were led away. Houri waited until the café was empty then left. She could imagine the beating her brothers were already receiving at the hands of the police. Sayed would die before talking. The other two, well, she wasn't so sure how long they would last under interrogation. Running through the streets of Alexandria, she knew there was little hope for them. She had to find Mohamed's son, Girgis.

Fall River, Massachusetts
October 10th

Derek opened the door of his modest raised ranch and entered the mausoleum silently. The broken screen door nipped at his heels. Somehow it made more sense to time the slam of the door rather then spend a few minutes to fix it. The wooden floors squeaked and echoed beneath his feet as he made his way into the bowels of the house. He threw his coat on a threadbare winged chair, dropping his keys and loose pocket change into a ceramic bowl by the telephone. Scuff marks on the walls marked the impact of his shoes where he kicked them off.

Spartan furniture and a few tokens of his past lay scattered around the living room – trappings of his life as a bachelor and widower. A mirror made from sand dollars and sea horses bought on his honeymoon hung on the wall of the main hallway. A small seashell vase sat on the fireplace mantle next to two empty beer bottles. He was surrounded by memories, which refused to be diluted. Then again, why bother? Interior decorating had always been Rose's forte. In many ways she still lived here. He appreciated her company.

It was another boring day at the precinct station – mostly paperwork, routine reports and administrative meetings; the very foundation of empires within his department. Time spent ass kissing and paper shuffling always bored him to death. The conflict of good versus evil had to take a back seat to the new OSHA guidelines on proper disposal of latex gloves in the work place. It was time to decompress.

He hit the refrigerator, popped a beer and began to sort through the day's mail. Nothing more then junk and bills. Of course, if he never wrote anyone why did he expect mail? Only the dual glow of the television and computer screen saver eased the darkness. The lights were kept off unless there was company, a carry over from the days his father use to yell at him for wasting too much electricity. The thought of becoming his father made him shake his head and smile. All the years of teenage rebellion and he still had morphed into the old man.

There was comfort in this daily routine. He went to the answering machine and scrolled through the usual telemarketing calls.

The first real message was from his mother reminding him that he wasn't an orphan. She warned he was in danger of becoming a poster child for paternal neglect. Tonight there was a message from Kelly thanking him for his help in the ACLS course. There was a not so subtle dig about John Brady's wounds as well.

Derek thought he heard more then a casual encouragement in Kelly's voice. He smiled thinking about the way her eyes twinkled whenever she looked at him. Maybe someday…his thoughts dissolved as he sat at his roll top desk tackling the pile of bills lying dormant for the past month. Several were on the verge of delinquency. Kasson's loan was just barely enough to take care of the stock margin calls. At his current rate bankruptcy might be a viable option.

He wrote a few checks to the limit of his balance and moved over to the computer. The machines and technology were clearly not his forte, but a necessary evil. E-Mail was a toy worth having. His years in the military had introduced him to a wide menagerie of people who now roamed the four corners of the world. Many times he lived vicariously through their adventures. Plus there was his Godson, Al, Junior, the autistic son of his poker buddy and watch commander, Al Sherman. The teenager was his best Internet pen pal, waiting for him on line with the instant messenger service.

Mog: Hey, Uncle Derek, how are you?

Lone Ranger: Fine, Junior

Mog: I hate it when you call me Junior. My Internet name is Mog.

Lone Ranger: I know. That's why I do it. Where does 'Mog' come from?

Mog: Dragon Ball Z. What u doing?

Lone Ranger: Just got back from the station. Settling down for the evening.

Mog: See Dad?

Lone Ranger: Yep. He was coming on when I was heading home. Got to get some work done now and I know you have homework to do.

Mog: K. Are you going to listen to the CD I made you?

Lone Ranger: Always. Every night. Talk to you tomorrow.

Mog: K.

Derek signed off and shut down Windows for the night. His only Godson was a genius with computers; but, still considered autistic. Autism had layers like an onion. Concrete with poor verbal extrapolation, Junior found math and computers satisfied an entirely different area of the brain. He did not need verbal or social skills to work the magic of microchips and processors. The youngster had come to his rescue with this computer talent on more then a few occasions. So much of the world was computer dependent; yet, Derek felt like an alien in front of the machine most of the time.

The Bang and Olsen stereo LED cast a red glow of a fairy dance on the wall above his bookshelf. Derek's hands waved in front of the tuner. The CD player clicked on. Junior's CD was the only one on the carrousel. It was the only one he needed. The kid had customized all of Derek's favorite songs onto one disc. He sat back in his Adirondack chair, put on the headphones and listened in the darkness to Bread, Billy Joel, the Carpenters, Jimmy Buffett and Bob Marley. He held the neck of a cold Molson Ice with three fingers of one hand while he caressed a picture of his wife resting on his chest with the other. This was his routine every night as he rocked his nightmares to sleep, retreating into dreams when life was simple and perfect.

The last cut of the CD ended. It was Billy Joel's "Lullaby". Derek was still awake, in spite of alcohol and soft music. He held the picture of his wife in front of him and stared into her eyes, distracted by thoughts unimaginable the past two years. Only a few pale beams of moonlight penetrated his fortress living room. He still remembered the last time they kissed. What would Rose have thought if she could read his mind now? He pledged love only once. Soul mates from that first moment, their courtship was slow and deliberate, interrupted by college and then the military. When they finally did get married, they promised love would be forever. Then the accident. Shit happens and things change forever. God laughs when he hears the plans of men. Now he was almost forty years old. For the first night in two years he returned the photo to its place on the mantle before sunrise. Memories would live forever but it was time to move on. He kissed the face on the photograph and went to bed.

Somerset, Massachusetts
October 9th

Kelly lay curled up in bed, overwhelmed by a sense of longing she had not felt in years. Darkness surrounded her like a thick blanket – sometimes oppressive, sometimes reassuring. She was conscious of the warm body pressed against hers. His breath tickled the nape of her neck, his tongue more nuisance then pleasing. She cringed as the slobbering wetness creped up from her neck to her right earlobe. This was Max's usual routine. For some reason, his breath was unusually offensive tonight. There was a time and place for everything and now was neither. At this rate she was never going to get any sleep.

"Come on Max, cut it out!"

The black Labrador was oblivious to her commands and continued his playful attack. The more she objected the more he leaned his massive chest into hers; his snout tunneling under and above the covers in a choreographed attack. Soon the bed was a tussle of human and canine paws, hands and feet interlocking like a gigantic pretzel.

"That's it! You're out of here," she said, pushing the bulky form off her bed. The Lab looked back with deep brown eyes, temporarily wounded from the indignity. The insult faded a moment later and the dog bounded into the chair in the corner of the bedroom. Snoring soon followed. Kelly hated snoring either from man or beast. It was going to be a long night.

The bed was hers, alone, once again. She stretched out exhausted staring at the ceiling, but still craving the elusive arms of sleep. The swirled texture of the plaster above her head broke into tiny white lines. Those lines in turn disintegrated into still smaller segments. The little dots and dashes above her head began to wiggle. All she could think about were fly larvae, maggots, and pupae. She had pursued a hunch on her own, directly violating a direct order from Rafferty. Thanks to John Brady's astute observations she had spent the past three hours on line learning more about different species of flies then she'd ever wanted to know. The facts were absolute. The murder investigation needed reopening, but how? Sleep tonight would be a matter of chance.

Kelly got out of bed, put on her new terrycloth robe and paced the floor. Max opened one eye, looked up sleepily and then flopped back into his dreams. Lucky dog. The tiles on the kitchen floor were cold. Her toes curled in protest with every step as she maneuvered around the sink and stove. A few minutes later the teapot whistled. A cup of Earl Gray tea with two sugars and a wedge of lemon was the panacea for every crisis in her life since high school. Kelly sipped it in darkness, slowly, deliberately relishing the ancient ceremony shared throughout civilized time.

Nighttime was her favorite. Kelly relished the peace it gave to introspect. Her life was comfortable. She thought of her father and smiled knowing how proud he was of her. Yet her father's modest life had seemed to be much more satisfying. She was thirty-one years old and made more money in a month then her life insurance salesman father made in his most productive years. But life wasn't just about how much money you made. Her parent's home was always full of friends and laughter. She couldn't remember when her antique colonial had guests enough to even equal the total number of rooms. By her age her father already had a family of four. She had only one previous serious relationship in her life and it was an unmitigated disaster. Her father had a sixtieth birthday party last year attended by over one hundred friends. She just turned thirty-one and found herself celebrating with a few nurses from the ER after work. Her father was in church every Sunday and truly believed in something greater than any man. She picked up extra ER shifts on Sundays just to avoid religion. Her father knew his limits and never rocked the proverbial boat. She was always bucking authority figures and was about ready to challenge the system once again. Was it the legacy of the woman's lib movement? And in the end, there were always the nights alone. She was at the pinnacle of her youth and professional life and all she had to show for it was a snoring 100 pound Lab, drinking tea, alone. Always alone.

Rafferty never retreated on a case. Not once. If he signed off on a death certificate in his capacity as medical examiner, then as far as he was concerned, it was time to move on. Kelly wondered how best to pursue her findings or even if it was worth the bother. The dead man was a junkie after all. But then there was the headless girl and the baby whose life was cut short within her. Even though the position of assistant medical examiner was part time, it still helped pay the bills. The detective, Derek Ekizian, would be a possible resource, but the state police had closed the investigation. She wondered if Ekizian had the power to reopen the case. All she needed was confirmation from an independent lab and then she could make her move.

Kelly smiled at the thought of Derek's name, his laughter and especially, his eyes. The man was handsome and powerful. His shyness was just fine with her as long as he kept moving gently in her direction. She wasn't in any rush. A little baggage was good. She was not in any position to throw stones. Her face flushed with a curious mixture of desire and embarrassment. She wondered what he was doing tonight. She finished her tea and went to bed.

Alexandria, Egypt
1917

The streets of Alexandria were deserted. Heat either mesmerized or paralyzed every living thing. Houri worked her way through narrow alleyways, backtracking several times, while the sun reached its zenith. Occasionally she would detour to the bazaar, examining items of interest to no one. Around her the fragrance of coffee, coriander and cinnamon mixed with that of the human sewage flowing in the gutters. The meeting with Girgis, Mohamed's oldest son, was to be within the hour. It would be in a public place that would guarantee ample opportunities for escape, if need be.

Word of her brothers' arrest spread like the rising waters of the Nile in flood. The Abdel-Rassouls were the best and oldest families of professional tomb robbers. Their name was respected by everyone from their home in Gurnah to the antiquities markets of America and Europe. Their demise portended ill for the profession. Houri seethed with anger. If you were foreign born then you were called an archeologist or explorer. If you were of the land, then you were a grave robber or thief. If the police moved on the Abdel-Rassouls with impunity, then no one would be safe. Strangers were viewed with renewed suspicion. No home was spared the impact of the arrest. All grieved and feared as one, for in truth, all of their bloodlines were intertwined through marriage for a millennia.

Girgis was waiting for her as arranged. He paced the area around the communal fountain like an expectant father, oblivious to the heat. The foolish boy stood out like a sore thumb, she thought. He was practically waving a sign that read 'here I am come get me' to the legions of secret police who infiltrated every aspect of the people's daily life. A spindly boy of sixteen, a speckle of facial hair erupted irregularly from his chin. She had not seen him in months. He certainly wasn't a grown man worthy of the trust and burden now thrust upon him. She cringed watching him pace barefoot, kicking up small clouds of dust, dirt and an occasional stone with his bare toes. She circled the market square once more. The faces around the fountain were mostly familiar and no police uniforms visible. Houri approached her nephew cautiously. Speed was of the essence.

The boy greeted his aunt warmly, but fearfully, with kisses on both cheeks. She instinctively knew he had neither the courage nor the brains to understand the consequences of his father's arrest. All the boy knew was that little would ever be the same again. If he only knew the truth, she thought.

"Are you sure they are beyond help?" he asked plaintively, counting on her experience.

"They are as dead men even as we speak," she replied, fully aware of the impact of her words. The boys face turned to that of despair. It was not time to play with the truth. Still she felt some remorse. He was, after all, blood. "The secret police have been looking for the Abdel-Rassoul brothers for years. Now they have found them, they will never let them go. At least not until they have beaten them to death looking for the secrets our family holds."

Girgis was visibly shaken. The legacy of grave robbing and treasure hunting amongst the tombs was all the boy knew. It was a way of life. Families such as his would release bits and pieces of antiquity from their private hoards supplying museums and private collectors of the world. Wealthy European and American tourists supported this industry. Now his father and uncles were gone, possibly for good. "What would father have wanted us to do?" he asked with a deep sigh of resignation. Tears began to well up in his eyes.

Houri looked past the boy's fear and uncertainty. All her dreams rested on the back of this unlikely hero. She put her arm around his shoulders; "We must be strong for your father's sake. Did your father tell you yet of our family's secret?"

Girgis knew his aunt was referring to something far greater then the usual trinkets or minor treasures with which his clan financed their lives. It was the topic he remembered dreaming about as a child. He reflected on how many times he accidentally stumbled on conversations between his father and uncles where, when his presence had become known, their language magically switched form Arabic to Copt just to keep him ignorant of a great secret. "Yes, Aunty. He mentioned it once briefly. He said it was our legacy as well as our family's curse."

Curse? Such fools! She wondered how she could ever be related to such weakness. "Did he tell you or show you where he hid this 'curse?'"

Girgis stood up proudly. "I have never seen it. But I did accompany my father once into the desert. I know I could find the place again."

"Clever boy," praised Houri. This was going to be easier then she had originally thought. "Let us go together and see if you are half the man your father is," she said resting her arm around his scrawny shoulders.

Fall River, Massachusetts
October 10th

"What is this, some kind of joke?"

"No, this is on the up and up," Derek replied. He could tell by Kelly's voice she was waffling. He was stunned by his own brazenness.

"This is Derek Ekizian, Fall River detective, the drawer of cartoons and caricatures, the man who says 'I never rush into anything', isn't it?" Kelly's disembodied voice needed more encouragement. "It's not April fools day. I'm not on candid camera, am I? Your buddy, Nunez, didn't put you up to this, did he?"

"No, no and no again. You and me in one hour. I want you standing by your door. Be there or be square." He was definitely putting on the full court press.

Kelly hesitated. The seconds she took to deliberate seemed to last hours for both of them. "All right, I accept. But if you back out on me or if this is just a tease, I'll nail your gonads to the front door of the police station. Agreed?"

"Agreed!" Derek's smile was as wide as his mustache. "One hour. Bye." He hung up before she had a chance to change her mind.

At half past five Derek's Gallant VR-4 pulled up to Kelly's home and turned in the driveway. The moon crested the horizon giving the twilight an eerie, Halloween pall. Derek dismounted out of the car and negotiated the overgrown pathway to the front door. Kelly was waiting. He assisted her with her jacket and retraced his steps with her in tow.

Kelly hesitated as Derek opened the rear door of the sedan. Someone was occupying the driver's seat. "And this is...."

"Reverend Littlefield, ma'am, at your service for the evening," the driver answered in a quietly hypnotic voice. He was a tall balding man in his late fifties with speckled gray hair and pale translucent skin.

"Kelly, this is John Littlefield. John, this is Kelly Gill. John is our chauffer for the evening." Derek joined her in the back seat. "John and I have a little arrangement. He needs the dough and I wanted to make the night a little bit special. He will be our designated driver for the evening. Besides that, I expect total silence from him. Total!"

Kelly could see Littlefield's downcast eyes in the rear view mirror. "Why silence?"

"Derek believes I have a tendency to proselytize. John 16 paragraph two. You know, that kind of thing. But I have promised to behave myself for the evening."

"The good Reverend doesn't quite have a church, yet," Derek added.

"Yet," Littlefield retorted. "It's only a matter of time until the Shepard shall have his flock."

"And if he doesn't keep quiet he'll still be looking for pastures."

"Yes, sir!"

Fall River faded into the horizon as they crossed into farm country along Route 24 North. For a man of the cloth Littlefield possessed driving skills of Mario Andretti on crack cocaine.

Derek opened up a small wicker picnic basket filled with munchies 'Armenian style'. Imported all the way from Watertown, the Armenian hub located just west of Boston, he informed her. And to wash everything down, some homemade Raki, Armenian firewater, to toast their evening's adventure into the city.

An hour later, Littlefield pulled into the parking circle of the Boston Aquarium. "See you about midnight?"

"In front of the Union Oyster House," Derek said, taking Kelly's hand. The night air was a few degrees less then crisp. By seven o'clock the moon was well above the horizon, playing tag with them between the tall buildings of the waterfront; the streets bumper-to-bumper with cars and pedestrians.

Kelly looked down at her hand in disbelief and slowed her pace. "Are you holding my hand, Detective?"

Derek stopped and looked down at his hand as well. "Yes, ma'am. I believe I am." He released her fingers but she did not let go. He gently returned the grip.

They negotiated their way along Boston's Freedom Trail following the path of red bricks. Strategically placed placards explained the historical significance along the way. Their pace quickened or slowed in response to their interest, finally coming to a stop in the Old North Church of 'One if by land, two if by sea' fame.

"Don't think I'm not aware of how big of a step this is for you," Kelly said, arching backward to look up at the interior dome of the church. White was the predominate color of the Protestant interior;

each rock hard pew gated and dedicated to a family from the Revolutionary War period of American history. The choir gallery with its mahogany organ stood guard from the second floor. Kelly's ponytail brushed up against Derek's head as she turned from side to side taking in the beauty of the church.

"You're welcome. I appreciate your dedication to the emotionally handicapped," Derek said looking at the curve of Kelly's throat. The urge to reach over and kiss her was overwhelming. Slow down, he reminded himself. Slow down. He cleared his throat instead. "Hey, it's getting late. We don't want to miss our dinner reservation."

"Where are we going?" Kelly asked, rising from the pew. The North End was famous for its Italian restaurants.

"Just follow me." Derek took her hand again. "Nothing but the best for you tonight."

They walked past legions of the North Ends' finest establishments. The smell of sautéed garlic saturated the air. College kids and families mixed shoulder to shoulder with wise guys with slicked back hair and outdated ponytails. A twenty something model in painted on black leather pants and halter-top clung to the arm of a man who should have been her grandfather. Only the way they kissed revealed the true nature of their relationship.

"Go figure," Derek said nodding in the direction of the winter-spring couple as he entered Gasparo's liqueur store.

"Seeing them gives me hope," Kelly said. Love came in many shapes and sizes. Who was she to judge?

"What?"

"You're about that guy's age," she teased, poking him in the ribs. "Maybe we have a chance." She smiled nervously as he looked back at her with surprise. Did she go too far again?

Derek bought a bottle of Chianti Reserve. "I trust you like dry Red?"

"Depends. So we're going to a BYOB restaurant?"

"You could say that."

Their next stop was two blocks off Hanover Street. Sorbo's Grocery flashed in red neon. "What, now?" Kelly asked as they squeezed past wheels of aged parmesan cheese and one hundred dollar bottles of aged vinegar.

"Nothing but the best!" Derek declared. He picked out a loaf of fresh bread, two different kinds of Italian sausage and two small wedges of Italian cheese.

Their picnic area was in the courtyard of a small Catholic church. A street musician strumming a folk guitar anchored one corner. Twenty feet away a Peruvian band in traditional costumes played Andean music. Derek set up the wine, cheese and sausage on the lip of a massive fountain rising like a volcano from the center courtyard. From one pocket he removed a corkscrew and opened the wine, his Eddie Bauer knife sliced the sausage and cheese into more delicate pieces. Kelly assisted by tearing the loaf of warm bread with her hands.

"Napkins?"

"Never fear," Derek said, taking a few from his bag and handing them over.

"What about drinking in public?" she asked. It wouldn't do to be arrested on a first date.

"We're on church property. This place is run by Father Joe Vivieros, a good Catholic boy with roots in Fall River."

Derek waved over a strolling flower girl, a pubescent waif who was making a small fortune selling roses. There was something special about tonight and the whole world seemed to know. Everything was perfect, from the food to the music. Even the flowers in the girl's basket were perfect little buds. He spied one purple rose. Natural or dyed, it didn't matter; this was the one he wanted. He made the purchase and cut the stem to within a few inches of the flower. With a magician's flourish, he placed it in Kelly's hair. It matched her signature lavender scarf perfectly.

Kelly blushed as her hand brushed up against his, fumbling to secure the flower in her hair.

"You know, in Armenian circles this means we're engaged," Derek said confidently.

"I think you might have missed a few steps," Kelly laughed. Still, the words were not lost on her.

"You're right," Derek nodded in assent. "I think you're supposed to give me a cow, one pig and two sheep to seal the deal."

"Up your hairy Armenian nose. The man is supposed to pay the woman."

They laughed until they turned red then sat in silence, introspectively drinking from the bottle without wiping the top. They ate the bread, cheese and sausage quietly, lost in their own thoughts. Around them the streets of the North End ebbed and flowed with the pulse of the city. Today was a good day. Not bad for a first date, thought Kelly. Was he really doing this, thought Derek.

At the appointed hour they met the good Reverend in front of the Old Union Oyster House. They slipped in to the comfortable warmth of the car. Kelly leaned her head against Derek's shoulder while he gently stroked her hair. They rode back to Fall River in contemplative silence, each glowing with the possibilities.

Egyptian Desert
1917

Girgis leaned over the abandoned wellhead. "I believe it is in here," he said proudly. His father's desert robes hung loosely off his shoulders, the ends dragging on the ground.

The well was nothing more then a circular collection of a few rocks, stone and mud brick. The top barely projected out of the sand. Only a few scraggily patches of scrub brush marked this area with water in contrast to the desolate landscape that surrounded them. Houri looked around the canyon walls; it was a blind end. The cliffs rose hundreds of feet into the air, indistinguishable from thousands of others. Nothing living existed within the sound of her voice except for the two donkeys that accompanied them. The donkeys bobbed their heads like puppets, side to side, chewing on their mouth bits, their legs hobbled. Occasionally they would snort. They were silent witnesses to the unfolding drama.

Houri needed her nephew's knowledge of the hiding site. The treasure below teased her to the brink of insanity. Her mind raced with the possibilities of freedom and independence from those who oppressed her. There would be no need to share with anyone. "Go, nephew. Climb down quickly and bring it up," Houri commanded. She gave him a gentle nudge towards the bottom.

It was midday. The sun shone directly overhead obliterating everything except the thought of water and treasure. Its rays illuminated the well to at least a hundred feet. Beyond that depth remained a mystery. Girgis was ill prepared for a descent. His climb down into the depths of the well was painfully slow. The ancient steps carved out of the rock bed remained, but the toeholds seemed barely accessible even for his small feet. His thoughts were to the treasure that surely existed at the bottom.

It was a long trip back to their ancestral village of Gurnah. The business of the treasure had to be resolved this day. Houri had no intent on spending this night or any other with this youngster in the desert. She paced like a caged tigress listening to the subtleties and nuances of every echo from the well. After what seemed an interminable amount of time, she heard his voice from the bottom.

"I have it!" he cried triumphantly.

Houri smiled. "Good. Now strap it to your back and bring it up at once. And water. Don't forget to fill the water bags."

"Yes, Aunty."

One hour later Girgis climbed out of the well, first passing the water filled sheepskins and then a rough ancient leather bag the size of a small roasted lamb to his aunt's hands. Sweat poured off his body and his muscles ached from the efforts expended. He let his aunt drink first, out of respect. After she finished, he greedily quenched his thirst. "May I see it, Aunty?"

"Certainly. But first, let us cover up the well once again. We must not expose ourselves to the prying eyes of others."

Girgis looked disappointedly at the leather bag at his aunt's feet then turned his attention to the task at hand. His muscles strained to replace the limestone top. It had seemed so easy to remove before he began the climb down. He slowly rocked the cap back and forth in circular motions, progressively bridging the gap between the stones. Behind him, Houri approached.

"Here, let me help you," she whispered at his back.

"Thank you Aunty," Girgis said, muscles fatigued with his effort. He pressed his shoulder into the large capstone.

Houri looked at her nephew with eyes emotionless and determined. As the boy pushed his hardest, she took a knife from beneath her robes, aimed as she had been taught and plunged it to its hilt into the youth's back.

Girgis jerked upright and arched his back. His arms flailed futilely as he spun in a wild attempt to remove the knife. It was not within his reach. His lungs quickly filled with blood and collapsed. He fell forward onto the capstone, his only movement now short gasping breaths. He looked backward towards his aunt just in time to see her raised foot as she kicked him down the well.

"Thank you, dear nephew," Houri said, wiping the blood from her hands on the sand. Capping the wellhead now was just a matter of balance and patience. Houri dusted off her clothes and straightened out her smock. The only witnesses to her deed were the two mules and a lonely falcon that circled above her head. Horus protect her, she thought. As always. This was going to be a good day after all.

Fall River, Massachusetts
October 12th

Derek pitched a dime into the center of the kitchen table. "Ante up boys. If you want to play, you've got to pay."

It was Monday night at its sacred best: poker, football and beer. He scanned the table ferreting out each hand. Rick Nunez exercised his talent of precariously balancing a chair on two legs, rocking back and forth, a mocha cappuccino glued to his right hand. His cards were already facedown on the table. Nothing going on there, thought Derek. Bill Kasson sat hunched over guarding his hand against any spies, probably one card away from something big. Al Sherman and Steve Desrosiers had both just come off shift and still in their respective police and paramedic uniforms. Sherman sat glued to the Patriots-Jets game on the thirteen-inch kitchen TV and hadn't even looked at his cards yet. Steve Desrosiers played nervously with the last of his nickels and dimes as if that action would make the pile magically grow. If the man stopped talking long enough to pay attention, he might even win a hand some day.

"Anything wild?" Nunez asked, reaching into the salsa with a half eaten Nacho.

"Hey, no double dipping," Desrosiers protested, pushing back a mop of hair. With three kids at home and another on the way, even a haircut was a luxury he could ill afford. He was bulimic thin and had an antiseptic approach to everything in life. Years of friendship hadn't diminished his germ fetish. "I don't want your Spic parasites getting into my food chain."

Nunez snorted in distain. "You should be so lucky. Besides, it's not Spic, it's Castilian. Spanish royalty who taught my ancestors to speak the tongue of the gods with a lisp." He took another sip from his Dunkin Donuts mocha cappuccino.

"Fuck you and the horse you rode in on," Desrosiers said, using a spoon to scoop out a layer of salsa where Nunez had submerged his last chip. His eyes darted nervously around the table looking for support on his stance against the double-dip.

"Fuck you," Nunez said, repeatedly dipping his nacho to Desrosiers' horror. "The next time I see you in the ER, I'm giving you a rectal exam and I'm not gonna' use any gloves."

"He'd probably enjoy it!" Sherman noted. He was the only man at the table who was groomed to GQ perfection, even down to his mustache. "One card, please." He bit his nails.

"Come on, come on guys. It's getting late and I want to finish this up before morning," Derek said. "I've got to get up early tomorrow and do an in-service at the academy."

Sherman's eyes perked up. "No shit. What'd they ask you to do?" he asked, spitting out something minute onto the kitchen floor, oblivious to Desrosiers disapproving stare.

He's got nothing, thought Derek barely exposing a smile. "Crime scene preservation so the rookie cops won't fuck up the next conviction."

"They'll still fuck it up. They're always stepping on their cocks."

Kasson straightened out his bow tie. His perfectly starched collar was always just a little bit too tight around his neck, accentuating his prominent Adams apple and bulging neck veins, his bow tie futile in camouflaging either. Once a week he would descend from the martini and country club crowds in the Highlands and exchange chump change with the old gang. Afterwards he would drive his 911 Porsche Carerra home to his shrewish wife. "Hey, nice article about you in yesterday's *Herald News*. Carl Furtado et al. It'll be another feather in your hat for the next promotion cycle."

"Get a few more and you'll have a headdress," Sherman quipped.

"Why do you always use the Latin?" Desrosiers interrupted. "We all went to the same school. We all played in the same parks, kissed the same girls and smoked the same joints. But you always have to come on with the affected speech. What's wrong with good old U-S-of-A English?"

"Because a man in my line of work deals only with the most refined and educated members of our community," Kasson answered, cleaning his thick glasses with an embroidered handkerchief.

"You're a jerk, " Desrosiers grumbled. "I knew your old man. I know your brothers. None of them are like you. This city is dried up. The only people around to talk to are the poor greenhorns. For that you don't need English; you need to *fala Portuguese.*"

"*Fala* yourself. The money isn't in the $6.00 an hour factory worker. I'll go wherever the money is. Money talks and shit walks. That will be the new motto on the People's Bank walls when I take over from my ungrateful father-in-law. And that, my good man, is what separates me from you losers. I'll see your ten and raise you another."

Derek cringed at their weekly exchange of class conflict. "Anyway, you're right," he interrupted. "It was a nice article. I'll see you and call. I hope it's not too premature. At least they spelled my name right for a change."

"No one's fault except your grandparents," Nunez said, returning from the bathroom. "Not too many Armenians in Fall River these days."

"Well, there were at one time, pal," Derek replied. "Came here from Turkey after the 1915 Genocide. Even before your people, I might add. Anyway, like I was saying before I was so rudely interrupted, it was a very good article. Too bad the Staties always take over the homicides. We do the dirty work at four a.m. and they get all the credit."

"Hopefully not this time," Kasson said. "Two pair, aces high."

A groan erupted from the losers around the table as they all threw down their cards.

"*C'est la vie,* my pathetic friends." Kasson scooped up the coins like Scrooge.

"English, damn it, speak English!" Desrosiers moaned. Even playing with quarters, nickels and dimes he had lost more then he could afford. Paramedic payday was still a week away. "Jesus, sometimes I think you're pulling those cards out of your sleeve."

"If I'm not mistaken, French was your mother's tongue," Kasson reminded not so gently, ignoring the insult. It wasn't the first time his honesty was suspect. "Desrosiers, Arcadian French. Chased out of France and pretty soon chased off the poker table." The phone rang, interrupting his sarcasm.

"Who's calling you at this time of night? You're off call, aren't you?" Nunez asked watching Derek pick up the portable wall phone.

"Never really off call. See my back up weapon?" Derek asked pointing to the gun strapped to his ankle. "Goes on first thing in the morning right after I take a piss. Last thing I take off before I go to bed."

"That's really comforting," Nunez replied sarcastically. "What's that for, in case we get into a fight?"

"Want to see mine?" Sherman teased standing up. He began the cleanup.

Only Kasson sat idly by as the rest of the men moved about the room. Chips were recycled in the original bag, nutshells went in the trash and beer bottles went back in the case. Derek listened intently to the caller repeatedly signaling his friends to keep the volume level down. The clang of dishes and chairs moving against tile forced him to move into the far bedroom.

"If I was getting a call at this time of night, I'd be worried about the kids," Desrosiers said. "Never know what's going to happen with drugs, car crashes and boyfriends."

"If it were me, it'd be my ex wife screaming about an alimony payment," Sherman said, unabashedly shifting some of Derek's pile of coins onto his own.

Nunez grabbed an equal amount of coins from Sherman's pile and transferred them back to Desrosiers pittance. Only Kasson failed to redistribute his winning horde. "This is the advantage of being single," Nunez said. "I've got nothing to worry about."

A couple of minutes later Derek emerged grim face from the bedroom and obviously distracted. He returned the telephone back to the cradle in the kitchen, then joined his friends at the front door.

"You got that 'Oh shit' look on your face, pal. What's going on?" Nunez asked.

"Nothing, just some problems with schedules at work," Derek lied. The look on his face betrayed his lack of experience at that fine art.

"Right, and Elvis still lives," Nunez countered. He zipped his ski jacket and played with his car keys, swinging them in a loop around his index finger.

"Well, in any case, it was a nice article about you, considering the department's reputation and especially since you're such a born loser," Kasson mocked, straightening his bow tie. "The only thing for sure is that Carl Furtado, Satanist exemplar, severer of heads, defiler of woman and children will never rise again."

"Amen to that, brother," Sherman echoed.

"Amen," they all nodded in assent.

Alexandria, Egypt
1917

The streets were deserted at midday as Houri, exhausted from her desert trek, walked unobserved into the two-story mud brick home of the Abdel-Rassoul clan. Her uncle was asleep in his usual drunken haze, oblivious to her absence the past two days. She would blame the boy's disappearance on the secret police. Tonight there was much work to be done.

The ancient treasure strapped to her back swayed with each step up. It was all there. She had seen the contents of the bag at the well and half a dozen times during the march home. Now, a new life awaited her. The bag jingled softly with each footfall. At the top of the stairs she turned right and entered her room, empty except for an old bed and a collection of dolls stolen long ago from the trunk of an English tourist. She bent down and rolled up the ancient oriental carpet exposing the floorboards. Slowly she maneuvered an old fork between the wooden planks and raised the pieces of her childhood hiding place one by one. The boards were replaced over the treasure and the rug unfurled again. Houri smiled at her own cleverness, stretched out on the wool mattress that was her bed and quickly surrendered to sleep.

Hours later she was jolted awake by the wailing of the village woman. Houri leaned out her window and received the news with an air of resignation. All three of her brothers had been killed attempting to escape the authorities said the official report.

"Bastards!" her uncle swore, spitting, cursing and drinking beyond his usual insatiable capacity. The old man paced his house like a caged animal, pounding the walls with his fist until they were bloodied, swearing vengeance against the police and authorities.

"Bastards!" Houri chanted, wailing with superficial grief with the rest of her village when the police dropped off the badly beaten bodies of her brothers.

"Bastards!" the village men and woman chanted in unison as they carried the coffins through the streets, firing ancient flintlocks and single shot German Mausers into the air. But dead was dead, and no one knew who the police would come after next. The rumors of informers within their midst ran rampant. Clan trusting only clan was again the rule.

Days later grieving faded. Life's routine of trade, barter and suspicion of anyone who wasn't blood returned. The talk of everyone now was of the war. The Turks were demoralized and had suffered repeated defeats in the Syrian Desert to the north. With defeat would come the inevitable collapse of the Turkish Empire. Native Egyptian and Arab populations would be helpless against the brutality of the deserters and refugees who follow in that wake. Internecine hatred between tribes and ethnic groups would spread even as far as Alexandria. Brutality came down to the lowest common denominator: women. A woman without brothers to protect her was an easy target. From now on, she could only count on herself.

Houri went to her room and locked the door. Only money would provide the means to escape the coming chaos. She rolled up the oriental carpet and removed the floorboards as she had done earlier, exposing the treasure then spreading the bag's contents on her bed. Many pieces of ancient Egyptian heritage had passed through the hands of the Abdel-Rassouls and she had been privy to most of them. What lay before her now was unimaginable by any previous experience. It was worth the life she had taken.

Slowly she lifted each piece and rotated them in her palms. The workmanship, the details, the sheer weight of the gold alone were all breathtaking. She recorded every detail on paper. Slowly, methodically, she drew pictures so she could recall the exact positions of the sacred objects on the crown. Her work was childlike and coarse; but the drawings were clear enough to recreate the designs. Gently she lifted up the largest gem that sat in the middle and rotated it clockwise. The giant ruby glared back at her, challenging, daring her to proceed with her plan. Another drunken uncle demonstrated the mechanism years ago. It was the key to locking the two halves of the crown of Upper and Lower Egypt. She removed the gold clasp and watched in satisfaction as the interlocking pieces of the double crown came apart in her hands. The winged scarab, Anun, and Re lay on the one side of the crown. The cobra dominated the front. The cobra head, itself, must have weighed at least a pound - a pound of pure gold. The Isis knot, the lotus, the Menit, the scarabs and the Shen fell to her uncle's handsaw one by one. Finally only the base of the double crown remained.

Houri paced her room frantically. The one large piece was now broken into many. The integrity of the crown, itself, no longer mattered. Only that which could be purchased with the treasure was real. The items had to be removed from her uncle's home at once. She would trust no one to share this secret. It no longer belonged to the Abdel-Rassoul family but was hers alone. Besides, after the old man was gone, there would be no family except for her. She would have to start a new bloodline and this time, the first-born son wouldn't take everything. Now, where to hide the crown was the overriding question. Someplace that would last for anther thousand years if necessary. She smiled. The choice was clear and simple.

Medical Examiners Office
Fall River, Massachusetts
October 12th

Al Sherman bit his nails nervously from the office side of the autopsy room. "You know, I hate this place. If I wanted to see dead bodies I'd have gone into medicine."

"Are you sure you don't want to see for yourself?" Kelly teased. She held one of the stainless steel morgue drawers partially open in case Sherman changed his mind.

Derek stood by Kelly's side and smiled at both his friends uncomfortably. It was Kelly's late night call during his poker game that forced this meeting. An inconsistency in the autopsies demanded his attention. Bringing Sherman was his idea. He was a good man for seeing alternatives to seemingly intractable problems.

The State police had already turned down his request to reopen the investigation. In their scenario, Furtado, the previously convicted cult murderer, and Ramierez, the juvenile, abducted the woman in Boston as a random act, performed their rituals and the rest was just details. Furtado killed Ramirez, in his usual *modis opporandi*, and then died in a self-administered heroin overdose. There was little funding and absolutely no interest to pursue Kelly's theories about the murders. The dead men were inconsequential minorities or had no living relatives who would protest to the governor. The medical examiner had signed off on the death certificates and no further investigation was warranted.

Derek leaned on the refrigerated door and stared at the dead man's face for a moment longer. "Come on, Kelly. It'll take an act of Congress to reopen this investigation. Make me articulate enough to present the case."

"Relax," Kelly said, closing the refrigerated cubicle. She led Derek back to her office and joined Al. "This isn't rocket science." She sat down at her desk and pulled out a folder with black and white glossy photos along with a large green medical text. "It's all about the maggots. All the bodies had maggots, remember?"

Derek nodded in agreement remembering that first night. How could he forget? "Go on."

"It's hard to speciate maggots even if you are a seasoned entomologist. First I fixed a few of the little buggers in hot water, not formaldehyde because they are so fragile. Their length told me how old they were. That gave me the approximate day the momma flies laid their little brood. I grew out maggots from each of the corpses. Ramirez and the girl matched. That means that the same species of flies laid their eggs at about the same time. But Furtado's maggots grew out Phaenicia Eximia, the green bottle fly. By the way, Derek, you can thank John Brady for observing the difference before I did."

The name, Brady, made the hair on Derek's neck bristle. "That self absorbed narcissist should be good for something, don't you think?" He asked grinding his teeth.

"And?" Sherman said, moving the conversation away from Derek's obvious jealousy.

Kelly ignored the dig. "And, I've run this by the folks at the University of Rhode Island and Cornell in Ithaca, New York. I've enlarged the photos from my lab." Kelly spread out the glossy photos and matched them with her reference text. "The entomologist confirms that one species is indigenous to New England, while the other comes from southern climates – very southern, tropical to be exact. So our friend, Carl, died at least a thousand miles south of here. Someone brought him here and placed him at the scene in Fall River, already dead."

Derek drummed his fingers nervously on Kelly's desk. "From Florida, Jamaica, Columbia – where?" He asked.

"Your guess is as good as mine," Kelly sighed, placing her research papers in a file and returning it to the desk drawer. "Personally, I believe the whole thing was a set up. Furtado was added as part of a play for our benefit. The Hispanic male was a seventeen year old from Roxbury. Except for a few misdemeanors, his record was unremarkable. I think your money should be on the girl. Someone with a medical background got to her before I did. My FBI sources suggest mutilators tear out organs. Her heart was much more deliberately and precisely removed. Follow her and you'll get the organization that set this up."

"Why do you say 'organization'?" Sherman asked.

"Simple. Think about it. To get a dead Mr. Furtado up here from somewhere south of the border, you'd have to drive a refrigerated truck or fly him in to the Boston area. You don't do that on a commercial flight. 'Excuse me, Mr. Furtado, would you care for some peanuts with your maggots?' Then transporting him to Fall River, carrying him up the stairs, arranging the other murders, the dismemberments and so on; this was a big time operation, gentlemen." Kelly leaned back in her chair and looked at both policemen expectantly.

Derek was proud of her. The presentation was succinct and well thought out. He fixated on Kelly's face. Every time she turned, he found a new perspective. The way she moved, her confidence and, particularly, her eyes, drew him in deeper. The details of her argument were the same as she had outlined last night, just in more scientific terms. He focused on her eyes, her legs and the way her sweater clung to her waist whenever she turned.

"So, what's your next move?" Sherman asked.

"I don't know," Derek replied, sitting on top of Kelly's desk. "I've brought this to the chief this morning but he blew me off. Too many people want this over. The last thing the state tourism board wants to see is a series of unsolved cult murders. Kelly has actually been suspended for a week for deliberately disobeying orders. Seems Dr. Rafferty has a fragile ego when it comes to the command structure of his department."

"Sexist pig," Kelly muttered grumpily.

Derek raised the Venetian blinds on Kelly's office window and peeked out the narrow slits. "I'd love to poke around some on my own. Maybe I can find something that will convince the chief or get the FBI involved. Something a bit more tangible than worms."

"Maggots," Kelly and Al corrected simultaneously.

"I need something a bit more specific then maggots and green spoon flies."

"Bottle flies," Kelly and Al chipped in at the same time.

"Bottle, spoon, dish, knife or fork. I don't care. I need something else."

"Your call," Kelly said. She needed Derek to take the initiative with her new found evidence otherwise everything she had worked on the past few weeks was futile. There was a greater evil at work here that needed to be ferreted out. It was their responsibility.

Derek scribbled out a quick cartoon. This one was of a sailboat and a pirate flag. A female pirate with a skimpy costume stood watch on the ship's bow. Her face was remarkably like Kelly's. The bow of the boat had a face with a mustache, remarkably like his own. He tore up the drawing before anyone could see it.

Kelly's voice became firm. The room hung heavy with inertia. She had to take the initiative. "Hey, Detective! Follow me for a second. Boerner, the dead girl, lived in Florida. The bottle fly I grew from Furtado's body comes from warmer climates like Florida. I've got some vacation time coming up - actually several if you count my recent suspension. Why don't the two of us take a little trip together and do a little Florida sight seeing? I did my residency training in Jacksonville – the same town Boerner called 'home'. We could just poke around a bit. No law says you can't explore on your own personal time, is there? You never know what we might stumble across. Besides, you owe me a real dinner."

Derek was surprised by her sudden aggressiveness. Was she interested in pursuing the homicides or was she after a second date? Her face was impervious to his stares, her motives impenetrable. The smile she always had for him was absent. Maybe this was just business after all. Derek turned to Sherman, "I'd have zero legal jurisdiction. Even if we find something, it would be very difficult to get it entered into evidence. What do you think, Al?" Challenging the chief might deep six any possibility of career advancement. He was surprised at his own timidity. Was he afraid of the woman or the case? Here was this incredibly beautiful lady within fingertip reach and he was intimidated. What if he went with her to Florida and she found him a bore or even worse? At least now he could count on her as a friend. He had everything to lose, it seemed.

"You know what will happen to you, career wise, if you're unsuccessful and the chief finds out you've been mucking around without permission," Sherman stated plainly. Both men stared at each other silently.

Kelly became impatient. Her voice rose an octave in protest. "Jesus, what a bunch of sissies! Whatever happened to your oath as a police officer, to get the bad guys? Besides, how many men get an offer to spend a few days in Florida with me as their personal tour guide?" Kelly taunted, leaning forward across the desk seductively, her bottom swaying slowly from side to side.

"Maybe if Al came along," Derek suggested meekly, retreating into a bashful mode.

"Hey, you can count me out," Sherman countered. "My wife happens to like the fact that I'm in line for a captain's position. Besides, people down there tend not to like guys with the name 'Sherman'.

"Down where?" Kelly asked.

"Anywhere in the south. Traveling with a Yankee with the name of Sherman would doom your investigation from the beginning. We'd be shark bait in an hour."

Kelly shook her head incredulously, but Sherman wasn't smiling. "You're really serious, aren't you?" Of all the potential arguments anticipated before their meeting, this was not one. "The Civil War was over a century and a half ago."

"Tell that to anyone from south of the Mason Dixon line. There are rednecks everywhere. I don't relish the thought of exploring that neck of the woods on any professional level unless I change my name to Lee."

Kelly turned to Derek. "Well, I guess it's just you and me, babe. That is, if you'll have me." She saw him waffle. "Don't make me beg," she said smiling coyly. "Whadda you say, big boy?"

Derek hesitated for a moment, then smiled. It was time to grow up.

Alexandria, Egypt
1917

The summer sun baked the residents of Alexandria. Houri swam through the oppressive heat, wandering in and out of the labyrinth of streets and alleyways – the ancient catacombs her final destination. Her biggest fear was being followed. She worked her way from the central market district to the edge of the old town. The pace of the city slowed the further she walked; tourist and military vehicles giving way to the ubiquitous horse or donkey carts that served as the engines of commerce.

The catacombs were a fixture of every major city in the Roman Empire. Alexandria was the center of commerce for countless Mediterranean empires. Levels upon levels of burial chambers were carved into the limestone; a final resting place for the citizens of the city for millennia. As a child, Houri played in them and learned the complex of caves and tunnels like the back of her hand. She knew entrances and exits still not catalogued by the museums and explorers. Some were plainly in the open while others masqueraded within basements of shops or private residences, sprouting around the portals through the centuries.

Cautiously wary of secret police, Houri approached a remote entrance near a minor canal and kissed the blue bead on her bracelet to ward off the evil eye. Just in case, she thought. She lit her oil lamp to guide her way in the darkness and began her journey down into the earth's bowels. The air became refreshingly cool and damp the further she descended. The fear of being followed dogged her heels. Occasionally she would stop and listen for the tell tale sound of footfalls behind her; but only her anxious breathing and pounding heartbeat penetrated the narrow corridors of the burial grounds.

Houri slowly worked her way down to the third level of tombs known only to the local antiquities dealers. They served as a tremendous resource of ancient artifacts; quickly and easily marketable to the museums and private collectors of Egyptology in Europe and America. Pushing a reed basket ahead of her, she crawled through spaces increasingly more claustrophobic. At what appeared to the uninitiated eye as a blind end, she pushed a keystone up and back, revealing a chamber the size of a small room. Scattered inside lay small childhood treasures sequestered by her brothers; and now they were dead. A momentary weakness washed over her as she touched the scraps of cloths and cartouche fragments she had not seen in a dozen years. Her will was forged with a new conviction as she exchanged the magnificent contents of her basket with those items that lay scattered on the dirt floor. Slowly Houri backed out of the vault and began her ascent to the surface. Along the way she placed a myriad of objects that littered the floors of the catacombs into her basket. Western tourists were getting more numerous and she did have the future to think about.

It was dusk by the time she emerged from the catacombs. Houri patted off the dirt and debris of the ancients from her dress, replaced the oil lamp on a cradle strapped to her waist and began her assent up the dirt ramp. She needed to hurry back home before the streets became unsafe. Alexandria took on a whole new persona at night. Refugees and deserters emerged from their hiding places and took back the streets from the rightful owners of the city. A rough hand that grabbed her by the back of her hair halted her scramble up the dirt embankment.

"Not so fast; my little flower," the crude male voice said behind her. The man reeked of body odor, stale urine and garbage.

Houri reflexly reached for her dagger at her waist but realized, too late, that it still lay imbedded in her nephew's back. She tried to spin around to look at her assailant but all she caught was the color of a dirty military uniform. She was rewarded with a blow to her face knocking her to the ground, dazed and bloodied.

"Feisty today, aren't we?" the uniformed man said pulling at her clothes.

Houri kicked and screamed but she was no match for her assailant. Her mouth and nose were covered with his big dirty paw. She tried to bite his hand and was greeted by more blows to the face and head, each sending her deeper into oblivion. Her efforts to resist her attacker became weaker as she fought futilely against his massive strength. She could feel her skirt being removed against her will. Now the pain in her head was making her sleepy. She did not care anymore.

Fall River, Massachusetts
October 15th

Monday night was poker night. Always was and always would be. Squabbling, boasting and threatening each other like a WWF grudge match only lent credence to what they already knew – they were friends. Poker was a man's game. They would be here forever.

"I'm done," Desrosiers said. "Karen's gonna' bust my chops for sure tonight. Got to keep at least a little for the groceries. I've lost my limit."

"Again?" Kasson asked, smirking.

"You should know," Sherman said, biting the nail of his index finger to a millimeter from the tip. "Most of the lad's disposable income keeps going to you.... as if you need it."

Kasson fiddled with his bow tie. "Maybe he needs some private lessons. What do you say, little man? I'd be happy to give you a few pointers."

"For a small charge, I'm sure," Nunez laughed. The conversation was drifting towards the uncomfortable. He took some leftover munchies to the sink and munched on a pretzel.

"It's just a streak of bad luck," Steve replied, getting up to put on his jacket.

"Yeah, a streak of bad luck that's lasted your whole life," Kasson sneered unkindly, pocketing the money. His pockets jingled like Scrooge. The amount involved wouldn't have covered his cigarette bill for the week. Still, he loved winning. His neck veins bulged from a hard chuckle as he readjusted his bow tie.

"Fuck you," Desrosiers said, his usual parting words to Kasson. "Fuck you and the Porsche you rode in on." He paced the floor and drained the last of his Molson ice beer.

"Turbo Carreira Porsche, to be exact," Kasson retorted. He starred at his adversary from his usual throne of kingship, relishing in his victory.

"Now, now children. If you can't play nice, you shouldn't play at all," Derek said, getting up from the table to join the cleanup.

Everyone, except for Rick, took off early tonight. Nunez rearranged the kitchen chairs and dumped the garbage. It was midnight but neither man was anxious for the evening to end. Being single often meant being bored.

Nunez sat backwards in the kitchen chair, his stomach leaning on the metal back, and began his trademark rocking. He looked at Derek expectantly. "The good stuff?" he asked.

"The good stuff!" Derek answered in the affirmative, removing a dark green bottle of 1977 Cockburn Reserve port. The bottle was worth a quarter of his weekly net paycheck and had been around so long that he forgot how it entered his possession. There were several more for backup behind this first, if needed. Still, it was the kind of drink that one sipped, slowly, deliberately relishing each maroon drop on the tongue while the brain gave homage to the master port makers in Portugal.

The night air was appropriately chilly for October. Nunez lit the kindling to start the fire while Derek brought out two aperitif glasses to partition the divine beverage. The friends moved closer to the fireplace and stretched out on the hardwood floors. Flames caught on the kindling and quickly spread to the oak and apple wood nestled in the wrought iron cradle. The odors of burning fruitwood mixed in almost gastronomic delight. Yellow, red and green flames swirled with waves of smoke riding the draft up the flue. An occasional spark flew towards them as air cavities exploded in quick pops. Soon, both the embers and the alcohol had the men toasty warm inside and out. Their bonds as friends grew more in the ensuing silence than any woman's gossip group.

"Did you ever hook up with Paula?" Rick asked in between sips of port. The question was out of the blue.

Of all the women Rick could have asked about, why Paula? "Hardly. Did you?" Derek answered promptly, leaving no doubt as to his innocence with regard to the nurse at Hatfield Memorial.

Nunez hesitated, taking another sip from his glass. "Well, actually one night after work we...."

Derek interrupted. "More than I need to know." He knew his friend was fishing for the blessing of a potential competitor. A true friend was hard to find and harder to keep. For Nunez, sex was neither.

They both returned to silence. Flames danced rhythmically, hypnotizing their heartbeats and breathing to the same cadence. Derek poured out another measure of port.

Nunez turned his face to that of his friend, the rest of his body immobile. "You know, this has to stop," he said waving his hands around the room. He yawned and stretched on the hard floor trying to get comfortable.

"What does?"

"You know what I'm talking about. This martyrdom for the past is for fairytales. Rose would have wanted you to begin again. You're almost forty."

Derek's face hardened, his eyes focused on the fire. "Leave me the fuck alone."

Nunez sombered with his new tack. "Not this time, bud."

Both men adjusted the couch pillows underneath their necks to better see the fireplace. Only the comforting click, click, click of the ancient grandfather's clock in the hallway disturbed the silence separating them.

Minutes passed. Derek raised his head and looked back at his friend. "Big fuckin' deal. You're almost thirty-five. I don't see you engaged yet."

"Look around you, bud. This place is like a shrine, a mausoleum."

This time the silence was painful to both men. They stared at the glowing embers seeking comfort in the port and the flames that turned their faces red. Each wanted to speak their true feelings, but neither was trained to do. They had to rely on silence as a medium of communication - as an active third party mediator.

"I like Kelly…a lot," offered Derek quietly.

The revelation took Nunez by surprise. Rick looked at him full in the face and smiled. "Well, well, well. Maybe I've underestimated you all along. Seems I've been worried about the wrong man." The two men clinked their glasses in a universal toast and returned their stare into the flames. "She certainly is a classy lady."

"How come you haven't hit on her?" Derek asked. "You hit on everyone."

"Because she's a one man woman. Not my type. Besides I've known all along that she has the hots for you. More to the point, we work together. You don't shit where you eat."

Derek suspected the relationship he was cultivating with Kelly could blossom. He still wasn't clear how he should deal with their mutual attraction. Was the other night in Boston an exception or was it a harbinger of things to come? And what about this trip to Florida? He thought about Rose. Her face was burned in his memory like a branding iron. Roses' cheeks had been just a bit too high. Her nose just a smidgen too long and her lips just a hair too thick. She was beautiful. He thought about Kelly, the way her mind clicked, her eyes and the way they made him melt. Her eyelashes were as thick as a paintbrush. He thought about how both women looked at night when their eyes were caught in the glow of a streetlight, when they sipped a cup of coffee or when they laughed. His brain slid back into neutral. "Do you believe that love comes only once in a lifetime?"

"Like there's only one person, one soul in the world that's supposed to be your partner?" Rick replied, knowing full well where the conversation was headed.

"Soul mate?"

"Soul mate, room mate, sex mate, check mate. It's marriage that's the issue for me. From what I've seen, it's only after being married that you can fully appreciate the advantages of homosexuality," Nunez joked, downing the rest of his port in one swallow. He reached over to fill up his glass again, this time almost knocking down the bottle. "Still, the world is full of people who can't connect at any level. It's just a matter of you opening that little door in your head and then your heart will follow. Take me, for instance, though. I'm a loner. Have been and probably always will be. My time for just one broad hasn't come yet. Maybe it never will. But for a man like you, being by yourself is a death sentence. You've tasted the elixir of life. I'm forever jealous."

Derek moaned and shook his head in comedic disbelief. "God, you sound like Dear Abby." Derek downed the last of his glass. A few more minutes of silence followed. "Do you believe in a heaven, an after life?" he asked charting a new direction.

Rick looked back into his friend's face. "My, aren't we just chock full of Neitche today." He pondered the question for a moment. "Like a physical place where we stand around and play the harp all day? No. But I do believe there is something special and unique about each one of us. Call it the spiritual essence, a soul, warm glow, nuclear resonance, whatever. And when we are gone, it moves on to those who remember us. If you are lucky enough to be loved, that is. Sort of gets spread around like fertilizer. That's immortality." Nunez stared into the dying fire, exhausted from his pontificating. "What do you believe?"

"I don't know," said Derek quickly. He had spent the past two years thinking about that question. "I use to think I'd be holding hands with Rose in the afterlife forever. Now, I just don't know."

Rick smiled and patted his friend on the head like a puppy dog. "If you did, we all would be lighting candles at your alter and praying to the almighty mustachioed Armenian, the great one who knows all and sees all."

Both men sat silently watching the fire exhaust itself.

Alexandria, Egypt
1917

The pain was unbearable. Each heartbeat pounded in her brain. Houri tried opening her eyes. Slowly the lids parted, then closed, then parted again. Nothing focused, everything a blur of gray and black. Waves of nausea rose from her gut. Slowly she tested body parts and, one by one, they responded to her commands. She had no idea where she was. The mattress on which she rested rocked on an unseen frame, rickety and feeble as she attempted to turn. Houri slowly reached up to her face and explored. She could feel the swelling and pain, but nothing seemed to be broken. Terrifying memories suddenly interrupted her search for shattered body parts. She quickly reached down to her waist and was relieved to find she was still clothed.

It was night. The illumination in the small chamber came from a single oil lamp and one struggling candle at opposite corners of the room. Houri saw a man, about her age, asleep in a chair next to her bed. She studied the stranger carefully, making sure she did nothing to awaken him. His face was totally unfamiliar, almost exotic and clearly not Egyptian. The nose was too long and narrow. His skin was too fair; his hair, red and wavy, like the clay used in making her pottery. His clothes were coarse and apparently home made. She saw no evidence of a uniform of any kind. Hand made leather shoes lay on the floor next to his chair instead of the ubiquitous sandals of the natives of her land. There was no evidence of any weapon in the room. Houri slowly raised herself up on her elbows. She tried getting out of bed, but the pain from her head made her release a small moan and she quickly fell back on her pillow. Waves of nausea followed again.

The noise of her movements woke the stranger. His head lifted off his chest and his eyes darted around the room anxiously as he assessed the situation. It seemed, he, too, had something to fear. Seeing the surroundings undisturbed, he relaxed, yawned and stretched his arms and legs simultaneously. He rose from his chair and stood next to the bed, leaning over her like a good parent does to a child.

Houri cowered pulling the covers to her neck. Although the man's eyes were kind, he was still a man - and a stranger.

"*Ne craints pas*, do not be afraid. *Vous etes sauf*, you are safe," he said in French. He reached over to a small basin of water at the side of the bed, moistened a small towel and applied the wet cloth to the woman's head.

Houri grabbed the stranger's wrist with her small hand as he touched her face. The effort to resist was futile. She gave up and let him touch her forehead. The cool water felt wonderful. Droplets of water cascaded down her temples and cheeks. "*Ent mine*, who are you?" she asked in Arabic then again in Turkish. His face revealed his knowledge of both languages. "*Esmak ey*, what is your name?"

"My name is Nerses," he replied pouring a glass of water. He held it up to her lips as she warily took a sip and then a large gulp.

She looked at the man and his glass of water suspiciously, then drained it completely. The pain in her head was still there but slowly dissipating. Her voice was clearer now that she had quenched her thirst. "Turkish?"

"God, no. *Yes hye em,* I am Armenian."

"Are you with the refugees from Der Zor desert?"

"*Eye yogh,* yes," he said simply in Armenian, moving towards the single window in the room. His face was turned away. He became suddenly lost in his own memories.

"The man who attacked me…."

"He is dead. I heard you cry out and saw him trying to have his way with you. His uniform reminded me of what his kind did to my family, my people, my sisters and mother. I only struck him once. I didn't mean to kill him, just to get him off you. May God forgive me."

"Did he, was he able to…"

"No, your honor is intact. Perhaps you will have a headache for a while, but nothing else."

Fleeting images of the ancient treasure, the labyrinth of the catacombs, the evil man in the uniform all swirled in her head. The more she wanted to stay awake, the weaker she became. She fought the fatigue futilely as her eyelids became heavy once again and slowly closed. Her head slumped back onto the pillow in defeat but with relief. For the moment she was safe. She forced herself to look deeply into the stranger's eyes. Then smiling peacefully, fell back asleep.

Jacksonville, Florida
October 18th

"Welcome to Jacksonville. Thank you for flying US Air." The smile on the stewardess' face was plastic.

Derek looked at Kelly and felt a comfort he had not experienced in years. Kelly had just finished a night shift and slept almost the entire way, using his shoulder as a pillow. The weight of her head had left his right arm numb, but he would not have moved her for all the tea in China. The way she nuzzled and snuggled in her sleep was remarkable in its sensuality.

The plane disgorged its passengers like a bulimic, exposing them to offensive one, two, three punch of heat, humidity and the rancid smell of nearby pulp mills. This was Jacksonville after all. For Derek, the odors were repulsive. "God, this is awful."

"Don't worry, you'll never get use to it," Kelly laughed. "We just hope the prevailing winds change and blow all this back into Georgia!"

Even in the air-conditioned environment of the airport terminal, the unifying constant was sweat. Shirts stuck to backs, skirts and pants to legs. Everything and everyone moved at a languid pace at this latitude. Baggage pick up took forever, the carousel making a full circle for each piece of luggage slowly unloaded. Derek traveled with a single canvass duffel bag in contrast to Kelly's suitcase labeled 'heavy load'. "Christ, we're only here for a few days. What could you possibly have in here?" he asked struggling with the weight.

"Girl stuff, you know," Kelly answered. "Besides, just do your job and don't complain." She wrapped a scarf and her jacket on his shoulder as well. "Follow me," she commanded.

Derek followed obediently, hauling suitcase, duffel bag and winter jackets in his arms like a pack mule. He followed Kelly's footsteps to the car rental agency where she chose a convertible, something similar to the Miata she had during her residency days. Alamo Rentals was happy to offer her a Mitsubishi Eclipse Spider.

"And just where do you expect me to put your 'safari trunk'?" Derek asked looking at the miniscule trunk space and the burden he seemingly dragged half way across Florida.

"Hey, that's why they invented a back seat. Here, slide up the passenger side like this and just let it sit upright. Trust me, it'll fit," she said guiding his struggle. She was right, as usual. Seat belts strapped, Kelly lowered the convertible top. The windows all lowered simultaneously as well. "Shall we get started, Detective? We've got 40 miles to the beaches." She stepped on the accelerator before he had a chance to respond.

Derek was flung back in his seat. "You know, Kell, I still don't know why you rented this little jet, here. A compact car would have been a lot cheaper," he said adjusting his seatbelt.

Kelly suddenly swerved off the road, brakes grinding and tires spitting out a shower of chalky sand. She looked directly at him. "Look, detective, let's get a couple of things straight from the beginning. You're here at my invitation. This whole trip was my idea. This car is on my credit card, not yours. And none of this male chauvinist pig stuff either. I make a pretty good living and I can afford to be nice to you. Besides this is my vacation, too."

Derek looked at her eyes and saw a fierce determination. "Have it your way," he said turning towards the front. His body was pressed back into the seat by her sudden acceleration as she ran through the first three gears in a blink and merged onto 95 South.

They listened to a radio station specializing in Motown. Kelly steered more often with her knees then with her hands as she repeatedly tied back her hair with her lavender scarf. The wind played havoc with her hair; but it only seemed to increase her pleasure in driving.

"Hey, that's a highway interstate sign, not a speed limit," Derek noted critically as they zipped past a line of cars. "Ease up a bit." He loved the rush of wind as it cooled his sun-roasted face and arms. For October the Florida sun was blazing hot.

"What's good having the power if you don't use it?" she answered disarmingly. "Besides I heard that one cop will never give a ticket to another."

Derek wished he had brought his sunglasses. "I don't know you. I'm gonna tell the man you just kidnapped me." He glanced at Kelly's legs, so conveniently stretched out courtesy of Mitsubishi. Their taper was perfect. Her skirt was tucked in above her knees. "Where are we going first?"

"We're in Florida. To the beach, of course, silly rabbit."

They took the first bridge across the St Johns River. The regional differences between north and south were glaring. The south did not have a monopoly on the poor; it was just the intensity of the poverty that amazed. The older section of the city still reeked of post Civil War despair. Along the St Johns they came to other areas gentrified by the insurance industry. Rows of unemployed poor filling porch steps in futile attempts to escape the heat and humidity were replaced by new condos and one-of-a-kind boutiques and restaurants.

"Where's the beach?" Derek asked.

"Foolish man. You're still a good hours drive away from surf and sun of Jax beach."

Forty-five minutes later, they crossed the barrier island causeway and exited Atlantic Beach Blvd onto Ocean Drive. Now it was Kelly who felt disoriented. Multimillion- dollar mansions had largely replaced the simple homes and cottages she knew from her residency days. Apparently, single homes had been bought side by side, and then demolished to make way for much grander residences. Ten-dollar-a pound taffy, fancy boutiques and ocean side restaurants were clearly displacing the arcades and peep shows of the boardwalk that catered to the Mayport Naval Base sailors.

Kelly slowed to a crawl as she looked for landmarks that no longer existed. Her head focused on the right side of the road as she pointed the car south along the ocean. Ubiquitous ocean front condominiums sprung from the sand like wild mushrooms. Finally, something clicked. "This is it," she said confidently, pulling into the driveway of a nondescript cottage.

"Now, one more time, please. Who are these folks we're spending the night with?"

"Joanie. J-O-A-N-I-E and Allen. Geeze, I think you need a CT scan of your head. That's about the millionth time I've told you the same thing!"

The home was simple, a couple of blocks off the beach. Derek looked around curiously. There wasn't too much difference between this place and those on the Cape he knew from his youth. Several palm and citrus trees, their branches heavy with fruit, graced the yard. Sand was everywhere, the yard looking more like a golf course sand trap then a tropical showplace. Peeling paint and a dangling gutter completed the picture. A small lizard darted in between his feet as he exited the car. Kelly walked in front. He hurried to be by her side. "And she was your...."

"Boyfriend!" Kelly said, doing a poor imitation of Madeline Kahn in a Mel Brooks movie. She saw immediately the comedic reference was lost on him. "Relax. She was the head nurse in the ER during my residency days before I finished up my program.

Remember I spent four less-then-wonderful years here. She was an inspiring mentor and friend. She's the one that got shot in a cross fire between two rival drug gangs in the ER. Can you imagine – in the ER, itself? Anyway, she lost her spleen in the ensuing melee and quit her job. Gave up emergency nursing. I can't imagine."

Derek lost himself in the visual images of stretchers, gunplay and blood in the middle of an ER. He returned his attention back to Kelly. "And we're staying here because...."

"We're welcome and it's free."

"Now you're talking. That's more my style." Derek said, removing their luggage from the miniscule trunk and back seat of the convertible. The lady certainly didn't travel lightly. He had a couple of changes of underwear and a pocket full of quarters for a Laundromat.

"I have to warn you of a couple of things, though," Kelly said, whispering in his ear.

Her breath was warm and luscious against his face. He wondered if she realized the impact on him. "Now what?" Derek said, shaking his head in anticipation of a worst-case scenario. In truth, though, she could have said anything as long as she kept blowing in his ear. The sensation was driving him nuts.

"They take their religion very seriously down here. These people are no exception."

"Like what? Orthodox Jews with unshorn locks? Muslim fanatics with chadors and unshaved beards? Come on. What could be so terrible?"

"I never said 'terrible'. I said 'seriously'. You're in the south. They're either all Baptists or born again Christians. I'm really not sure which one."

Derek snorted. "Is that all? You said a couple of things. What's the other thing?"

Kelly smiled and took Derek's hand as she rang the doorbell. "Her husband, Allen, is a little different. A wonderful guy, but a little different."

"Like how different?"

"You'll see," Kelly said, giving him a small peck on the cheek.

Alexandria, Egypt
1917

The morning light pierced the narrow window like a dagger; alternating shadows of light and dark kindly caressing the face of the man asleep in the chair in front of her. Houri stared at her rescuer and apparent benefactor studying his face carefully as she surveyed the room. The man with the red hair sat in the same chair as before. There was no other furniture in the room besides her bed, his chair and a small wooden table. No decorations adorned the walls. A torn curtain of uncertain cleanliness guarded the window from any intruders. Why was she still here? Why did he stand over her like a watchdog?

Nerses awoke and stretched, smiling in response to her smile. He rose from the chair and poured her a cup of water from a pitcher on the table.

Houri drank greedily and returned the metal cup to him. Strangely, when his hand touched hers in the exchange, she did not recoil.

He removed a large knife from the wall hook and cut her a piece of almost stale bread and some unidentifiable cheese. She expressed her gratitude with a smile. He apologized. "I am sorry, but this is all I have to offer you. I did not feel it wise to leave you alone to get something else." He sat down in the chair again and looked at her face. "Do you feel well enough to go out today?" he asked.

Was this an invitation to leave? Was she a hostage? Questions floated like clouds aimlessly crossing the sky. Her head still pounded where she had received the blows from her assailant. Still, when she looked into his eyes, she felt no fear. She followed his lead. "I have no where to go. The police have killed my brothers and now this. They may still be looking for me. I am alone." The stranger looked at her with great sympathy. She enjoyed his attention.

Nerses leaned over to her bedside and took her hand in his. He, too, was now alone in the world. He felt a kinship with this woman of uncertain circumstance. There was much to say after having sat alone with her for the past two days; but his words would wait. He stood. "What do you want to do? I will help you the best I can."

Houri sat quietly for a moment. How much had this man seen

before the attack? Was he aware of her trip to the catacombs? She doubted that he was inside the curial chambers at the same time she had been; but, no one could be trusted. She had come too far to lose it all now. No one and nothing would come between her and the treasure she had just hidden. It was her destiny. She would take no chances, especially a stranger, no matter from what evil he had rescued her. "I must return to the ruins and retrieve a package."

He looked at her incredulously. The woman could barely sit up by herself. "What could be worth your health? Are you strong enough to go? The police might be waiting for you. They could be waiting for me, as well," Nerses said in rapid staccato. He shook his head in disbelief. This girl had been nearly beaten to death and almost raped just the other day. Now she insisted on leaving his protection and returning to the scene of the crime.

"The world is a dangerous place to live these days. The streets are no different. I have lost my brothers. I need something they left me inside the catacombs to secure my future. I am, now, all alone in the world. I must go." Houri sat up and her feet found her sandals. Even that small activity drained her; but, this she kept hidden as best she could or so she believed. She swayed just enough that Nerses was forced to lean forward and catch her from falling forward. She slowly eased herself back into bed with his help.

There was a new silence between them. Houri noticed Nerses in deep thought looking out the small window at the human activity below. Agitated, he paced the cramped room again. She watched the way his arms swung from side to side with curiosity. Why this man's movements intrigued her so was even more of a mystery. Finally he sat down on the bed and put her hand in his own – a bold move for a stranger. This time there was no boundary between them. Again, she did not recoil. Her brothers, had they been alive, would have been mortified.

"If you must go, then I will go with you."

Houri smiled as a simple village girl who was lost in the wilderness. This was exactly what she wanted to hear. "*Enshalah,* as God wills."

Jacksonville Beach, Florida
October 18th

"Go ahead, hit me as hard as you can," Allen instructed in a thick southern drawl. He rolled up his T-shirt for the challenge exposing his abdomen.

Layers of taunt muscles rippled in front of Derek's face. The last time anyone ever invited him to such a test was back in high school. "What?" It had been a long drive.

"You got a problem with your hearing, son? Go ahead and hit me in the stomach as hard as you can."

Derek shifted his weight on his chair uncomfortably, his eyes looking to Kelly for guidance. She ignored him, engaging instead in non-stop gossip with Joanie. The two women faced each other on the couch, lost in time, chattering like old ladies at a bingo hall. Their hands moved in unison while recounting stories about an old friend or coworker.

Derek looked at his hosts. The Floridians were quite a mismatched couple by outward appearances. The woman was languid, flowing out onto the furniture like molasses. Apparently she rarely left her home, a consequence of agoraphobia. Derek imagined he could see indentations in the seat cushions from years of reading every novel on the New York Times fiction bestseller list. Genuinely sweet, Joanie chose to live vicariously through the fantasies of the printed word or the exploits of her husband. Her speech was molasses with a hint of chocolate. Her motions were slow and deliberate.

Allen, on the other hand, was a whirling dervish of energy. Although bald, he was delusional enough to drag his few remaining hair follicles from ear to ear in the belief that the world could be fooled with this illusion. A foot shorter and perhaps twenty years older then his guest, his speech was as intense as his universal distain for politicians.

Allen slapped his washer-board flat stomach with his own bare hand. "Down here we call these babies a 'six pack'," he said proudly. "Now come on, Yankee boy, hit me!"

"We call them a 'six pack' up north, too," Derek said uncomfortably.

"Just do it," Joanie interrupted from across the room. "At least that way he'll shut up."

"Let it be your way," Derek said. He pulled back his fist and landed a relatively soft blow to the midriff. He had to admit, Allen looked to be in amazing shape for a man of his years. Still, hitting someone you've just met was not considered polite in too many circles.

"Harder, you damn Yankee girly man!" Allen commanded.

This time Derek landed a solid punch to the solar plexus. His blow rocked Allen several inches off his midline stance. Surprisingly the man's face did not flinch. Tough little bastard, thought Derek. "That certainly is quite an amazing display of muscle."

"Thank you," Allen said, smiling. He had once again proven he was king of the hill. He strode into the kitchen with renewed confidence. "Now what can I get you folks to drink?"

"A beer will be fine," Derek said, hopefully, dying for something cold and foamy. It was hotter then hell. Apparently being ocean side, his hosts had sworn off air conditioning.

"I'm sorry hun, but the Bible says we're not to put any fermented juice to our lips," Joanie said. She dropped her right leg down from her throne on the couch and searched for the TV remote with her toes. "Perhaps some Coke or lemonade?"

"Coke, please," Kelly requested.

"That'll be just fine," Derek added, taking a seat across from Kelly. She gave him a reassuring smile then returned to her gossip.

Allen brought out two Bud Lites and two Cokes. He popped the flip tops and passed out the cans with two glasses for the ladies and none for himself or Derek.

"Didn't you just say you don't believe in drinking alcohol?" Derek asked.

"Shush," Allen said, raising his index finger to his lips. "There's so little alcohol in this stuff that the Lord would surely forgive me if he were lookin' down on us right now. This is from my special stash. Seein' as how you are a friend of Kelly's, I'm proud, no, make that honored to share it with you," Allen said, ignoring the visual barbs from his wife.

A pragmatic born again Christian, thought Derek. He was beginning to like this guy.

"So, Derek, Kelly's been telling me all about this case," Joanie said. "Quite an interesting story of maggots. What do you expect to find down here that our local boys haven't?"

Derek took a long heavy swallow and drained the can of beer. "I don't quite know." How much had Kelly revealed to her friends? The way Joanie asked, probably everything. "A little of this and a little of that. It's Kelly's idea, actually."

"Well, young man, we're ready to help you. Allen will drive you both to the poor girl's apartment before we have dinner. It's actually not too far from here."

"Would you mind?" Kelly asked. "I really want to get this out of the way before we get into the fun stuff."

"What fun stuff?" Derek asked, enjoying a second beer that miraculously appeared in his hand. Allen was looking better and better.

"You know, like looking for sharks teeth," Kelly said.

"What kind of sharks teeth?" he asked. What did sharks teeth have to do with their murder investigation?

"Fossilized sharks teeth, to be exact," Joanie answered. Her stretch on the couch almost pushed Kelly aside. "Anywhere from twenty to two hundred million years old. They're all over the beach, especially since the Army Corps of Engineers pumped oodles of sand from a mile off shore back onto our beaches a couple of years back. Stunk up the beach for almost a year. At least now we have something to walk on. Erosion is a terrible thing. Anyway, it's great fun looking for them during a romantic sunset walk." The reference to romance and sunsets was an apparent breach of trust. Kelly glared silently at her friend.

"Hey," Allen said, moving the conversation from an embarrassing pause. "Wanna' hear the latest scuttlebutt about the old guard from your UHJ days? We've been keeping track."

"I'd love to hear about the old guard," Derek said, finishing his second beer. He was much more relaxed. "Nothing like old gossip. Just like on the *National Inquirer*, I'll bet. Who knows, maybe they know something about John Brady, too."

Kelly threw a pillow. "What? You tell me that you don't sit around with the boys at the Down Under Pub and smirk when you hear about which guy from your station is fooling around with someone else's wife? Give me a break. And, by the way, John had nothing to do with my program here at UHJ."

"Actually, I was thinking more about what kind of job everyone has," Joanie said, revealing a semi-wicked smile. "But, since you brought it up, I've got the low down on pretty much everyone - kids, divorces, scandals, all that kind of stuff."

"There you go again," Derek said feigning embarrassment. "I am stunned. Your mothers would be mortified. The dark side always comes out in the end, doesn't it?"

"Are you kidding? My mother lives around the corner. She's gonna' be mad that I didn't call her up and invite her over to hear all the good stuff," Joanie said gleefully.

"Anyway...," Allen said, giving Derek another beer.

"Anyway...," Joanie began in a low whisper as if the room was bugged. She began the litany of the University Hospital residency graduates.

Derek actually found the tales interesting, especially after beginning his third beer. His hosts weaved images of passion and intrigue around faceless names, constantly interrupting and correcting each other with their own versions. Of the original seven emergency medicine residents, 'the seven dwarfs', three remained in Florida. Another had returned to his home in Missouri and tragically succumbed to the debilitating effects of Alzheimer's at the age of thirty-five. Kelly was the only graduate north of the Mason-Dixon Line. One lucky man hit it big on the multilevel marketing circuit and had retired from the practice of medicine altogether. Another ran a sports fishing camp on the Gulf Coast of Florida.

"Maybe we could give him a call," Derek said, hopefully. "I'd love to go fishing."

"I hate fishing," Kelly said, quickly. There was no doubt in anyone's mind where she stood on that idea. "Besides, we're on the wrong side of Florida."

"Who says you're gonna' be invited? We don't generally bring our women along unless they agree to clean the fish," Allen teased.

This time it was Allen's turn to be hit with pillows thrown from both women at once.

Derek looked out the window and drained the last of his beer. No beer, no fishing and no privacy. Something told him this is going to be one very long week.

Alexandria, Egypt
1917

The full moon hung low over the cities abandoned streets. Those who emerged from hiding at this hour often had good reason to seek out the dark places in the light of day. Men slinked out of doorways and alleyways of the casaba, each to their own purpose. Sometimes it was by choice that they lived this way. Sometimes it was a matter of fate or just bad luck. They fed off of each other with only an occasional foray into the mainstream of society. Even drunken sailors and prostitutes knew better then to venture into this no mans land.

Houri leaned on Nerses leading him down the rubble-strewn paths into the bowls of the catacombs. He gladly shared her weight and, for this, she smiled inwardly - this was going to be easier then first imagined. She leaned on him more then was really necessary; letting out an occasional moan perfectly timed to guarantee his attention. Below their feet cobblestones dissolved into dirt roads then to dirt paths. They double backed on their trail, constantly wary of the police.

"Are you sure you want to do this now?" Nerses asked, totally disoriented. Only the moonlight guided their path. He was a stranger in Alexandria and knew he could never find his way back alone.

Houri smiled her best, helpless feminine smile. "The police are asleep or drunk. Better now. Better before the city wakes. Now we are both wanted by the authorities. If we are discovered and captured, neither of us would survive the interrogation."

A catacomb entrance loomed in front of them, but only Houri recognized that the side door to a Coptic chapel accessed the underground. She kissed the blue beads and blue eye of her bracelet to ward off the evil spirits. Removing a small oil lamp from her skirt pocket, she lit it and handed it to Nerses then lit another one for herself. Beneath her dress, she felt comfort in the handle of a kitchen knife that pressed against her breast. It was the same one that Nerses had used the day before when serving her bread and cheese. She removed it from his room without detection just before they left on her mission to the catacombs.

They entered the first series of tombs standing upright. Mosaics of Greco Roman princes and commoners stared back at them from the walls. Soon they found themselves stooping forward so as not to strike their heads on the low ceilings. Carvings in Latin, Greek and Copt decorated the walls and chambers as they descended through history. Occasional rats scurried away from their approaching lamps. They made frequent stops to rest and again to ensure they had not been followed to Houri's secret.

"How much further?" Nerses asked, eyes anxiously darting around the tunnel.

Houri smiled coyly. Good, he does not know about my hiding place. "Not too much longer," she replied. The thought of suddenly abandoning him deep within the bowels of the earth was tempting. It would be easy to just disappear into the side tunnels leaving this man to starve to death in the labyrinth. On second thought the situation called for a more decisive move to guarantee the treasure would be hers, alone. She demanded finality. Houri leaned on an outcrop of limestone. "I feel weak. Please go ahead of me. I will follow."

Nerses squeezed past her to lead the way. "Whatever you ask, I will obey," he replied. He took her small hand in his own and led the way.

Changing places, his body brushed against hers. Houri felt a tingle in her spine, a sensation new to her; but this, she quickly ignored. She removed the knife from the space between her breasts and held it behind her back. The blade was serrated and at least eight inches in length. The wooden handle balanced nicely in her small hands – not quite as evenly as her own that now lay at the bottom of a well, but good enough for the task at hand. She smiled, to think that just yesterday this knife cut bread and cheese. The man in front of her was large by any Egyptian standard. He only wore a simple shirt. There would be no problem with a jacket or coat that could interfere with her blow. Her thrust would have to be up and in to his heart if she were to be successful for a quick kill.

Nerses turned and looked at her. His eyes were gentle but determined; his voice lush with strength and sincerity. "This is foolishness. You are getting weaker. There is nothing here that is worth your health. Come, take my hand and we will go back. You should rest and regain your strength. I will take care of you."

Houri hesitated in her mission. For the first time in her life she faced a conflict between years of training, of loyalty to her clan, and some new part of her being that defied recognition. Her determination to finish the act of murder, of self-preservation, as was her natural birthright, began to ebb. His eyes, her gaze always returned to his eyes. Then she knew. It was she who would surrender. "You are right," she said. "Let's return to the surface."

They made an about face and began their assent, slowly, hand in hand. The knife that could have defined Houri's life for all eternity lay discarded in an abandoned crypt. "You never did tell me your full name," she said.

"I'm sorry. It is Bagdasarian, Nerses Bagdasarian."

Ponte Vedra Beach, Florida
October 19th

With 240 turbo charged horses, Allen's Subaru Impreza WRX, had a body of a Nash Rambler and the heart of a screaming turbo Porsche. Joanie's agoraphobia and intrinsic knowledge of her husbands driving habits kept her at home. The man drove in and out of the back streets like a maniac, narrowly missing pedestrians and other traffic alike. 'The Lord will protect us' was his mantra, a trail of beach sand flying in his wake. But who's going to protect the rest of the world, thought Derek, his body alternately pressed into the seat back or thrown forward as his host double clutched.

It was a short ride to the murdered girl's store. The address the Florida state police had provided was in a beachside strip mall. The store was an empty shell with a large 'For Rent' sign hung across the front window. Only bare carpet and a random shelf bracket remained of the woman's business. The interior window ledge was covered with dead flies and spiders.

Derek looked at a second address in his notebook and gave that one to Allen. This was Boerner's beachfront condo and was further south by a mile. The difference in communities was amazing. A sprawling menagerie of eclectic cottages morphed into an upscale planned community with hidden mansions and golf courses that melded into each other.

Boerner's condo sat oceanfront at the end of a row of identical units. The WRX pulled into a 'visitor' parking space. All three passengers exited the vehicle, following Derek as he confidently strode up the walkway. The front door of the condo still had one single yellow police tape across it and resisted only a few seconds before it succumbing to Derek's jiggling credit card. Ducking underneath the tape, he led the way inside. The unit was amazing. Two thousand square feet of marble, tile and glass overlooked the Atlantic Ocean. Outside double sand dunes, wild sea grass, sea grapes and purple beach roses spread out between the first floor deck and the narrow strip of boardwalk that lead down to the sea. After brief instructions the three intruders separated to explore on their own.

Derek turned his back to the magnificent view and looked around the living room. It was clean. Amazingly clean, considering the owner lay in a morgue drawer 1500 miles north for over a month. He opened the kitchen refrigerator. Everything inside was new, unopened and neatly arranged.

A toilet flushed somewhere on the second floor. Kelly came downstairs, each footfall leaving a barely perceptible indentation on the perfectly white carpet. She noticed the stares of her two friends. "What?" She looked back and forth between them, slightly embarrassed at the attention. "So I had to go to the bathroom. Is that a crime?"

"How's it look," Derek asked, enjoying her embarrassment.

Kelly adjusted her skirt. "Perfect, just like the rest of the house." She sat down on a leather love seat. "The closets have a few dresses perfectly hung up. The bureau drawers are full of clothes perfectly folded. A brand new toothbrush and unopened tooth paste sit on the bathroom sink."

"I hope they left ya'll some toilet paper and soap," Allen quipped. He sat down on the seat next to her. "Even a poor southern boy like me can recognize this place has been wiped clean." He turned his head behind and around. "Look, see there. How can you have a computa' desk without a computa'?"

Derek was impressed by the thoroughness of the sterilization. Someone had gone through a whole lot of trouble. Even the vacuum marks all went in the same direction. He knew it wasn't the state police because they would have mentioned it in their report. Nothing personal remained: no bills, no diaries, no ledgers and no scraps of paper on the refrigerator. It was the refrigerator that bothered him the most. You could always tell about a person's life by looking at their refrigerator. This one had magnets but nothing attached to them. He walked up to the double sliders that faced the ocean and stared out into the horizon. The findings today suggested a conspiracy that extended into two states, Massachusetts and Florida. Even Kelly's house wasn't this clean and she was obsessive-compulsive in her housekeeping.

"Might as well head on out," Allen said. "We're gonna' be late for dinner. Don't want to get Joanie pissed off at us."

Heading out the door they were assailed by a woman's angry voice. "What are ya'll doin' here?" Petite, in her mid twenties and clearly on a mission, she blocked their path with a stance reminiscent of a bad karate movie. Her fiery eyes darted back and forth between the three trying to figure out the leader. Dressed in a sports bra and jogging shorts and dripping sweat, she held a small dog in her arms. The dog, too, was panting in the heat, tongue dangling out of the corner of its mouth.

"Easy there, sister. My name is Derek Ekizian. I'm a detective from Massachusetts. " Derek extended his right hand with his Fall River police ID. He waited until the woman matched the photo with his face and then he returned the wallet to his rear pants pocket. "And you are…."

The woman relaxed her combat stance. "My name is Pat Mendes. I'm Carol's friend. I mean I was Carol's friend until well, you know. No matter. What's your business? The State police told me no one was suppose to go inside of her condo. No one."

Derek didn't know the extent of this woman's relationship with the murdered girl. His forte was not bluffing but he started anyway. "Just cleaning up some loose ends. You know how that kind of thing is. Both of her parents gone and we can't find any living relatives. I'm in charge of probate for the estate." He was beginning to get lost in his own lies.

"You, too?" A few weeks back some other guys came around and said the same thing. Seems like the Florida and Massachusetts legal systems need to get their acts togetha'. You guys should talk to each other and save yourselves a trip." She shifted the dog in her arms and placed in on the ground. The animal sniffed the legs of everyone on the walkway then shuffled over to the grass, squatted and pissed. The woman looked at the three of them and a sudden smile crossed her face. "You know something, I'm glad you're here. I've had her dog for almost a solid month. It's old and I'm tired of it shitting and peeing on my floor. Let it be someone else's turn now. Carol, God rest her soul, promised I'd only have to dog sit for a few days when she went to Boston. You folks have just solved my dog problem." She placed the trembling dog in Derek's arms and stepped backwards, ignoring his feeble protests. "Follow me," she ordered. Shrugging their eyebrows, they all obliged.

"Wait here," she instructed. "I might as well give you the mail, too. That way I'll be done with the whole thing. Never wanted to get this involved in the first place," she mumbled.

Kelly took the dog from Derek's reluctant arms. "The other 'officers' who got here first and moved a few things, did they take her mail, too?" She asked.

"Don't know. No one bothered to ask me. Just saw them out of my car window as I was pullin' up. They didn't seem interested in me or anything I had to say. I never even got around to askin' them about the dog." She left them at her front doorstep for a few minutes and returned with a large shopping bag of mail, a bag of dog food and a small bowl with the name, Cricket, on its side. "Already threw out all the junk mail. You'll need this for the dog. Carol said to use only this bowl 'cause her dog won't eat out of nothin' else." She handed over all the bags, turned around and closed the door behind her.

"What are we going to do with a dog?" Derek asked, shaking his head in disbelief.

Allen stroked the dog's stomach as it lay curled in Kelly's arm. "S.P.C.A. shelter is just around the corner from my house. They'd take the animal in. Probably only last a few days before they decide to put it asleep."

Kelly pulled away defensively, cradling the dog tightly in her arms out of Allen's reach. "Whoa there, partner. Just wait a minute. Why are we talking putting this animal down?"

"Advanced case of breast cancer," Allen replied with somber confidence. "Feel here and here," he said stroking the trembling animal's chest and abdomen. "Feel these lumps? Yorkies are prone to that nasty problem as they get older. Too bad, seems like a nice enough little fella'."

The dog stretched and began to lick the side of her face. "Oh, look!" Kelly said. "It's trying to kiss me!" She turned toward Derek. "We can't just get rid of it. It's got feelings."

"What do you expect me to do with it? I'm not a big fan of dogs. Besides we've got a 1500 mile trip back home," Derek said scrunching up his mouth. The dog looked at him with big sad eyes. Against his will, he watched as his right hand extended itself towards the dog and began stroking the small terrier behind its ears. The dog responded by pushing off Kelly's arms and jumping into Derek's. "Great, now look at what you've done. The damn thing likes me!"

Kelly smiled as the dog stretched out to lick Derek's face. "Hey, you're the one who scratched its ears. Don't blame me. Let that be a lesson for you. Never scratch behind the ears of a woman or a dog. We'll both do the same thing." She smiled at Derek's blush. "Besides, who knows, maybe it'll help us solve this case."

"Right," Derek snorted. What else could go wrong with this trip?

Allen chuckled at their predicament. "Come on guys. Joanie's a' waitin'."

Modern Alexandria, Egypt
October 20th

He dropped the massive lion headed doorknocker again, this time more loudly then the first. "Let me in, sweet sister," he cooed. He stood impatiently in the street listening to her move around inside. American and Middle Eastern music wafted through the windows of the surrounding homes, clashing incongruously. The neighbors were already looking out their windows at the big American car with its diplomatic plates. Most knew the siblings were estranged and they anxiously anticipated another round of screaming and cursing.

A bolt released, the door cracked open a few inches. The clink of a chain reminded him entry was unlikely. "What do you want here?" a cautious female voice whispered within.

He could barely make out a pair of saggy eyes on the other side of the entryway. "What! Am I no longer welcome in my father's home?" he demanded.

"Father has been dead for over five years. This is my home now. What do you want?" she repeated, still barring his entrance. Older then him by ten years, her manners were course, her voice heavy and crude. No wonder she had remained unmarried.

"Nothing dear sister, nothing at all. I just wanted to see you and visit a bit."

"Like the last time? I still carry the scars from your anger." Her voice was now agitated.

"I am a new man," he said simply. "The world has changed and so have I. You are the only family I have in the world." He could hear no response after his last entreaty. "Here," he said pushing a box through the narrow opening. "I even brought you a small present, a box of *lokkum*, it's your favorite. Please, dear sister, don't make me beg."

She took the box from his hand. For a few moments there was no other response. He shifted his weight, nervously from foot to foot. Suddenly the door closed then cracked open again, the sound of bolts and chains clanging against each other on the other side. It responded to the pressure of his hand and he slipped inside. Walking directly into the living room he sat down on the couch, still not looking at her inflated face and obese body.

"The big shot has come back to his poor relatives. I'm blessed," she said sarcastically, closing the door behind him. "Are you going to hit me now or later?"

He ignored her, leaning back into the massive cushions of the antique furniture, slowly breathing in the memories. The house stood unchanged for centuries. Within the walls, time stood still. Oriental rugs covered the three- foot thick walls. The plastered ceilings were eight feet high and supported three large ceiling fans that slowly rotated in the heat. Elaborate furniture and ornate pillows stuffed the room to overflowing. He involuntarily winced as old conflicts and the memory of his father's harsh discipline blended with his current reality. "So, sister, how have you been?"

She looked at him suspiciously. "Not that you really care, but I am just fine. Does that disappoint you? Besides can't you use your friends in the CIA to find that out?"

"You know I just wish you the best," he protested. Their mutual animosity made the ensuing silence viscous. He rocked his top foot back and forth across his crossed legs, his eyes wandering around the room. "And don't overestimate my contacts. I am just a simple soldier who's lucky enough to be able to visit his native land now and again." He wondered if she was alone in the house.

"Sometimes I wish father had never sent you off to America for your education. You were so much nicer when you were a little boy." Her voice softened.

He hated her more when she slipped into the maternal mode. "Dear sister, we all must grow up." He stroked his red mustache. "Perhaps if he had sent you instead of me, things would have been different between us." His real thoughts were incompatible with this conversation. "Might you offer me something to drink?" he asked wiping the sweat from his forehead.

She excused herself and returned with a glass of *tan* - yogurt, salt and ice water. She handed it to him. Their hands brushed against each other as they made the exchange.

He hated her touch. He took a sip of the classic drink and placed it down on a coffee table at his side. If she had to get the beverage herself, that meant there was no maid and she was alone in the house. Cautiously he began his inquiry, stammering and stuttering the words. "I was just wondering ...."

Her face curled in a snarl. "So is that what this is all about?" She snorted in disgust. "I knew there was something else you wanted." She rose out of her chair in anger.

He feigned ignorance looking at her wide-eyed and apologetic. The situation needed to be defused immediately. "I'm sorry. I was just wondering if you had anything stronger to drink, like *Raki*?" he said innocently. "That's all I was going to ask."

His response caught her off guard. Her shoulders eased as she unclenched her fists. "*Raki?*" she stammered. "Of course." She disappeared into the kitchen and returned with a half opened bottle of the high alcohol brandy and one glass. She placed the bottle in front of him and let him pour his own drink.

"Won't you drink with me?" He saw her frown. "At least if not with me, then to the memory of our mother and father. We, you and I, must try to break this impasse between us."

The invitation was unexpected. She looked at him intensely suspicious. His reputation preceded him. Still, he had asked, and not commanded. That, in itself, was unusual and must count for something. She returned from the kitchen bringing another glass.

He poured her a shot as well. "No water or ice, right?"

"Right, just like our parents and their parents before them." She locked her eyes on him defensively.

She was more masculine in movement then most of the men he knew. It made him nauseated even being in the same room with her. He forced small talk, inquiring as to her life and daily activities. He pretended interest and smiled as she slowly opened up her sorrows from the past five years. They were on their third shot of *Raki* before she sat back in her chair relaxed enough to talk freely. By the fourth shot she had taken off her shoes and curled her feet on the couch. He was disgusted by how hairy her legs were. By the fifth shot she had retreated into the kitchen and returned with thinly sliced wafers of spicy cured *Soojuk* and *Basterma.* Few men could have drunk so much and remained coherent.

Slowly, deliberately, he steered the conversation back to his true interest. He talked about the ancestral home and old photographs, Egyptian artifacts scattered in the room, relatives who had passed away and the pressure of being a single woman in modern Egyptian society. Finally, he broached the topic so dear to his heart." It must be a heavy burden."

"What?" she asked.

"You know. Having something so valuable beside your bed. Looking at it every night knowing that if you sold it you could leave this life, travel, explore the world."

"What makes you think I haven't sold it already?" she slurred.

"Because I know you. You are true to your word. You promised father that you'd never sell it and keep it in the family forever."

"Perhaps." She stared at her glass then drained it. "As usual, you are right, though. I still have it. In fact, it's very close. You'd die if you found out how close you are to it." She giggled uncontrollably and then frowned, pointing a bony finger at him and waving it in front of his face. "It's mine. No one else's, but mine. Do you understand that?"

He feigned a wound to his sensibilities. "Sister, I came to visit you. Please don't ruin this chance for us to get together." He saw the words begin to take affect. She must have been lonelier then he first thought. "I know that it belongs to you. I was just making conversation. There are just the two of us left out of all the family and I know how important it is to you, how you have been protecting it all these years. I'm sorry. Just forget that I even brought it up. What is important is you and I as brother and sister."

She softened and sat down again. In a society that was based on family, she had been alone for years. "Yes, it means a lot to me. Would you like to see it?"

He smiled inwardly. "Only if you want to show it to me. I wouldn't want to put you through any trouble." He was so close, that he could taste it. "Is it too difficult to get?"

She smiled, lost in her sudden position of power. Life had been unkind to her in many ways; but this was her reward for years of empty love, loneliness and being born looking more like her father then her mother. "It won't take but a minute," she babbled like a little girl. She could barely stand up without help. Slowly she disappeared up the stairs pulling her obese frame along the railing with both hands.

He could hear the sound of doors opening and closing, of floorboards being removed. He looked around the room again now that she was gone. He felt a visceral connection to everything within his sight. There was much that he regretted over the years. This woman, who he detested, held the key to his future. Was he prepared to sacrifice her to acquire an object, a thing? The thought was unimaginable; but, he did imagine it, over and over until it was real. Her footsteps down the stairs sounded like a man. Even the way she walked disgusted him.

She returned with a large box and plopped down next to him on the couch. Her fat fingers fumbled with the ropes that bound the top. Clumsily she opened the container, removed the straw packing and displayed its contents to her brother, still holding the box in her lap.

"May I?" he asked politely. His eyes were glued to the treasure. Two large jewels, each the size of an eyeglass case, were encrusted in a border of five thousand year old gold. Their existence had been rumored for millennia but only the two of them knew the truth.

"Of course." She smiled like a little girl. Her feet tapped ever so gently on the floor as she had done in her youth. She looked proudly at the contents and not at her brother's face. It was a mistake.

This was the final piece of the puzzle. Everything else had come to his possession over the past years. With each piece retrieved, his extended family became smaller and smaller. People disappeared frequently in this society. Few questions were ever asked; and, those that did, resolved with a few dollars of US currency. He took the box from her surprised hand and placed it by his own side. "Thank you, dear sister. I've seen enough."

She looked up from the floor and then at her brother's face. The look in his eyes was now unmistakable. She tried to stand up but it was too late. At least she would feel no pain..

Jax Beach, Florida
October 19th

"So, what do we have?" Kelly asked, stroking the neck of the Yorkie on her lap.

Derck sat in front of a coffee table on his host's screened porch sorting through Boerner's mail. Two piles formed around his feet: one for bills and the other, personal correspondence. Three empty cans of coke and a small bag of potato chips floated between the floor and Kelly's couch. The mechanics of his task was complicated by the lack of privacy in the small cottage. Bible hour blared on every TV and radio between the hours of six and eight pm.

"Electric bills, telephone bills, credit card statements and a couple of discount coupons to Burger King. Nothing much of substance," Derek commented, stuffing another pile of non- clues into the garbage bag. There was no guilt in sorting through the debris of another human being's life; Boerner was, after all, dead and he was a homicide detective.

Allen poked his head into the porch. "How ya'll doin'? Need anythin'?" he asked.

"Maybe another Coke, please," Derek said without looking up.

"What do you make of those other folks who cleaned out her place before we got there? Think they were real cops?" Allen loved his foray into the world of police work.

"Bet my pension they weren't," Derek said, opening Boerner's credit card statement. "I don't think they were post mortem parasites, either. Local or state cops wouldn't sanitize a potential crime scene to that degree; at least we wouldn't do that up north unless the case was still active. Remember, as far as the rest of the world is concerned, this case is closed."

"But all they took was computa's and personal papers."

Derek stuffed the last of the mail into the garbage bags. "And refrigerator magnets and anything handwritten and personal photographs and every bill and scrap of receipts the woman had." He was frustrated at his own ineffectiveness. "The things missing from her condo suggest she had information so critical, so threatening that someone went to a lot of trouble to set up what appears to be an elaborate charade up north."

Kelly interrupted indignantly. "'Appears to be'? What do you mean 'appears to be'?"

Derek caught his slip too late. "I'm sorry. You're right. Kelly has proven that it was a charade. They, whoever they were, wanted this girl out of the way with no trail back to Florida. And, if someone was lucky enough to find out who she really was, they cleaned out any proof of her life except for pastel sun dresses in her closets and a used toothbrush. If I had been a bit more aggressive with this case in the first place, we would have gotten to Florida before now and might even had caught these guys."

Kelly reached down from the couch and massaged Derek's neck and tense back muscles. "Hey, don't be so hard on yourself. Besides, we got to make this into a bit of a vacation, too. If nothing else, consider yourself a lucky man to spend a few days with me," she laughed.

Derek moved from the floor to sit next to Kelly. "I know, I know, you're right," he said draining the last of his soda. "I'm just mad. I'm mad because you were right all along. I'm mad because neither of our bosses believed you. I'm mad because I didn't have the courage to follow my own instincts from the beginning. I'm mad because we seem to be weeks if not months behind the trail of whoever did this. And you know something, unless we get real lucky, they're going to get away with it."

"What about now?" Allen asked, sitting across from them in a wicker rocking chair. In the background they could hear Joanie requesting his presence in front of the TV; the television evangelist was nearing a climax. "Be there in a moment, hun," he yelled across the house. He returned his attention to Derek. "Ain't you got enough to go back and see if the bosses will reopen the case?"

Derek shook his head in the negative. "What do I tell them? That I broke into a crime scene that they still don't acknowledge is a crime scene; that some next-door neighbor saw some folks removing a few truckloads of potential evidence? That'll go over like a lead balloon with my chief. I have to get some hard evidence or I might as well forget it."

They were alone again, Allen retreating into the kitchen with his wife. "Anything I can do to help?" Kelly asked leaning her head against his shoulder.

Derek shook his head in the negative and stroked his mustache. He scanned the dead girl's credit card statement for any obvious or not so obvious clues. "Key West, Key West, Key West. This girl spent a lot of time in the Florida Keys. For a Jacksonville working girl, she certainly had a lot of vacation time. Look, these statements go back into August and early September. They end just before she came up to Boston. Almost every charge is from Key West, not Islamorada or Key Largo, just Key West. Hell, there's even a veterinary bill from the Keys. Seems she took her dog on vacation there, too."

"Is there a hotel or guest home or bed and breakfast bill?" Kelly asked reaching into a bag for a dog treat. The terrier wiggled in her lap with anticipation, stood up and locked its eyes on her hand.

Derek scanned the credit card statement again. "Nope."

Kelly gave the dog the treat, just missed being nipped by the animal's enthusiasm. "So she either slept in her car or knew someone pretty well down there."

"Would seem so," Derek said. "Looks like you have a new friend." He watched the lap dog bury its head in Kelly's armpit, sniffing and tunneling away in play.

"She must have really loved this dog," Kelly noted, rubbing the dog's neck again. "A personalized dog dish, vacation to the Keys, even some jewelry with the name 'Cricket.'"

Derek frowned. "What a waste. You've got to decide about that dog pretty soon. Maybe a kennel or the SPCA. Maybe your friends, Joanie and Allen may have an idea."

"Not a chance," Kelly replied defensively. She worked the dog closer to her chest. "I think the three of us will do just fine."

"The three of who?" Derek asked.

"Why, Cricket, me and Max," she said, making kissing baby noises to the dog. The dog responded in kind, trying to lick Kelly's face. "Maybe I'll even have to get Max some jewelry, too. I don't want Max to get jealous."

Derek snorted. "I don't get how you can give this little nothing of a dog the time of day, never mind even thinking of bringing him back to Massachusetts. The only kind of jealousy you have to worry about is making sure that your killer Labrador doesn't eat him."

"How many times do I have to tell you, Cricket is a 'she', not a 'he'. Besides, I give you the time of day, too, and you are no Max, either," Kelly said giving Derek a whack to his ribs with her elbow.

Frustrated in his search of Boerner's mail, Derek sat forward on the couch deep in thought, arms resting on his knees, fingers interlocked. "Hey, Kell, what kind of jewelry is this dog wearing?"

Kelly held the dog at arms length then laid it flat on her lap and began to sort through the various tags. "Let's see: Flea and tic collar, a dog tag with her name, address and phone number, rabies vaccine, license number. Ah, here it is, a nice heart locket."

"Do you mind if I take a look?" Derek asked leaning over towards the dog. "Sometimes these things are hollow. Let's see if there's anything inside this baby." His fingers fumbled with the small piece of gold.

Kelly pushed his hands away. "Here, let me do it. You men can be so helpless sometimes."

He was successful before Kelly gave her assistance. "Well, well, well. Look at this!" Derek said, looking inside the locket. He unfolded a small piece of paper inside.

"What is it? Let me see," Kelly insisted, pressing forward.

Derek turned the paper over and over. On one side was '5817'. The other side held a series of hand written numbers and letters. "Y-O-G-I-P-6-1," he read aloud.

"The mystery deepens,' Kelly said. She smiled, rubbing the dog's ears absentmindedly.

"Do the numbers mean anything to you?" Derek asked.

"5817. 5817," Kelly repeated over and over in a drone. "In a strange way it seems familiar but I haven't a clue. It's not Pi, or Avagadro's number. Nothing medical. Certainly nothing to do with a Yorkshire terrier. And Y-O-G-I-P-6-1…doesn't mean anything to me either."

Derek folded the piece of paper, returned it to the dog's locket and pried off the gold clasp, separating it from the rest of the dog's collar. He placed the locket into his shirt pocket. "Do me a favor, Kell. Let's just keep this between us, OK?"

"Sure, but why? Joanie and Allen are the only other folks who are here. It's not like they are involved or anything."

Derek broke into a whisper. "Look, Allen used his car to drive us out to Boerner's house. He was inside with us. A neighbor saw the three of us together. I'll bet you a week's pay your friends are discussing this case right now, or, at least, they will be when the Bible hour is over. I don't want anyone else possibly getting in trouble or worse."

"What do you mean, 'or worse'," Kelly spoke up quickly.

"If you haven't noticed, several people are dead. Let's just keep this our little secret for now."

Kelly hesitated then placed her one free hand on Derek's.

"You're the boss."

"Yeah, right," Derek said, stuffing a handful of potato chips into his mouth.

Their conversation was interrupted by the arrival of their hosts. Joanie spoke up "All right, boys and girls, time to get some shut eye. Girls follow me and boys follow Allen. You're lookin' at a Christian house here," Joanie said. "Won't be no hanky-panky under my roof. Now get a move on," she said pushing Derek in front of her.

Derek looked at Kelly inquisitively. She shrugged her shoulders and smiled. This was one aspect of their Florida vacation that had not been defined before they left Massachusetts; yet, he knew that sleeping arrangements could be spontaneous and he had left the details deliberately nebulous. When was an invitation not an invitation? What did the words 'join me' really suggest?

"Never *assume* anything," Kelly quoted smiling as she followed Joanie. "It makes an *ass* out of *u* and *me.*'

Allen grabbed Derek by the shoulders. "Come on, friend. Looks like neither of us will be getting' any ta'night," he said leading Derek away.

Nasser International Airport, Egypt
October 20th

Grinding his teeth impatiently he inched forward with the rest of the maddeningly slow line boarding the aircraft. The air conditioning in the concourse was broken – again, and the terminal was sweltering. A chaotic bazaar of pastels from western tourist clashed visually with white robed Saudi princes and their entourage of black chador clad wives and daughters. Sweat was the common denominator as everyone waded through security checkpoints. Now he faced a machine gun toting soldier who blocked his path.

"I'm sorry sir, but I have to inspect your carry on baggage," the man said in Arabic. Full bearded, his uniform was Egyptian army special forces. He expertly cradled his weapon.

This had never happened to him before. The soldier, not yet in his twenties would not easily be intimidated. "I beg your pardon, are you talking to me?" he asked in a huff. The man did not blink. "Do you know who I am? I'm the military attaché for the United States government. I have total diplomatic immunity. Now get out of my way before I have you transferred to a post in the Sinai desert."

"I know who you are, sir." The soldier stood like granite. "I have my orders."

It was hot. Odors of unwashed third world citizens saturated every molecule in the airport. There was no time for this nonsense. He had to take the upper hand immediately. "I insist on speaking to your superior officer."

A moment later another soldier appeared, this time with the rank of a colonel, the same as himself. The two Egyptians whispered to each other and then the senior officer approached. "I understand you have a problem with understanding Arabic."

The American snorted. "I was born speaking Arabic before I learned English. Tell your man to get out of my way."

His counterpart stood firm. "We have our instructions from the minister himself. Since the latest Intifada uprising, we have been given direct orders to inspect all baggage. The minister insists that the fundamentalists will not be permitted to sabotage any additional flights to the United States. It is for your own safety. If your satchel is confirmed to contain only papers, then you will be permitted to board the aircraft. Every suitcase must be fully inspected and only then will you be permitted to leave the country."

Every contingency had been prepared for except for the unthinkable, and this was the unthinkable. Diplomatic immunity worked for everything. He had used this route to transport innumerable items in the past. If he permitted a search of his luggage, the consequences were unimaginable. Without a search, he would not be permitted to board the aircraft. His mind raced. There was no alternative. He turned resolutely to the colonel. "What is your name? I will make a full report to the ambassador, himself."

The Egyptian officer politely obliged him with the requested information. The American pivoted and left the queue of passengers preparing to board the airplane. There had to be another way; but, not today. He began the long walk through the terminal back to the VIP lounge.

"Hello my friend," a deep voice bellowed behind him.

Pivoting, he found the face of the General looming within inches of his own. The pot-marked aberration of a human being loved to invade personal space – better to intimidate. This Egyptian reputation as an animal was well deserved; he was a man comfortable with violence. Indiscriminate brute force was his trademark. "Are you responsible for this indignity to the government of the United States?" the American asked aggressively. There was little to lose.

The Egyptian stood with his hands behind his back and slowly rocked on the balls of his feet. His smile beamed a patchwork of terrible tobacco stained teeth. "Actually, it wasn't me. It's the prime minister himself. Terrible the way he has insulted your government. I'm so sorry," the General said mocking his prey in heavily accented English. "Actually, if things were left up to me, I would encourage a few more bombs. It tends to keep your people a bit closer to our reality." He smiled again. "Can I be of some assistance with your bags?" he inquired, extending his tree stump of a forearm towards the American's luggage.

He clutched the satchel firmly in his hand. "Diplomatic sensitive documents only. My orders prohibit me from accepting your kind offer. No, thank you."

"By the way," the General said, alternating his gaze between the luggage he so desperately wanted to open and the eyes of his potential victim. "My sympathies for the passing of your sister. Aren't you planning to stay for her funeral?"

Burial arrangements were made before he left the city. Her

body had already been cremated; no need to give any inquiring minds an opportunity to get nasty. He suspected the house must have been under surveillance for years. "Tragically, no. There's an urgent matter I must attend to back home."

The General matched him step by step to the VIP lounge. "That's a shame. Oh, I have to tell you that I was speaking to your ambassador, himself, today. I've brought a few things concerning your extracurricular activities to his attention. He was quite surprised when I told him we have some very interesting surveillance tapes and cell phone intercepts." The General waited for his words to sink in. "Oh, I'm sorry. The look on your face suggests you didn't know. I thought you Americans knew everything. Anyway, I understand he has a surprise for you on your return to the States. Something about the status of your diplomatic immunity." A master of his profession, the General bathed in his victim's anxiety.

The possibility of having his diplomatic immunity revoked racked his body with waves of nausea. He would have to move quickly if there were to be any possibility of success. "I have no idea what you're talking about," he replied, teeth and fists clenched. If the General had some real evidence, he would already be in custody by now. Then again, the General must have known something of his operations; otherwise, they wouldn't have had the balls to insist on an inspection of his luggage.

The General broke out in his tobacco stained trademark smirk. His hunch was right. The man in front of him did have something to hide. Well, there are more then a few ways to skin a cat, he thought, even if the cat had diplomatic immunity. Now was the time to begin a squeeze. "See you soon," the General said, waving goodbye.

The American caught himself grinding his teeth once more. This was definitely not good, he thought. Fixable but not good.

Matanzas Beach, Florida
October 20th

Twenty yards off shore huge gray-brown pelicans swooped low against the water's edge. Derek counted seven of the birds flying wingtip to wingtip in a perfect V formation within inches of the ocean's surface. The glare from the water made him wish he brought sunglasses. He turned his attention to Kelly probing her historical knowledge, enthralled with the way her eyes darted whenever she answered. "So, who was it that got wiped out?" he asked, a mouthful of food garbling his speech. He took another bite of a fried chicken leg and washed it down with a long swallow of an ice cold Dr Pepper; his greasy fingers wet with condensation from the soda bottle,

"I think it was either the British or French," Kelly answered. She leaned back on her arms on the beach blanket at a forty-five degree angle, face turned towards the crystal blue sky soaking in the sun. They were a long way from Massachusetts. "I'm not that great with my history. Someone sent an attack force to capture St. Augustine a few miles north of here. You know, the Spanish founded St. Augustine. In fact, it's one of the oldest continually occupied walled cities in North America. Or, is it Quebec City in Canada? I forget. Anyway, something went wrong with the invasion and the attacking fleet ran aground just about here. The Spanish got wind of it, sent some troops and wiped out the survivors. Thus, the name Matanzas; I think it means massacre in Spanish."

Derek looked down the spectacular coastline in both directions. The beach was empty of the usual wall-to-wall condos synonymous with the Florida oceanfront. It seemed they were the only human beings within light years. "Hard to believe such a beautiful place was the cause of so much bloodshed." He absentmindedly drew another cartoon in the sand with a chicken leg. He hated the violence men perpetrated on each other in the name of national pride, religion, or worse, the egocentricities of politicians. He could almost hear the screams of dying men, musket fire and the clash of steel against steel in the wind that gently rustled the sea oats growing along the dunes. A small lizard poked its head up and down at the edge of their blanket; a tiny red sack alternately inflating and deflating at the base of its throat in territorial display. It scurried back into the dune grass satisfied that the humans were no threat. "How much longer before we hit the Keys?"

Kelly lay backwards on the beach blanket, stretched out, fingers locked behind her head. She unconsciously wiggled her bottom to create a more comfortable depression in the sand. "Depends on which way we go. The density of the local population and concrete begins to pick up a few miles south the closer we get to Daytona. Oh, you can still see the ocean at times; but, you'll have to do it peeking between the high rises. I think we might as well head inland now. We'll cut west a few miles and pick up 95 south. After that it'll be another six hours."

"Six hours! I didn't think it was that far away." Derek took a piece of chicken skin and threw it towards the direction of a hovering seagull. The bird caught the tribute and began to fly away. Suddenly a dozen more white and gray winged birds descended from the sky competing for the feast.

"Jacksonville is almost 400 miles from the Keys and remember, Key West is only 80 miles or so from Cuba. We've got a long way to go." Kelly turned towards Derek. She picked up a handful of sand and let it run through her fingers like an hourglass. "What's our plan of action once we get there?"

"Good old fashion detective work. Door to door kind of stuff, I imagine. I brought along the only photograph we have of Boerner, a blow up of her Florida driver's license. We have credit card receipts from her last month in the Keys. We'll go store to store if we have to and see if anyone can remember anything about her. I want to paste together a collage of her life the past few months before she ended up in Boston. Maybe get a better picture of who she really was and why she ended up dead. Somewhere along the line, she pissed someone off royally."

Kelly took a handful of crackers and threw it to the waiting seagulls. Most of the pieces disappeared before they hit the sand. "Don't forget the shop in Jacksonville. It held an import and export license. The Florida state police listed the store as selling crystals and minerals from Brazil and some knickknacks from overseas. The records from Tallahassee said it was one of two stores licenses by the Pyramid Group. The second store is in Key West. I would be interested in knowing why they closed down the Jacksonville store just because they lost their manager. Doesn't make sense that they'd close down 50% of their business just because they lost one individual;

unless, of course, she was that critical to their operation."

"As good as any place to start," Derek agreed. He watched Kelly stretch out on the blanket again. Tiny grains of sand reflected off her bare thighs just below her pink shorts like sugar on a freshly made donut. The taper of her ankles was perfect. A gentle breeze weaved in and out of her hair in spite of her lavender scarf. She was oblivious to his stare. It was better that way.

Kelly's movements mesmerized Derek as she packed away their picnic lunch. Her hair, her face, the length of her fingers all moved in a magical cadence to the gentle sounds of the ocean waves at her back. He watched the curve of her back, the occasional peek of a belly button and the way her t-shirt stretched across her breast as she turned left and right collecting the last few items off their picnic blanket. Time slowed as primal forces outside his understanding overwhelmed him. He reached over, pulled her surprised face towards his and kissed her softly on the lips. It was the first time he had ever kissed her that way, not as a friend or a sister, but as a *lover*. It was a kiss that curled and danced like a candle flame when passion blew through a window, making the flame flare for just a moment. It arose not from logic or need, but from magic. As their lips touched, the certain knowledge of a conjoined future seeded both of their subconscious. Their faces flushed and their heads pulled back simultaneously, as they shared this mutual surprise.

"Hey, what was that for?" Kelly asked, her lips and cheeks flushed red. She leaned forward, hands clasped around her knees, astonished at this sudden turn of events. A bashful smile caressed her face. She looked into Derek's eyes inquisitively and then, just as suddenly, avoided his direct gaze.

"Just because," Derek said, shyly. He was amazed at his own audacity. "I just wanted to know what you taste like."

"And?"

"Just like chicken," he said, leaning forward to give her another kiss.

Cairo, Egypt
October 21st

The reception desk at the dental office was modern even by western standards. A lone secretary sat behind a Formica counter top dominating the center of the room. Walls decorated with photographs of friends, family and traditional tourist sights surrounded her station. Recessed lights accented tropical plants strategically placed in each corner. The receptionist's eyes were theatrically layered with makeup, something very much against the teachings of the clerics. She barely looked up from her typing when the General and his entourage entered. "I'm sorry sir, but he is with a patient. You can't go in right now," she said, either oblivious or ignorant to the power represented by the military. She drew her long hair away from her face and unconsciously twirled it in a knot.

The General stood in the center of the office basking in the hushed whispers of patients sitting in the waiting area. A moment ago he was soaking up fear like a sponge. Now he was furious. Orders, especially his orders, were never disobeyed. And for a mere woman to ignore him was unthinkable. This was just another example of Western decadence infiltrating the very fabric of Moslem society. He made an almost imperceptible gesture with his head to his lieutenant. Within seconds the dental office was filled with uniformed soldiers, automatic weapons fully displayed.

The waiting room emptied spontaneously. No further demands on his part were necessary. Even the silly little girl who blocked his way disappeared. He crossed the threshold into the examining area and stood in front of the one closed door. This time he motioned with his hand. His lieutenant opened the door with enough force that the top door hinge snapped, the drama of his entrance paralyzing the occupants of the suite. The dentist stood with his hands buried wrist deep in the mouth of a rotund middle-aged man. A beautiful young thing of a dental assistant froze against the far wall, barely breathing.

The General alternated his glare between the captive patient and the dental hygienist until both quickly excused themselves, bolting out of the room. "Dr Sayour, so good of you to spare me a few moments of your time," the General said surveying the office. A rotating dental chair dominated the center. Above, a high intensity light could be manually or automatically directed. "It's Richard, right? Isn't that a Christian name?" the General asked.

Dr Richard Sayour, a balding middle-aged man of average height, powerful build and a thin hooked nose, surveyed the extent of this sudden catastrophe. He shuffled his size 7 EEE feet on the linoleum floor. Professionally, it would take weeks for his practice to recover from this disruption. Sayour knew the man's reputation intimately; there would be no witnesses to whatever the General had in mind. He was at the man's mercy. "Good afternoon, General. What can I do for you?" Sayour said politely, ignoring the religious intimidation. He resigned himself to the man's authority and sat down in his own dental chair. He did not have long to wait.

The General played innocently with the hand-directed ceiling light, finally focusing it at the head of the dentist. Suddenly he brought his face within inches of his victim's. "Your friend is on the move again. I want to know how and when he is going to transport his next package." He pulled back just as suddenly as he had leaned forward. His one hand slowly twirled the dental chair in small circular motions while his other hand fingered the dental tools at the side of the chair.

Sayour kept his breaths shallow. The smell from the General's mouth was horrendous. Hostage, his eyes darted nervously about the room, a small bead of sweat forming on his bare upper lip. The man who blocked him in his own dental chair was twice his size. Even if he could stand up, two other uniformed henchmen stood with their backs to the door. "I have a lot of friends. Which friend are you referring to?" Sayour asked carefully. There was much at stake. It would be prudent to listen and be cautious.

The General looked into the eyes of his captive and saw the truth. That was his talent and the basis of his success all these years. He stepped back away from the chair and strolled between photographs of the man's family adorning the walls. "Beautiful children you have here, Richard," he said, accentuating the non-Egyptian name. "If I remember correctly their names are Bassem, Hani and Reema. Two are at the University, correct?"

Sayour blanched, waves of fear sweeping through his body. Nothing was outside of the reach of the man who stood before him. If he was going to bring the children into this, then all bets were off and the game had no rules.

"Did you know he killed his sister two days ago?" The General studied the impact of his words carefully on his prey. "I will prove it soon. She was the last of the Abdel-Rassouls, the last of the clan who knew more about the resting place of our kings and pharaohs then even the director of our Cairo Museum. He extinguished his own bloodline. Can you imagine? Amazing, isn't it? I thought I was the only one who could do that." He paced the room, hands behind his back. "We've suspected his activities for years. For a while he fooled us with his diplomatic immunity; but, I too, have friends in government agencies of the United States." His heavily accented English spit out the last two words in disgust.

Things had definitely taken a turn for the worse. Sayour didn't doubt the veracity of the man's comments. Still, there were more pressing matters then a few dead Abdel-Rassouls. If his boss wanted to make himself an orphan, that was his business. "Sir, I still don't know what you are talking about," he said slowly. The fingers of his right hand drummed nervously on the armrest of his chair, suffocating under the breath of the human beast before him.

The General looked directly into his captive's eyes and smiled, fingering the dental instruments on the metal tray next to the chair. He always hoped that someone would resist, even in small measure. It always made things that much more interesting. Before his victim had time to react, he swung a dental probe in an arch, impaling the man's left hand into the leather armrest. Sayour's screams were muted by the General's hand covering the smaller man's mouth. The dentist squirmed ineffectively, his right hand fighting and clawing to remove the small piece of stainless steel from his own flesh, his efforts futile against the General's bull strength. The two soldiers who guarded the door gloated in amusement as they watched the drama unfold.

"Tell him I am waiting," the General said, his words coming out slowly, staccato and venomous. "Tell him I have men in every port and in every airfield in the country. There is no road he can pass, no ancient goat trail or slave route that he can leave this country without my men being there. He has something that belongs to my country, to Egypt and we want it back." The General accentuated the significance of each word by twisting the dental probe in the bloodied hand. He was done for the day. He stepped back and composed himself, wiping his victim's blood off his own hand. His voice was now almost kind. "I think you need to take some time out from work. You don't look well." With that, he exited the office, his entourage obediently in tow.

Miami, Florida
October 22nd

By any measure the Blue Flamingo Motor Lodge was unpretentious. On the fringe of the Art Deco quarter and looking across the broad white sands of Miami Beach, thirty-three pastel rooms rose up two stories from street level. A blue neon sign advertised 'best price on the strip' and 'military welcome' to anyone who cared to look between the Howard Johnson's and the Holiday Inn.

The Mitsubishi Eclipse was a fabulous car to drive on the open road with the top down and music blaring. It was, however, unkind to backs on drives of any great distance. The two occupants exited the vehicle stiffly, each stretching in their own way, shaking off the miles with every step forward.

"Now who's this guy, again?" Derek asked looking at the palm trees and hibiscus.

"Zagara. Joe Zagara. "He's the chief cook, maid and bottle washer. A one-man operation. He's my uncle, sort of. This is his place."

"Well, either he is or he isn't. Which is he?" Derek persisted removing his duffel bag and Kelly's suitcase from the car's back seat and trunk.

"Actually, both. Our families lived next to each other outside Philadelphia. He was married to my mom's cousin. After she died and the kids grew up, he moved down here to Miami." Kelly played with her lavender scarf and adjusted her ponytail. A touch of lip-gloss completed her makeover. "I haven't seen him in years."

Derek looked down A1A in both directions. The street was awash in high-rise condominiums. The two-story motel was definitely out of sync with the rest of the neighborhood. "Nice piece of real estate; across from the beach and next to some pretty substantial properties. Is he connected?"

"What do you mean by 'connected?'" she asked defensively.

"Come on. You know, to the mob. All the Philly boys with vowels at the end of their last names are connected," Derek teased.

Kelly pivoted, swinging her head from side to side as if to check for eavesdroppers and whispered, "In fact, he is. Witness protection program, I think. How did you know?"

Derek pulled back, momentarily startled.

"Just teasing." She wished she had a camera just then. "Gotcha!" She watched Derek's shoulders ease back. You could take the boy out of Fall River, but it seems as if you could never take the detective out of the boy. "Actually, he made quite a small fortune selling fruits and vegetables."

Derek looked around. This was not a fruit stand address. "Come on, how much dough can you make selling a head of lettuce in South Philly?" he asked.

"Ah, very good question, grasshopper," Kelly replied in a feigned Chinese accent. "I often asked the same question. Then one day Uncle Joe put things in clear perspective. He reminded me that it wasn't what he sold, but how much it cost him to buy on the wholesale side. If he bought something for a quarter, then he sold it for a buck. Every day he would double or triple his money. Just think of it as compound interest."

"Interesting," Derek nodded opening the office door following Kelly inside. A blast of refrigerated air walloped his lungs. He could almost see his breath with each exhale.

A small counter divided potential customers from the sole occupant sitting underneath a three foot black and white 'no smoking' sign. The man's face was shriveled and tanned to the texture of well-worn leather, his perfectly coiffed gray hair swept back into a small ponytail. A nasal canula sprouted from his nose and dangled to a green Oxygen bottle on the floor. His head bouncing up and down between a small TV on ESPN and a newspaper on his lap opened to the horse racing section. A large clamshell covered three deep in smoldering cigarette butts sat next to a Dunkin Donuts coffee cup. A telephone cradled against his ear, he seemed oblivious to their presence.

Kelly hesitated to interrupt his concentration. "Ahemm..." she cleared her throat.

"Sixty bucks a night, plus tax," he said without raising his head. "I give a ten percent AAA or AARP discount. No smoking, no drugs, no booze. Check out is at noon."

"Unk..."

Zagara looked up, startled. Two gold teeth flashed as he smiled from ear to ear, "Kelly! I can't believe it's my Kelly!" he said almost leaping across the counter to give her a giant bear hug. "Honey, I wasn't expecting you for a few more days," he added apologetically stroking a small earring on his right ear.

Derek was startled by the speed of the man coming towards them dragging the oxygen tank. In their own little universe, Kelly and her uncle exchanged greetings, kisses and family news all in one breath. Genuinely affectionate, a 'dems, deez and doze' kind of guy in speech, the man was giddy with the appearance of his niece. Within minutes he had arranged for a delivery of a massive spread from Moe's Delicatessen.

"This section of town is like a little Israel," he joked. "Might as well take advantage of it." He spread a huge slab of corned beef and hot pastrami on fresh rye bread, sprinkled it with a little mustard and handed it to Derek. The newly lit cigarette in his hand sprinkled the sandwich with a touch of ash.

"I see you like the ponies," Derek said between mouthfuls. The uncle's paper was filled with horse's names that had been circled with cryptic notations on the margins.

"Nah, my luck has been so bad lately I couldn't pick my nose." He handed another more delicately arranged sandwich to his niece and took another long puff on the cigarette. Two hours later they had caught up on years of family news.

Zagara turned to his niece, "Look, Honey, I know it's late and you've had a killer of a ride from Jax. Give me a few minutes and I'll get your rooms ready. Why don't you guys take a walk on the beach? Relax a bit before you turn in. Go enjoy the entertainment from our local population."

"What kind of 'entertainment'?" Derek asked.

"Come on, you know. We got the largest population of queers this side of San Francisco," Zagara noted mater of factly.

"Unk!" Kelly reprimanded.

Zagara snorted as he lit up a cigarette. "Excuse me, I'm sorry. Homosexuals, gays, light in the loafers, whatever the politically correct description you'd care to use." He took a long drag from his cigarette and let out the smoke from his nostrils. "Most are really fine people, but at night, oh my God, are they a sight to see! Now you take them and mix 'em up with the college crowd, the Cubans and the bikers and you couldn't get a better show even if you were at the Moulin Rouge in 'gay Pari'," he said, smiling from ear to ear.

Taking the uncle's suggestion they negotiated a harrowing cross to the beach on A1A, dodging a parade of drunken tourists and senior citizens whose licenses should have been pulled twenty years before. On the ocean side lovers of every sexual persuasion leaned against palm trees, roller bladed, scootered and even jogged together. Many were dressed in exotic costumes that rivaled Mardi Gras time in New Orleans. Others were simple tourists like themselves who were captivated by the alluring rhythms of the ocean and the sight and sounds of nightclubs that dotted the street.

Derek picked up a large piece of abraded coral and threw it into the waves. Cargo vessels lined up along the horizon preparing to enter the port of Miami or Ft Lauderdale. He took Kelly's hand and headed towards the water's edge carrying their shoes as they walked barefoot into the surf. The water was amazingly warm. Every few steps he playfully kicked up a spray of water that caught Kelly's skirt or blouse. Her annoyance grew until she reciprocated, pushing him unexpectedly into the water, soaking his clothes. His instinct was to pull her in, too; but one look at her face and he knew better. He was about ready to go for a nocturnal swim when Kelly intervened.

"Remember, sharks come out to play at night. This is their prime feeding time."

"You're kidding, right?" Derek said, standing bolt upright out of the water.

"This face does not kid," Kelly laughed. "Look around you. See anyone else in the water?"

The contrast to New England's bone chilling water temperature was amazing. What a waste, thought Derek. Soon they were lucky enough to witness an ocean moonrise. Moonlight shimmered from the horizon into forever. He felt her fingers lock tightly onto his. He looked into her expectant face and time just stopped. Shadows from the sky, or was it from wind-stirred palm fronds, danced across her cheeks, her lips and her hair as the gentle tropical breeze pushed their bodies together. She, too, felt the moment, turning her face into his. They kissed once, briefly, but deeply.

Derek pulled his face away from hers, feeling a sudden wave of confusion. Kelly's face looked so much like Rose. No, they looked nothing alike. What was he thinking? It was impossible. He tried to recapture the moment. The more he strived, the more unnatural the whole scenario became.

Kelly pivoted in tandem with him as he turned away. "Derek. Are you OK?" she asked, sensing a sudden abandonment.

He stood silent, looking past her into the moonlit horizon. "Yeah, sure, it's nothing. Too much pastrami, probably. I'm sorry. Where were we?" he asked, putting his index finger on her chin, projecting a smile that was 99% natural.

She looked into his eyes and knew. Kelly leaned her head against his shoulder. "Come on, it's late. We'd better be getting back before my uncle sends out a search party. We have a long day tomorrow."

Derek feigned a weak protest as they returned to the Blue Flamingo in silence, still holding Kelly's hand somewhere between never-letting-go and tender. They stumbled up the sand dune embankment to the reality of A1A and the Blue Flamingo. It was Derek's turn to take Cricket for her evening's constitutional. When he returned Kelly was fast asleep. Or so he thought.

Key West, Florida
October 22nd

The Keys formed a chain of islands jutting out 130 miles from the mainland, porous to every kind of contraband imaginable. Seven Mile Bridge was really seven miles long. You could hear Jimmy Buffett sing in Margaritaville while getting drunk in Hogs Breath Saloon. Tarpons were huge 300-pound fish that broke the water's surface like dolphins but, unfortunately, tasted like sardines. Speaking of dolphins, the kind at Sea World were mammals, like a whale. Mahi-mahi served up in restaurants was a dolphin fish and unrelated. Conch, was pronounced 'conk', and, for a few buck, you could get a fantasy passport stamped with that logo. All the coral for sale in local shops came from the Philippines. Yes, there was a disproportionate number of gays in the Keys; but, hey, no different then Provincetown, Massachusetts. And would you like some grouper or yellowtail with your fries? Derek got the lowdown on it all.

The convertible was bred for this adventure. Basting in UV-forty sunscreen, they cheerfully roasted in the sun, blowing past slower vehicles on the single lane highway. Nothing mattered other then the feel of the wind in their face. If Florida was all about sun, then the Keys were all about water. Only God could have created this pallet of blue and green. Every turn on A1A revealed a new vista and a beach begging to be swam in.

He arched back his head into the car's headrest. Kelly's running commentary blurred into scattered fragments the more he thought about her uncle, Zagara. Uncle Joe had hugged them near to death as they prepared to leave that morning. The man's parting words were thought provoking, observing that everyone tended to live as if they had two lives: one for practice and one for real. The secret to life was knowing the number was one. The old guy with the ponytail certainly knew more about life then just how to sell a twenty-five cents head of lettuce.

Three hours after they had begun their journey, Derek sat in the Conch train's metal bench, soaking up the local sights and sounds, reflecting on this eternal truth. His back needed a break. He stretched his legs on this uniquely Key West tourist attraction; but, his focus was on his travel companion sitting next to him, not on the palm trees or the ubiquitous halter-topped coeds who littered the city's streets.

He was drawn to Kelly for reasons that went beyond the obvious, studying her carefully while she was distracted with the tour. She was unpretentious in makeup and dress, a lavender scarf her only fashion accessory, Alliage perfume her signature fragrance. There was certain intensity with her speech that dissolved into a smile whenever she made her point. She had a certain way of tilting her head when she listened and another way when she was just pretending. He was conscious of her presence without looking at her often finding her hand while walking even before it was offered. He slid closer to her on the metal seat, stretching his arm behind her shoulder.

Kelly was busy adding vignettes of her own experiences to those of the tour guide as favorite spots came to view. This beach was where she woke up to the morning sunrise after a weekend of partying. This was where she bought the carved candle that still sits on her piano to this day.

A portly Cajun tour guide chuckled at his own sexual innuendoes as if hearing them for the first time while he recounted tales of rumrunners and conch-heads, Naval barracks, artist cemeteries and cigar factories. Conch Train company photographers grabbed quick shots along the way to post at the end of the ride to sell at exorbitant prices. Hawkers passed out discount tickets for restaurants and snorkel trips along the way. Derek loved every minute of it. His hand was now unconsciously stroking Kelly's hair. She leaned back into the caress.

All too soon the ride was over. Lunch had to wait until the dog was given its afternoon constitutional. They were both nervous dog sitters, its bladder tested by them only to the three-hour limit. So far, Cricket had a bladder of steel. Even Derek felt jealous. "Probably a bad prostate", he guessed out loud.

"Cricket's a girl," Kelly said, shaking her head. "Some detective you are."

The only Cuban restaurant on Mallory's wharf served them up black beans and rice, shrimp and beer. Bagpipers and jugglers entertained the moving crowds that ebbed and flowed like the tide. Henna tattoo artists offered their talents at a dollar a letter. Derek felt light-headed in the tropical heat. Was it the beer and sun, or was it the company, he wondered. He preferred rice pilaf Armenian style the way his grandmother used to make it; but Kelly was infinitely better company then his grandmother any day.

Florida was certainly something he could get use to. Maybe he had spent too many years in the cold of Massachusetts. His eyes refused to open as he turned his face towards the sun. The sun and beer, the beer and sun; was it the wind touching his face or was it Kelly's breath? He felt himself being shaken awake.

"Come on, Detective, it's time we get back to work."

He opened his eyes and saw the determination on her face. "Yes ma'am." It wasn't quite what he had in mind.

Key West, Florida
October 22nd

The marquee read *Abdul's Nick Knacks and Antiques.* "Here it is." Kelly stopped in front of the store, replacing her palm pilot in her purse. "According to Tallahassee, Pyramid Enterprise shares the same tax ID number for this store as the one Boerner worked for in Jacksonville."

The beer was wearing off. Derek's mind focused on the investigation. The smell of sandalwood incense and the haunting sounds of Middle Eastern music greeted them as they crossed the threshold, dividing Florida from Baghdad. "Ever been here before?" Derek asked. An *oud* and *dombeg* played a haunting melody in the background.

"Nope," Kelly said entering the shop. "Remember, it's been a few years since I've been down in this neck of the woods. Stores come and go a dime a dozen."

Derek introduced himself to the girl behind the counter and showed her his police credentials. Her face registered no surprise. He left his official card next to the register. Spindly with purple and green hair and a mouthful of gum in perpetual motion, the girl's multiple tattoos and nose rings reinforced the regional differences in merchandising between New England and Florida. She was totally indifferent to his presence.

"I barely knew the girl," she said ringing up another purchase. "Come again, folks." She waved good-bye to the new owner of an 'authentic' antique genie lamp. "I use to work here part time. Now I'm a manager – least ways until I fuck up. Besides, I've already told everything to the other cops. You know, the ones with real jurisdiction," she said accentuating the last two words.

"Did Carol Boerner ever work here?" Derek asked ignoring the insult.

"How do I know? I'm busy. If you wanna talk to me, go see my lawyer."

Derek was surprised at her belligerence. It was certainly out of character for all the conch heads he met on this trip so far. I know nothing I see nothing, thought Derek. "Seems like it shouldn't be too hard finding someone to help out here," he commented. "Must be a lot of kids looking for work these days."

The clerk relaxed her defensive posture. "Most are pot heads. Wouldn't trust them further then I could spit," she replied playing with her nose ring.

"Neat stuff," Kelly said examining a large quartz cluster in the window display. "What kind of shop is this, exactly?"

"New wave. You know; crystals, meditation, fortune telling, alien secrets of the pyramids. A lot of reproductions but some real things he keeps in the back." The clerk became distracted by the sound of someone moving in the curtain drawn room behind her. "Look, if you're not gonna buy something, I'm gonna have to ask you to leave," she said slowly backing away to the opposite end of the shop.

"This is wonderful," Kelly said, ignoring the girl's threat. She picked up a model of an Egyptian falcon, rich in patina. "How can you tell the difference between real and fake?"

"It's like buying a yacht," a deep male voice said from behind the curtain. "If you got to ask, then you shouldn't be looking."

Kelly's eyes lit up. "Lance?" She strained to see the origins of the voice.

"Who's Lance?" Derek asked turning his head between Kelly and the curtain.

A tall man of about forty emerged from the shadows. "Lansky, Jerry Lansky," he said introducing himself. Thin as a railing and with receding blond hair, he enveloped Kelly in his spider arms.

Kelly reciprocated the greeting, then pushed Lansky away holding both his hands in her own. "Look at you! You haven't changed a bit!" she exclaimed, stepping back and surveying Lansky from head to toe.

"Madam is too kind," Lansky replied in a fake French accent.

"Well, maybe a little less hair," Kelly teased. She noticed Derek standing next to the counter, both arms crossed. "I'm sorry. Derek, this is Jerry Lansky. Jerry, this is my good friend, Derek Ekizian." Both men shook hands. "What are you doing here?" Kelly asked incredulously. He was the last person in the world she expected to see.

"I'm kind of stuck here," Lansky said. "This is, in fact, my store. Why else would I be spending time behind curtain number three?" he asked, pointing to the back room.

"Get out!" Kelly's mouth almost dropped to the floor in surprise.

Derek took advantage of the pause. "How do you guys know each other?"

Kelly sensed her lapse in social graces. "Derek, I'm sorry. Jerry did his residency with me in Jacksonville," she said still smiling at her old friend. "I haven't seen him in, I don't know, at least five years. Isn't that about right?" she asked smiling fondly at Lansky.

"Five years," Lansky concurred mentally counting backwards.

Derek looked around the shop. "You sell these things while practicing medicine on the side or visa versa?" he asked giving his mustache an unconscious twirl.

Lansky sat down on a high barstool next to the cash register. "Actually, gave up medicine years ago. Retired from the Air Force. Medicine and I just didn't get along. In fact, the military and I didn't get along either. I found I had more of a knack for business instead. By the way, do you like that statue?"

"It's lovely, Jerry. Is it real?" Kelly asked holding it up to the light.

"Egyptian. Middle kingdom. About four thousand years old," Lansky replied.

"How much?" Derek asked, trying to establish some kind of presence.

"I'm afraid it's more then you can afford on a policeman's salary," Lansky quipped. "But considering this is Kelly, here, I want you to have this as a gift. Think of it as something for old times sake."

"I couldn't possibly..."

"Hey, it's only half my money," Lansky said. He took the statue from Kelly's hand and began to wrap it in bubble wrap and Styrofoam chips. "The other half belongs to Bags. I'm sure if he knew you were in town he'd insist as well."

Kelly's eyes glazed over as an awkward smile touched her face. She reached out and put her hand on the box that Lansky was preparing. "Thanks, but no thanks."

Lansky looked amazed that his generosity might be refused. "Really, Kelly, it's something I'd like you to have."

Kelly ignored his offer. "Sounds like you overheard us talking to your employee. We're down in the Keys working an angle on a murder back home. The victim's name was Carol Boerner. Apparently, she worked for a shop in Jacksonville that shares the same sales tax license as yours here in the Keys. I take it you own both places."

Derek snorted softly in amazement. When the girl meant business, the girl meant business. He leaned against the wall and watched her go to work.

"Pyramid. Yep. That's ours," Lansky nodded matter of factly. "Barely knew the woman. Terrible the way she died. Just signed her payroll checks, though. Don't like mixing with the help much."

"Anything you can tell me about her that might shed some light on our investigation?" Kelly asked intently.

"Anything I could think of I already told our own state police down here. I'm sure it's all in the report they shared with your friend here. Besides, I understood that the investigation was closed," Lansky answered. He finished wrapping the box and then placed a lavender ribbon on top. "See Kelly, I remembered it was your favorite color."

Derek intervened, "We have access to some records that showed she spent most of the last month of her life down here in Key West. Did she cover this store for you as well?"

Lansky pondered for a moment in thought. "Don't rightly know for sure. Like I said, I write the checks, I don't usually spend much time here. It's just a fluke you found me today." Lansky removed a schedule log from beneath the desk. "Our employees are flexible. I would imagine there might be an occasion for that poor woman to have to cover this shop here as well." He flipped through a few pages. "Can't help you today. This log begins in October. Maybe our accountant has the original volume that goes back to the beginning of the year. Or maybe the State police have it, I don't really know."

An elderly couple came into the shop walking a small poodle.

"I'm sorry folks, no dogs allowed," Lansky said. As soon as the couple left he muttered "SFD."

"What's SFD?" Kelly asked.

"Stupid Fuckin' Dog. Can't stand dogs."

"By the way, who's Bags?" Derek asked. "You mentioned earlier that the two of you own this place."

"Oh, just another one of the guys from our residency in Jacksonville," Kelly said.

"Just another one of the guys, heh?" Lansky said sarcastically. "Kelly's only telling you half the story, Eric. They practically lived together during the good old days."

"It's Derek, not Eric."

"You are such an asshole," Kelly interjected, staring down her old residency classmate. She pushed the package back into Lansky's hand. "Besides, I never lived with him. We just dated for awhile, that's all."

Lansky was obviously enjoying Kelly's discomfort. He looked back and forth between Kelly and the detective. "Could have fooled me." The conversation was hitting a shoal. "Well, neither here nor there. That was all in the long forgotten past, isn't it? Why don't you folks have dinner with us tonight? That is, unless you have other plans, of course."

"Hey, I didn't even know you were married!" Kelly said wide-eyed.

"Me? Hell no! Not for years. I was referring to me and Bags."

Derek jumped at the opportunity. "Nothing wrong with being gay. Some of my best friends are gay."

Lansky scowled. "Very funny. Maybe you should come alone and leave Eric behind."

"Derek. With a D," Derek responded, fighting to keep his smile. This guy was a real ball buster. "Come on, Jerry, I was just kidding. We'd love to come, right Kelly?"

"Boys!"

Lansky looked at Kelly and eased back the throttle. "Well, if you insist. O.K. Kelly, bring your shadow. I'll pick you folks up at six and give you the grand tour. We'll go to my place first for a couple of drinks and then head over to Bags' house at seven-ish."

"Great, I'd like that," Kelly said. She took Derek's arm and waved good-bye as they turned and left the store. She scribbled their hotel on a scrap of paper and placed it back on the counter. "Come on Derek, let's go for a swim."

They left the shop, walking hand in hand back to their hotel along the cobbled streets of old town Key West. Derek thought Kelly was happily reminiscing about the good old days but he was wrong. Her thoughts were uncomfortable and centered around one man from her past. Crowds began to pick up as tourist and natives awoke from their afternoon siestas. "I'd kind of like that," Derek said parroting Kelly, hoping a tease would return her back to reality.

Kelly turned laughing off his jealousy. "Oh, get over it! That was another lifetime. Besides, since when did you start getting jealous?"

"Me! Jealous? I don't think so." Derek unconsciously ground his teeth. "Just remember why we're here in the first place." He ran to keep up with her as she entered a sunglass booth.

"Sorry, Sergeant, I thought we were here to explore more than just a crime," Kelly replied. She took his arm. "Don't be afraid of what you might find."

Key West
October 22nd

"We should have brought the dog," Derek said. Both hands buried in his pants pockets, he aimlessly jingled keys and loose change. They stood outside the hotel waiting for their pick up. Sounds of southern rock and strolling jazz troubadours gently wafted over the palms and bougainvilleas from all directions. The non-stop party for which Key West was famous, was in full gear.

Kelly glared "You heard him back in the shop; SFD: stupid friggin' dog. That's how he thinks. We're going to be his guests. We should respect his feeling even if we disagree," Kelly said. She played with her lavender scarf and ponytail, nervously readjusting the loop.

Derek snorted. "All the same, we should have brought the dog. I would have loved to see the look on his face when the little mutt pissed on his floor."

"You're such a jerk!" Kelly said, enjoying the persistent undercurrent of jealousy. She leaned over and kissed him gently on the cheek. "Besides, it's not a mutt. It's a Yorkshire terrier, a Yorkie. And it hasn't had an accident, yet. We're up to five hours."

"Jerk? Is that what I am now! You sound like Nunez. That's something he would say. If you think I'm a jerk now, wait until...."

Kelly interrupted him with a firmly planted kiss. "Isn't Key West wonderful?" she said. Inhaling deeply, she smelled the ocean, nowhere in sight but permeating every fabric of the island. Orion, at full apogee, dominated the night sky. Betelgeuse shone in vivid red glory. "I wonder what the peasants are doing tonight?"

A metallic green Porsche 911 convertible pulled to the curb. Lansky leaned his head out the window. "You folks know the way to Boston?"

"It's that away," Kelly said pointing to the sky. "About three IRS audits and two ulcers away from anyplace in the Keys."

"No matter. Why don't you hop in and join me you sexy thing."

Opening the door Derek eyed the tiny cockpit of the sports car. There was barely enough room for one adult, never mind both of them. "Why, thank you very much. I'd love to," he said, mimicking Norm's lisp on a bad day.

"You again!" Lansky grimaced. "I'll tell you what, I'll take

Kelly now and come back for you later. I don't want your underlying sexual insecurities to disturb my driving."

"I'll keep my lust for you under control," Derek said, plopping into the passenger seat. Leering at Kelly, he patted his thigh. "Come to Pappa, baby. Plenty of room for us both."

Without hesitation, Kelly followed Derek into the Porsche. Laughing, she perched on Derek's lap, giving him a poke in the ribs with her elbow. "Keep your hands where I can see them at all times," she ordered her human seatbelt.

The brief ride to Lansky's home was sprinkled with references of mutual friends and patients who haunted their memories. Derek had trouble concentrating on anything other then Kelly's body as she shifted her weight on his lap. He pushed away a strand of Kelly's hair from his face when she leaned into him. Please accelerate, he silently ordered Lansky. Too bad Key West was such a small island.

Shortly, they arrived at Lansky's beautiful but modest home. It was vintage Keys, across from the ocean, layered in Mahogany and Teak even down to the toilet seat. The white exterior was almost completely overwhelmed by the green of natural plants and vegetation, leaving only the front door visible. White hurricane shutters flanked narrow 19th century windows. A porch with three white rocking chairs completed the picturesque setting.

They followed their host inside the parlor, taking seats in oversized rattan furniture. Lansky was cryptic about the details of his life, slowly opening to Kelly's probing. Teasing them with innuendo, he admitted the nightlife in the Keys was more to his liking then anywhere else in his travels.

A petite and striking Japanese girl in full kimono entered the room and joined them, kneeling at Lansky's feet. "She speaks no English, but seems to understand everything." Her expression did not change when Lansky gave her a playful pat on the rear end. "Best of all, she'll do whatever. Obedient and silent. That's the way I like them. Can't find that combination in a wife."

Derek smiled imperceptibly watching Kelly wince at the chauvinistic comment. He found victory in silence. Even the 'seven dwarfs' had their warts, thought Derek. The two classmates melded in the past, leaving him in limbo at Kelly's side. Bored, his eyes wandered the room. World War II memorabilia covered the walls of Lansky's study. Most carried the insignias and service medals of the US Army Air Corp, precursor to the US Air Force. Photographs, drawings, and models of vintage fighter and bomber aircraft hung from the ceiling, reminding Derek of a teenager's bedroom. Derek stood to examine a framed piece of silk, a pilot's map of a Japanese island.

"You like that?" Lansky asked, interrupting Kelly.

"Love maps," Derek replied. "Haven't seen anything like this, though."

"Belonged to my father. He flew bombers in the Pacific theater during WWII, the 'big war' he used to call it." Lansky paused, reflecting. His eyes darted to a model B-29 hanging from the ceiling. "I'm a military brat, you know. I grew up with this stuff. The old man never made the fast track for promotions. He left the service as a major." Lansky smirked, staring into the distance. "I got out as a Colonel." He pulled out a model airplane from the shelf and blew a dust ball off the wings. "Actually, a lieutenant colonel," he corrected himself. "The review board didn't think I was worthy of eagles. Hey, but what the fuck do they know, huh?"

Lansky's maid brought in a round of beverages: beer for the men and a cosmopolitan for Kelly. The Asian beauty took a place at Lansky's feet, held there as if by magnetism. Derek found the relationship between servant and master enigmatic and compelling. Distant sounds of tourist trams and an occasional car interrupted the cadence of guitar music from the next-door neighbor's home. The ocean filled the view across the street.

"Do you remember that crazy old drunk who kept calling out 'Jesus is comin' to get me'?" Lansky asked, changing the subject.

Kelly broke into hysterical laughter, almost snorting into her empty drink. "And how you stuck your head through the drapes and said 'I'm here, my son. I'm coming to take you now.'"

"What's so funny?" Derek asked, alternating his gaze between the two.

"I'm sorry, Honey," Kelly said, putting her hand on Derek's arm. "Back then, Jerry had a full head of hair and a beard. He looked just like the Jesus Christ you see plastered on billboards and advertisements for revival meetings all over the south. He nearly scared the poor guy to death."

"Shit in his pants, if I remember correctly."

Derek chuckled politely. He expected a long night if the two continued to reminisce. Every few minutes he attempted to broach the subject of Carol Boerner and the murder investigation. Lansky deflected the inquiry with a curt but polite series of 'I don't knows', focusing instead on Kelly. The only hint of interest he could draw from the man came when he mentioned their visit to Boerner's condo.

"Find anything interesting?" Lansky asked, downing the last of his beer. The girl at his feet began to rise from her canine position, probably to get her master another beverage. He pushed her back to the pillow cushion on the floor, hands stroking the woman's hair while he focused on his guests.

"Not really," Kelly replied, finishing her drink. "We did come away with the cutest little dog. The dead woman's neighbor was dog sitting for over a month. Had no interest in the job at all." She placed her empty glass on the driftwood coffee table. "Poor thing was just dying for affection."

"Who, the neighbor or the dog?" Lansky joked.

"Probably both," Kelly answered.

"Aren't we all?" Derek muttered. He doubted anyone was paying attention.

"Who's got the dog now?" Lansky quizzed Kelly, ignoring Derek.

"She's guarding the motel room," Kelly laughed at the thought of a three pound guard dog.

Lansky grimaced. "Good. Just keep it away from me. I hate the little fuckers." He rose from his seat. "For your sake, I hope it doesn't piss on the floor. Hotel managers dislike dogs with weak bladders and guests who sneak them in."

"You a dog lover?" Derek asked.

Lansky headed down the wooden porch steps. "Yeah, right," he mumbled. He beeped off the electronic kill switch on his Porsche. The threesome squeezed into the sports car one more time.

"Where to now?" Kelly asked. She held onto Derek's arms, comfortably wrapped around her waist, his lap and hands a human seatbelt.

"Bags is back in town." Lansky paused for affect. "Returned this evening from a mission in the Middle East. When I told him you were in Key West, he about jumped out of his skin. We're going over to his place for dinner."

"Fantastic, Jerry. About time I meet this mystery man," Derek said.

Kelly looked at the visor mirror and studied her reflection. It was blanched. She turned her head towards the open window begging the night air to restore her color before either man noticed.

Gaza, Palestinian Territory
October 23rd

His left hand ached like a bastard, the pain relentless and throbbing. His hands were everything to him. Now this. The Dentist stuffed his bloodied bandages in his sweatshirt pocket hiding them from view of those in the bar around him. Still, red seeped out from the dressings, staining his clothes. Percocets and apricot brandy did nothing for this kind of pain. Hopefully Keflex would halt or even slow down the infection. Time was of the essence. There was a job to do. He would not fail the Colonel.

Arab workers came in from the end of their shifts and the bar grew noisier. Tobacco smoke, alcohol and laughter mixed to form the universal ambience. Now it was time for friendship and maybe even sex. These men worked the Israeli territories sending desperately needed money home. Their families were on the wrong side of the West Bank, so their loneliness grew. So did homosexual activity in this quarter of town.

A young man approached his table. Dressed in old jeans and a tattered Nike tee shirt, the youth was barely old enough to have hair on his face. "Are you looking for some company?" he asked in Arabic. His eyes were wide in anticipation of an evening's meal. Everyone had to live and for him sex was a means of survival.

"Sorry," Sayour frowned. "I'm waiting for someone," he said firmly. Disappointed the youth moved on to another prospective table. Sayour downed his beer and chased it with an apricot brandy again. The alcohol helped to ease the throbbing.

The bar grew more crowded. Sayour watched beverages consumed and conquests made. Small tables would fill and empty in the time it took to down a glass of beer or drink the thick native coffee. Finally, Malouf, joined him at his table. He had met the man several times from prior operations. Malouf was only about half his age. Tall and muscular with a fashionably shaved head, his eyes were hazel blue, his nose African wide. Neither man extended their hands. Sayour kept his good right hand in his pocket, his fingers playing with the handle of a stiletto knife, his weapon of choice.

"Almost got lucky, heh? I was watching you from the corner for the last half hour," Malouf said in near perfect English. He ordered a demitasse of coffee with a single hand motion to the circling waiter.

"Very funny. Do you have the package?" Sayour whispered impatiently.

Coffee appeared and Malouf took a sip of the steaming brew. It had the consistency of mud. "There has been a change in plans," he said cautiously leaning forward. It was clear from Sayour's demeanor he had not yet been informed. All communications had been disrupted since Monday's incident at the airport, so it was not unexpected. "Relax. It's sitting in the Israeli embassy in Cairo as we speak. The Colonel had it delivered this morning by special courier." He took another sip of coffee and placed the delicate demitasse on the table. "That Egyptian bastard is watching him like a hawk. By the way, how's your hand? I heard you had a little problem of your own with that piece of shit."

Sayour felt waves of nausea just thinking about the General's visit to his office. Or maybe it was just the massive dose of antibiotics he had taken. "Just fine. Thanks for asking." He pushed his recently impaled left hand deeper into his jacket pocket as if that action could push the pain out of his consciousness.

"There is just no way he's going to get access to it on this side of the Atlantic. The Colonel always accompanies his pieces personally; but, I guess there is a first time for everything. They put a new plan together and you, my lucky friend, have the honor." He shifted his chair speaking so closely in the other man's ear that their heads almost touched. "Seems that the Americans are threatening to withdraw the Colonel's diplomatic status if he is caught with any more antiquities. Whatever it is he's got this time, it's got to be pretty important. In any case he is on his way back to the States even as we speak carrying an empty diplomatic pouch just to throw off the bloodhounds."

"Why the Jews? " Sayour asked with complete distain. He hated anything Jewish, and was hard pressed to acknowledge their usefulness in matters such as this. He had been in the service of the Colonel for years; but this was the first time the Israeli's were brought into play. There was no way he could reach the Colonel now for any clarification.

"The Jews work closely with our Turkish brothers. You know how it goes – the enemy of your enemy." Malouf almost spit out the words. As an Arab he hated the Turks almost as much as the Armenians and Greeks, grimacing at the memory of a hundred years of abuse at the hands of the Turkish Empire. "They will pass the package along to the Turks who will return it to the embassy in Jerusalem. Here are your new passports and documents," he said, surreptitiously placing an envelope on Sayour's lap. "You are to pick up the Colonel's package there and take a freighter from Haifa."

"What flag are we sailing under?" Sayour inquired taking another shot of brandy.

"Israeli, of course," Malouf said. "The ship is perfect for your needs. The Egyptians and Syrians can't check the freighter because it sails under an Israeli flag. The Americans won't check because it sails under an Israeli flag. The Jews don't care what we do as long as there is hard currency involved. The freighter is loaded with cargo containers and is registered to take ten passengers. If anyone does bother to check your manifest you have nothing to worry about. The entire ship can be checked from bow to stern. Everything, and I mean everything, is legitimate."

"Are all ten the Colonel's men?"

"Of course, the captain, too. All their papers are in perfect order as well. The crew is main land Chinese. They won't bother with anyone." Malouf replied with confidence.

"Fully armed?"

"Of course, the usual complement of weapons. And everything will be disposed of before we hit Halifax, as usual."

"As usual," Sayour replied closing his eyes. He rubbed his forehead to ease the pounding. If he didn't know better he would have gnawed off his own hand by now. The pain was incredible. Some day he was going to kill that son of a bitch sadist who masqueraded as a general. "Good, let's go. I need to get going as soon as possible and cross the border."

"Take your time with the instructions in the envelope. You'll be making a different kind of delivery this time."

"I can't go back when this is done, you know." Sayour cringed at the thought of returning to his former life. "I'm going to need some help to get my family out and get started somewhere else."

Malouf grinned. "Don't worry. I'm going to take care of everything. You will be able to make holes in people's teeth again, soon. I promise."

For the first time in days Sayour smiled.

Key West, Florida
October 23rd

Gated estates hiding behind Spanish moss and carefully coifed Bougainvillea blurred in their drive along Ocean Avenue. Derek hoped they could see a sunset. The need to see a flaming ball of red splash into Caribbean blue-green was overwhelming. Not too many places back in New England that faced west over the water.

"These homes are gorgeous," Kelly said craning her neck to get a better angle.

"Just another day at the beach," Lansky replied. He pulled the Porsche up to the entrance of an oceanfront mansion and accessed the gate's keypad. Security cameras conspicuously monitored their every move.

Derek gave his mustache a frustrated twirl. This much wealth made him insecure. "How long have you guys been living down here?" he asked politely.

"Almost since the end of our residency days," Lansky answered. He drove up to the front door and parked. "Everyone out, ladies and gentlemen." He threw Derek the keys. "Have this washed and waxed, boy. We'll be out in a couple of hours."

Derek opened the driver's door. "Oh, wow, mister. I've never driven a stick before. Let's see, I think it's a big 'H', isn't it? First gear is here and second gear is here."

Lansky grabbed the keys. "On second thought, you might as well come in."

Derek's head maintained a perpetually upward forty-five degree angle as he inspected his surroundings. The house was palatial. Two stories of marble and glass faced oceanfront, due west. Multiple fountains and rustling palm fronds surrounded his ears as they crossed an open courtyard. A tall but unpretentious man with receding red hair and a large droopy mustache intercepted them from a side vestibule. Derek immediately picked up on his Armani shoes and Piaget watch.

"*Parev,* welcome!" the man said in traditional Armenian.

Armenian this far south? Derek stood wide-eyed watching Kelly disappear into the man's arms under an avalanche of kisses.

Face flushed, she pulled away, composing herself. "Derek, this is Jack Bagdasarian. Jack, this is my dear friend Derek Ekizian," she said standing between the two men.

"A fellow Armenian – down here n the Keys. I love it! My friends call me Bags," he said with a trace of an accent shaking Derek's hand as if he were priming an outdoor water pump. "All my friends do. And I hope you will consider me a friend."

"Pleased to meet you," Derek said. It never crossed his mind Kelly's old boyfriend was Armenian. He noticed his host's eyes were blue. Red hair and blue eyes on an Armenian! That was a first for him.

They were ushered into a massive central foyer surrounded floor to ceiling in glass and cut crystal chandeliers. In the corner, ghostlike and attentive to Bagdasarian's hand signals was an olive skinned servant woman who moved silently among the guests, anticipating everyone's needs. Her face was plain and ageless with silver and black hair tied back in a tight bun.

The mansion's insides were cavernous, rivaling those in Newport, Rhode Island he loved to tour at Christmas time. Antique oriental rugs hung from every wall. Shelves and isolated pedestal stands were strategically placed to display museum quality artwork. Recessed lights accented oil paintings he suspected were originals. Bagdasarian's study impressed him the most. It's walls were lined with the man in photographs accompanied by faces Derek recognized from years of Time magazine's Who's Who in the Middle East. He talked freely of his years in the service of the US military - Air Force intelligence to be specific. Although an American citizen, he was ethnically Armenian, born in Cairo, Egypt. Both sides relied on him through thirty years of Arab-Israeli negotiations. Bagdasarian explained what everyone saw on television was just for show. The same players would get drunk and eat at the same table or, at least, close by, in spite of their public persona and display of mutual hatred. It's just a game, he repeated over and over. It's just a game.

The hour was late. "*Hrametsek*, please join me at the table," Bagdasarian requested in Armenian," ushering them into the dining room..

The table was massive Brazilian teak with spectacular rosewood inlays. It was covered in piles of shish kebob, rice pilaf, stuffed meatball kufta's, eggplant and tomato baba ganoush, cracked wheat tabouleh salad, stuffed grape leaves sarma and dolma. There was nothing else left in the Armenian dietary lexicon, thought Derek.

Only Lansky abstained from the feast, taking a few bites of

bread and butter. "I'm just a plain meat and potatoes kind of guy," he claimed. "Don't go for this foreign stuff, much," he grumbled. He sat with arms crossed impatiently until a hamburger wrapped in Burger King Styrofoam magically appeared on his plate.

Dessert came in waves: multi layered phyllo-dough baklava, shredded wheat khadaief, cheese filled borags and candied lookum rotated from plate to plate as everyone, except Lansky, sampled the avalanche of sweets. Derek was won over by his host's gracious hospitality. He had not seen a spread like this since his grandparent's days. Raki was brought as an after dinner drink and toasts were made all around. Derek turned to his host and took another sip from the aperitif. "You know, Jack, the reason we came to the Keys in the first place was to investigate a murder case we've been working on in Fall River. Seems there was a connection between one of the victims and your business here in Florida."

There was a noticeable pause in conversation. Kelly voiced a weak protest on this mixing of business and pleasure. She was silenced by a wave of Bagdasarian's hand. "Bags. Please call me Bags." The servant woman brought over a humidor, undoubtedly of Cuban origin. Only Bagdasarian took a cigar, the rest of his guests politely declining. "Mind if I smoke?" he asked staring only at Derek. He cut the tip off the cigar and puffed on the flame in his servant's right hand. "Tragic about the girl. If you're asking whether there was a connection because one of my holding companies and the check we gave her twice a month, then, yes, there is a connection. But I have no knowledge of the personal or private affairs of any of my employees and this young lady in particular. Besides, I was led to believe by my sources that the case was officially closed," Bagdasarian said focusing his attention on Kelly.

If Derek heard the phrase 'case was closed' one more time, he was going to puke.

Kelly was giddy with Raki. She became uncharacteristically open with the details of their investigations, babbling like a teenage girl at a prom dance while going through a point-by-point outline of the autopsy. She proudly revealed the key discrepancy of the two different maggot species. Both Lansky and Bagdasarian became newly attentive with this revelation.

"You know, fly speciation is difficult even under the best of circumstances," Bagdasarian said calmly. "Could be a million and one explanations why the maggots came from different kinds of flies. The little bastards could have been blown by storms, hitchhiking on cargo transports, escaped from someone else's laboratory – I could think of a lot more if given half a chance."

Kelly continued with the politics of opening a closed investigation and their search for the truth in Florida.

The mention of a fourth victim, the fetus in utero, tweaked Lansky's interest. "About how far along in the pregnancy was she?" he asked intently.

"Somewhere between ten and twelve weeks as best as I could tell," Kelly answered. She began to discuss their adventures in Jacksonville.

Derek attempted to restrain her monologue. "No need to bore your friends with details," interrupted Derek firmly.

"Ah, but if the investigation is closed, what harm could it do to talk about it?" Bagdasarian said, reading the eye communication between his guests.

"That's just the point," Derek answered politely. "We're trying to find something tangible to reopen the case. I'm sure you understand how delicate this is."

Bagdasarian leaned back in his chair exhaling an 'O' ring of smoke. "I thought the Massachusetts state police had final jurisdiction. I didn't know you had the authority to open anything at the local level. Well, if there is anyway I can help, just let me know."

Derek was flustered. In one breath, his host revealed intimate knowledge of the workings of police hierarchy. How could he know from shit about the Massachusetts major crime unit? If this had been a game of chess, he would have been in check.

Kelly noticed the rising tension between the two men and Derek's discomfort in particular. "Read my cup like you use to do in the old days, Jack," she asked.

Bagdasarian graciously agreed. A *jezzva*, a small bronze coffee pot, appeared by his side. Sugar was added to the coffee and a thick liquid poured into miniature demitasse cups. Again, only the three of them drank, Lansky preferring a Starbucks. When they finished drinking, they ceremoniously inverted the cups and waited for the residual paste to dry. After a few minutes of inconsequential conversation, it was time to read the cups. Bagdasarian began with Kelly's. "I see a long trip," he began.

"That's a no brainer," Derek interrupted, laughing at the stereotypical beginning. He was ignored.

"With a letter or two arriving soon. Perhaps an invitation to a far away land," Bagdasarian continued. "I see plenty of money and happiness."

Kelly smiled and giggled. The heavy anisette of the Raki made her giddy.

Derek felt frustrated surrounded by the ghost of old lovers. "What about mine?" he asked trying to regain momentum. There had to be some place for him this evening.

Cups were exchanged. "Hmmm," Bagdasarian pondered, turning the demitasse in small increments to better see the secrets of the future. "I see a long road for you, too, my friend. No letters or money, though. But I think I see a satisfactory resolution to your visit here. You will leave in peace." His smiling demeanor was unflappable.

"Thanks," Derek said distracted by the look Bagdasarian was now giving Kelly. The man was trying to read her face with the same intensity with which he had read her coffee-cup future a few moments before.

They retired to the ocean deck for more aperitifs. The views to the west were totally unobstructed. Red and green marker buoys lit up the shallow channels of the waterways. The stars shimmered with the effects of ocean currents while pleasure crafts of all lengths worked their way back to the harbor for the night. The conversation began innocently enough but quickly degenerated to Derek's worst nightmare, the 'old guard' and the 'seven dwarfs'. He slumped over noticeably.

"I'm sorry, my friend. I've forgotten my manners. Sometimes I forget not everyone is interested in our youth in Jacksonville. My home is your home," Bagdasarian said. "Please feel free to explore. We'll come find you when the coast is clear and we return to more civilized conversation that might not be so exclusive."

"Thanks." Derek perked up. He wanted Kelly to intervene on his behalf, but she did not. "Don't mind if I do," he said disappointedly. He rose from his seat and left the three classmates return to their private past walking through double French doors and away from the ocean deck until he could no longer hear their voices. Retreat seemed wise.

He ended up in Bagdasarian's study. The man's library shelves were filled with aircraft flight manuals, multilingual historical documents and medical journals. Both Lansky and Bagdasarian appeared to share a passion for World War II aircraft. He searched the bookshelves, walls and plaques futilely for anything with '5817' or 'YOGIP61'.

Working his way around the room he ended up behind Bagdasarian's mahogany desk. Massive, it was empty of paper, stacks of bills or cryptic documents. A multi-line stainless steel phone sat next to a small memo pad and pencil. Indentations on the paper showed it had been in recent use. The room was still empty. With a quick tear, he removed the top paper and stuffed it in his pocket. No telling what he could find on it with a little pencil tracing. Sometimes his detective work harkened back to the days of Sam Spade and the Maltese falcon. He knew this was an ungrateful behavior as a guest, but the policeman in him would not let go.

On the left side of the desk was a flat screen computer monitor. He followed the wires below the desk to a Dell model on the floor and a cable line to the wall. Only the fastest Internet communication for this guy, thought Derek. The screen saver was something unique, photographs of the Pyramids and the temples of Luxor. He tapped the keyboard once and was stunned to see his own face staring back at him, only twenty years younger.

Derek heard Kelly's laughter echoing from the front porch. He stared at the information on the monitor. It was a DD214, his Department of Defense discharge papers and an outline of his military service. This was confidential information. He tapped the back key. This time he saw his face again, but only ten years younger. It was his Internal Police File from the Internal Affairs office in Fall River. That was also supposed to be totally confidential and accessible only with a subpoena.

He smiled and grimaced simultaneously. Bagdasarian was a slimy bastard after all. Voices came closer. He looked up to the door of the study. How much time did he have before the screen saver came on again to cover up his intrusions?

Bagdasarian appeared with Kelly and Lansky close behind. "Oh, my friend!" I did not expect you to be commandeering my desk," he laughed nervously.

Derek raised his left hand. "Stop right there. I'm almost finished," he said, scribbling furiously on the note pad by the telephone.

Bagdasarian and Lansky stopped at the doorway unclear how to proceed. Kelly came up to the front of the desk and nodded appreciatively. "It will be worth it, guys. Trust me," she said.

Derek drew while keeping one eye on the computer monitor. "Almost done. Just one more minute," he begged. His profile was still up on the screen. If the computer was on a three-minute cycle, he would have it made. Anything longer then that and he was toast.

Bagdasarian moved, circling the desk and coming up behind him. The screen saver flashed back on just in time. No harm done, thought Derek. "A present for you," he said tearing off the drawing and handing it to his host.

Bagdasarian stood frozen in his track. "This is truly remarkable," he finally said sheepishly, looking at his caricature with sincere interest. "Jerry, come look at this."

"You're welcome," Derek said exiting the chair and then office.

Bagdasarian stopped him at the door, turning him around firmly with one hand on his shoulder. He looked Derek in the eye and hesitated briefly. "Derek, my friend, Kelly told me of a little secret passion you and I share." He paused just long enough to see if the other man would sweat. Seeing no reaction he continued, " I understand you like sushi."

"Of course," Derek replied without flinching. "I also like raw *khreema.*

"I happen to have a friend who owns one of the best sushi bars this side of Tokyo and it's right here in Key West. Why don't you go there while you're here? In fact, let me give you my card. When you get there give him this and he'll take care of you."

"Why, thanks, Bags. Maybe I'll just do that," Derek said, tucking the card into his pocket.

Key West
October 23rd

"It was a wonderful evening, Jack. Thanks again," Kelly slurred, hugging her host.

Derek impatiently counted their farewell in seconds. The couple in front of him had a history. "Yeh, thanks again," he echoed wondering where he stood with Kelly.

"You sure you don't want a lift back into town?" Lansky asked jingling his car keys.

Derek took Kelly's arm, almost prying it off Bagdasarian's neck. "No, thanks. It's such a beautiful night and, besides all of Key West is just a few blocks wide, isn't it? Just point us in the right direction." His hosts accompanied them to the end of the driveway and punched in the requisite security code for the gates. It was too dark for Derek to see the numbers. "You know, Jack – I'm sorry, I mean Bags. I had some relatives in Alexandria, Egypt. I'll bet we're related somewhere along the line. Give me your e-mail address and phone number and I'll send you a copy of my family tree."

"Gladly, my friend," Bagdasarian replied. He removed a personalized card from his wallet, scribbled a few words and numbers and passed it back. They shook hands once again. "This is my private line. Call anytime. As a friend of Kelly's and a fellow Armenian, you will always be welcome."

"That's great, Bags," Derek said gritting his teeth. All he could think about was the DD214 staring him in the face on Bagdasarian's computer screen.

"And don't forget the sushi. I'm going to give my friend a call tonight and tell him to expect you," Bagdasarian said waving goodbye.

The mansion faded out of sight as they walked in tandem on the seawall. Kelly leaned against Derek for support. "Wasn't that great?" she asked.

Derek gratefully accepted her weight while avoiding the three-foot drop to the beach below. "Yep, nothing like Armenian hospitality," he answered navigating the streets by dead reckoning.

"Someday, I hope you'll cook like that for me." Kelly said looking seductively into Derek's face. Her usual emotional armor dissipated under the influence of the Raki, fueling the embers of desire. The more she protested intellectually, the more her body could not be denied. Every time she looked at Derek and her old love that evening, the more confused she became. She was attracted to the Detective. The taste of his kiss on Matanzas beach lingered in her mouth. The more she attempted to rationalize her feelings, the more she was becoming obsessed with him.

Derek stopped and turned. Had he misjudged her all evening? His hands rested on both of her shoulders. "You mean you have no great déjà vu with this Bagdasarian fellow? I thought for sure you wouldn't be coming back to the hotel tonight. You were hanging on him like a lap dog."

Kelly swayed seductively between his arms. "There's only one lap I'm interested in tonight," she cooed. Suddenly she stopped her movements, her eyes opening wide in a moment of lucidity. "Oh, oh."

"Oh, oh, what?" Derek said smiling at her innuendo.

"Speaking of lap dogs, guess who's been waiting for a toilet run for six hours?"

Derek sobered with the image of cleaning up dog poop tonight. "Six hours or six hours and another fifteen minutes, it's not going to make any difference at this point."

"Easy for you to say. You're not a girl," Kelly said, laughing.

They walked in silence for several blocks. Real parties were just beginning as quiet residential neighborhoods yielded to the noisy honky-tonk of downtown. Derek couldn't take the insecurity anymore. "What's the story between you two, now?" he asked solemnly. "Do you still have feelings for this guy?"

Kelly stopped short of the curb, pivoted and looked at him straight in the eye. The man really wanted to know. She was giddy with the attention. "Bags? Ha! Show's you how much you know." She reached over and kissed him firmly, deeply on the mouth. The detective's demeanor changed, reacting with genuine pleasure as the kiss rippled through his body.

Walking metabolized the alcohol faster, pushing her to the other side of intoxication. She hated losing control but this was different. The feeling was exhilarating. She didn't care about anything except for the man by her side. When they reached the motel, she headed directly for the pool.

"We ain't got noooo bathing suits," Derek protested in spite of himself. "Besides, it's after midnight and the sign says the pool is closed after ten PM. And the dog. What about the dog?"

"Don't you ever break any rules?" Kelly laughed. She stood poolside, her toes playing with the water, dipping in and out. "Come on. Take a chance. Be brave. Be naughty." Suddenly she dove in, clothes and all.

Derek sat down along the pool edge, feet dangling in the water. They were the only two there. He marveled at Kelly's beauty as she broke the surface of the water. She was the closest thing to a mermaid he had ever seen. Her blouse, once a translucent white, was now transparent, clinging like saran wrap. Her breasts were clearly outlined, her nipples erect with the cold of the pool water. Even her stomach, back and chest shone through, looking like they were carved from a Bernini marble.

"Come on," Kelly laughed, splashing him. "Last one in is a rotten egg!"

"No fair! You're already in." Derek protested feebly.

"I know, that's why I said it," she laughed. She dove underneath the surface and broke by his feet at the pool's edge.

Derek hesitated briefly then unceremoniously jumped in. The pool was unheated, and the water was refreshingly cool. Every time he attempted to grab her, she slipped away like an otter. Clearly she was the better swimmer. He could only hop around, floundering aimlessly in a sidestroke. Soon they found themselves floating on their backs, right hand holding left. The night sky revealed a spectacular display of stars and constellations easily recognized even in their mutually impaired state. A few more splashes and a turban headed hotel clerk showed up, putting an end to their midnight swim.

They walked back to their adjoining rooms dripping down the entire length of the hallway. Kelly's room was first. "Would you like to come in?" she slurred seductively.

"I promised my grandmother never to take advantage of a girl who's had too much Raki," Derek replied, kissing her lightly on the lips. "But in this case, I think I might make an exception," he said kissing her deeply.

Kelly's eyes were awash in Raki and desire. "Silly rabbit," she answered, kissing him back.

Their lips met firmly as she pressed her body into his. He could feel her breasts against his chest, the movement of her stomach against his as she breathed in and out. Her breath was sweet and laced with the lingering taste of anisette. Their tongues met as she wrapped her arms around his neck. For the briefest of moments, time stopped. Then Kelly went limp in his arms. Derek hung his head in defeat. Too much damn Raki, he thought.

Derek carried Kelly in his arms and laid her on the motel bed, doing his best not to get entangled with the Yorkshire terrier nipping at his legs. No obvious leaks on the floor. For that he was grateful. He removed Kelly's wet clothes, peeling them off one by one as she lay immobile on the bed. He knew it was somehow wrong but he could not tear his eyes away from her naked form. She was gorgeous. Shaking his head in disbelief at his lousy luck, he dumped the wet clothes on top of the bathroom shower curtain rod. Returning to her side reluctantly drew the sheet around Kelly's neck. She mumbled incoherently and rolled over, oblivious to the world.

The dog joined him outside for a brief walk. When he returned he unbolted the dividing door between their rooms from both sides, keeping the door slightly ajar. His life, like the room, was sterile. For the first time in years he longed for something different. He stepped out on to the balcony and watched the sun rise over Key West in silence, his fingers playing with the piece of paper he had taken off of Bagdasarian's desk.

Key West
October 24th

"Did I say anything? Did I do anything?" Kelly whispered grabbing Derek's forearm across the diner's Formica table, her fingernails digging in like talons.

"Depends on what you mean by 'anything,'" Derek replied, looking at her coyly. He delighted in having the upper hand for once. Teasing was in his blood.

"Come on, buster, no games. Did I embarrass myself?" she asked again. "And who took my clothes off?"

"The dog. Isn't Cricket you're roommate?" He watched her eyes. She really didn't know. "Actually you were pretty good," Derek said pouring ketchup on his scrambled eggs. "And you told me I was fantastic!" he added, stretching out the last syllables.

"Ohhh, men!" Kelly exclaimed lowering her head and avoiding eye contact. "You are such a jerk. I hate you." She gave him a double kick to the shin.

"Ow! That's not what you said last night," he continued, tormenting her for everything it was worth.

Kelly reached over the table and gave him a solid punch to the biceps.

"Hey, that hurts!" He rubbed his arm. "That's battery. I could have you locked up."

"Not half as much as it's going to if you don't knock it off, buster," she said layering cream cheese on an onion bagel.

"Just don't drink Raki anymore and you'll be fine."

"You still didn't answer my question. Did anything happen last night? Please tell me the truth," she pleaded. This time she looked directly at him, not releasing her radar lock.

He knew the game had just about gone too far. "Come on, Kelly. I'm just teasing. Nothing happened. You were a perfect lady."

The truth set her free. "Good. Because you're a jerk." She washed down the bagel with freshly squeezed orange juice and kicked him again for good measure.

"Love you, Kelly," he winked, blowing her a kiss across the table.

"Some day, I hope you'll mean that," she replied, sticking her fork in his plate for a quick taste. "I didn't know anyone else liked ketchup on their scrambled eggs."

Derek sipped his coffee, waiting for the waitress to refresh his cup. "Kelly, I need to talk to you, serious like. No joking around, now. We got a big problem."

"What do you mean 'we'?" Kelly replied eating a piece of Derek's buttered toast. She really craved bacon, but he had eaten it all. "I see nothing but sunshine and happiness. This is the Keys. It's Florida, man. Nothing matters except for today."

Which part to tell her first? "I didn't want to upset you last night. You were having too much fun and, besides, you were drunk." He needed to break the news about her old lover slowly. He wasn't sure which side of the fence she was on.

"Upset me with what? We both had a wonderful time last night. I could tell even you did in spite of your Neanderthal guy thing. Isn't it against your Armenian code of honor not to have a good time with a fellow blood brother?"

He took a deep breath. "These guys are connected to your missing maggots," Derek said firmly. She deserved the truth. "They are up to their butts in everything."

Kelly starred at him in total disbelief. The pain couldn't have been any worse if he had slapped her. "Look, we came down here looking for clues to a murder. What we found were some old friends, great food and good times. Don't ruin that for me, please."

Derek reached into his wallet and slowly removed the piece of paper he had taken off of Bagdasarian's desk. His pencil tracings filled in pressure indentations on the paper. "Take a look at this," he said, pushing aside her coffee cup.

"I see a set of numbers. What does this have to do with a murder 1800 miles north of here?" she asked defensively.

"It's a federal routing number for a bank. I checked with Al Sherman earlier this morning while you were sleeping off the Raki. Anyway, he's traced it to a bank in the Boston system."

"So what? You still haven't answered my question. What does that have to do with anything?"

"I took it off your buddy's desk last night while he was plying you with Raki."

"Who?"

"You know, the red headed Armenian with a handlebar mustache. Dr Bagdasarian, 'Bags' to his friends, 'Jack' to his lovers,

'Sir' to anyone below whatever his rank is in the US Air Force. That's who."

Kelly looked at him blankly, scrunched up her face and shrugged her shoulders. "So what? There could be a million reasons why he would have banking connections in Boston. Beginning with a million dollars. You saw how the man lives. Most of the mutual funds originate on the east coast and many, like Fidelity, are based in New England." She got up abruptly from the table. "I think you're just jealous."

Derek reached over and grabbed Kelly by the wrist. "There's more." She glared at him until he let go of her arm. "I accidentally touched his computer keyboard when I was drawing my cartoons," he lied. "Your friend had my DD214 and my Fall River Internal police file sitting on his screen. Both my military file and my police file are confidential. There's no way he should have had either of them." Kelly looked at him stone faced, oblivious to his words. He could have had a videotape of Bagdasarian killing someone at high noon on the courthouse steps in front of a dozen witnesses and she still wouldn't have believed him.

"Look," he began again. "You're the one who started this whole thing with your stupid green bottle fly and maggots. You get me thinking your way, entice me to join you on a quest for the truth and suddenly you're not interested anymore? Come on!"

"Entice? Did you say 'entice'?" Kelly bristled.

"I'm sorry, maybe that was a bad choice of words," Derek corrected himself too late. "Look, Boerner worked for your pals. She ends up in Boston. Her condo is stripped clean. There's a code of some sort tucked inside a jeweled pendant on a dog collar. There is evidence of a wire transfer of funds from the Keys to Boston. Your dog-hating friend is suddenly interested in the well being of this one mutt. Your friends know more about the workings and pecking order of the Massachusetts State police then I do. Come on. Think. Connect the dots. I don't know how or why, but somehow your two pals are tied to this Boerner girl's death."

Kelly fumed pacing back and forth in front of their table. "Great. Let's talk about you're so-called evidence. I already explained why Bags might need to wire money to Boston. I don't know why he had you're life story on his computer. All kinds of things that aren't supposed to be on the Internet are on the Internet these days. And now that you mention it, what about the dog?" Kelly asked.

"What do you mean?" His coffee was as cold as Kelly's eyes.

"Did you find 'Y-O-G-I-P-6-1' on anything in either house?

Come on, I know you were looking. Even I did when we first started. And what about '5817'?"

"No, but...."

"But nothing! Not on a phone or the Internet or a street address or a license plate. Nothing. I saw you snooping around. Show me a real connection and I'll reconsider your so-called evidence. These guys have more money then God. Why would they be involved in a murder? Why?" she demanded leaning forward to within inches of his face.

Derek needed to slow the avalanche of words. He had lost control of his most important audience. "Look," he began softly. "I know how important it is to you not to have your friends involved. People get murdered usually for only three reasons: love, money or sex. I don't know. Pick one."

Kelly was silent. She stood up and tossed her unfinished bagel on the table. "You pick one," she huffed storming out to the restaurant parking lot.

Everyone in the restaurant was staring. Derek threw a twenty-dollar bill on the table and followed her. She was fumbling with the car keys, her eyes filling with tears. He gently pried the keys out of her hand. "Look, this is not a vendetta and it's not personal. A lot of folks are dead back home and it is my job, no, *our* job to sort things out. I'm going back to Boston tomorrow. Can I count on you?"

Kelly seethed, not sure whether to cry or punch him in the face. Why did he insist on tormenting her? This trip had turned into a disaster. What happened to Matanzas Beach? She had come so close with this man and now a dead girl, a federal reserve banking route and a DD something-or-other was coming between them. Who cared?

He had lost. "O.K. Fine. I'll go home alone. I won't ask you to do anything you're not ready for," Derek said. He kissed her on the top of her head, turned away and slowly headed back in the direction of the motel.

The walk back was miserable. The entire island was filled with lovers and people smiling and happy for no damn reason what so ever. Why hadn't he stayed in Fall River where he belonged? Without an apology the trip was going to be a disaster. Kelly was special. The thought of losing her to an investigation was absurd. And what about her old boyfriend? Maybe she was right and he was putting a case together out of nothing just because Bagdasarian was an old love. Furtado was the devil incarnate. What could he ever have had in common with a man of Bagdasarian's stature? The case was officially closed anyway. No one cared. He had to apologize to Kelly now. She was waiting for him in the hallway outside his room, sitting on the floor, back to the wall. He helped her up. Her cheeks were tear stained with mascara.

"Look, I'm sorry," she said, touching him gently on the arm.

"No, I'm the one who's sorry," Derek said. "I should have left all this Furtado stuff behind. I wasn't being fair to you or your friends."

Kelly stared at the floor. "I know you have to go back. Just don't go angry. I believe you think you're right, but I'm sure there is an innocent explanation somewhere. Go home and check it out. I'm going to stay here and just think about things for a while. I've got plenty of vacation time." She looked into his eyes. "I may even do a little snooping on my own under the auspices of the Fall River police department, of course."

Derek gave her a strong hug, stroking her hair rhythmically. She had given him an out, a way to protect his integrity and still leave a door open for them as a couple.

"Remember, Kelly, even though this is a closed case, I'm still conducting an active investigation. Murder cases can be reopened officially any time. I know you're close to your friends but please don't talk to them anymore about this. Be careful with the past. Sometimes it can bite you in the ass."

"You know, you're the only one I want to do that," she teased regaining her smile. "You're right. They are my friends. I'll tell you what, though; I'll be careful and keep my distance. I promise."

The thought of Kelly remaining behind in the company of potential suspects left him suddenly uncomfortable. "If you insist on staying, then I insist you contact me every day. Call, e-mail, pony express, telepathy, I don't care what or how you do it, just do it."

Kelly leaned her face closer to Derek's. "Do you want me to do it like a spy or because you really care about me?"

Derek didn't hesitate for a moment. "Both."

"Aye, aye, captain," Kelly said giving him a kiss on the lips.

Business was over. "Great. How about dinner tonight?" Derek asked.

"Let me guess, sushi?" Kelly asked resigned to eating raw bait.

Derek smiled. "But of course." Sushi, Kelly, Florida sunshine and the crystal waters of the Keys, what else could he ask for in life.

Key West
October 24th

The noise at the sushi bar was typical Keys – a mix of pickled ginger, Wassabi and Jimmy Buffett in a Kimono. Halter topped and muscle shirted patrons surrounded three sushi chefs working magic with something that would be considered 'bait' in any other culture. Sapporo beer and Sake washed everything down. The walls were painted with scenes of samurai warriors, geisha girls with pretty umbrellas and cranes, lots of cranes. Tiny sushi boats floated in front of salivating customers in a perpetual circle, stopping first in front of the chefs who prepared rolled rice and seaweed.

Tonight Derek was a reluctant patron. Accepting anything from the hands of Bagdasaian made him uncomfortable. Still, sushi was sushi. At Kelly's insistence he presented Bagdasarian's card to the hostess who buzzed between the kitchen and tables like a dragonfly. The card had a remarkable effect. She brought them to a premier seat across from the head sushi chef.

Derek ordered his usual Hamachi, Unagi, and Yellowtail. The menu was loaded with local fish that never appeared on the menus up north. The restaurant's seat of honor brought the privilege of being served by the head chef, himself. Wizened and ancient, he shuffled among the patrons, extending handshakes and sushi simultaneously, an enigmatic projection of his culture. A sushi boat was not unusual; but this was something special. Derek couldn't wait until he could gloat about the experience to Nunez.

Kelly opted for tempura shrimp in a Bento box. "Something cooked, please," she insisted. The closest she came to sushi was a California roll - rice, avocado and a small piece of cooked fake crab rolled up in seaweed. She took a sip from a glass of plumb wine. "Yuck! I can't imagine you eat this stuff," she said pointing to a sliver of raw sea urchin just before it disappeared into Derek's mouth. "If you had any idea what parasites are sitting in your mouth right now, you'd just die."

"That's why only real men eat sushi," Derek replied taking a swig of Sapporo beer. "More ginger, please," he called out to the waitress. She nodded and disappeared into the kitchen. "These guys fly all over the world to be at the docks when the big ones come in.

I remember a pal of mine catching a 900 pound tuna off of George's Bank. The Japs met him on the dock in Marshfield, offered him ten bucks a pound for the fish undressed and had the fish loaded off to Tokyo within an hour. Undressed! That's $9000 cash. They paid that much money for the fish scales, fish guts, fish head just so they could get the sushi grade fish to folks like me. Now that is something special!" Another plate arrived, complements of the chef. "I think he likes me," Derek gloated working on his third beer.

"I betcha' Jack has something to do with it," Kelly said staring at the shoes of a woman seated at the next table. There was no accounting for taste.

"Jack?" Derek mumbled in between a swallow.

"You know, the guy who set up tonight's dinner. Bagdasarian. Bags," Kelly said driving home a point. "Not too shabby for a suspected murderer."

Derek turned and shook his head from side to side. "Let's see. It's dear old Jack at the door, Dr Bagdasarian, mon Capitan Bagdasarian in service of the government of the good old US of A, Bags if he's a friend and back to Jack when you have a particularly special relationship."

"Oh, give it a rest," Kelly reprimanded rolling her eyes.

"Sorry, I just can't be held responsible for my actions or commentary when I'm gorging," Derek said joking his way out of another tight spot. Foot-in- mouth disease seemed to be his forte this trip.

Kelly nursed the same glass of plum wine for over an hour before Derek finished eating. She kept the conversation superficial and deliberately void of any potential stress between them. The man just wouldn't let go.

When it came time to pay the bill, it was on the house. "You're money is no good here," the waitress said smiling and bowing.

Derek took out a twenty and left it on the table as a tip. "Maybe I have misjudged your pal." They exited the restaurant walking out hand in hand back to Division Street. Southern rock and Jimmy Buffett blared at them from every corner bar. College students on a rampage and married couples with small children in tow blended comfortably on the sidewalks. They stopped in front of a calligrapher working magic using butterflies, dolphins and palm trees instead of letters of the alphabet. Along side someone hawked the opportunity of having your photograph taken with his pet boa constrictor.

Derek swayed catching himself on Kelly's shoulder. "Whoa,

Nellie!" He tripped on the curb coming to rest against a coral fence.

"Hey, what's the matter?" Kelly joked. "Too much booze?"

"I don't feel well," Derek complained, repeatedly clearing his throat. "Kind of tingly all over. And my heart's racing to beat the band." The feeling passed. He stood fully upright again and touched Kelly on the chin. "I think I'm in love," he smiled. His countenance changed again as he swayed and reached backwards to hold onto the fence.

"Awe, you're just a big baby. Give me your hand," Kelly said taking his hand. A look of surprise crossed her face the longer she felt his radial pulse. She reached over and felt his carotid pulse at his neck. "Geeze, Derek. You're going a mile a minute."

"Kelly, I'm having a hard time breathing. I really am." Derek blanched.

"Take it easy, Derek," she coached. "Slow your breathing down. You're beginning to hyperventilate." Her new patient struggled, uncomfortable with his symptoms and projecting a perceived weakness to his date. Without the tools of her trade she felt naked. She couldn't even take his blood pressure. "Come on, I'm taking you to the hospital."

"What do you think is wrong with me?" Derek asked rising to his feet. He needed Kelly for support just to stand.

"Hey, what do you think I am, a doctor or something?" she said nervously leading him to a taxi stand.

Derek turned and smiled at her genuine concern. It was clear she really cared. A sudden wave of nausea brought him down to his knees again. He vomited uncontrollably on the pavement splattering Kelly's shoes while sweat poured off his forehead.

"Great. Just Great. Another romantic evening out," Kelly said. She opened the back door of the taxi, pushing Derek into the cab with her hip and told the driver to step on it. The cabbie needed no encouragement.

Key West
October 24th

Derek counted the ceiling tiles – again. Options were limited considering the presence of two 18-guage IV needles in each forearm and a one-size-fits-no-one hospital Johnny exposing his naked rear. His stomach felt as if he had gone ten rounds in a ring. Every joint in his body ached. He wanted Kelly at his bedside, all right, but not this way. EKG machines, telemetry monitors, IV bags, bedpans and cardboard urinals were the legacy of the past ten hours. Kelly stayed by his side like Velcro asleep in a reclining chair brought in as a special courtesy – ER doc to ER doc.

A head poked in between the curtains. "How are we feelin' this morning?" asked Dr Leersen, ER attending at Monroe County General Hospital. Sandy blond hair swept back in a ponytail, the man's stomach preceded him everywhere.

"Just great," Derek answered, his voice rousing Kelly into consciousness. "What's the verdict, Doc? Am I going to live?" He wanted the IV's out now. This was his third liter of fluid. If the nurse came over with a couple of more bags, it would mean at least another four hours before escape would be possible.

"Yes sir, you'll live. In fact, I'd love to get you out of here before the end of my shift. That means we've got about 30 minutes to make up our minds." Leersen reached down and slowly scratched his pendulous stomach as if scratching the stomach of a favorite hunting dog. "Just a touch of scromboid poisoning." He finished scribbling his notes, his voice booming like a jolly green giant. In an ER as small as Monroe County General, any hope of privacy was impossible.

"Scromboid?" What's that?" Derek asked accepting his discharge instructions. Only the word 'poison' was in his lexicon.

"Too much damn sushi," Kelly interjected, now fully awake.

"Well, ma'am, that's not quite accurate," Leersen corrected. "It comes from fish all right, but poorly handled fish. When you catch something in these waters, or in most waters in fact, the fish must be refrigerated immediately or put on ice. Otherwise bad things happen. The heat releases certain toxins." He stretched and yawned. It would be seven o'clock in about five more minutes and his shift would be over. The man looked exhausted. "Where did you say you folks ate last night?"

"At Soli's, down by the wharf area," Derek said.

"Funny. I know the place well. Never had a case of scromboid there, ever. The guys who own the place are doctors, themselves. They have a reputation of being meticulous."

"Doctors?" Derek asked. "Seems like everything down here is owned by someone in the medical profession."

"Doctors, lawyers and drug runners for sure. Sometimes you can't tell the difference," he laughed. "These boys are on the up and up. They got an antique business in town. One of them even works for the government. It's strange, though."

"What?" Derek asked wincing as the nurse removed the IV's from his arm.

"We're the only show in town. I was the only doc on duty last night and you're the only case of scromboid poisoning I had. These things almost always end up in clusters. When we have an outbreak, half the town ends up in my ER."

Very strange, thought Derek. He looked back at Kelly. She deliberately avoided his eyes.

Key West Airport
October 25th

"Thank you, Officer." Kelly pulled her car curbside at the airport just behind the state police vehicle.

"No problem, ma'am," the Florida State Trooper said, smiling behind his polarized sun glasses. He tipped his cap with his index finger in a salute. "The Colonel said to take care of you, and, take care of you we will. You can leave your car right here. No need to rush. I'll keep an eye on it personally."

Derek slung his large canvass duffel bag over his shoulder. Half the clothes had never been used. His wet bathing suit smelled as if it was beginning to ferment. Everything would need to be double washed when he got back home. A sky cap lifted the bag off his shoulder before he had taken a few feet towards the check-in counter.

"How ya'll doin' today, sa?" the sky cap asked in a thick drawl. "The Colonel told me to bees on the look out for ya. I gots your ticket all taken care of. You's cleared all da way to Boston." The man slapped on a luggage tag to Derek's duffel bag. "I's gonna carry this here bag myself to the air-o-plane."

Derek thanked the sky cap and handed him a five dollar tip. Damn. Bagdasarian's thoughtfulness was making it hard to dislike the son-of-a-bitch. "Isn't there anyone in Key West that doesn't know this guy?" Derek asked.

Kelly smiled weakly. "Awe, come on, Derek. You got to admit it was pretty nice of him to arrange all this. Otherwise, we would have had to come here an hour early so we could park in the garage. At least this way you got another swim out of the trip. Even a bit of snorkeling." She rearranged her scarf. "Besides, he said it was the least he could do. Jack felt so badly after our experience at Soli's last night."

Derek snorted. "If you can call that snorkeling. Should have gone out one last trip to the reef. Now that would have been something." The memory of Dr Leersen and his last night in the hospital made his blood percolate. "And your pal should feel guilty. Damn near almost killed me!" Derek said unconsicously flexing his forearm. The sites of the needle sticks still hurt like a bastard. "I should sue the S.O.B."

"Derek!" Kelly frowned.

They worked their way to the small waiting lounge in uncomfortable silence. The area was filled wth naugahide seats locked in the shape of a gigantic 'L'. At least the area was airconditioned. Sitting side by side, they alternated Cricket between them, staring at the counter and waiting for Derek's flight to be announced. All around men and women came and went about their business, arriving and departing the Florida dream, oblivious to their incubating emotions. Derek and Kelly each took a turn stroking the little Yorkie's head. It wasn't clear who derived the most pleasure, man or beast. The past week had witnessed a remarkable catharsis between them. Once the barriers and defensive networks had been put aside, they had discovered something about themselves originating in another human being - each other.

Now it was Derek's turn to hold on tightly to Kelly's hand. It was a very conscious act derived from fear and loss. A detective's salary would only go so far. He had to return to work in Fall River. The thought of Kelly staying this close to an old boyfriend was almost as unnerving as the possibilty that some of her friends were involved in the murders back in Massachusetts. "Where will you be staying?" he asked.

"Jack owns a couple of cottages near the center of town. He offered to let me have one for a few days."

"I'm surprised he didn't insist you stay with him at Versailles Palace East," Derek grumbled.

Kelly took a deep breath. "In fact, he did." She watched Derek's face scrunch up in anxiety. "But I declined. No need to stir up old memories when there's no place they can go," she said rubbing the top of his hand. "And there is no place for them to go," she said reassuring.

"What will you be doing?" A vacation without structure was incompatable with his experience. This place was just a few strokes short of temptation island.

"Actually, I'm going to spend some time in their store. Going to learn as much as I can about Egyptology. Maybe even be able to tell the difference between real and fake."

Derek's flight was announced on the loudspeaker system. He slowly got up from his seat holding onto Kelly's hand while tucking the dog underneath his armpit. "Don't forget me," he pleaded. "I'm real. Your life back home in Fall River is real. Most of everything down here isn't."

Kelly looked at him and smiled shyly. One look into his eyes and she knew the truth. He was hers for the asking. He just didn't quite know it, yet.

"Keep a close eye on her for me, Cricket," Derek instructed, rubbing the back of the dog's ear. He leaned over and gave Kelly a farewell hug.

Now it was her turn. "Silly rabbit," she said, giving him a deep, long kiss.

Key West
October 25th

The cell phone vibrated at his waist. The caller ID registered an oversees number. "Lansky," he said opening the top drawer of Bagdasarian's desk and turning on the scrambler. "You're clear. Go ahead." Listening intently, he moved his hands as if writing in the air and motioned for a note pad and pen. "Fine. Third trap. "Give me the coordinates again." He wrote down the data then repeated them back to the caller. "Got it. Thanks." He clicked off the scrambler. "Give my best to mom. Goodbye." He turned off his cell phone.

"Are we on schedule?" Bagdasarian asked impatiently.

Lansky removed a World War II vintage model airplane from it's stand on the bookshelf. Holding it in his right hand, he made flying motions with the toy moving it up and down as if in aerial combat. "Yep. It's all taken care of as we speak." He returned the plane to its stand. "The Dentist is riding shotgun on this one." Lansky sat down in the leather high back chair and drummed his fingers. "You really pissed off the General this time. He's got both the Alpha and Beta teams under arrest on a bunch of trumped up charges. The embassy is waiting for the General's evidence. They promise to withdraw all dipolmatic immunity for our guys if he comes up with enough evidence."

The mention of 'the General' made Bagdasarian scour. "The bastard almost got me the last time. Now he's shutting down our operation in Egypt. All those years gone to waste. Shit!" He poured another glass of Raki, sniffed it and downed it in one swallow. "I'm going to kill him! I swear it, I am!" He took the glass and smashed it against the wall. Hearing the noise his maidservant rushed into the room. "Bring me another glass!" he demanded. The woman silently backed out.

"Do you have our guys covered? I don't want this coming back to us."

Bagdasarian snorted. "Standard protocol. The cells are independent of one another. You are the only connection between them and you're here with me. We've used secure communication lines and encrypted technology. When the time comes I'll get them out. Until then, they are just going to have to cool their heels."

"The ship is on it's way. There's no stopping it now." Lansky moved to the six foot colorized world map on the wall. "Your plan is the only one that's viable. For all we know they're following the ship as well with satellite and real time imagery. Interpol, CIA...after 9/11 who knows who's sharing information anymore." He removed a magic marker from the desk and drew an eliptical path between the Mediteranean and coastal New England. "I've had the box modified to your specifications. The radio transmitter beacon is set. I even have just the right man in Boston to do the pick up. Ross, remember him?" Lansky massaged his own neck with the palm of his hand. "God, this hurts. Where's my geisha girl when I need her the most?"

Bagdasarian ignored the complaint. "Wasn't he the scout on our first mission to Somalia?"

"One and the same. Taken to the sea these days living the life of Reilly."

Bagdasarian finished the bottle. "He's a good man. Or was. It's imperative there be no mistakes," he said, twirling the handlbars of his red mustache. "My buyer is just off the 495 high tech loop in Boston. One billion dollars is a lot of money. I wouldn't want anything to go wrong."

"Like I said, this time there will be no mistakes."

Bagdasarian snorted. "You said the same thing the last time. When you got careless with your pecker, I had to go out of my way to clean things up. Now I've got a new problem. The girl is smart. Don't underestimate her. The detective is a typical small town idiot. We can lead him anywhere."

"Isn't that why you picked him in the first place?"

"What about the dog?" Bagdasarian asked. "I can't believe you missed the dog."

Lansky snorted. "I've checked out that little piece of shit while they were swimming today." He waved a bandaged index finger to prove his bravery under canine attack. "Can't find anything there that would be a problem."

"Would have been nice if the dog and the girl went together, don't you think?" Bagdasarian pointed out. "I told you a fire would have been preferable. I keep wondering if we missed anything. She did have the codes, you know."

"I know. I know. That's why she had to go." The memory of the woman's death gave him pause. What had been pleasure now proved to involve infanticide. The bitch never let on about the pregnancy. Not once.

"I don't want anything getting in my way this time. Do you understand me?" Bagdasarian's voice rose to a crescendo. "No loose ends."

Lansky flexed his fingers one by one. If it wasn't for the meddling of Bagdasarian's ex girlfriend, the entire case would have been wrapped up a month ago. Of course, he was in no position to throw stones. Now, with these continued intrusions, there was a risk, even just a small one, of failure. It was only because of the woman's past with the colonel that she still lived. The lives of many others had been forfeit for far lesser offenses. "What do I kow about maggots? Who would have thought?"

"That my friend, is just the point. We have to think. We have to out-think, in fact. Nothing can be left to chance. Nothing." Bagdasarian paced the room It all had to come together perfectly; or, it wouldn't come together at all. "When are you leaving for Boston?"

"I've got a couple of days before this goes down Got some business to finish before the pick up. Catch my drift?"

"Be careful." Bagdasarian returned to his chair resigned to a waiting game. "Remember, it's better to be lucky then good. Our two friends here have, unfortunately, been too lucky of late. They're working as a team. If the detective is out of the picture, then the girl may fold on her own. I want his luck to run out."

Lansky smiled. "I've already taken steps to ensure that scenerio." He checked his watch. An unstopable cascade of events was just a phone call away.

Bagdasarian twirled his droopy mustache again. Everything depended on the Dentist and Ross now. He had already begun to close down his non-essential operations. It was time to deal with the General once and for all. "Long distance operator, please." The line went static for a few moments while relays connected. " I'd like to make a person to person call."

Logan Airport, Boston
October 25th

Seat 32 E was right between a screaming toddler in seat 32 D and a plugged up toilet in the rear of the plane. The child was inconsolable on both takeoff and landing, but a pleasant nuisence the remainder of the flight. The odors from the obstructed bathroom were unrelenting. Derek slowly walked up the exit ramp cradling a farewell bag of navel oranges in one arm and an arthritic, blue-haired grandmother in the other. There was no rush. Half the city was asleep at this hour. No one waited for him and he had nothing to do besides take a shower when he got home.

By the time he arrived at baggage claim, the platform was empty and the rotating luggage caroussel frozen until the next flight. His duffel bag sat in a corner next to several other pieces of abandoned luggage. Reaching down he picked up his bag, juggling the citrus on one shoulder and his duffel bag on the other. Two men approached him from the far corner of the baggage claim area.

"Excuse me, sir. Is this your bag?" a formal voice asked politely.

The men in front of him were wearing three piece suits. No one flew in clothes like this. These guys were on the job. Derek nodded in the affirmative.

"Agents Tavares and Rimel. Would you mind coming with us for a few moments." Tavares, the shorter man extended his Federal ID and then quickly folded it back into his jacket pocket. Rimel, the taller of the two men by a head, had a Kel receiver in his left ear, a wire disappearing into his shirt collar and down the back of his neck into a good old fashioned government issue walkie-talkie and recorder. Both men sported crew cuts and had the weightlifter physiques.

Derek looked impatiently at the two men who delayed his shower and soft bed. It had been a long flight from the Keys with two different connections and hours of layover time. He was dirty and tired and craved sleep in his own bed with his own pillow. Both of the federal agents projected the stone faces of experienced middle-aged veterans, perfectly starched and humorless. "Certainly," Derek replied. He slung his canvas bag over his shoulder. He extended his Fall River police ID. "Is there a problem?"

The agents ignored his efforts at camaraderie. Neither agent avoided eye contact as they tried to stare down the Massachusetts detective. It was a pissing contest no one would win. Their continued silence was their only indication of an issue that needed to be resolved in private.

Fuck ‘em, thought Derek. “Sure, let’s go, fellows,” he said with an air of resignation. “It’s been a long day. Let’s get this over with ASAP. I’m tired and I’ve got a long way to go tonight before I hit the sack. He followed the two men into the airport security office one level up from the baggage claim area.

The room was small and windowless, worn layers of checkerboard green and white linoleum on the floor. A metal table dominated the center of the room, its legs bolted to the floor. A six-foot tall one-way window covered a wall. Derek wondered if anyone was looking at him from the other side.

The man who identified himself as Agent Rimel placed Derek’s beat up canvas duffle bag on the table. “Is this your luggage, sir?” he asked in a monotone.

“Of course it is. You guys watched me pick it up downstairs. It’s got my name on it, see?” he said pointing to the luggage tag.

“Would you mind opening it, sir?” Rimel asked. Tavares stood mute as concrete with his back to the only door in the room.

Why the mystery? At eleven o’clock at night he wasn’t in the mood for games. “Of course not. But will you guys tell me what this is all about?” He unzipped the bag, his request for clarification ignored. The smell from clothes wet with seawater mixed with his dirty underwear exploded in the room reminding him of a junior high gym locker. Derek smiled sheepishly. “What, my dirty shorts set off your dogs?”

Rimel donned a pair of latex gloves. One by one each article of clothing was removed and placed on the counter adjacent to his bag. His shaving kit was opened. Razor, fingernail clippers, dental floss and a small freebee shampoo bottle from a long forgotten hotel stay were dumped on the counter for apparent inspection. The tube of Crest toothpaste was squeezed. The can of shaving cream tested as well for legitimacy. Rimel used a pen to hold each article of dirty clothing up against the high intensity ceiling lights, and then returned them to an already examined pile. The duffle bag was even inverted in their search. Next he took out a small dental probe and explored the seams of the bag. Apparently his search was turning up empty and he motioned his frustration to his partner.

Derek grew impatient. “Come on, fellas. What do you think; I’ve got cocaine on board? It’s late and this is getting a bit much.

Can't you hurry it up?"

Agent Tavares stepped forward from his position against the door and explored the 7-11 bag that held the snorkel, mask and fins. Each piece was placed on the table for examination. He held up the snorkel to the light then blew through the top. Finding an obstruction, he manipulated a probe into the mouthpiece and pulled out a roll of plastic. This was followed by another and another. Both agents smiled knowingly. Similar plastic bags filled with a white powdery substance were extracted from his flippers.

It took just a moment for the significance of their discovery to click in Derek's fatigued brain. Now it all made sense. "Awh, come on. What is this, some kind of joke?"

Neither agent said a word. Rimel took a sample of the white powder from the snorkel tube and mixed it with a solution in a small vial from his pocket. The color of the liquid changed with the introduction of the new substance. "Is that a needle mark in your forearm, sir?" Tavares asked.

"Looks like track marks in both arms, if you ask me," Rimel said.

Derek looked at the faces of the two agents nervously. "Jesus Christ! I spent last night in a hospital in Key West getting a couple of gallons of IV fluids." The whole scenario was coming into focus. He shook his head and smiled knowingly. "I get it. Nunez, it was Nunez, wasn't it? He's always doing practical jokes." He heard the 'click' of a handcuff before he felt the first shackle on his right wrist. The recitation of his Miranda rights echoed from somewhere behind him. Everything moved in slow motion. This was insane.

Cairo, Egypt
October 26th

Interpol's fax confirmed his suspicions. Reading the memo, the General smiled and nodded his head knowingly. The dates of shipments, thefts and intercepts from the Museums in Cairo, Delphi, and Crete matched the activities of the two mercenary teams in his custody. He knew it! He took a bite off the tip of his cigar, rolled it between his lips and teeth and began to gnaw.

His office was simple. The walls were unadorned except for a three-foot picture of Egypt's president. His desk was as uncluttered as his mind. The world of electronics and computers stayed reserved for the staff outside the office door. One lonely air conditioner blasted full throttle in a futile attempt to combat the circumstance of geography. Things in Egypt moved at the pace of the desert -.either slowly or not at all.

A series of aggressive knocks disturbed his concentration. "Enter," he commanded, recognizing his lieutenant by the man's characteristic knocks. "What is it, Emir?" he asked without looking up.

"The minister is here. He's waiting for you in the conference room," replied the aid. He was a narrow man of limited imagination who always dressed in combat fatigues ready to defend the state against its enemies at a moment's notice.

"I'll join him in a moment. This is very interesting reading. I'll show it to you soon."

The aid didn't budge. "You know the minister doesn't like to be kept waiting." He stood with his hands behind his back unconsciously spinning his worry beads.

The General grinned. "Yes, I know. That's exactly why I do it," he quipped.

The younger man nodded in appreciation of his superior's wisdom. There was much he needed to learn. He waited patiently for the hand signal that would be his dismissal, pivoted and exited the office.

The General returned to the file on his desk. Twenty years of following the American and now he was finally getting close. How many untold national treasures disappeared into the hands of this former citizen? Intelligence reports suggested a new object rumored to have been in the hands of the Abdel Rassoul dynasty for generations was being moved. The American embassy was helpful but diplomatic immunity was still an issue. Now the Jews were getting involved. It was time to present his case to the minister.

He shuffled the papers and tapped them lightly into order. The half chewed cigar would keep until after the meeting. He tucked it into his top drawer. He removed his military dress jacket from the seat back of his chair and exited the office, instructing his secretary to hold his calls. The woman refused to cover up her face as the Imam instructed. The Koran was very specific. Unfortunately, she was the niece of the Minister, himself, and, therefore, outside his authority.

The walk down the hall was brief. As was his custom he entered the meeting unannounced. There was something to be said for a dramatic entrance. The minister and his entourage occupied the dozen seats in the conference room. His aids had prepared a slide show on the new computers. The younger generation certainly knew how to make the technology of the Jews and Americans work towards Allah's will. *Allah Akbar.* Praise Allah. With this new data, he would put an end to the American Colonel's pillage. The General sat down and motioned for a cup of coffee. All eyes were directed towards his lectern.

Across the street, a man received a phone call from his informant. Removing a device from his jacket pocket, he entered a four-digit code. The detonator was pressed and a massive explosion rocked the entire third floor of the intelligence ministry across the way, dissolving the conference room and all those in attendance. Glass and concrete sprayed pedestrians and motor vehicles for blocks. A cloud of dust and debris rose from the former government office site that could be seen for miles. Tourist and native Egyptians stopped their daily activity puzzling over the echoes of the explosion.

Satisfied, the man removed his cell phone and made two calls. The first call was to the local office of the Arab news office, *Al Jazedrra.* In perfect Arabic he made a claim of the bombing in the name of Jihad and Allah against Western influence in Islamic life. The second call was a long distance international number to Key West. He waited for the scrambler and relayed the good news.

Fall River, Massachusetts
October 26th

Kelly's voice seemed disengaged. He was using the landline at the Precinct station so the connection was technically perfect. The problem at the receiving end was in the cerebral cortex of the listener. Derek repeated the word again so there could be no misunderstanding. She had to believe him. His voice was bordering on agitated.

"Cocaine?" she asked.

Why was she distracted? "Cocaine!" Derek yelled again. "Cocaine as in Miami Vice, drug lords, cartels, Columbia, blow, crack, snort, shoot. Cocaine as in 26 ounces. Cocaine as in I spent the night in jail. Cocaine as in two more ounces and I would have been arrested under a trafficker statute as a felon and never made bail. Cocaine as in I'm suspended from my job until Internal Affairs makes a report," he said excitedly.

"Cocaine?" she asked again, the sound of her voice trailing off into the distance.

Derek's words came out pressured. "Kelly, please listen carefully. This was a set up. It was in my snorkel. A couple of DEA agents were waiting for me when I got off the plane. Someone called the Feds and told them to look for me." He took a breath and waited for a response. The line was silent. "You there?" he demanded.

There was a noticeable pause. "Yes, I'm here," she said quietly.

"Your boy, Bagdasarian, told us were to go, where to park and even had someone personally hand carry my bag at the airport in Key West. I'm telling you this was a set up all the way. Who else had the motive or opportunity?"

"I don't know," Kelly mumbled. "I can't believe Jack would have anything to do with this."

He wasn't getting through to her. Across from the interrogation table he could see Al Sherman waited patiently on the other side of the door "Look, I gotta go now. Call me tonight at home. And be careful, just be careful." He hung up the phone.

"Hey, bud, what's the scoop?" Sherman asked biting the nail on his index finger and spitting it out onto the floor. "Can I get you a cup of coffee or something?"

Derek collapsed forward in his chair in a frustrated heap. His clothes were the same ones he had worn on his return flight from Florida two days before. He was dirty and disheveled, with matted hair, a two-day stubble on his face and in definite need of a bath. "I'm set up by the rat bastard in Florida and no one believes me. I'm suspended pending the outcome of the investigation from the DEA and Internal Affairs. Suspended!" His friend's eyes were sympathetic. At least someone was listening. "I hate coffee. Black. Please. I gotta wake up."

Sherman stepped outside the doorway and just as quickly returned with two cups of steaming brew. He sat, hands folded on top of the table ready to listen. The difference between his impeccable grooming and Derek's was dramatic. His friend of ten years was a picture of defeat. "Everyone is talking about it. I've heard more about you today then you know about yourself."

Derek shook his head knowingly. "Shit, Al, what am I going to do? The Chief suspended me. I'm suddenly a pariah in my own department. No one will talk to me or look me in the eye all day. Everyone's got me pegged as guilty. I can't investigate the fucker who did this to me. I can't even leave the state until after my arraignment on Wednesday. They want me to just sit on my ass until this whole thing is over."

"Who do you have for a lawyer?" Sherman asked.

"Haven't even given it a thought. I know it sounds corny, but I didn't think I needed one because I'm innocent. I didn't do anything!" Derek pounded his fist on the table.

"Easy there, fella. I'm on your side. I spoke to Nunez and Desrosiers last night. We're going to meet you at Rick's place in a couple of hours so you better show up." Sherman put his hands together fingers extended as if in prayer and tapped his bottom lip with both index fingers nervously. "I'm afraid you've got more trouble on the way."

Derek raised his head and looked up cautiously. For just the briefest of moments he had a sense of hope. "Now what?" he asked.

Sherman leaned forward and spoke just above a whisper. "Rumor has it that they have your safety deposit box. I spoke to one of the boys in Internal Affairs and he told me Judge Coppa gave them the go ahead while you were in the slammer last night. Seems they're afraid you're going to bolt."

Derek snorted and for the first time in hours he smiled. "Ass holes. I don't have a safety deposit box."

"According to the bank you do," Sherman said frowning.

Key West, Florida
October 26th

The tropical sun evaporated the afternoon's downpour almost as soon as it hit the pavement. Kelly watched curiously as Stacie, her nose ring and rainbow hair bouncing, reversed the open sign on the shop door and closed the curtains. "We done for the day or is this just a lunch break?" she asked.

"While the boss is away, the mice will play," Stacie answered. She finished closing the window shades and locked down the cash register. "Lansky is out of town for a few days. No need for us to suffer needlessly."

Kelly still didn't quite get it. "What about Bagdasarian? Aren't you afraid he might come down and surprise us."

Stacie recognized the mentality of a Northern refugee. 'Work all day' was their mantra until they suddenly woke up one morning and realized life was over. "Lansky is the only one that ever shows up. With him gone, no one else is going to come, period." She reached into her purse and took out a handful of pills, shoved them in her mouth and washed them down with a mouthful of tequila. "Do you like getting high?" she asked.

This wasn't quite what Kelly expected for her first day on the job. She was looking forward to lessons on crystals and Egyptian artifacts. The invitation was unwelcome but presented an opportunity as well. "Not in years," Kelly replied cautiously. "I'm a doctor, you know. I don't want to be doing anything that could get me in trouble with the state licensing board. But don't let me stop you."

Stacie broke out into a roar and looked as though she was going to pee in her pants. "Come on, girl. You're in Key West. Fuck the government." She took Kelly's hand. "This is your lucky day. You're coming with me. And no charge for the lesson."

They took the back steps up to a second floor apartment above the shop. The three-room residence was deceiving. The outside was classic Keys, all white clapboard and shingles. The interior looked as if it had been outfitted from a classic 19th century cross Atlantic pleasure ship. Everything was made from Teak, Brazil wood or mahogany. Wide planked floors and beveled glass accentuated the open space and arched ceiling windows. Her hostess went directly to the high-end Bang and Olsen surround sound stereo and turned it on. Kelly felt she was suddenly at the Fleet Center in Boston.

"Pretty nice digs, huh?" Stacie lit up a joint and passed it on to her guest. She was relieved to see Kelly take a short drag.

"I'm surprised you can afford the rent. From what I've seen around here it's got to be pretty steep. They got to be charging you an arm and a leg for this place."

Stacie slumped back into the arms of a beanbag chair and broke out into a hysterical laugh, jostling the beans back and forth in a rustle of bean rain. "It's not costin' me nothin'. All I gotta do is give him a blow job or let him take me in the ass a couple a times a week."

The thought had never crossed Kelly's mind. "Lansky or Bagdasarian?" she asked cautiously, surprised at the girl's frankness.

"Lansky, of course. The other guy? Nah, never seen him around." Stacie took another long drag on the joint. "Can't keep his fly zipped long enough to give it a rest." She slid back into the beanbag chair and let her head fall back. Her eyes were getting heavy with the effects of the pills. "If it bleeds once a month and has long hair, he'll stick his dick in it." She held her breath in order to maximize the effects of the smoke. "This is pretty good stuff. He gets me only the best. No stems or seeds. I got other things, too, things that aren't even on the market yet. Where did you say you're from, Boston? Do you want another hit?"

"Sure," Kelly said taking a small drag. Instead of relaxing, her mind churned. Lansky supplied this girl with drugs. Derek was caught with drugs in Boston. If Jerry traded freely in the market, he could easily have been the one to set up the detective. The thought of Derek alone and in trouble made her miss him terribly. She exhaled. "What's the scoop with the Boerner girl from Jax? Was he having an affair with her, too?"

The nose ring twitched as Stacie woke up from the sound of her own snoring. Her mind returned to reality. "Whadda ya think? He let her stay here for nothin'? They use to go everywhere together, as if I didn't know. Do you have any idea how many times I was sent home from work early? With pay, no less! I see things. I hear things. I'm kind of invisible. People like me just fade into the walls, sometimes. Just because I have a few more holes in me now then when my mother spit me out doesn't mean I'm stupid." Her last words were barely audible as she slipped into a dream that would last the rest of the day. "Scum," she mumbled. "All you doctors are alike, scum."

Kelly stared at the ceiling, her head arched backwards in the headrest of a leather chair. Lansky had always been a pig, but this was beyond anything she had imagined. Was it obstruction of justice or was Lansky just hiding an affair? Even a few presidents did the same thing and never paid a price for their indiscretions. But drugs and murder? That was a different story.

Fall River, Massachusetts
October 26th

"I call the meeting of the Derek Ekizian defense league to order," Al Sherman said, tongue in cheek. "The first order of business is the introduction of today's guest of honor. Derek, you have the floor," he said taking a bite of pepperoni pizza.

The four friends sat around Nunez' kitchen table, all eyes riveted on Derek as he reviewed his trip to the Keys. The only details he omitted were those personal ones involving Kelly. Everything else was open for discussion.

"Got you an appointment with Manny Correia tomorrow," Nunez said. "He's the best criminal lawyer this side of New York City."

Derek grumbled. "I can't believe I need a lawyer in the first place. I didn't do anything! And his fee. What about his fee? I can't afford anyone like him."

"We got you covered, pal. That's what friends are for," Desrosiers said. He would have offered more from the baby's fund if it hadn't been on such short notice.

Sherman wiped the corners of his mouth with a napkin. "We know that, bud, but as far as the rest of the world is concerned, you're just another dirty cop. And you know what the world loves to do with dirty cops," he said simply. "Keep your appointment. That's an order."

Derek nodded in assent. He already confided his next move to Sherman. He had to see Kelly again, soon. It was all he could think about on his return to Boston. It was all he could think about sitting in jail waiting to make bail and every waking moment since then. His friends risked all to be with him and all he could think about was Kelly. By the terms of his bail he was forbidden to leave the state until his arraignment. Still he had made arrangements for a ride on a FedEx cargo transport out of Providence to Miami at three o'clock in the afternoon. Dave Pelletier was a commercial pilot and a friend of his in spite of the trumped up drug charges. Or maybe because of them, he wasn't sure. It was a non-stop flight and after that it was only a hundred and twenty miles to Key West from Miami. There would be no records of any ticket purchase so, if all went well, he would be back in Massachusetts within twenty-four hours, no one the wiser.

He returned his attention to his friends. Al had gone beyond the call of duty and the brotherhood of blue. Derek knew that he was exposing his friends to catastrophe if things didn't go well. Sherman traced the bank routing number he lifted surreptitiously off of Bagdasarian's desk to the People's Bank in Fall River, his bank. Sherman was the one who called his Poker buddies together to help him out. Only Kasson had failed to show, begging off because of a FDIC inspection he couldn't postpone. It was time to kick it up a notch and get their collective brain juices flowing.

Derek wrote down the two sets of numbers removed from the locket of the dead girl's dog. "Does this mean anything to you guys?" he asked putting the information at the center of the table. All three friends focused on the new data, pinging the numbers and letters back and forth between themselves in hopes of picking up a cadence or rhythm or maybe even a rhyme.

Nunez was the first to answer. "5-8-1-7. Can't do much with that. It's probably something very personal. Maybe a social security number or birthday. We've got to know more about these two guys first. Let's work with the second group of numbers and letters, Y-O-G-I-P-6-1," Rick chanted. "YO GIP 61, Y OGIP 61, YOG IP 61, the combination is extensive. Seven to the power of seven to be exact."

Desrosiers jammed the last piece of pizza in his mouth. "Didn't you mention something about both of those guys being World War II aficionados?" he asked, the words barely distinguishable through his chewing. "I know a little something about those times."

"Yeah? Like what?" Derek asked, his interest piqued. Even the idea the paramedic had a special talent that went beyond eating like a vacuum cleaner had never crossed his mind. Still, the Lord worked in mysterious ways.

"P61 was a night bomber. Built by Northrop in the last days of the big war. They used it extensively in the Pacific theater," Desrosiers said nonchalantly.

Something clicked in Derek's memory. "Steve, did it have a twin tail? Something like this?" he asked drawing a rough rendition from memory on the tablecloth.

Nunez protested. "Hey, not on the tablecloth, man. It was a gift from my mother last Christmas. She checks up on me once a year."

Desrosiers studied the sketch briefly. "In fact, it did. It had a twin boom and a twin tail. Very unique for that era of aircraft. How did you know?"

Derek stood up and walked to the big slider overlooking the backyard. The dog was chasing something. He'd have rather been the hunter rather then the hunted. "The walls in Lansky and Bagdasarian's study were covered with photographs of all kinds of aircraft. Pictures of that one plane in particular were repeated over and over. I'd never seen anything like it, so it stuck in my mind."

Steve grabbed a pen and wrote a combination of numbers and letters down. "You know, those numbers you gave us could represent call letters. When those guys went on a mission, they'd have to be in communication with their base. They would use a nickname and plane identification in their radio transmissions so they wouldn't alert the Japs. YOGI P61. YOGI bear, like the cartoon character. It was big back then."

"Heyyyyyyyy Boo-Boo," Nunez imitated in his best cartoon voice. "I watch it every Saturday morning. God bless Hanna-Barberra."

"So, part of the mystery is solved," Sherman said looking at his watch. He had another hour left before he had to pick up his kids from school. "Now the question still remains what might those call letters be used for?"

"Beats the hell out of me," Desrosiers said. "You're the detectives. Go figure it out."

"Computers!" Nunez said excitedly. He felt a sudden inspiration. "Of course!"

"What about computers?" Derek asked.

"The whole universe is run by computers. What you've got there is probably the man's access codes," Nunez said, triumphantly.

"How can we find out?" Derek asked.

Nunez stood up. "There's only one way, and you are looking at the master." He stretched and yawned. He had worked the previous night shift. "Follow me," he said leading his friends out of the kitchen to a plywood computer desk. His PC was top of the line Pentium with speed in the multi-giga-something range. Everyone hovered next to him flanking the chair on each side.

"You got the search warrant?" Sherman asked grinning the whole time.

"Right here," Derek answered tapping his empty shirt pocket. "Judge Judy was very cooperative." This was the first sign of optimism in 36 hours. Bagdasarian's calling card was in his wallet, containing the man's street address, a phone number and e-mail address as well. What his friends were attempting to do was illegal and inadmissible in a court of law. He needed more evidence then a few slippery maggots, a bank routing number and two sets of cryptic numbers taken off the collar of a Yorkshire Terrier. The facts so far weren't enough for an indictment or to convince Kelly her old friends were even remotely connected to anything deadly. The thought of her broke his concentration. It took a few moments to refocus on the job at hand.

Nunez connected to the Internet. "This is so much fun I could just shit," he said rubbing his hands gleefully, mesmerized by the glow from the 21-inch flat monitor.

Derek was amazed at his friend's audacity. "I saw something like this on *60 Minutes* once, but I never really believed it would be so easy," he said pacing the hallway.

"That's because you are technologically impaired, buddy," Sherman said handing Nunez a program from the top shelf of the desk.

Nunez made a flourish as he pressed the enter key. "O.K. folks, just follow the bouncing ball." He leaned backwards in his chair and locked his fingers around his neck waiting for the computer to do its thing. "Guys like him always keep their computers on. They have dedicated lines in their homes all the time. Basically, we are going to spoof the guy's IP address by pinging his DNS name to give us a static IP address. We need to authenticate. We'll use key cracker software recently obtained from the 2600 Internet site loathed by western companies but beloved by hackers all over the world. That will help us seed his codes. This will even work around firewalls. At least, that's what someone once told me." He looked at his friends sheepishly. "I wouldn't know of course, since this is strictly illegal unless you're the FBI or CIA or Interpol or an Alien from the planet Krypton."

"What's a firewall?" Derek asked pressing his face over Nunez's shoulder.

"That's his defense against hackers. But we'll beat him. Just watch and learn, little buddy," Sherman said biting his nails.

The key cracker software program worked perfectly. A few tweaks later and Nunez announced they were in the hard drive of Bagdasarian's computer. "E-mail, bank transactions, Quicken accounting programs, what is your wish my lord?" Nunez quipped.

"Shut up, Rick. Just copy everything. We'll sort it out later," Derek said nervously.

"Not that easy, little buddy," Sherman said frowning.

"Why not?" Derek asked.

"Too much time in his files. His computer will recognize a visitor in his system sooner rather then later. Conceivably he could even trace us back here." Sherman turned to Nunez and touched his shoulder to get his attention. "Do you think we should have scrambled?"

"Too late now, bro," Nunez said nodding his head in agreement. "On this T1 line we can download his entire hard drive in minutes."

Derek's voice climbed a few octaves in anxiety. "Fine. Just do it, god damn it. Do the fucker's e-mail, the Quicken anything and everything." His focus was supposed to be on Nunez's computer; but, all he could think about was Kelly, the beach, the way grains of sand clung to her skin, her smell, her touch, the way she laughed and her eyes, always her eyes. The computer screen glared back at him snapping him back to reality. "How many floppy discs do you need?" he asked Nunez.

Sherman and Nunez both snorted simultaneously. "Floppy discs, indeed," Nunez said incredulously. "You are light years behind the times. This is all going on my hard drive and then we'll burn a couple of CD's. You'll get a copy in just a couple of minutes."

"Make an extra for safekeeping," Derek said. His hands were sweating. That was not a good sign.

"What are you, the fucking CIA?" Nunez asked shaking his head in disbelief.

"Insurance," Derek muttered. "Just insurance."

Sherman bit down another nail. "Rick, just do it before he starts whining again." He turned to Derek, "I'll put a lock on them only my son could know."

"Just in case?" Derek asked.

"Just in case, what?" Rick laughed. "This is Fall River not Russia."

Key West, Florida
October 27th

Derek squeezed himself in between a couple of unassuming good old boys returning from a gig in Hawk Cay. As payment for the ride, they asked him to critique their demo CD. He hated southern rock but by the time they dropped him off at Mallory Square he had grown to like both the young kids and their music and was sorry to see them go.

A fine mist turned to a downpour while he stood in the empty dock area contemplating his next move. It was past midnight. What was he doing down here in the first place? He had never broken the law as a cop. Never. Now he was almost a fugitive. And for what? To see some girl who might not even give him the time of day. For all he knew she was back in the arms of her old boyfriend. The thought made him cringe. He had to see her, that's all he could think about – just like lemmings rushing to the sea.

He pushed his wet hair out of his eyes. Few things are more beautiful then a tropical thunderstorm, unless you happen to be caught in one unprotected. Derek had seen the black clouds roll in on the horizon about half way down from Marathon Key. Lightening played tag on the edges of the cloudbanks slowly enveloping the night sky, devouring moon and stars alike. When the wind driven rain came, water rushed at him horizontally penetrating nose and mouth alike. He stood in front of the cottage address Kelly had given him two nights before and rang the doorbell again.

Kelly's sleep was restless. It didn't take much to wake her up. She put on a robe over her Victoria Secret silk pajamas cautiously approaching the front door, her feet making the barest of squeaks on the narrow planked pine floor. A solitary figure could be seen through the frosted glass. "Yes. Who is it?" she called out tying her bathrobe.

Derek took a deep breath. God, what was he doing here? "Kelly, it's me."

The detective should have been 1800 miles north. "Derek?"

"Yeah. Please open up. It's cold out here."

His voice was out of a dream. Her fingers fumbled with the latch until she opened the door. The man looked like a near drowned puppy. "Oh my God! Oh my God! What are you doing here?" She put both hands up to her face in surprise. "Come in. Come in. Get out of the rain." Cricket raised its head at the disturbance then went back to sleep.

Derek sloshed in, dripping puddles of water. He focused on Kelly, embarrassed at his own sudden appearance, shifting his weight from foot to foot like a little kid who needed to go to the bathroom. He kept his eyes locked onto hers. What could he say? What was he supposed to say? He could always talk about the case, Bagdasarian or cocaine. There was no shame in that. But those things were the furthest from his mind. It was all about her. He needed to say something before he exploded. Kelly interrupted his thoughts by giving him a hug, sopping wet and all. The feel of her cheek against his was maddening.

"Oh, Derek, I'm so glad to see you," she said holding on to him for dear life. "I've got so much to tell you." She released her hold around his neck and planted a solid kiss on his lips, her arms still hanging loosely around his shoulders.

The best way to say something was just to say it. "Kelly, I've got something I need to talk to you about, too." He kissed her back lightly, reached up and removed her hands from his shoulders holding them securely in his own. "It's very important."

Kelly's eyes dropped down and stared off into space. "I know. It's got something to do with Jack and Jerry, isn't it?"

Derek noticed the change in her demeanor. "No. In fact I don't give a rats ass about anyone or anything in Key West except for you."

She didn't understand. The detective was never one much for initiating a conversation. "I don't get it. Why are you here then? Why didn't you call and let me know you were coming? Why the surprise?"

Derek took a deep breath. There was no other way to do this without just coming out and saying what he felt. "Please sit down with me," he asked. He took her hands and sat down on a beat up Futon couch. He was oblivious to the water dripping from his clothes saturating the furniture. Kelly followed his lead sitting quietly by his side.

"Derek, what is it? What is wrong?"

He put his head down and stared at his feet. "I came here because I wanted to see if you were real, if what I felt all last week was something real. I have to be sure." His face flushed noticeably red. "All I think about is you. I wake up in the morning and I think about you. I go to bed and I think about you. I can't help myself.

I'm risking jail time even being here and I just don't care. I can't eat. I can't sleep. All I think about is you."

All this took her by surprise. "Why, Derek Ekizian, what are you trying to say?" she asked cautiously. Boyfriends and serious relationships were far and few between, but she had never seen anyone act like this before.

"Kelly, I think I'm in love with you." There. He had gone and said the 'L' word at last. It dripped off his tongue and hung in the air like a balloon. He closed his eyes when he told her. Now he opened them slowly, not sure what her reaction would be. The wait was painful. Every breath brought him closer to the oblivion of rejection.

She had tears in her eyes, her right hand partially covering her mouth. She stared into his face and then raised her gaze into his eyes. "Me, too," she said. A smile broke out on her quivering lips. "Oh, Derek, me too."

His eyes opened wide. "You do? I mean, you do!" He leaned forward on the couch smothering her in kisses. His enthusiasm yielded a clash of teeth.

"Ouch!" Kelly said smiling and laughing and crying all together. She rubbed her front tooth were they had just clicked. "Whoa there. I don't want any dental work down here right about now. Don't know if I can trust southern dentists."

Derek smiled and leaned backwards on the couch. "Do you have any idea how miserable I've been the past few days? I never thought love could hurt so much." He smiled as Kelly leaned forward and placed her head on his chest. He stroked her hair gently. "Kelly, will you marry me?" he blurted out.

"What?" she asked raising her head. Being in love and getting married were very different things.

"You heard me. Will you marry me?"

Kelly resumed her snuggle. "Yes, Detective, I'd be honored to be your wife."

He was even more surprised. "You would? I mean you would! That's fantastic." His life was now on autopilot. "Kelly you're making me the happiest man on earth."

She reached up and kissed him firmly. "Silly rabbit." Only now did she realize how wet her future husband was. "Hey, big fellow, we've got to get you out of those clothes before you die from pneumonia. Then I'll never get a chance to be Mrs. Ekizian. Or should I say Dr. Ekizian-Gill. Then again, maybe it sounds better if it's Dr. Gill-Ekizian. What do you think?"

Derek smiled. "I think you're right. I'd better get out of these wet clothes."

"I've got a washer dryer here. You can borrow my bathrobe until everything is dry," she said leading him up to the bathroom shower.

He began to unbutton his shirt. "Hey, a little privacy please," he demanded.

"Now you're playing bashful?" she teased.

Derek stepped into the 1950's shower stall with its frosted fishnet pattern glass door and turned on the water. The temperature was steaming hot.

"Is it safe to turn around now?" Kelly asked politely.

"Care to join me?" Derek said lathering up with her tangerine peach shampoo.

"I thought you'd never ask," Kelly said.

Derek saw the white of her long legs enter, first one then another as she stepped over the edge of the tub. She was naked. Her breasts were perfect. Her hair clung to her back as the water cascaded down her neck. He slowly lathered up her back and then her front while she made tight circles toward the spray of the showerhead. It was crowded in the stall and for that, Derek was even more grateful. He didn't have to look down to know he had an erection the size of Florida.

"Is this for me?"

"Til death do us part."

Key West, Florida
October 27th

There comes a pivotal time in life that marks a transition between the 'before' and the 'after'. The detective's words of love germinated in Kelly's heart as if they were her own. Every fabric of her being wanted to be with him forever. They planned a future in their few hours together - when they were going to get married, where, who they'd invite and who they wouldn't, their favorite colors, the kind of pillows they preferred, how many kids each wanted and how late they liked to get up on Sunday mornings.

Happiness was impossible until the murder and drug investigations came to a satisfactory conclusion. Derek's personal and professional survival rested on the pending drug charge. Suspended from his job and officially banned from any further investigating, he needed Kelly's help. At least that was her official position. She adamantly refused to leave the Keys until he was cleared of all charges. For that to happen she would have to be his eyes and ears in Key West while he returned to Boston.

"You don't own me, mister," Kelly said. There was much work to be done before this was over. She wasn't an ornament; she was going to be his partner for life.

There wasn't enough evidence to get the Florida State or local Monroe county police involved - yet. And there was always the hope of 'yet' if all went well. Derek's two prime suspects were powerful; he probably couldn't trust the local cops anyway. Still, someone had to do the footwork. He swallowed his male pride long enough to lock in his cell phone number on Kelly's voice activated phone so she could check in with him daily. Then there was the matter of the dog. She would stay in the Keys but he had to take Cricket back to New England. Would anyone look for a smuggled dog on a FedEx cargo carrier? Derek removed the gold cross from his neck and gave it to Kelly in return. It was not a fair exchange. Kelly's gift was work and needed to be walked at least three times a day. He insisted on something else.

"What?" Kelly asked.

Derek scouted the room for something of hers that was special, something that would remind him of her every day. "This," he said triumphantly, pointing to a small gold sand dollar from Kelly's key chain. "It'll do just fine." He reached over and removed the sand dollar from her key chain, transferring it to his own. "Now we are engaged!" he laughed. She hit him with a pillow while burying him in an avalanche of kisses. Then, as quickly as he entered her life, he left at dawn, hitchhiking back to Miami to catch a FedEx flight.

That afternoon Kelly was once again a luncheon guest of the Bagdasarian household. She sat on the deck overlooking the water eating cottage cheese and fruit salad.

"See, Kelly my love, I still remembered," Bagdasarian said flashing a toothy smile. He dug into his own plate of steaming pasta and clams then wiped the corners of his mouth.

"Jack!" Kelly reprimanded. His subtle attempts at rekindling their relationship had not gone unnoticed. "You know how that makes me feel." She spoke with confidence and conviction. There could be no misunderstanding.

"I'm sorry, *hokis,* my soul," he replied in Armenian. "You can't blame me for trying, though." The look of rejection on his face was palpable.

Kelly sighed and put down her fork. "Come on, Jack. Now you're being a real shit in Armenian, too. You're making this harder then it has to be."

A cool breeze helped to break the sun's heat and peel back layers of her anxiety. Even their brief confrontation over the past disappeared in the presence of the sea. Feelings of wonder and passion for her old flame were replaced with mistrust and suspicion. She needed to challenge him soon but hesitated. That reluctance to go on the offensive bothered her more than anything. She was never one to avoid the truth under any circumstance. She took a sip of iced tea and went on the offensive. "Jack, I need to ask you a question," she said plainly.

He had seen this look before. "Whatever I can do to make you happy," Bagdasarian said. He swirled the ice in his glass of Scotch with his finger then licked it dry.

"Did you know Lansky was having an affair with Boerner, the girl from your shop? Look me straight in the eye and tell me the truth."

Bagdasarian paused and swallowed a mouthful of his drink. Damn this woman. "This silly murder investigation again? Humph!" He saw the look on her face and knew it was the wrong answer. "If he did, I was unaware of it," he answered softly. "I have strict rules about fraternizing with the troops, so to speak, both with my private businesses and in the military. Any deviation from Federal or State guidelines is cause for dismissal, court marshal or summary execution," he joked. He saw his words were having little effect on her. "You know, I'm out of the country a lot. Sometimes things happen and I'm the last to hear about it. But I'll tell you what. If it makes you happy, I will speak to Jerry myself and get the truth, even if I have to beat it out of him," he said smiling behind his mustache. She was bending, he could tell.

Kelly sat quietly and stared at the tablecloth. "Thanks. That'll be great."

"Now it's my turn," Bagdasarian said rising from the table and extending his arm. "There is something I want to show you. Come. Follow me."

She followed him inside the house, their footsteps echoing against the twelve-foot ceilings and stairwells like the hoofs of Clydesdales.

"Carved right out of the coral rock and reinforced with steel," he boasted leading Kelly through a vaulted chamber. "We are actually about fifty meters below sea level and about twenty yards past my sea wall on my property line. Truman had this built in the final days of his administration in case of nuclear attack. Key West was his summer white house, you know. Bullet proof, bomb proof, fire proof, even flood proof; only the best top of the line construction for the government of the United States of America back in those days. It had been abandoned for almost fifty years when I bought his place. I stumbled on the original plans when I was sorting out old top-secret documents for declassification. You can say I built what you see above ground because this was here in the first place."

"Is this where you keep your booze?" Kelly joked deliberately ignoring his arm.

"Something even better!" Bagdasarian approached the door that stood in the way of his surprise. He punched a code into the electronic keypad to the right of the door and watched it slide open. Inside a battery of lights ignited in response to a wave of his hand bathing the room in a multicolored spectrum of primary and secondary colors.

Kelly's first response was one of relief. The code that opened the door had nothing to do with the numbers '5817'. Crossing the threshold her breath was taken away at the most amazing display of antiquities she had every seen outside the Metropolitan Museum in New York. Every piece was professionally lighted and labeled with markers that indicated Old, Middle and New Kingdom timeline in linear order. The sheer complexity and magnitude of this collection was stunning. Even the walls were covered with limestone hieroglyphs. Basalt, marble, soapstone, limestone, gold, bronze and silver objects stood side by side. There was barely enough room to walk through the narrow isles. "Where...?"

"Just look and enjoy," Bagdasarian interrupted.

"Jack, are they real? Is it all real? Is it even legal?"

"Of course. Every bit," he said putting his hand on her shoulder. "It's been in my family for years," Bagdasarian replied.

Kelly shook her head in the negative. "Wait a minute, pal. You're Armenian. Everyone knows that the Armenians were chased out of the Turkish Empire and suffered one of the first genocides of the 20th century. Every Armenian I know came to this country with the shirt on their backs and precious little more."

Bagdasarian smiled through the veil of his floppy mustache. "Ah, you're only partially right my *hokees,* my soul." He noticed she didn't flinch this time with the use of the word of affection. "My great grandmother's family was Egyptian. Thus you see the treasures around you."

Kelly soaked in the experience with a newfound rapture for Egyptian antiquities. She strolled the narrow isles overwhelmed by the sheer magnitude of the vista. At the far end of the room Kelly noticed another electronic touch pad and another door. "Where does that go?" she asked.

"If I show you, I'd have to kill you," Bagdasarian said smiling.

Was he joking wondered Kelly?

Fall River, Massachusetts
October 28th 7am

The law firm of Correia and Shaffer had a lock on the criminal practice in Southeastern Massachusetts. They were the best, period. Correia represented first and second-generation immigrants and Shaffer, his blond thirty something partner and sometimes lover, the white bread population of the city. Derek wondered where he would fit in as an Armenian. No one went to trial unless they refused the expert advice of their attorney. Everything was settled by a handshake in the judge's chamber well before that final aspect of the jurisprudence system could be engaged.

Manny Correia, the principal in the law firm, heard it all before. When Derek protested his innocence and the drugs in his snorkel a set up, Correira waved his hand and begged off any series of explanations. "The truth is for God. I'm here to get you through the American legal system without you being squashed like a bug." He watched Derek's eyes steel up. Until today it had been the detective's sworn duty to protect the system. "Look, if someone is really out to get you and went to all this trouble to set you up, then you're up against some pretty big boys."

Derek's head nodded in assent while starring out the window into the streets of downtown Fall River. All he wanted was Kelly. This was standing in his way. What kind of future did he have unless he was able to make this all disappear. He couldn't live his life in constant fear. "I'm listening," he said resigned.

Correira smiled. He was finally getting through on a level the cop would understand. "Let's just say you're right in your convictions and we go to trial and by some act of my genius or the benevolence of God you're acquitted. What then? I've got a paper here from the DA that tells me you've got a quarter of a million dollars in a safety deposit box in your name you claim you know nothing about. So someone out there thinks your more valuable then a quarter of a mill to keep off the street. Do you know how much a thirty-caliber bullet costs these days? Hell, half the people that walk through my doors would plug you for free just to say they knocked off a cop." He let the words sink in. "If you're lucky and I'm good, and, most of the time I am, you're going to walk out of court this afternoon a free man - and a target. You'd better have on your running shoes."

Derek squirmed in his seat. "But if I take a drug test, blood, urine, hair samples, wouldn't that prove I've never taken any drugs? Then they would have to believe me. I could go back to work and then have the department behind me."

The man was naïve. Correira laughed. "What good have they done you so far? If you're not using, then you're dealing. You want the DA to call you a trafficker instead. That's a felony, son. Do you know what they do to cops in jail? How many ways of saying 'pass the soap' do you know? Now, please, let me do it my way. I don't know who you pissed off. In fact, I don't want to know. But it seems to me, you're best chance to get your life back is to get out there and nail the bastard. Let me make short work of this my way and I'll leave hunting down the bad guys up to you. Agreed?"

He had no choice and he knew it. Derek sat in the back of Correira's Ford Explorer and followed his master to Superior Court like a sheep dog. The next few hours were critical, but all he could think about was Kelly. She might be in danger and worse, alone. He wanted and needed to protect her. He trusted Correia blindly. From the moment they entered Judge Coppa's private chambers it was all fluff and bluff and good old boy networks that ruled the show. The DA was young and loaded for bear, relishing the thought of nailing a dirty cop. The two agents involved in his arrest represented the DEA. Derek felt like Custer, preparing for certain annihilation.

Correira made short work of them all. "Your honor, we demand dismissal of all the charges." The DA and DEA attorneys snickered only for a second. The principal of evidentiary rules, Correia pointed out, demanded his client have possession of the baggage. Someone else had removed them from the luggage carrousel. The bag was never locked and, in fact, didn't even have a lock attached to the luggage. Undeniably there was a break in the chain of custody. Agents Rimel and Barber agreed on the facts, sheepishly nodding their heads. Derek walked away less then a half hour later a free man, at least as far as the Feds were concerned. Internal Affairs in the morning would be a different matter. A handshake at the bottom of the courthouse steps was all the time Correira gave him on the way out. "Go get 'em, tiger," the attorney's final words leaving Derek to fend for his own ride home. "See you in the chief's office tomorrow for the Internal Affairs review. Be there or be square."

Derek shook his head in disbelief. The whole process took less then 90 minutes. For the past three days he was tortured with every miserable possibility of ruination. Now he was at least half way home and could pursue the dragon on his own terms. A man without wheels in the middle of Fall River, he flagged down a cab for the brief ride home, activating his cell phone. "Kelly," he said into the microphone. Two rings later he was relieved to hear her voice. "Hey, babe, how ya' doin'?" Even at 45 cents a minute peek airtime, he could have listened to her breathe for hours.

"Derek? Is that you? Thank God!" Hearing Derek's voice had her on the verge of tears. She was tired of playing detective without the real McCoy by her side. Only separation made her realize how much she loved the man, telling him so in the syrupy effervescence of lovers.

Derek was all business. "Look, Kelly, I'm out of the jam with the Feds and now I've got to face Internal Affairs. Anything I can get on your boys down there will help my case. Until then I've got to hang around here. Then I'm going to come get you."

The news of his delay was crushing. Kelly valued her relationship with Bagdasarian but his repeated attempts to rekindle something that died years ago were wearing thin. Lansky boré the brunt of her suspicions. She could almost feel Derek salivate when she relayed the news of Lansky's affair with Boerner. How much more involved was he in the whole sordid affair? The stakes were raised, but he needed more then an affair to tie in the Pyramid partnership. Or was it the actions of just one man, she wondered? Only ancient loyalties shrouded Bagdasarian's undersea vault from revelation. Yes, she would do whatever it would take to win Derek his freedom. She would keep her appointment tonight.

Derek's hopes rested on the computer discs in Nunez' home. "Gotta go, hun. I'm almost at Al's house. Going to pick up the dog and then head on home."

"Derek, please be careful."

"Of course, babe. I won't be doing anything to jeopardize my honeymoon night."

The thought of their last night together made her smile. "I love you," she said. She clicked off the phone.

Key West, Florida
October 28th
3 p.m.

Love is mysterious and ephemeral, traveling between souls in constant search for the 'other'. Kelly was one of the lucky ones, and she knew it. Derek needed her help more now then ever and she had to focus. Cocktails and dinner at Jack's was on today's itinerary. Dodging passes from an old boyfriend was not an ideal way to spend the evening, but someone had to get closer to Pyramid and sort out truth from suspicion and innuendo. And the door. The images of the sealed door in Jack's subterranean vault teased her like a Pandora's box, beckoning, enticing.

The massive wrought iron gates at the mansions entrance were open as Kelly pulled up in her convertible. She came to a stop at the end of the circular driveway right next to Jack's Mercedes. He was waiting for her by the door eager and impatient, greeting her with his usual barrage of kisses. She moved her face just enough that all he caught was air. Her new demeanor did not go unnoticed but Bagdasarian let it go for now.

It was another perfect Key West afternoon. The drinks appeared if by magic at the side of her lounge chair. She nursed them along listening to Jack's stories of the past and those times they spent together as more then friends. It was clear he still had a thing for her. Kelly wondered who else shared his bed in the past five years. Certainly it wouldn't have been Stacie. Jack had better tastes then that, or at least she hoped he still did. But then again, who knows anymore, she thought. Bagdasarian's friendly banter blurred into a monotonous drone as her thoughts drifted to images of Derek's face and their last kiss.

Her distraction morphed. "Hey, Jack, would you mind terribly if I might look at your collection in the basement again."

The request took him by surprise. "Of course not," he smiled. "Follow me." He led the way once more taking her arm but not her hand.

This time she observed everything. No detail escaped her notice. The numbers from Cricket's locket were fixed in her mind, 5-8-1-7 and Y-O-G-I-P-6-1. She counted the steps, the tiles, the number of railings, anything and everything that might reflect on a pattern, any pattern, any sequence. She stared at the keypad in front of the vault and focused on his fingers as they moved on the touch pad. Again, nothing connected the locket and anything she had seen so far. The door opened and the room was enveloped in a spray of color and light that took her breath away. She was transfixed by the collection in front of her. "Jack, I just don't know how you can live with all this and not spend your whole life in this room."

Bagdasarian's head danced. "*Hokkees*, I grew up with these things; but I never take any of this for granted." He noticed that she didn't protest this time with the affectionate word. "But, please feel free to enjoy this at your leisure." The cell phone at his waist hummed a Bach melody. He opened the phone and turned it on. "Excuse me for a moment, please." He turned his back and went to the door's threshold, leaving her alone in the vault.

Kelly could hear only the staccato of his words. When he turned he was still smiling, but she recognized the plastic nature of this particular smile.

"I have some news for you," he said. He stared at the floor for a moment. "My sources in Boston tell me that your Detective friend has had all the charges dropped on his recent arrest for cocaine."

"How..." her voice trailed off startled with his connections.

He raised his head and now focused on her eyes. "Oh, yes, I knew about that little problem he had at the airport. I make it my business to know as much as I can when it comes to you. You never know about people, Kelly. I wouldn't want anyone hurting you. You never know what kind of fellow this Ekizian person is, even if he is an Armenian and a police officer. You'd be surprised to learn how many people use cocaine these days."

Kelly composed herself. "Thanks for your concern, but Derek was innocent all along. In fact, he had a concern that he was set up by someone down here in the Keys." She went on the offensive. "By the way, what did you find out about Jerry?"

Now it was his turn to be surprised. Nothing could be taken for granted with this woman. "I'm glad you brought that up. Jerry has been out of town away on business for the past few days. I haven't been able to talk to him directly about this; but it seems your sources were correct. He was having an affair with this Boerner woman. I am humiliated, just humiliated. No, appalled is a much better word. How something like this could have gone on without my knowledge is an embarrassment. He's going to have some pretty serious explaining to do when he returns," he said nodding his head confidently. Kelly listened without saying a word. "Now you must excuse me. I have some business to attend to. It won't take more then a few minutes. Please, stay here and enjoy yourself."

Bagdasarian's footsteps echoed up the stairs. Kelly stood alone in the chamber of the ancients, her focus on the far wall and its forbidden door. Her fingers traced the margins of the keypad, a standard ten digits with a pound and a star key flanking the zero. No alphabet letters were present. The possible number of combinations was twelve to twelfth power. She conjured up Cricket's locket again. 'YOGIP61' would not fit on a numerical pad. There was something about '5817' that stuck in her mind she just couldn't place. Then she remembered. '5817' was the address for her beachfront shack during her residency days in Jacksonville. She and Jack had spent almost the last year of their residency together at this address when they were off duty from the hospital. Was the code that simple? The words 'my love' and '*hokkees*' rolled off of Bagdasarian's lips as easily as the phrase 'my friend'. But could he still be obsessed with her?

Kelly punched in the code and stepped backwards in surprise as the door to the second chamber opened expelling a blast of refrigerated air. The darkness within was impenetrable. Footsteps accelerated down the stairwell alerting her to imminent danger. She punched in 5817 again and the door to the second vault closed just in time for her to pivot towards a Middle Kingdom stella on the adjacent wall. Boerner and Lansky were an item. Boerner's dog held at least one code that belonged to Colonel Jack Bagdasarian, MD USAF, military attaché to the American Embassy in Cairo, Egypt. The knowledge that he had lied to her all along cut like a knife. Derek's instincts had been right all along. It was she who was blinded. Were other explanations possible? Maybe Boerner had the codes because she was planning on stealing from Jack. Kelly had been intimate with Jack for one very special year of her life and felt she knew him well. There was a fine line that even Jack wouldn't cross. At least she kept reassuring herself this was so.

Entering the vault, Bagdasarian smiled. "*Hokkees,* I'm sorry for my absence but it was a delicate matter of some urgency that could not wait. Dinner will be served momentarily on the veranda. Please allow me to escort you upstairs." He extended his arm and immediately noted the temperature difference between the front of the vault and the rear portion where Kelly stood. Somehow she had accessed the second vault. How much had she seen? His smile did not change as he took her arm directing her up the stairwell his teeth grinding with every step.

Drinks were continuously served with dinner. Each course

more exotic then the next and each course accompanied by a different wine from his private collection. The wines were truly magnificent. The effects of the alcoholic beverages accumulated, even though she had consciously attempted to limit her intake. Bagdasarian's maidservant appeared and disappeared in complete silence. As hard as Kelly tried to engage the woman in conversation, she was met with a blank stare. Kelly learned that this woman was of Arabic descent and had come to this country as Jack's personal maid from the 'old country'. "What are you two speaking?" Kelly asked. She had another sip of a special reserve Chardonnay.

"Copt," Bagdasarian replied, looking out the window to the ocean, lost in thought. "Ancient Egyptian if you will. It is nearly a lost art. Nowadays only priests and a few villagers from the desert towns speak that tongue. It's actually the language of my childhood." He felt miserable to the bottom of his soul but had to control any display of emotion.

The wine was going to her head. Ancient artifacts, treasures and secret vaults all jumbled in her head. If she didn't excuse herself soon, she'd never be able to contact Derek. She was past due for their nightly phone call. He had to know of her discovery, her confirmation of Jack's involvement at some level in this whole sordid affair. She'd let the detective sort out the truth. "Jack, dinner was lovely, but I must be going soon."

He had to try one last time. "Kelly, my love, do you ever think of me? I mean to say, do you ever think back to our time together and wish we could just pick up where we left off?" The only emotional vulnerability he had in this world sat by his side. The woman's face blurred with the chemicals clandestinely placed in the wine. "I know that I regret not having you in my life everyday."

Kelly swayed in her seat and shook her head to stay awake. She didn't have that much to drink, she thought. "Jack, you are so kind. I do love an Armenian with all my heart, but it is not you." Her words trailed off as she slumped forward onto the table.

He sat there blinded by fury, a gnawing pain in his chest. This woman held a key to his heart and she had thrown it away. He would never have her again, at least not of her own free will. Still he was never a man to give up. He nodded his head giving permission for his maid to move Kelly's obtunded form. "Gently, please," he said in Copt.

Fall River, Massachusetts
October 28th
3:30 p.m.

Dressed in her nurse's scrubs, stethoscope slung around her shoulder, Rhode Island hospital ID badge dangling from her front pocket. Betty Sherman looked her usual harried self. "Derek, you're such a doll for doing this," she said giving him a quick peck on the cheek. "Now remember, junior will be waiting at the rear of the school. You've got to go to the main office though to sign him out, first."

"I know, I know, Bett." It wasn't the first time he had played temporary chauffeur or nursemaid to his Godson. Al, senior, and his wife, Betty, worked opposite shifts. Sometimes mandatory overtime prevented one or the other from being able to pick up their son from school. That's where he came in.

"Ohhh, I'm so late they're going to kill me." She looked at her watch and hopped on one leg as she tried to squeeze her sneaker on her right foot. "And congratulations." The Shermans were one of the few couples who unflinchingly stood by his side the past four days. She grabbed her jacket and keys. "Tell Big Al the roast is in the fridge. All he has to do is heat it up in the microwave. Oh, and don't forget Cricket's doggy treats."

Embarrassed about the whole sordid affair, he mumbled an acknowledgement. The news of this afternoon's court proceedings had already spread. The Shermans had agreed to dog sit Cricket while he was in court. "Bye Bett," he called out to the blur of a figure flying out the door.

He grabbed the dog, tucking it under his arm, leaving the other one free to carry the bag of dog food, leash, and food bowls. Standing on its hind legs to look out the passenger window, the dog seemed genuinely happy to be with him. He pretended to do the speed limit on his way to pick up Al, junior. All wheel drive, all wheel steering, the turbo Galant VR4 purred up President Avenue.

Ten minutes later he was inside Hope Highland Middle School to pick up little Al. At fifteen years old, the boy was the oldest child in that system, but at least he was mainstreamed. The diagnosis of autism no longer carried the stigma of special education classes; but that trend in education was a mixed blessing. It wasn't easy being fifteen years old under any circumstance, particularly if your classmates were only eleven or twelve years old.

Derek produced his photo ID and logged in. The dour faced secretary, verifying his signature against the one on file, was no-nonsense. Security in the school was tighter then in the police department's evidence room. Al, Jr. greeted him with a hug as Derek assisted him with his school backpack and loaded him in the front seat with the dog. It was only a ten-minute ride back to the Shermans'; but Al, Jr, forced an hour's worth of Ninteno on him before he could head back to his own home.

Calls to Kelly's cell phone remained unanswered. They usually contacted each other at night when she was alone. Still he missed her terribly. Pulling into his driveway he recognized the nose of Nunez' Mazda RX-7 poking out of a side street. Next to this was Sherman's Dodge Caravan and right behind that, Derosiers beat up but fully functioning 1988 Subaru Legacy with its 250,000 original miles. Who had called this meeting to order, wondered Derek with a smile. It must have been a congratulation party. If Betty knew of his newfound freedom, then so did half of Fall River.

He stumbled several times walking up to his front walkway as Cricket weaved and bobbed between his legs. The screen door was open again. Which one of his jerky friends had forgotten to close it? They all knew how much leaving it open pissed him off. Sleeping with a mosquito buzzing in his ear was perhaps his least favorite way to spend an evening. Of course his friends could fault him for being too cheap to get the door fixed, but that was his business.

"Hey, Jerks!" Derek called out standing on the threshold. "Close the damn screen door!" The stupid dog, Kelly's betrothal gift, was barking nonstop. Is this what he had to look forward to until she returned? Maybe they left the door open on purpose. It could be a legitimate surprise party. For all he knew he was making an ass out of himself in front of a houseful of guests.

The temperamental door slammed behind him. Derek turned to the right. Except for his measly furniture, the living room was empty. He pivoted to the left flicking on the dining room lights. That room was empty as well. Shit! Nunez and Sherman were great ones for horseplay and practical jokes. How could he forget the stripper when the last promotion list came out? He wouldn't put it past either of the two men to try and humiliate him with something they would preserve on video for a later party. "Come on guys. If you're going to be jerks, I'm not in the mood."

Only the sound of his voice echoed in the house. Where were they? Not too many places to hide in a simple raised ranch. A knowing smile broke out on his face. Then he remembered. Between his trip to Florida with Kelly and his recent problems in court, their usual poker game had been preempted for the past two weeks. And poker was always played in his kitchen. Desrosiers would be half way through a bag of chips by now arguing with Nunez on matters of oral hygiene. He'd have to act surprised or he risked hurting their feelings. Cricket growled continuously as he crept up to the kitchen. The damn dog was going to give away his location. Next time he'd have to break in the dog easier with strangers.

Derek came up to the two swinging saloon doors that separated the kitchen from the dining room and gave them a quick shove. "Hey, guys..." he called. He stopped in mid sentence. The chair and table had both been overturned. Broken glass was everywhere. In the far corner Al Sherman sat on the floor, slumped over like a broken marionette. The police lieutenant was still in uniform. He had been shot at least once in the head. A pool of blood congealed by his side on the kitchen linoleum.

Instinct and training took over before the paralysis of fear. Derek hit the floor and rolled towards the center of the room. Broken glass fragments scraped his hands as the only reward for this maneuver. Reaching for his service revolver he remembered too late his primary and back up weapon were surrendered with his arrest over the weekend. The guns were still in the chief's safe. Sweat beaded on his forehead, his heart pounding clear through to his brain. Someone might still be in the house. He jumped up and grabbed the largest knife from his steak set sitting on the counter above his head and hit the floor again. This time he held his breath and just listened. The house was as dead as his friend.

Lying on the floor wasn't going to get him anywhere. Wiggling like a snake, he performed a quick belly crawl to Sherman's body and removed his dead friends gun out of the holster. It was a standard issue semiautomatic. The clip was full. Derek smelled the barrel. It hadn't been recently fired. He knew if he stayed on the floor he would only make an easier target. At least if he moved around the house he would have a better chance. With Sherman's gun in one hand and the serrated knife in the other Derek went from room to room looking for the intruders, crashing through each room of the house rolling on the floor with his gun arm extended to shoot anything that moved. It was only when he opened the door heading to the basement that he saw Rick and Steve's bodies at the bottom of the basement stairs. Both had been shot execution style in the head as well. Otherwise the house was empty.

Waves of nausea percolated, the impact of his friends' deaths slowly overwhelming him. His mind raced manic. His best friends were shot dead in his own house. Why? What was he going to say to Betty and Karen, their wives? And little Al, how would the boy understand? And Karen was pregnant. Stupid thoughts crossed his mind. Who would work Nunez' shifts at the hospital? Who was going to take care of A-hole, Nunez's dog? Insane thoughts began to manifest themselves as well. What was the name of the cleanup company the department used in similar situations? Would blood ever really come out of linoleum? And what if a bullet went through Al's head and struck the wall? Would he have to paint and plaster the whole kitchen or would a patch and a little Spackle do just fine?

He shook his head and returned to reality. Derek took his cell phone out and activated it. He dialed the station house directly. "Communications," he requested quietly. His breaths came in shutters as his voice shook. A rookie dispatcher answered. "This is Ekizian. Who's the sergeant on for tonight? Blackmore? Good. Put me through." He heard his voice echoing in his head, the words empty of emotion. Tears blurred his eyes. He attempted to wipe them away with his right wrist even as the gun lay glued to his fingers. If it had to be, he was glad Blackmore was on duty tonight. The man was a cop's cop, loyal to the blue uniform first and to whatever came next, second. Blackmore would make the coming nightmare of the preliminary investigation just a bit easier to survive.

Steve Blackmore got on the line. "Hey, Derek. Good going. We all knew you'd beat the rap," he said cheerfully. "I've got some...."

Derek stroked the head of the little Yorkie as he cut off his friend in mid sentence. "Steve, shut up God damn it and listen!" He could tell Blackmore was flustered by this sudden rudeness. "Send some units over to my house. There's been a shooting. Notify my office, too."

"Sure, Derek, sure," Blackmore answered somberly. "I'm calling dispatch now."

Derek moved outside to the front steps. The screen door was jammed open again but this time he didn't give a shit. He placed Sherman's gun on the concrete and sat with the dog on his lap, stroking it just behind the ear in a rhythmic pattern of man and dog through the ages. "Kelly," he commanded his cell phone. The phone rang a dozen times before he gave up and severed the call. The sounds of police sirens came closer.

Central Police Station, Fall River
October 28th
5 pm

They moved him from interrogation room to interrogation room as if anticipating a sudden inspiration or divine revelation. Perhaps the homicide detectives assigned to this case hoped to catch their fellow officer in an inconsistency or an outright lie. They checked the taxi schedule and the middle school sign out sheet, calculating the amount of time it would take him to drive back and forth, comparing that against the medical examiners preliminary time of death. State and local police measured trajectories, angles and calibers of the recovered bullets. He was with his attorney from when to when? What time did the clerk of courts log in the dismissal of all charges on the cocaine bust? The challenges to his honesty and integrity were non-stop.

The Chief made token appearances while Derek rotated between the informality of private offices to the stark gray of the interrogation room. Some voices oozed sympathy while others were loaded with innuendoes and blatant accusations. Fall River's most gruesome butchery since the days of Lizzie Borden and her famous ax occurred in the kitchen of one of the cities finest. Derek could only imagine the looks of his fellow police officers peering between the slits of the blinds to the office or through the one-way mirrors of the Quiet Room. How many were sympathetic and how many wanted nothing to do with him ever again. First the cocaine charges and now this. How many lives did he have?

Derek's eyes were red and bloodshot. Dark circles betrayed his fatigue. He had perhaps a handful of hours of sleep in the past four days. There were just too many things happening for him to close his eyes in peace and not end up awake, sitting bolt upright in a cold sweat. His movements were lethargic and responses to questions became dull – nothing was funny anymore. They read him his rights. No, he had no wish for a lawyer or for a Fraternal Order of Police monitor, he assured them. Yes, everyone in the city was a suspect including himself, but no, he was happy to learn, he was not under arrest, at least not at this time. Just don't leave town, they said.

Brain Tsang, lead investigator for the State police major crimes unit, asked the same question again. "Tell me what time you returned home this afternoon," he pushed. One of only a handful of Asians in the department, his aggressiveness characterized his career.

Tsang was violating his personal space - a standard technique for this type of investigation. Derek had previous occasions to break bread and spill a little beer with the state police officer. Tsang was always considered 'all right' and a 'stand up kind of guy' by the local cops in Fall River. Today, though, was a different matter. Derek knew the man was only doing his job but right now he hated the bastard – supercilious piece of shit that he was. "About five years ago, ass hole." He was just plain fed up. "What the fuck is wrong with you. Instead of crucifying me you guys should be out there trying to find out who did this to my friends!" Derek yelled. He was exhausted, but still feisty enough to enter into verbal combat, especially when his opponent was a bone fide shit head.

Joe Tondreau, the lead Fall River homicide detective on the case, put his hand on the State Policeman's shoulder and pulled him back away from his quarry. "Come on, Tsang, can't you see the man is beat? He's one of ours. Kick back a little and give him a break."

Tsang snorted in disgust. "It's because he's 'one of ours' that we have to take a hard line. If you think I'm hard wait until the Feds get their hands on him." He turned towards Derek. "They're already crawling in your house, photographing, fingerprinting sketching, interviewing neighbors and otherwise dismembering your house and your so-called life. They're going to make mince meat out of you by the time this is all over."

"Don't you mean chop suey?" Derek said sarcastically.

Tsang pivoted and came at Derek, fist clenched. Only Tondreau's presence kept the two men apart as he stood between them.

The Chief entered the room. At least ten years past retirement age, Wayne Shea was massive and still looked like he could bend steel with his bare hands. His presence was always intimidating. He had been watching all along. "O.K., boys. I think we've had enough for today."

Tsang dropped his arms by his side stepping back against the table. "I don't think so," he answered angrily. "I'm just getting warmed up."

"I said, you're done and you're done," the Chief replied simply. He never took crap from anyone. "Now wrap up your report, son, and move on." The State Police did have the authority, but there was no question who was the boss in this town.

Tsang closed his notebook and headed towards the door. "You'll be hearing from the Governor."

"I'm sure. Do what you gotta do but keep away from my man here." Both of the lead detectives left, leaving only Chief Shea and Derek in the room. The Chief turned off the microphone so they could talk privately then turned to his Detective. "Jesus, Ekizian you look terrible," he said resting his hand on the Detective's shoulder. He went to the corner coffee pot and poured a cup of coffee, black. "Here, drink this down nice and slow."

The paper cup was the cheap kind from some bargain outlet, standard department issue. It barely held the coffee in, never mind prevented scalding. Derek shifted it repeatedly between his hands to prevent them from getting burnt. The hot liquid singed his insides on the way down. Within a minute, the caffeine began to kick in. His eyes opened wider. His brain began to process information more clearly.

The Chief gave him a minute." Al was a friend of mine. The department will miss him."

Derek sat down, head cradled in his own hands. "He was a friend of mine, too."

The Chief let out a sigh. "I know son, I know." Little could be said to make either man at ease. "Let's look at this together, shall we? First the maggot thing. You go traipsing off to Florida on your own. Then the cocaine. Internal Affairs wants to know how a cop gets a quarter mil in a safety deposit box. And now this. You're up to your ass in alligators, son." Shea sat down next to Derek. "Did any of those boys ever mention anything to you suggesting they were in jeopardy or being threatened by anyone?"

Derek turned his head and looked his boss in the eyes. "Sherman was a lieutenant. He had a desk job. What could he have possibly done, pissed off a pencil? Nunez was a single guy who worked the ER. Steve Desrosiers was expecting a new baby. They were all princes. Absolutely the most honorable human beings, the nicest guys I ever knew."

Shea turned his back on Derek. "I know you were working some angles down south. I've got to assume your medical examiner friend was onto something. What's her name again?" the Chief asked having another senior moment.

"Gill, Kelly Gill," Derek answered, thinking about his love. He would try calling her again. It was imperative he reach her.

"If she was right with her conspiracy theory, then I've got to assume you did something to attract attention to yourselves?"

Derek didn't say a word. He just looked at the Chief and nodded silently. His boss sighed and leaned back in his chair taking in the details one by one, from a dog's locket to computer codes, bank routing numbers and Kelly's old residency friends. What Derek didn't mention was successfully hacking into Bagdasarian's computer. Was it fear of recrimination or the potential loss of his only ally?

The Chief stood up and paced the room. "You are on official leave, with pay of course. Trust no one. I want you to disappear but with a modicum of some common sense, too. Do not go back to your house under any circumstance. Besides, the state police will be sealing it for weeks, trust me." His voice broke into a whisper. "Son, who ever did this is still out there. It takes a very different kind of man to kill a cop. To kill a cop in uniform is even worse. If they had the balls enough to go inside a policeman's home, then there is no telling who they are or what they're going to do next. Protect yourself first. Together we're going to find them," the Chief said putting his arm around Derek's shoulder. "Come on back to my office. Let's get your weapons out of the safe and back into your hands. We're both going on a hunting trip."

Fall River, Massachusetts
October 28th
11 pm

Fatigue gnawed at his bones while he activated his cell phone. "Kelly," he said agitated. A dozen rings later he gave up keeping the phone on standby incase Kelly tried to call. Somehow Bagdasarian and Lansky were connected to the carnage in Fall River. He had to warn her. He hadn't come this far to lose the love of his life at the hands of some maniac.

Derek had no choice. Kelly was sitting in a den of thieves and murderers. They might turn on her next. Dialing directory assistance he was connected to the Monroe County Sheriff's office. He identified himself, requesting the night supervisor and waited. What could he tell them; that six people in New England were dead and maybe, just maybe, two local physicians, one a high-ranking USAF intelligence officer, were somehow involved? What proof did he have? Who could he trust? Half the Key West police force was probably in the pocket of his adversaries anyway. If the Florida folks checked his own credentials, they would discover he was a suspect.

A woman picked up the line on the transfer. "Jodie Lee, here. How can I help you?" she asked politely. Northern cops were always asking for favors when they found themselves in a jam down south. Someday she was going to get paid back for all the kids she got out of jail for underage drinking.

Derek hesitated then identified himself again. He briefly outlined his inability to contact a certain physician by the name of Kelly Gill for a medical emergency, keeping the conversation deliberately vague but using those key words that would engage an officer of the law to go above and beyond the usual call of duty – 'physician', 'medical emergency' and 'urgent message'. The Monroe County Sheriff became genuinely attentive with the mention of Lansky and Bagdasarian.

She was relieved the request had nothing to do with a juvenile delinquent. "I wouldn't worry about a thing, sir," she assured. The hour was late and she hated to wake anyone up. "I know those two gentlemen personally. If she is with them, then I'm sure she's in good hands. Can't this wait until the morning?" The Massachusetts detective would not let go, seemingly desperate in his tone. "Well, sir, if it makes you feel any better, I'll send out a couple of the boys to check things out." She was tired and cut his thanks short, promising to call him with any news.

Derek's exhaustion level was at critical. He could do no more at a distance of 1800 miles and desperately needed a place to crash for the night. Only one man in Fall River could help him now. Four men played poker at his house on Monday nights and now three of them were dead. There was only one friend left from his inner circle. It was past midnight when he knocked on the door of the mansion. He needed a place to stay and he could think of none better or safer then Bill Kasson's.

The Porsche was still in the driveway, Kasson rarely bothered to garage his vehicles. All his toys were expendable. Derek parked behind the sports car. He wasn't sure how much he'd be welcome, never mind if he came armed with a dog. Cricket was chomping at the bit to get out of the car. He opened the passenger door and watched the Yorkie jump out sniffing around in the grass. Three clockwise circles later the animal relieved itself on Kasson's blue fescue lawn and Derek tucked her into the backseat of his car, hopefully for the night. Now if only he could get the same opportunity.

Surprisingly Kasson answered the door himself, still wearing his trademark bow tie even at this hour. The angle of the man's nose accentuated his paper-thin lips giving him the look of a startled turtle when he saw Derek's face pressed against the screen door. "I thought...." Kasson croaked meekly.

"What?" Derek interrupted ducking beneath his friend's outstretched arm and into the wide planked oak hallway of the foyer. Kasson looked as if he had just seen a ghost. Derek had never seen the man frazzled, even when losing a sure hand at poker. "Aren't you glad to see me?"

"They said you were all dead," Kasson replied. He craned his skinny neck beyond the doorframe to see if anyone lurked in the shadows.

" 'They' were slightly misinformed. Enough chitchat. It's cold out here. Invite me in, God damn it. I need a safe place to sleep tonight." The request seemed to take his friend by surprise.

Kasson glanced furtively down the driveway, regaining his composure. "I'm sorry. Sure. Sure come on in." He took Derek's coat and hung it in the front closet.

Although poker buddies for years, Derek couldn't remember any invitation to socialize in the rich man's house. The insides were churchlike with flying buttresses, soaring ceilings, skylights and deep dark wood. Plush leather chairs inhabited the cavernous living room mimicking the layout and décor of Kasson's office at the bank. "Look, I hope you don't mind me asking, but I need a place to stay tonight. I haven't had a good night sleep in a light year. The Chief doesn't think I'm safe anywhere in town until this is over."

The bedroom levels were apparently forbidden to him. Kasson brought down sheets, blankets and a pillow to bunk on the couch in the living room. It was a peculiar kind of hospitality, but Derek was grateful for anyplace tonight. He had learned long ago not to judge others by his own values or expectations. Hillary, Kasson's bipolar wife, was nowhere to be found, apparently visiting her mother again. It was a very codependent relationship, assured Kasson vaguely starring into space. Derek thought of his own relationship with Kelly and prayed that he would never feel that way about his wife to be. God, he hoped she was all right. His cell phone was on continuously and still not a word from her. It would need recharging soon.

One question nagged at the back of his mind: "Bill, what were the guys doing at my house yesterday?" Everyone who played poker was there except for Kasson. "I thought you were all planning a congratulations celebration of some kind. Did anyone call you?" He looked Kasson in the eyes. Maybe it was the poor lighting, or the hour or his fatigue, but there was something unsettling in his friend's response.

"Geez, no Derek. Maybe the guys were planning something and tried to reach me, but honest to God, I never heard anything from anyone. Otherwise it could have been me laying on your kitchen floor, too."

Derek believed because he had to. It was a matter of survivor's guilt. If it weren't for the dog, or picking up little Al from school he might have walked into the same slaughter. "I know what you mean."

A telephone rang somewhere in the bowels of the house. Kasson excused himself momentarily then returned. His demeanor changed. His eyes looked like he did when he was one card away from a straight. "You know something, you're right. This will be perfect for you," he said confidently almost frothing with enthusiasm. "Stay here for as long as you want. No one ever stays here. Hillary will be gone for God knows how long. This would be the last place anyone would look if they wanted to find you. It'll be just fine."

"Thanks, pal," Derek said. Something felt not quite right. A cop's instincts are his primary weapon and often the edge he needs for survival. He was suddenly getting nervous and couldn't put his finger on the 'why'. "Look," he said to Kasson. "I've got to pick up a few things. I'll be back in a jiffy," he said excusing himself. There was something surreal about the whole scenario. Questions swirled in his head as driveway gravel crunched beneath his shoes. What was it the man said about the kitchen? He jingled the ignition key in his hand. This paranoia had to stop now, he thought turning the key. He didn't have too many friends left.

Key West
October 29th
1 a.m.

In Key West, sexual orientation defined the person. Captain Jodie Lee, fifty something and vertically challenged, was a police officer first and a lesbian second. The telephone of the AWOL doctor rang unanswered. The doc was probably just one of a legion of Yankees lost in a drug or booze haze. The last thing the Monroe County Sheriff's office needed was getting involved in any domestic dispute. This professional courtesy thing was a pain in the ass. Angrily she rose from her chair. Both of the other night shift officers were tied up with a boating accident in the harbor. If anyone was going to check out the Massachusetts detective's request, it was going to have to be her.

The name used as a reference point for her search was that of Colonel Jack Bagdasarian, MD USAF. That man kept a low profile in town, but everyone knew he was connected to intelligence agencies and big money concerns. Still, she thought, if the situation was reversed and she had called Boston looking for a favor cop-to-cop, she would hope someone there would pay attention to her concerns.

"Forward my calls," she ordered Robin, her sister's daughter and part time dispatcher. It was after midnight and things were just about percolating on the island. She reached for the leather holster and strapped it on her waist. The utility belt weighed in excess of ten pounds and there was no satisfactory position to attach the weapon without making her prominent hips more noticeable. It was just another cross she had to bear in this job: incompetent relatives and a fat butt.

Key West was surrounded by water. Problems had to come to her rather then the other way around; unless of course she had to make a trek up A1A to the upper Keys. The drive to the doctor's bungalow was a quick one. The cottage was off the party circuit in a quiet community of one hundred year old homes. Repeated knocks on the front door went unanswered. It was unlocked. She announced herself then entered cautiously. The bed was made up and had not been recently slept in. Several dishes remained unwashed from breakfast. She had one more stop to make before she could honestly say she had given the search for the doctor her best effort.

Returning to the cruiser she detoured to the wealthier side of the island. The large wrought iron security gates to Bagdasarian's mansion were open. A U-haul truck was parked at the top of the driveway, it's loading ramp extended to the mansion's front door. Good, she thought. At least she wouldn't be waking anyone up. Her cruiser's headlights caught the glimpse of the rear end of a Mitsubishi Eclipse convertible, just like the model the young female physician had rented. Bingo! Mystery solved and case closed. All she had to do was deliver the message and she could return to her office.

Jodie Lee exited her cruiser, adjusted the obnoxious holster on her hips, put on her hat over her butch haircut and walked up the front steps of the mansion. A woman was coming down the stairs carrying a large box that obstructed her view of anything except for the half a dozen on her right side. She had seen the woman in town before and recognized her as the household servant. Clearing her throat she announced herself. "Officer Lee to see Doctor Bagdasarian, please," she requested, removing her hat.

The maid reacted quickly but silently, placing her burden in the bowels of the U-haul truck and escorting the sheriff into the foyer.

A moment later Dr Bagdasarian entered, greeting her with a vigorous pump of her hand. "Jodie, so good to see you. What brings you around this evening?" he asked, his smile toothy and confident. There was a good foot difference between their heights.

"I'm sorry to disturb you at this time of night, sir," Jodie said. She was getting a pain in her neck as she looked up at the Colonel. More importantly she hated being called by her first name when she was on duty. "Our office received a call from a detective in Massachusetts. He wanted to pass on an urgent message to a Dr Kelly Gill. He sounded pretty desperate to reach her. Your name was mentioned. I told him I'd do my best to track Dr Gill down."

Bagdasarian grinned knowingly. "Of course I know the young woman, Jodie." He put his arm around the uniformed officer's shoulder and brought his voice down low and soft. "In fact, she's here as my house guest. I think she's going to switch boyfriends," he winked.

"That is her car then in your driveway?"

"Why, yes," Bagdasarian said distracted by a noise in the living room. "Can I get you something to drink?" he offered steering her in the opposite direction. The damn woman was taking her job too seriously. "You know I'd be happy to pass on any message you want."

Jodie maneuvered out of Bagdasarian's friendly grasp. "No thank you, sir. Would you mind terribly if I speak to her? Just to close my report out."

"Not at all." There was another series of noises coming from the living room and now both their eyes looked in that direction. "I think that she's indisposed at the moment; too much to drink in the hot Florida sun, I imagine. On second thought I promise to have her call you as soon as she recovers, so to speak." Bagdasarian twirled the ends of his mustache nervousnessly.

She really didn't give a rat's ass who the doctor was sleeping with but there was a job to do. A sudden loud crash echoed from the living room followed by a muted voice. Sliding past Bagdasarian she followed the noise. On the floor next to the maroon leather sofa was a disheveled young woman lying on her back, moaning imperceptibly. The Colonel pushed her aside as he rushed to the young woman's assistance. Helping her back on the couch, he mumbled something barely coherent about too much Key West cheer.

"I understand, sir," Jodie said. She had seen similar scenarios with adolescents and booze. It was just as embarrassing when an adult was involved. "When she wakes up, please have her call her office in Massachusetts and the police department in Fall River." She was about to withdraw from the room when she noticed that the woman on the couch was lying on both hands beneath her bum. That was peculiar. As she leaned forward for a closer look, the woman on the sofa turned to roll off again revealing a plastic cord binding the woman's hands. A grateful but desperate look exploded on the young woman's face followed by a look of terror as her eyes darted to something behind Jodie's field of vision. The shadow of another woman silently drew up behind the sheriff and ended her life with a quick circular slice around both jugulars. The Monroe County police Captain collapsed towards the floor.

Bagdasarian grabbed the dead woman's body under each arm before the impact and eased it into a sitting position next to the couch. The body had to stay upright no matter what. Otherwise the sensor on the sheriff's communicator would go off alerting the central dispatch in her office. As long as she stayed vertical, they had some time. "*Halthat drory,* was that really necessary?" he asked in an ancient tongue. Bagdasarian shook his head in frustration. Now his timetable had to be moved up. "We could have found another way."

His servant woman just looked at him, blankly, and starred.

"Go into the vault and bring up two bodies that will match, mine and Ms Gill's here," he said pointing to the girl. "We can leave the good Captain's body here. The explosion will make it all look like a tragic accident." He looked around his house with it's priceless collections. Inside he wept at the loss. But the certain knowledge of a greater reward when the jewels finally reached his hands gave him comfort. Most everything would have to remain. They had neither the time nor the space on the U-Haul truck to even make a dent in his collections. "Come, we must hurry."

Key West, Florida
October 29th
2 a.m.

Colonel Jack Bagdasarian, MD, USAF, hated change. The polished coral surface of the stairwell ran cool underneath his fingertips. Cold War paranoia built his Key West fortress. Covert operations helped pay the bills. It was only by chance he came across documents revealing these series of underground and underwater vaults that made this life possible. Power for the vaults came courtesy of the Naval base next door. Of course, they were totally ignorant of that fact. Now it was all coming to an end.

He entered the code to the second subterranean vault and watched the door slide open for perhaps the last time. The blast of refrigerated air that struck his face was cool and refreshing, originating in a series of heat exchangers that served his private morgue. Derelicts and an occasional runaway disappeared off the streets of Miami or the Keys with no one the wiser. Who would miss them? They were kept on ice and recycled as circumstances required. Clients with the proper financial resources could disappear with impunity and begin a new life. Pyramid Enterprise provided near identical body types to match whatever scenario required. In the aftermath of a perfectly calculated explosion or fire, only the sex and an approximate age was necessary to convince all but the most ardent medical examiner to sign off on a death certificate. It was, in of itself, a very lucrative business.

Years ago charges of C-4 and accelerants were strategically placed through out the main house in anticipation of tonight's activities. To have it all end this way was a shame. Bagdasarian waved his hand in front of a photo sensor on the interior wall of the second vault. The object in the center of the room was bathed in blue, red and gold florescent lights. It was spectacular. He had spent years accumulating each piece of the ancient double crown of his ancestors and now the crown of Upper and Lower Egypt lay almost complete. All that was missing were the two large jewel clusters representing the Eyes of Horus, the ancient falcon god, which flanked the central Cobra head.

His obsession began quite by accident. When his father died his inheritance included a portfolio of original drawings and letters from his great grandmother, Houri Abdul Rasoul. The legacy of the Abdul Rasouls and Bagdasarians tantalized him from the beginning.

It was in his nature to hunt and hunt he did. Relatives or collectors who made purchases for the Abdul Rasouls would get an offer they could not refuse, either one way or the other. Many times he would arrange a purchase. Other times, a reluctant owner would join the legions of those who disappeared in the normal course of his personal or professional occupation. The crown was his by primogeniture.

Time was short. The female sheriff's disappearance would not go unnoticed for long. Too many trails led to his home and to his person directly. It was time to move on. Gently he removed the crown from its rostrum wrapping it in felt, and then placing it in a Lands End backpack. Slinging it over his shoulder he sealed the vault. A hundred years from now the stainless steel chambers and his collection would still be there.

Bagdasarian's maid loaded the last box in the U-Haul. "Your command?" she asked her master in the language of the Copts.

Things were only getting more complicated. Bagdasarian reflected on his options. Years of loyalty were weighed against the need to begin a new life. It was this woman's foolish response to a temporary inconvenience that forced him into this hasty retreat. It wasn't in his nature to lose graciously. He had originally planned on leaving two bodies behind, one for himself and the other for Kelly. It was a shame to lose her. She did make the best *dolma* he ever had. As Shahin knelt over Kelly's moaning body, Bagdasarian reached around her neck and snapped it like a chicken. The motion was simple and well practiced. She crumpled instantly to the ground in a lifeless heap. Kelly was beginning to awaken and that would not do at all. Removing a prefilled syringe from his pocket, he injected a vein in her right forearm. She slumped backwards in a coma. Slinging her body over his shoulder he set the timer on the C-4 explosives and retreated from his Key West mansion for the last time.

Minutes later he drove the large U-Haul truck across the causeway out of Key West. A large explosion and a plume of white fire lit up the southern most sky of the island. Kelly was secure in the rear of the truck protected from all but the most serious jostling by layers of shipping blankets. Bagdasarian mentally reviewed the scene the investigators would find. Between the cordite and accelerants there would be little left for them to sort through. Four bodies would be found. Two stand-ins would represent Kelly and himself. Shahin, poor woman, would be there too. The unfortunate police Captain, officer Lee, would be found along with her police cruiser. Clean up would come from a foundation administered by trustees from the Cayman Islands. The property would be bulldozed only to ground level. The vaults would never be exposed. Taxes for the property had been escrowed for years in advance. The land would stand vacant forever.

Marathon Key
October 29th
4 am

They bypassed the main entrance of Marathon Airport by using the unmonitored security gate on the lagoon side of the runway. On one shoulder Bagdasarian clutched his backpack and on the other, the unconscious body of his old flame. The U-Haul was parked in an underground bunker a quarter of a mile north of the airport marked with the sign 'government reservation do not trespass'. At this hour not even maintenance personnel were around.

Opening the massive doors of the hanger one by one, it was all he could do not to drop Kelly as he pushed the sliding panels. She was a lightweight, but the inertia of the doors proved awkward considering he chose not to put either of his burdens down. Inside the hanger was cavernous and shrouded in darkness, his personal Cessna 185 Sky Wagon waiting. It was always fully fueled and ready to go on a moments notice.

Bagdasarian strapped Kelly in the copilot seat then moved to push the plane out of the hanger. It was a task he had performed solo many times before. His hands felt secure on the cool aluminum struts that supported the wings. The vibrations of the tail wheel bouncing on the concrete runway felt reassuring as he moved the craft. He climbed into the pilot seat and placed the charts on top of Kelly's lap. The key was under the seat as usual. He turned on the master switch and kept only the panel lights on. Even at this hour the less attention he drew, the better. Opening the throttle a quarter inch, he turned the key to start, holding the brakes with his toes as he hit the auxiliary fuel pump. He watched with satisfaction as the propeller torqued over a few times and sputtered until the engine finally caught.

This was a private strip, not a controlled airfield. Bagdasarian turned on the radio to Unicom 122.8 and began to monitor any conversation of incoming aircraft. It wouldn't do to be T-boned by another plane or careless air jockey on the runway. Slowly he taxied out to the run up area, then, holding the brakes with his feet, he advanced the throttle and felt the engine surge. The airplane pulled against the brakes begging to take to the air. He plantar flexed his feet, depressing the rudder pedals all the way and ran the engine to

1700 RPMs, checking the mags and cycling the prop. The tanks were full, the altimeter was correctly set and all the engine gages were in the green. Pulling back the throttle, he released the brakes and taxied out to the active runway. Reaching down between the seats, he pulled up two notches on the flap lever and released the emergency brakes.

Runway 15 lay ahead. He taxied out to line up with the runway while adjusting his head set and looked for any incoming traffic. Tapping the right brake, he pushed the right rudder pedal and swung the airplane into position. With one smooth motion, he advanced the throttle. The engine torque was so powerful that it pulled the aircraft. Bagdasarian maneuvered the right rudder pedal to prevent the plane from going left and felt the familiar and rewarding forward surge. The tail rose as he applied forward pressure on the control wheel, the plane rapidly achieving a climb rate of 1500 feet a minute. Slowly he retracted the flaps, came back on the power and the prop and established a cruise climb. Eight hundred feet off the tarmac he banked into a sharp left turn and headed north. It was time to begin a new life.

Lansky should have the package before noon and would be checking in as soon as the jewels were secure. But for now he had other things to worry about. Sounds of the prop and engine would alert everyone from a mile away a plane was taking off. Key West had many private aircraft that took advantage of the local airstrips for legitimate and sometimes illegal activities. No one would care unless the fire burned itself out prematurely and the truth of the bodies left behind came known. And that hadn't happened since he perfected his technique, so there was little need to fear.

Bagdasarian looked at the unconscious figure of the woman in the adjacent seat. Kelly was beautiful even after spending the last eight hours in a drug induced haze. Although she was with him involuntarily now, he still had secret hopes for her in his future. He recognized this unhealthy obsession, but first things first. He had a package to retrieve. Now it was up to Lansky.

Fall River, Massachusetts
October 29th
3 p.m.

Sea turtles make love in the undulating ocean. When the moon is full the female comes ashore to lay, on average, one hundred eggs. Sixty days later silver dollar sized hatchlings make their way back to the surface and crawl to the sea. Sixty days of sleep. Derek was jealous of any creature that had that luxury. He remembered watching Kelly's eyes while she lay on Matanzas beach identifying the creatures surrounding them.

Sleep was essential - somewhere safe, somewhere no one would look for him. He gave lectures at the academy on the unimaginable things sleep deprivation might make you do or say and now time was working against him. Derek had spent the last four hours parking on side streets or in playground driveways trying to sleep in his car only to invariably waken from a passing car headlight or a cramp in his neck. He had to find a real bed. He pinched and slapped himself repeatedly to stay awake, the windows of his car wide-open, stereo blasting to some obnoxious punk rock tune while he scrolled through the numbers on his cell phone.

"Hey, Paula, how ya' doin'?" Derek asked. There was dead silence at the other end.

Finally she spoke, her usual wisecracking effervescence absent. "Derek, is that you?" she asked cautiously. "Oh my God. Are you all right? We all heard about last night. That's all anyone is talking about. Where are you?" she babbled.

At least she could be trusted. "Yeah, darlin', I'm O.K." He had to get some sleep. He was way past overdrive and if he didn't pull over pretty soon he was going to crash his car and save a trigger man the trouble of having to hunt him down. "I've been driving around and around looking for a place to crash for a couple of hours. Look, I'm sorry for calling you so late, but I'm in a bad way. I was just wondering...."

What do you need, you big hairy Armenian? Anything. Just name it."

The lady was a bit crazy but at least she was genuine. Derek explained his predicament. He had to be honest with Paula. There was always the potential that he was being followed. She had to know that he might bring trouble. The mention of danger only aroused her. She loved anything that pushed her to the edge. All he wanted was some shut-eye, a few Z's, a siesta, a long slumber, to catch forty winks or he'd be worthless to himself, to the investigation and, most importantly, to Kelly.

He pulled in front of Paula's apartment complex like a drunk, nicking the curb and probably put a slice into the sidewall of his Pirelli tire. Patting the steering wheel in regret, he couldn't even focus on the digital clock on his dashboard, but the eastern horizon was beginning to lighten up. It must have been near dawn.

Paula's complex was a standard six or eight unit brick building constructed in the sixties. She was waiting for him at the front door in a bathrobe and curlers. Under any other circumstance the sight would have been comical but he used her help to get out of the car. "Paula, I've got to get some sleep. All I need is a few minutes."

Paula didn't hesitate. "Hey, big boy, come to mama. Follow me." She helped Derek stagger up her stairs, taking a good portion of his weight on her shoulders.

It had been just too many days without sleep. "All I need is a couple of hours," he mumbled collapsing on her bed, shoes and all. "Just lock the door and don't open it for anyone. Oh, and one more thing, babe. I've got this kind of friend in the front seat that's gonna need a little attention. If you don't mind, would you take her for a walk?" he said throwing Paula the keys to his car. Within seconds he was asleep.

Kelly's arms caressed his face as she softly called out his name. He dove under the water avoiding a shark fin. It would only be a matter of time before the attack. And an attack was coming for sure. Kelly was chum bait for a bigger score. Who threw her in the ocean? His eyes opened and tried to focus on the face above his. Hey, Kelly, when did you change your hair color? He looked again. Why, it wasn't Kelly at all. What did you do with Kelly? He reached up to touch her.

"Wake up, Derek. Wake up," Paula whispered softly. She put a wet washcloth on his face and shook his shoulders again.

Derek sat up on his elbows turning his head from side to side disoriented. The sensation was only momentary as he quickly recognized Paula's face. Then he remembered - everything.

"Come on you big hairy Armenian. Your beauty sleep is over. You've been out for over ten hours," Paula said shaking him again. "You're not going to catch anyone if all you do is stay in bed."

He looked around and sat bolt upright. How many hours did she say? He stood up and looked outside. It was light all right.

Children were playing on some swing sets behind the complex. School must have been out. It was probably late afternoon. He had lost track of time.

"I'm sorry Derek. I didn't have the heart to wake you. You were just dead to the world."

He had only wanted a couple of hours, but it looked like she had let him sleep all day. What's done is done. He probably needed it more then he knew. "O.K. I'm up, I'm up. No need to shout." The room smelled of perfume and skin-so-soft. The pillow, Paula's pillow, smelled all girl. He moved his head from side to side as he stretched, orienting himself to her bedroom, his eyes focusing on his host. She was dressed in her nurse's scrubs and her hair was straight. No more curlers thank God. Coffee. Lots of black coffee. The hell with the palpitations. He had to wake up quickly. Paula obliged his every whim. When this was over, he was going to have an ulcer the size of France. He stood up. "I owe you, big time, sister," he said kissing her on the cheek.

"Kelly is one lucky girl."

"What do you mean," he asked defensively. He didn't remember her name coming up in any conversation."

"Anyone ever tell you that you talk in your sleep?" The look on his face suggested he thought she was teasing again. "No, really," she reassured him, smiling the smile one woman gives a man when she realizes she has been bested by another contender. She blushed, probably for the first time in her adult life. "Come back safe," was all she could say, choking back a tear.

Fall River, Massachusetts
October 29th
4 p.m.

The turn of the century Victorian sat deep in the woods at the top of a circular driveway on the Dighton – Fall River boundary. Three and a half stories high of candy colored turrets, wooden shingles, and slate roof had enough history behind it to warrant several books from the historical association. Nunez joked there were so many rooms he could make love to seven different girls seven days a week and an eighth house guest would never know.

Derek pulled into the driveway. The brother he never had was gone. The sound of gravel popped against his wheel rims as he made the turn up the hill. It took several minutes before he had the emotional strength to step out of his car. He missed his friends terribly and Rick most of all. There would be no more stories of Castilian lisps, no more tales from the bowels of the emergency room, no more practical jokes, no one with whom to drink Port on a cold winter night.

Cricket jumped out of his car door as soon as he opened it and took off for somewhere in the yard. He let the dog go. No telling when it would get another chance of freedom. Slowly climbing the stairs to the stained glass front door, he listened for the familiar sounds of Nunez's jazz collection blaring from his surround sound stereo; but the house was silent. The key was under the front mat. Why anyone ever locked their doors when they hid a key in such an obvious hiding place was always amazing to him. Entering the house he turned on the lights. The place was neat as a pin. Derek instinctively pulled out his gun even though he knew the house was empty.

What did his friends say the night they hacked into Bagdasarian's private files? Something about downloading the entire hard drive of one computer into the other, then making copies of those files on CDs? This was not the time to be ignorant of the technology. He went to Rick's computer room hoping against hope that his friend had left clear instructions on how to access those records. All he found was an empty desk – no computer or discs. Now he knew for sure why his friends were killed.

Returning to the kitchen, he opened the refrigerator, took out a Coke and sat down on one of the massive iron chairs he had helped Rick pick out from Filenes last year. It was time to rethink. Again he was hours behind whoever did this. Something else was missing and he couldn't place exactly what it was. The silence in the house was ominous. Then he remembered why the quiet was so bothersome. Rick's dog, A-hole, was missing. The big loveable black Lab was always slobbering or trying to hump his leg. Now there was nothing, no whimpering, no sounds of nails on the wooden floors as the dog slid from a full gallop into a sudden stop. He put away his gun and went from room to room calling the dog's name.

Derek mentally retraced his friend's steps the day of the murder. Rick wouldn't have kept the dog inside if he were going to play poker or attend a party for the day. He must of anticipated being out late. Derek went out the back steps of the kitchen into the rear yard. A large immobile form lay at the end of stretched out dog chain. Cricket sat quietly next to the larger animal. The dog made a better detective then he did. Slowly he approached the animal on the ground and touched it's head. It was cold. Someone had shot the dog even though it posed no possible threat being that far from the house. Who hated dogs that much, wondered Derek pushing back the bitter taste of bile. The tool shed stood just behind the dog run. He selected a large shovel and a pair of his friend's work gloves. How many times had he given Rick a hand with some manual labor and worn these same gloves? The earth was rich and black as he turned over the dirt. He was surprised the local population of wild animals hadn't already begun to dismember the dog's body. He would make sure they never got the chance. Thirty minutes later he gave the dog it's final resting place, picked up Cricket and carried her back to the car.

Al's house was next. He needed courage to face Betty and the boy. Perhaps if he called them first it would warn them he was on his way. The message box on Rick's portable phone on the kitchen wall flashed with the number six. It was just outside the boundaries of ghoulish to pry into the life of a recently dead friend, but Derek was also a police officer. This was routine in any investigation. Message number three was the one that took him by surprise. The answering machine had apparently kicked in after the fourth ring and then Rick had picked it up. The conversation was recorded. It was Bill Kasson's voice on the other end inviting Rick to a surprise poker party in honor of the recent dismissal of all charges against Derek. Why did the man lie to him last night? Bristling with questions, Derek locked the door of Nunez's home and began the drive to the Shermans.

A blue Mercedes 190 lurked in his rear view mirror. Or did it?

It could have been his imagination but he wasn't prepared to risk a confrontation; at least not yet. Several last second weaves and turns and the Mercedes disappeared from sight. He gave the Mercedes no further thought as he worked his way from the outskirts of the city across the Taunton River to Al Sherman's home in Somerset. Several patrol cars were parked in front of the modest colonial, men on duty undoubtedly paying their respects. He parked just out of sight of the house waiting for a bit of privacy. It wasn't long before the patrol cars left. Shift change was coming up. He left his car, cringing with each step up the small walkway. How many times had he come for a party, a christening, or just to baby sit? He was ultimately responsible for everything that happened to his three friends. And now he wasn't just going to pay his respects he was looking to retrieve a package. What balls!

Al's wife, Betty, was alone in the house when he rang the front doorbell. It was the first time in years he just hadn't knocked and barged right in. Even in grief she was beautiful. Starring at him across the screen door, the look on her face was a mixture of surprise and anguish. She stepped back from the door without opening it, turning away without a word.

The moment was awkward and he wasn't sure what the proper thing was to do. Derek let himself in following her into the living room. "I'm so sorry, Bett," he said. Her back was still turned towards him as if he didn't exist, the sounds of her crying muted. His words came out stiff and self-conscious. He needed absolution and she was the only one who could give it. The clock on the mantle ticked for the most uncomfortable minute of full silence in his life.

Without a warning Betty pivoted and slapped him full in the face. "You! It's all your fault!" she spit vehemently. Her face was filled with rage, her eyes widening with hatred. Slowly one hand then another pounded him on his chest in windmill repetition, each swing picking up speed but lessening in physical intensity until she was exhausted. "I hate you, I hate you, I hate you," she screamed, the words slurring into her river of emotions. Then, just as suddenly as she attacked, she collapsed in Derek's arms, sobbing uncontrollably. "Why, why, why?" she kept repeating, her words and body shaking as she held onto him for dear life.

Time stopped. When it resumed they were family once again. "I wish I knew, Betty. God, I wish I knew," he lied. There were tears on his face as well. He did know why. He just couldn't tell her the truth, at least not yet.

She pulled back and wiped her face. The man in front of her

felt as badly as she did. She was ashamed for being so unfair to him. "God, you look awful," she said patting down her dress and tying back her hair.

"You don't look so great yourself," he teased back somberly. "How are the children?"

Betty became silent again as she took a deep breath. "As best as can be expected. Carrie understands more at age nine then her brother does at age fifteen."

There was no time for beating around the bush. "Look Bett— I can't stay. The folks who did this are still out there. I've got to find them. I'm looking for something Al may have left for me. A package, a letter, perhaps a manila envelope—something large enough to hold a couple of compact computer discs."

"You want me to look for a package now?" she asked incredulously.

"Believe me, I wouldn't ask unless I thought it was important. It may have something to do with the murders," Derek pressed.

Betty searched her memory. Too much had happened in the past few days. The terrible phone call from the Chief, going to the morgue to identify her husband's body, the phone calls, the children —it all swirled in a jumbled mess inside her head. Everything seemed to be hazy, in a fog just outside reality. Her eyes suddenly lit up. "In fact Al did give me a couple of CDs a few days ago. Said that someone at work made a copy of some of his favorite songs. It did seem odd at the time because it's something he never would do. He's so tight assed about breaking any law, you know. He was always afraid the copyright police would find out and turn him in. Could that be what you are talking about?" she asked proudly.

"It's got to be. Can I have them please?"

Betty went to the stereo unit right behind Derek. She flipped through the stack until she found the CDs in question, then removed them from the pile of Country Classics and Nineteen sixties Motown. They stared at it each from their own perspective. What she held in her hands represented both life and death. "Was this worth his life?" she asked.

"That's what I need to find out." The hardest question of all remained. "Where's little Al?"

"What's he got to do with this?" Betty asked defensively.

"Your husband knew I was computer stupid when he made up these copies. He told me he locked them with a code only your son would know. If I'm going to get to the bottom of this, I'm going to need his help to sort through the files." He could see Betty's reluctance. "Believe me, Bett. If there were any other way, I'd do it. Please, where is little Al?"

Betty knew he was telling the truth. She let out a deep sigh. "The kids are at my sister's. Please be gentle with him. This has really hit him hard. He doesn't understand why his father isn't coming home anymore. Goddamn the autism! Jesus, Derek what am I going to do?" She collapsed on the couch, holding her head with both hands fighting back the tears again.

Derek never felt so helpless. Dropping down on his knees beside the couch, he stroked her head sympathetically. "One thing at a time. I want you to go to your sister's house, too. Get out of town until the dust settles." He stood up to leave, the critical package in his hand.

"Promise you'll get these bastards, who ever they are," she pleaded.

"I'll do my best, Bett. I promise," he said, kissing her on the forehead. Derek had one more question before he left. "By the way, Betty, did Al get any phone calls from Bill Kasson before he left for my place?"

Betty smiled. "I'm sure he did. Bill was always so concerned about you when you had that problem at the airport. He would call most every day checking on you to make sure you were all right. He's a wonderful friend to you all. I'm sure he tried to do everything in his power to help you when you were in trouble."

I'm sure he did, thought Derek. He turned and left.

Fall River, Massachusetts
October 29th
5 p.m.

Derek had met Sherman's brother-in-law only once and that was during little Al's christening years ago. Jim Lewis was a physician's assistant at Hatfield Memorial. Tall and very Irish, Lewis was bald with a crown of curly white hair that blended into a Santa Claus beard. He always had a smile for everyone within fifty feet. His wife, Barbara, was rollie-pollie and at least ten years younger. Her career was trying to get pregnant.

Lewis greeted Derek at the partially opened front door, a hunting rifle in his hand. "Can't be too careful," he said, releasing a series of chains letting in the detective.

On one hand Derek was happy that the boy was with Jim Lewis. He was an ex grunt who worked his way up from corpsman to physician's assistant the hard way. At least the man knew how to use the weapon if necessary. Carrie, Al junior's sister watched TV while her brother played a game of fish at the kitchen table with his aunt.

Derek needed to access the data on the computer discs. Betty Sherman had apparently called ahead alerting her sister to his request. "Come on, honey," Barbara said to her nephew. "Let's play on the computer for awhile with Uncle Derek." She turned towards the detective, "If he wants to stop, you stop," satisfied with his nod in the affirmative.

The boy greeted Derek with an affectionate hug. "Hi, Uncle Derek. What game do you want to play? "

Derek handed his godson the two computer discs. "We're going on a treasure hunt. Let's see if you can find the secret codes so we can get the bad guys."

Al junior was enthusiastic. His Uncle Jim's computer was newer then the one in his bedroom at home. As they waited for the computer to warm up, the boy turned and looked at Derek perplexed. "Mom says Dad isn't coming home anymore. She said bad people hurt him. Why?" he asked tearless.

Derek looked into the eyes of the man-child who would never grow up. The look on the boy's face was devastating. There were no tears or sadness, just a vacancy that betrayed his underlying illness.

Al junior was retreating into dark places known only to him. "I don't know. I wish I did," Derek replied. "The world is full of good and bad people. Sometimes the bad ones hurt us."

"How come you didn't stop them?" Al junior asked, typing in a computer command.

Barbara and Jim looked at him and waited for his response. Everyone suspected he was somehow at fault.

"I wasn't there. Otherwise, I would have done my best to protect your dad and my other friends." His last words were lost in a series of musical notes from Windows.

The boy sat down at the desk and took on the persona of an adult. "O.K., I'm ready."

The screen went blank as he loaded the discs. "Oh, oh. We're in trouble."

Derek put one hand on Al junior's shoulder turning his godson's face towards him. "Your dad told me that you would be the only one who would know how to open the files. There's a lockout code he put in only you would know."

Al, junior, looked at him puzzled and then smiled. "I know! Dragon Ball Z, my favorite show!" he said. He entered the code and Bagdasarian's files opened. "Where should we go first?"

Derek had to readjust his thinking. The discs were a snapshot of Bagdasarian's hard drive. It would take the experience of a computer forensic specialist to dissect all the files. He didn't have the time. Where to go first, he thought. His fingers moved the mouse across the screen searching for a place to begin. What he wanted was names and addresses. "Outlook Express," he ordered. It was the equivalent of a phone book.

The file was opened. Inside were the names, addresses and phone numbers of over one hundred individuals important enough to reside in Bagdasarian's electronic world. Many of the names were of foreign origin with overseas addresses such as Syria, Egypt, Jordan and Israel. He needed something closer to home. Something or someone he could investigate in the States. He scanned the files for anything with a local connection, searching for the 617, 508, 781 or 978 area code prefix of the metro Boston area.

Then he found one. The name, Bill Kasson, caught in his throat as he read the phone number and address he knew by heart. The significance was immediate. It was time to move to a more implicating area on the hard drive - Quicken with all Bagdasarian's financial records. They needed another password to gain access to the accounts.

"What do I do now, Uncle Derek?" Al junior asked.

The boy's face was a spitting image of his father. Derek had not come this far to be stonewalled. The information he just unveiled about Kasson was enough to tie the two men together. But he wanted more. He needed more. He recalled the jeweled locket on Boerner's dog. "Try 5817," he suggested.

Al junior, punched in the numbers. Access was denied.

Where was Rick, Steve or Al, senior, when you needed them? Thinking about his friends made him angrier. He thought of the other side of the locket. Most people used the same code for their computers and home security systems probably just out of laziness. He knew he did. It couldn't have been that easy, could it? "Try YOGIP61."

"We're in, we're in!" Al junior said jumping up and down in his seat.

In front of him was a log of the financial comings and goings of each calendar year. Derek used Quicken for his own financial records, so he was comfortable moving in and out of the flow sheets. Bagdasarian was very meticulous. Only one account was listed and it held transactions for the last three years. He ignored those mundane categories such as electricity and gas bills. Derek was after bigger fish. Bagdasarian had specific categories for wire transfers and deposits. Names followed route numbers in the 'memo' section. Derek smiled - this was it! His prey was obsessive compulsive and that was going to be his ruination. Derek scanned for one specific routing number that matched the paper he had originally copied off of Bagdasarian's desk. He found the transfers without difficulty. Every entry was listed as going into Kasson's account. A quick mental addition of the amounts transferred to Kasson in the past month alone was over three million dollars.

More important then the numbers involved was the 'memo' section next to each entry. Derek read a summary of names that read like a who-done-it from a dime store mystery book. The names of Furtado and Boerner appeared two weeks before the bodies were discovered. The sum of one million dollars alone was posted along side that entry. His own name appeared twice. The first time on the day he returned from Key West on the day he was arrested for cocaine. A figure of a hundred thousand dollars was logged in. Another transaction was listed for two hundred and fifty thousand dollars. He could only assume that money was transferred to a safety deposit box currently waiting for Internal Affairs. His name appeared one more time. This entry was along side the names of

Al, Rick and Steve and dated two days before the attack on his home. He and the boys were apparently worth one million dollars.

His mind raced with possibilities. Hatred and pure blind fury percolated in his veins. A dead girl from Florida, green bottle flies, millions and millions of dollars swirling in the electronic air of the Ethernet all to a little known bank in Fall River. He could see the blood smeared bodies of his friends lying in his own home. And Kelly, what about Kelly? He couldn't reach her. She was alone in the Keys with those slimy bastards. Derek's fists clenched. All he could see in front of him was Bagdasarian's face, his red mustache and sneer. Reflexively, he punched the computer monitor, shattering it in a million pieces. He hit it again and again and again in rage until the pressure of Jim Lewis' hand restrained him.

Al junior, was crying and probably scared to death at his uncle's display of violence. Derek looked up at Jim and Barbara embarrassed at his loss of control. There were cuts on his hand that needed attention. He flexed his fingers. Everything worked.

"Here, let me take a look at that," Jim said, leading him away from the ruins of his computer monitor.

"Forget it," Derek growled pushing back his chair. All he needed to know was whether he could hold a gun.

Fall River, Massachusetts
October 29th
8 pm

He cradled the cell phone against his chin while driving down Robeson Street. "Kelly," Derek commanded. He repeated the call four times, ignoring the standard 'no one home' or 'not available' message from the wireless carrier before he gave up. Opening his wallet he pulled out Bagdasarian's personal card. If he called, the bastard would be warned, but he had no choice. Kelly had to know the truth about her old boyfriend. Dialing the number on the card to Bagdasarian's home he got an automatic response - 'the number you have dialed is temporarily out of service. No further information is available at this time.'

The Monroe County Sheriff's department was his last option. Waiting to be connected he caught a glimpse of a blue Mercedes 190 in his rear view mirror. This time he was ready. He was tired of being the prey. From now on he was going to be the hunter. Derek removed his semi-automatic from its holster and placed it on his lap with one hand and executed a one hundred and eighty degree turn with the other. The VR-4, with it's all wheel steering and all wheel drive, responded perfectly to the maneuver. This time it was the Mercedes turn to disappear. A cavalcade of cars honked him angrily for this cowboy stunt, several drivers flipping him the middle finger. The possibility of becoming a trigger happy paranoid was looming more real every minute. He dwelled on this for a moment when his call to Florida came through. Derek pulled off onto a side street and identified himself to the Florida communications officer. Asking to speak to Captain Jodie Lee he was placed on hold.

A minute later a male voice picked up the phone. "John Ortiz, Florida State Police," he said simply. "What's your business with Captain Lee?"

Derek outlined the urgent need to find Kelly and the probability that a warrant would be issued for the arrest of Jack Bagdasarian and Jerry Lansky, both on state and federal charges for murder and racketeering.

"You're a bit late, friend," Ortiz said. "There was an explosion at Dr Bagdasarian's estate late last night. Looks like a leak in the gas main. Our dogs came up with four bodies, all pretty badly burned up. Captain Lee was one for sure. Three are waitin' at the medical examiners. We're pretty sure one's gonna be claimed by the Air Force and the other's gonna be his maid. We were wondering who the last woman was. Do me a favor and fax down some dental records on Gill." He rambled a series of numbers believing Derek was copying them down as he spoke. "We need to notify next of kin so we can release the body. Ain't a pretty sight, though. If someone comes for her they'd better have a strong stomach. You know how they look after somethin' like that. Sort of barbequed and all."

Derek's universe collapsed. He ended the call without acknowledging the State Trooper. His blood lust for Bagdasarian was over. He grabbed both sides of his steering wheel and just squeezed, his head slumping forward against his hands, fighting back the tears. To mourn and to grieve openly was unmanly. Choking back sobs, he fought the primal urge to scream or howl at the moon, those feelings burrowing deeper in his soul with every heartbeat. He would never love like this again. Derek sat frozen in his grief. Grief slowly morphed into hatred and seething anger. He could choose to live or die. Neither was an option until he paid one last visit to the remaining loose end.

It was a short drive to the Highlands, the rich part of town. "Hey bud, what's for dinner?" Derek asked, working his way past Kasson's slack jaw at the front door. Bet you didn't expect to see me you slimy bastard, he thought.

Kasson recovered from the surprise of seeing his friend again. "Derek! Thank God you're all right. When you disappeared last night I was worried sick about you."

"Had some last minute business. Can't be too careful these days, can I," Derek said taking off his jacket and slinging it on the back of the kitchen chair. His service weapon was now exposed in his shoulder holster. "Where's the beer?"

"Beer?" Kasson asked hesitantly, surprised at the request. He starred uncomfortably at the weapon. "Sure, one beer comin' right up." He went to the refrigerator and handed Derek a Molson. He noticed the recently bandaged right hand as the man put the bottle to his lips. "What's the story with your hand?" he asked politely. "Wasn't that way yesterday."

Derek took a swig and grabbed a handful of salted cashews that were already on the counter top. "This?" he asked looking at the blood stained bandages. "Aw, it's nothing. A little confrontation with a computer monitor, that's all." He looked around the couple of rooms within visual sight. "Any one else here?" he asked cautiously.

"Hillary is still gone. Housekeeper's gone. Only you and me, bud," Kasson replied leaning against the granite of the kitchen island. The first bottle was almost empty. He got up and brought a second bottle to his guest. He noticed an undercurrent of agitation in Derek's demeanor. "Mind if I make a phone call? Got some quick business myself."

"No problem," Derek said. He was in the middle of building a quick sandwich assembled without permission from Kasson's refrigerator. He was famished. Coffee could only go so far. Laying mayo, black forest ham and American cheese between two pieces of rye bread, he took a bite the size of Rhode Island out of the middle.

Kasson returned, this time with an open smile. "I'm done for the evening. Everyone else can wait for business hours in the morning. I promise no further interruptions all night. I'm even turning off my damn cell phone. Sometimes I think we're all slaves to technology," Kasson said, throwing the phone on the kitchen table.

"Yeah. I know what you mean. Thanks." His last few words came out sideways in between bites. "Hey, how about a hand or two of poker? We've got nothing else to do tonight. Say it's for old times sake in honor of our friends."

Kasson shook his head in amazement. Yesterday the man was dying for sleep and mired in grief for his poker pals. Today he wants to play cards. What the hell, the books said everyone grieved differently. "Poker? Now? Why the hell not," Kasson replied reaching for a deck on the top shelf. "I don't mind taking your money, and it certainly beats crying in our beers."

"We certainly wouldn't want to do that," Derek said sarcastically. "Table stakes, right?" His hands were itching to draw his weapon and just shoot the bastard where he stood. He let Kasson win the first two hands outright. By the third hand Kasson's play became a bit sloppy, the man's eyes darting around the room nervously with every sound or creak in the empty mansion. Kasson showed a pair of Aces. "I'll raise you a sand dollar," Derek said. He took his betrothal gift from Kelly, a little gold plated sand dollar off his key chain and threw it on the table.

"Hey, what's this? Only coin of the realm at this table," Kasson snorted in contempt. He fanned out a roll of twenty-dollar bills. "Like this, see."

Derek could barely contain his furry. He had been playing with this fool long enough. "Fuck your rules!" Derek said, holding up the small Florida souvenir to the light. He rotated it several times in his fingers as if he expected it to grow.

Kasson stared at him in disbelief. No one talked to him this way except his father-in-law. The only reason the old man got away with it was because he owned the bank. "What? You drunk or something?" he asked angrily.

"Humor me," Derek insisted.

It was a not-so-friendly challenge, thought Kasson. He lit a cigar knowing full well how much his guest hated cigarette smoke in general and cigar smoke in particular. "Fine. Let's make this interesting. What are the stakes?"

Derek paused. He reached behind his back and looked in his wallet as if checking on available funds. He returned the billfold and looked Kasson straight on. "Your life," he said simply.

The cigar almost dropped out of Kasson's mouth. "Are you out of your fuckin' mind? What's gotten into you tonight? I know you've been through a lot lately, but that is no excuse to treat me like this," he protested getting up to leave.

"Sit down!" Derek commanded his face flushed with anger. The man in front of him, the man who he once considered a friend, the man who controlled half the city was speechless and meekly sat down.

"Are you going to tell me what this is all about?" Kasson asked picking up his cards.

"Murder, conspiracy to commit murder, money laundering – do you want me to continue?" Derek answered.

"And who is it I am supposed to have killed?" Kasson said cautiously. "One card please." He didn't look his accuser in the eye.

"Carl Furtado, his teenage lackey, Hector Riviera and one girl by the name of Carol Boerner. And I mustn't forget Al, Steve or Rick you piece of shit." Derek gave him one card.

"You're nuts! Everyone knows Furtado did those murders last month. While you're at it, why don't you blame me for the Kennedy assignation, too. You've gone too far, this time buddy. I hear your name is first up on the very short list of suspects for the murders at your house. That's right, you," Kasson said focusing on Derek's eyes.

"Interesting," Derek replied coyly. "I've got your voice on Nunez' tape telling him to meet you at my house for a surprise. Betty Sherman said you called Al every day since I came back from the Keys." He watched Kasson's face scrunch up with the first lie. "I've got a million reasons you killed those folks. In fact, I've got three million reasons. Care to take my marker?" Derek pushed a piece of paper across the table.

Kasson read the numbers and paled. "Where did you get this?" he croaked, recognizing the routing number from the Cayman Islands to his bank in Fall River.

"That's not important. What matters is that I have the accounts and I have the codes and I have you." Derek let the words sink in with pleasure. "You, my former friend, are responsible for killing at least six people that I know about in the past two months alone. I don't know if you pulled the trigger or not, but you killed them all the same. How many others, I wonder."

"You're crazy. We've both been under a lot of strain the past few days. We've lost our friends. Go to bed now and I'll forget this whole thing ever took place," Kasson said getting up off his chair.

Derek pulled out his carry piece, a .45 automatic, from his shoulder holster and leveled it at his old friend. The arch of his hand was slow and deliberate. "Move and I'll blow your balls off where you stand," Derek said, his voice rising to a crescendo. The time for dancing with this piece of subhuman scum was over. "You killed my friends, you bastard. I want to know why!" He looked only at Kasson's eyes. It was the only way he could ever read the man.

Bill Kasson gently eased himself into his seat making sure he made no sudden movements. He didn't want to set the detective off any more then he had to. "Look, you're obviously disturbed. I mean that in a medical way, Derek. Let me call someone for you." He slowly reached for the cell phone on the table. "You need help."

Derek looked at Kasson and smiled. The man in front of him trembled and quivered like a rat caught out in the open. Fall River's moneyman exuded evil, particularly when he was afraid. The detective hated the man's beady eyes, the angle of his nose, the bulging Adams apple, the way his neck veins stood out. He even hated the air the man breathed. He thought of Kelly and what could have been. He took two cigarette stubs from the rich man's ashtray and methodically put one filter in each of his own ears. It was a trick he remembered from his days in the service. To Kasson he probably looked bizarre, but there was a method to his madness

"Hey, what are you doing now?" Kasson asked staring at this new apparition. "Now I know you're crazy for sure. You look like a fuckin' idiot," he laughed uncontrollably.

The words sounded muffled through the homemade earplugs. I'm an idiot? Ha! Derek calmly and deliberately moved his weapon to the right and fired one round into Kasson's left foot. The man fell to the floor screaming in pain. The noise from the gun's discharge echoed like thunder within the walls of the house and it's cathedral like ceiling. At that range the round penetrated the foot and cracked the Italian floor tiles beneath. Kasson didn't know whether to grab his ears or his bloodied foot. The pain was the same for both.

"You shot me! I can't believe you shot me!" he raged, a trickle of blood pooling out of his right ear.

Derek looked curiously at the damage wrought by his hands. He had never shot anyone before in all his years in the military or police. Blood now seeped from both Kasson's ears. Probably a small rupture in the eardrums, reflected Derek. He had seen that before when folks got careless around guns and discharged them inside without proper precautions. Blood was squirting from the man's foot as well. Derek watched Kasson agonize on the floor, smiling at his pain. It was a small payback for the loss of Kelly and his friends. Under any other circumstance he would have been ashamed at the satisfaction he received from watching the other man's suffering, but not today.

Shaking his head in surreal disbelief at the entire scenario, Derek took a swig of his Molson Ice. The beer had gotten warm and flat. At least he had Kasson's full attention. "Massachusetts doesn't have a death penalty for capital offenses, you know. The Boerner girl was abducted in Boston. I think they call that kidnapping. And a murder committed during a kidnapping carries Federal penalties. The death penalty, to be exact, I believe. I know you don't have the brains or balls to have murdered my friends by yourself, particularly Al Sherman. Derek thought about his friends and his resolve grew. I'm going to count to three and then I'm going to shoot you in the other foot; unless, of course, you tell me who was the triggerman on that job. One way or the other you're going to pay for the lives you took. Talk to me now, you bastard. I have no hesitation in neutering you on the spot if I have to."

The fear, pain and terror in Kasson's eyes suddenly evaporated. Looking past Derek's shoulder, he stopped screaming and broke out in one of his trademark sardonic smiles.

Derek felt the cold steel of a gun barrel against the back of his neck. The trick with the cigarette stubs had protected his ears from the shock waves of his weapon's discharge. It also made him oblivious to the more subtle noises around him. This was sheer carelessness on his part and it would cost him dearly. His ego made him go to Kasson's without backup. Now he was going to pay.

Fall River, Massachusetts
October 29th
8 pm

"Drop the gun and don't move."

The voice was familiar. "Lansky?" He was wondering where that piece of shit was all this time. The man's name never came up in conversation with the Florida Trooper when bodies were being counted from the rubble. "So, you're the other half of this enterprise." Carelessly dropping his gun on the floor, he half hoped the impact would discharge a round and kill someone. Nothing happened. No such luck tonight.

"None of your fuckin' business. Now your back up weapon, too. Reach down nice and slow like a good little boy. Yeah, that's it." Lansky kept the barrel of his gun glued to the back of the detective's neck the entire time. "Good, now lock your hands behind your neck and kneel." He slowly reached down and picked up both weapons. One he placed in his belt, the other in his empty hand.

Derek did as he was ordered. He had no choice. Escape was impossible.

Kasson rose off the floor, livid. "Take him in the back and do him," he screamed, punching Derek once in the side of the head. The banker was feeble, but it was enough of a blow to knock Derek down off his knees. He kicked the detective once to the face with his good foot snapping Derek's head to the right, causing a small trickle of blood from his nose.

"Is that the best you can do, you fuckin' girl?" Derek grunted between waves of pain.

The banker was foaming at the mouth. "I'm fed up with his constant interference. Drop him into the cesspool with Hillary that bitch! No, give me a gun. I'm going to shoot him in the foot first. Shoot him in both feet. Make that son of a bitch suffer!" Kasson's neck veins bulged volcanically the longer his tirade continued.

Lansky stood there and smiled, enjoying the show. "So, this is how friends play together?" he smirked. "Too bad I never got to see you guys play poker."

Derek lunged towards his tormentor from the floor, receiving another effeminate blow to his face from Kasson. He wiped the blood from his nose and face with his right sleeve. "Just tell me why. I want to know why before I die," Derek said.

Kasson leered. "It's all about money, ass hole. The boys here found me when I was in need. Hillary is a fat pig. My father-in-law is a demanding prick. But neither of those fuckers can bother me again, ever. The casinos at Foxwoods are unforgiving when you lose. Even occasionally requisitioning funds from the old man's bank wasn't enough to sustain my entertainment needs. I was fed up with kissing ass. All these folks wanted was a little sanitizing and suddenly I had my own source of income. Do you have any idea how much money is involved when your cut is ten percent of everything that flows through your fingers?"

Lansky cuffed his captive behind the ear with a glancing blow from the gun. "Come on. Get up. Let's get this over with," he said leading his captive out the back door.

"What did Furtado have to do with this?" Derek asked getting another shove in the small of his back.

"He was my heavy, my enforcer whenever I needed something. Even I need protection now and then. Shit, he'd scare the devil himself sometimes," Kasson spewed, limping after Derek and snapping at the detective's heels like a junkyard dog. He led the way to the cesspool. Kasson pried off the cover with a crowbar. The reek of fermenting human waste choked the air.

"Did he get too close at the wrong time?" Derek asked as Lansky kicked him behind the knees dropping him to the ground in front of the tomb.

"Yeah. Started to ask questions about the operation. Kind of like you. He got cocky and wanted a piece of the action. So we just decided to kill two birds with one stone. My friend, here, needed a little help with a girlfriend and I needed to dump an albatross. I sent Carl on an errand in Florida and they packaged him up and returned him via UPS."

Derek turned to Lansky. His face was stone cold. He held both weapons expertly. There was no chance of taking him by surprise. Clearly the man was a pro. "I'll bet you didn't know she was pregnant before Kelly told you." He watched Lansky's face change subtly. He was right on that point. "And to think you could have been a father. Ha!"

Kasson turned towards Lansky and began to laugh. "Come on, Jerry, tell me you didn't know. Shit, I thought you guys knew everything. You're not as smart as I thought."

Maybe he could get them going after each other, thought Derek. "Why my house? Why Steve, Rick and Al?" he asked Kasson.

"That was your doing, asshole. You hacked into the wrong man's computer. He had you traced before you even began the download. It was your poking around that got your friends knocked off. Too bad you weren't there at the same time everyone else was. You would have saved us a lot of trouble. Jerry, here, had another appointment up the coast and couldn't wait for you. You should have left things alone and followed the lead from the state police when they closed the case. Everything was set up perfectly. I even made sure the bodies were found on your watch. I was doing you a favor, pal. You could have come out with a promotion if you had just been as stupid as your reputation." Kasson looked on the wounded face of the man he was verbally torturing and smiled. "Aw, come on. Did I hurt your poor little feelings? What did you think; you were the brightest bulb on the tree? If it weren't for that stupid doctor friend of yours, we'd all be playing poker together, no one the wiser. There's a big deal coming up. Pretty soon I'm going to be able to buy as many friends as I'll ever need. This time tomorrow I'll be in the Caymans."

Lansky turned abruptly to Kasson. "You know something, you talk too damn much!" He fired twice with Derek's gun. Kasson spun and fell backwards with the impact of the two bullets. Lansky stared at his former partner, watching the man's blood ooze into the leaves. "You know something, I really enjoyed that."

"I have to inform you that you're under arrest," Derek said passively, looking at Kasson's twitching body. Death was becoming routine. The satisfaction of seeing this parasite dead was muted by the knowledge of his own impending demise. "Drop your weapon and surrender peacefully."

"You really are a comedian! Besides it was you who shot Kasson. They're gonna find your gun. Everyone knows the kind of stress you've been under. All that money in your safety deposit box will get them thinking. There was a struggle and he shot you. Case closed," Lansky said, dropping Derek's gun on the ground by Kasson's hand. "Time to say bye-bye."

"You're shooting a police officer. That's a federal offense guaranteeing the death penalty." Derek's words came out hollow, his head moving from side to side for any out.

"Fuck you." Lansky leveled the gun point blank at the detective's head.

Derek heard a single shot. He was still breathing and felt no pain. He cautiously turned towards Lansky. The man had a puzzled expression on his face, closed his eyes and then crumpled to the ground. The sudden quiet of the night was disturbed by the sounds of a jiggling holster belt with all the standard equipment of the Fall

River police department.

"Officer in need of assistance?" Wayne Peterson asked huffing and puffing his way to Derek's side. His weapon was in his hand.

Derek smiled. He was never so glad to see the fat bastard in his life.

A few feet away, Armand Lefevre came forward out of the darkness and holstered his weapon. "Not bad for an old fart who needs glasses to drive according to the registry, huh?"

"Let me guess. Was that your green Mercedes following me yesterday?"

Lefevre helped the detective up to his feet. "Metallic blue, if you have to know. The Chief was very specific. He insisted we keep an eye on you, until, of course, you spotted our tail. Besides, some of us have been luckier in the stock market then others. We can afford a Mercedes."

Derek tussled the balding head of his friend as a token of thanks. Reaching down he turned over the body of the man who was about to put a bullet in his head. Lansky looked better dead then alive any day. Derek felt incomplete. Was there anyone left to pursue? Kasson had made mention of a big deal happening within the next twenty-four hours. He made a quick search of the lifeless form. Except for a wallet and cell phone, nothing substantive was on the dead man's person. Lansky had over a thousand dollars of cash on him. Removing the money he placed it in his own pocket. "Expenses," Derek said. He took the cell phone and strapped it next to his own. The units were identical. "You didn't see this," he reminded Lefevre.

"Hey, leave me something to give to the Chief!" Peterson said.

Derek looked at the face of the dead man from the Keys. There was no one else to hate. "I'll give you something," he said. He kicked the dead man once in the stomach lifting the body a few inches in the air from the force of the blow. He turned back towards the house alone.

Wayne and Armand looked at each other and then turned away from the carnage. The downward spiral began with the four a.m. call they all shared two months ago. Their friend had crossed an unspoken line and would have to find his way back on his own.

Fall River, Massachusetts
October 29th
10 p.m.

It was amazing how much blood could come from a little hole in the foot. Derek didn't even remember shooting Kasson, but he knew it had happened. As his rage eased, sanity returned. It was an extreme effort for him to control the darkness of his thoughts. Bloodstains were everywhere on the floor, giving him some measure of comfort knowing he had extracted some little payback for the death of his friends. He stared at the footprints of blood and mud on the tile floor. Most belonged to his shoes – Peterson and Lefevre were carefully walking around the evidence and not becoming part of it. There were now two more dead bodies to be added to the list of homicides in Fall River for this calendar year.

"What's next, boss?" Lefevre asked. "There's a big mess outside we gotta clean up and now I have to fill out a firearms discharge report, too. Who's the guy I had to take care of for you? As much as I'd love to, it's not my habit to go around shooting people in the middle of the night."

"What goes around comes around," Derek said. These men had just saved his life. They deserved to know the details of the past twenty-four hours. He did his best to review the case and the players, working from maggots to computer discs in one semi-coherent summary. Everyone was now accounted for, but there was still a feeling of incompleteness. The story couldn't end like this. Too many people had died for a whole lot of money. In the world of Bagdasarian and Lansky, the figure of three million dollars was considered chump change for whatever the big score was going to be. "Look, guys, I'm almost to the bottom of things. I've come this far and I'm not going home until I see it through the end." He thought of Kelly. It was the least she deserved before he walked away and started a new life.

Peterson stood against the refrigerator arms folded across his chest. "Where are you going next?" he asked, throwing a few cashews from the countertop into his mouth.

"No idea," Derek replied. "Kasson said he was leaving town in twenty-four hours. I'm gonna start poking around the house and see if I come up with anything." The thought of searching room to room in an estate this big was unsettling, especially since he hadn't a clue what it was he was supposed to be looking for in the first place.

"How about right under your nose?" Lefevre asked, holding up a black brief case. "Found this right next to the door. You're buddy, there, probably put it down when he came in the house. By the way, how did he get the drop on you, hot shot?" he teased.

The memory of cigarette butts in his ears made Derek embarrassed. He reflexively checked his ears with a brush of his hands just in case the filters were still in place. "Not sure," he lied. The briefcase had no exterior identification markings. Was it Kasson's or Lansky's?

He placed the black leather case on the table and flipped open each latch. The sound of metal snapping against leather was followed by a soft pop as he opened the top. Inside was neatly wrapped bundles of one hundred dollar bills and one black leather memo book. Derek ignored the money and opened the book while Peterson and Lefevre both reached in and fanned the bills like they were the ATF. He recognized Kasson's handwriting from years of alleged friendship and this clearly didn't belong to the dead banker. It was Lansky's briefcase for sure.

"Drugs. It has to be drug money," Lefevre said with a low whistle.

"How much do you think?" Derek asked without looking up from the memo book.

"Got to be a couple a hundred thousand, for sure," Peterson answered counting the bundles of hundreds. His count ended at fifty.

Derek ignored the chatter focusing on today's entry in the appointment book. It read 'Ross, Elizabeth Rose, 5 a.m., Scituate, trap #3'. The entry date was the 30th of October, just a few hours away. Another entry followed 'Bos F.H. Auerbach 9 p.m..' The book's pages were blank after that.

"You goin'?" Peterson asked , already knowing the answer as he watched the detective stand up.

"You'll need some help," Lefevre said. He could already see the determination in Derek's eyes and he knew he was wasting the offer. The detective was on a one-man mission. They would only get in his way. "Be careful. These folks are bad boys. They don't play by the same rules we do."

"I know," Derek agreed. He had nothing else to lose. Kelly, his friends, his professional reputation were all gone. Then he smiled. "But neither do I, any more."

Armand removed the notebook gently from Derek's hand and

returned it to the briefcase. He snapped the latches closed then wrapped Derek's fingers around the handle. "I'll give you a couple of hours lead time while we write our report, then I've got to give this mess to the Chief," he said. "Make sure all the evidence comes back, he said tapping the black case." Armand looked into the Detective's eyes. "He's going to ask you to come in, you know."

"I suppose," Derek said pensively. "Thanks for the head start. You're going to find two more bodies in the cesspool. That'll be Kasson's wife, Hillary and her father. Don't know how long they've been there, though."

Peterson placed his hand on Derek's shoulder. "I'm tellin' you this as a friend. You're way too close to all this now. You need to back off and let someone else take over. You're not thinking or acting like a cop anymore."

Derek slowly removed his friend's hand and looked him straight in the eyes. "You're right," he smiled slowly grinding his teeth from side to side. "I kind of like it this way."

Beach Haven, New Jersey
October 30th
1 a.m.

A lone car headlight cut the night fog, shimmering ghost like in the fine mist. The mid Jersey coastal route along Route 70 from Long Beach Island was abandoned this late into the season. It was the first car they passed in ten miles. Bagdasarian took a small nibble of an Oreo cookie, brushing away the crumbs off his mustache glancing at his unconscious passenger. Kelly was securely strapped in the front passenger seat and hadn't moved since they landed at Long Beach Island community airport thirty miles back. Ecstasy was a good drug in the hands of a master and he was, by any measure, a master. Air traffic control was non-existent at unmonitored airports, especially those in seasonal facilities, and they were definitely off-season at this time of year.

The single lane road bordered the national preserve of the Pine Barrens. The Jersey sand made for the best tomatoes and asparagus on the East coast, but did little to support anything taller then a basketball pole. Gas stations were closed after midnight and the ice cream shops wouldn't open again until Memorial Day of the next year. He was famished and needed to take a piss, but there was no place to go. Besides, what was he going to do with the girl?

Bagdasarian suppressed the urge to contact Lansky. His plan's ultimate success depended on precision timing. There was to be no further communication until the package with the jewels was secure. Even with his successful disappearance from Key West, the potential intercept of an errant cellular phone call might ruin everything. Still, it would have been nice to keep tabs of his associate's progress. Lansky was tidying up some affairs in Massachusetts with the Detective and his nosey friends. How many more loose ends would have to disappear before he could begin a new life? Until then the only direction was North.

First things first. A vacancy sign for the Summer Breeze motel flashed ahead. It was perfect. He needed someplace nondescript where cash was the universal language. Ten ramshackle units sat back from the road, two rooms per unit. Several sixteen-wheelers were parked out front. The rest of the motel appeared empty. Kelly was still out cold. Bagdasarian patted her on the head before sauntering off to the front office. Several rings of the door buzzer later, a sleepy man staggered up to the window.

"Kind of late for traveling, mister, ain't it?" the clerk grumbled. Fiftyish and cue-balled he was dressed in a tee shirt and boxer shorts. A USMC tattoo with its eagle, anchor, rope and globe covered his burly right biceps.

Bagdasarian smiled ignoring his comments. "How much for one night?" he asked.

The ex-marine eyed him from head to toe. "How many?"

"My wife and I. It's just the two of us," Bagdasarian answered pointing to his beat up ten-year-old Chrysler Lebaron parked in front of the office.

The man appeared satisfied. "Got a room with a double bed; thirty-five bucks, payable in advance. There is a two-dollar towel fee and a two-dollar laundry fee for the sheets. Check out is nine a.m.. And I don't help with no luggage, either," he added.

Bagdasarian counted out thirty-nine dollars in small bills and accepted the key. The last thing he wanted to do was attract attention by flashing around larger denominations. The clerk disappeared. Bagdasarian could see the 'vacancy' sign had been switched to 'no vacancy.' He carried Kelly inside placing her on one of the twin beds of the ten by ten room. The air inside smelled of mildew and Lysol. The brown commercial rug was threadbare. He flicked on the bathroom lights. At least no scurrying insects, he reflected with some small consolation.

He lifted Kelly's prostrate form, sitting her up. "Here, drink this," he said putting a small white pill in her mouth followed by a tap water chaser.

Kelly opened her eyes momentarily and did as she was ordered. Her eyes darted back and forth in the haze of drugs but lacked any recognition or independence of thought. Just as quickly, she fell back asleep.

Bagdasarian stretched out her right arm to the bedpost. Even after being shuffled around like a sack of potatoes, she was drop dead gorgeous. It made him pause. He took out one handcuff from his jacket pocket and secured her arm to the headboard. His experience with ecstasy ended after a third pill. Kelly was already working on number five. How long would the effects last? Were the effects cumulative or did the body build up a certain resistance?

"I'm sorry *Hokees*," he said giving her a kiss on the lips. "But I must get some sleep and you simply can't be trusted." He lay on the bed next to hers starring at her profile. The motel's neon light penetrated the dust and grime of the curtains, casting a ruby glow to

Kelly's skin. Bagdasarian sat up and leaned over the void separating the mattresses. He touched her face, stroking it gently. "I still love you, you know. I could have ended your life long ago. You never would have known." He fell back onto his bed and starred at the ceiling. "A billion dollars will make me a king. There is still a chance for you to be my queen."

Outer Cape, Massachusetts
October 30th
2 a.m.

Richard Sayour leaned over the railing as the ship pitched back and forth in the ten- foot seas. His face was turning green, the same color of the water below the wind stirred foam. He had always felt uncomfortable in the open ocean. What he wouldn't give for the company of a civilized bartender. Swallowing a mouthful of apricot brandy from his flask, he focused on the hand held LORAN, the long-range navigational unit. The fingers of his hands worked the digital keys stiffly. Antibiotics taken to repair the damage from the Egyptian General had proven only marginally effective. In a few minutes he was going to have a rendezvous with a lobster trap.

The Chinese captain passed by and tipped his hat in a polite salute, issuing orders based on Sayour's coordinates. Halifax was still eight hundred nautical miles due north. As long as they kept on this present course and stayed outside the American three-mile limit, their next official contact would be Canadian customs. This was the last leg of *Sassoonnie David's* voyage that began in South Africa six months earlier. The captain grappled mentally with his manpower needs for the return trip home. The crew of thirty-two would dwindle in Nova Scotia as half the men jumped ship while its cargo of plastic toys and dialysis equipment were unloaded. That was an acceptable attrition rate. Hopefully the ship would pick up an equal number of Mainland Chinese crewmembers rounded up by the Canadians for deportation.

Sayour worked his way back to his quarters and unlatched the half rusted steel door. Large gray paint chips flaked off of everything. The bottom lip of the door caught his foot, pitching him into his room like a drunken sailor. The cabin contained a double bunk bed, a small metal writing desk, a large safe and an enamel head. Years of neglect had left large brown rust stains on every surface of the toilet. He unlocked the five-foot tall safe inside his room and removed the metal box containing the package entrusted to his care by the Colonel.

The plan was simple. Under cover of darkness, the object would be placed in an American fishing trap just outside the three-mile limit, then retrieved by one of the Colonel's cohorts in the local commercial fishing fleet. The North American crustacean industry was so finely developed that this package was deemed safer in the hands of the local lobstermen then by any other route of transportation. These lobstermen could legally shoot trespassers or poachers who violated their private traps. The Colonel's diplomatic immunity had been lifted. Parcels sent by long established routes or in the hands of experienced couriers were being intercepted. Everyone on board realized they were being shadowed. Occasionally a plane would skirt their wake. Sometimes another ship would parallel their course, even picking up garbage thrown overboard. The Chinese Captain did his best to zigzag and change speed but how could you hide from a satellite?

A walkie-talkie call later, Sayour summoned an armed escort. "Follow me," he instructed, leading the guards down the corridor into the entrails of the ship. The four men walked silently, single file down two stories to the water line and then detoured aft of the engine compartment. The lobster traps were there, lined up perfectly in a row. He logged onto the marine LORAN location unit then placed the package into the designated trap. They were skirting Stellwagon Bank; the waters depth was suitable for lobstering. One last pull on each line to confirm the integrity of the ropes and the traps were ready for discharge into the ocean, single file, line tethered trap to trap, on his command. "OK boys, we're done," he said smiling to Immir, the team's commander and his childhood friend. "Let's give the traps a shove and go home."

He began the climb up the steps when he heard the click of a bolt from an automatic weapon behind him. Sayour turned his head just in time to see a spray of precisely aimed bullets from an Uzi strike down two of the mercenaries below. The weapon fired belonged to Immir, the teams' commander. Sayour's hands began to sweat profusely. He knew of death, but never this closely. "*Lemaza,* Why?" he shouted in Arabic, his breath coming in short bursts.

Immir ignored his question for the brief moment it took him to wrap weighted lines around the bodies of the two men he had just executed. A man of medium size and enormous strength, his personal appearance was defined by two front teeth missing after contact with a rifle butt years ago. He worked silently and efficiently pushing the first trap into the chute and watching it sink below the surface, dragging the bodies down. The crustaceans would have a different kind of bait this time. Immir turned towards his friend and answered in Arabic. "*Endy Awamer,* I had my orders. The Colonel is closing down his entire operation. He wanted no loose ends," he said simply. "I am saddened, most were like brothers to me." He looked up the ladder at the Dentist; his eyes hollow of remorse.

Sayour stood frozen on the steps each heartbeat pounding as if it were going to be the last. "And me? What about me? *Hal ana elly bado*, Am I next? Am I part of the loose ends you were ordered to dispose of?" he demanded.

Immir turned his head and avoided eye contact with his childhood playmate. "Yes, but I could not," he replied. He clicked on the Uzi's safety. "See, my weapon is disarmed." He looked once more at Sayour and began the climb up the ladder without waiting for a further response. "We have some serious matters to discuss."

Sayour's position was untenable and totally at the mercy of his old friend. He waited for Immir at the top of the ladder keeping his sweaty hands inside his jacket pocket. On one side he could feel the reassuring coolness of the apricot brandy flask, in the other his stiletto. Options and consequences raced through his mind. He was a deliberate thinker not use to making decisions on such short notice. The man in front of him was climbing the final rung. With one bold quick thrust he impaled the tip of his knife into the throat of his childhood friend. Immir flailed wildly for the knife, but it was too late. He fell backwards ten feet to the metal deck below, his body thrashing for seconds like a fish out of water then laying silent, a pool of blood oozing from the fatal throat wound.

Now what? Sayour sat on the top rung staring at the body. At least he had time to weigh his decision carefully. He didn't know about the remote charges timed to destroy the entire vessel in twenty-four hours time. The Colonel really did want to close down the entire operation.

Scituate, Massachusetts
October 30th
4:30 a.m.

The constellations of the eastern sky faded one by one. Men of the sea were already on their way to a full days work, their fishing vessels tethered together like so many sardines, all sporting the names of wives or children. A series of swells penetrated the sheltered inner harbor bobbing the docks in rhythm to the wave crests. Seagulls lined up on railings and adjacent rooftops waiting to pounce on discarded donuts or spilled bait boxes. The smell of fuel oil, frozen baitfish, and salt air combined to create a potent mixture saturating the wharfs. He felt at home.

Derek pulled into a parking spot next to the Harbor Master's office, cracking the window open a few inches for the benefit of the dog sleeping on his front seat. Across the docks files of men followed each other like ants loading their vessels with ice from the main ice shack, everyone dressed in knits and waterproof yellows. He gently closed the car door so as not to wake the dog. Drawing the parka hood tighter, Derek worked his way down the series of free floating ramps, now set at a steep sixty-degree angle, to begin the search for the Elizabeth Rose. Lansky's black briefcase, loaded with the bundled one hundred dollar bills, weighed ominously in his hand. His baser instincts said take the money and disappear forever. Still the mystery of the unknown could not be resisted.

After several inquiries he found the Elizabeth Rose on the far side of the pier. A lobster trawler of about forty-five feet, years of hard use had left a history of former owners like the rings of a tree on her railings and decks. It was unassuming like the rest of the local fleet, her name hand stenciled by someone with a good heart but only a modicum of talent.

Derek navigated the steep ramp holding the briefcase by his chest. Was 'Ross' a first or last name? Did he know Lansky's face? The memory of the bastard's last breath brought a brief smile. Was there a code word? Was he being foolish with his life twice in one day? A kid in his early twenties bumped into him with the edge of his bait box. "Ross?" Derek asked.

"Over there," the man replied in a classic Boston accent, pointing to the back of someone sitting on the railing across from the Elizabeth Rose.

Derek walked to the other side of his quarry. "Ross," he said as a matter of fact.

The man in front of him didn't budge. A wild stock of reddish blond hair oozed underneath the man's knit cap, a full red beard flowing down his cheeks and chin. "I don't know you," he said flatly returning to his knot making.

"Lansky's indisposed. He sent me instead," Derek said giving the briefcase a slow jingle. "Now cut the shit. Can I come aboard?" His brazenness caught the big man off guard.

The lobsterman looked at him suspiciously. "I don't know what you're talking about," Ross insisted shifting his gaze back to his handy work.

Derek was working on little sleep and lots of adrenaline. This wasn't going well. If the fisherman didn't bite, then the trail would end here. There had to be more. The lives of Kelly and his friends demanded closure. "I guess then you don't want this," Derek said throwing the briefcase over the railing into the water below. "I'll just go tell the Colonel."

Ross looked up at the sound of the splash and rushed to the railing. With one clean swoop of his pole he retrieved the briefcase and put it by his side. "Come aboard," he said without looking at Derek.

Good, at least we're getting somewhere. Was it the money or was it the mention of the Colonel that turned the man? Derek jumped on deck ignoring an offered hand and followed Ross to the pilothouse. "Don't you want to count it?" Derek asked.

"Don't need to. The Colonel gave his word. That's good enough for me." Clearly suspicious, Ross gave Derek a once over. "By the way, how is the Colonel these days? Still charming the girls with his English accent?"

Derek froze. Which Colonel was Ross referring to? What if there were other players he didn't know about? Better to find out now rather then a few miles out to sea. He didn't relish the idea of wrestling the big man for his life outside the three-mile coastal limit. He took a guess. "Who the fuck you talking about?" he said indignantly. "The Colonel's Egyptian. The only thing English about him is the Earl Gray tea he drinks."

The big man relaxed. "Can't be too careful these days. Welcome aboard." His handshake was simple but firm. Ross looked carefully at Derek's clothes. "You'll need something a bit warmer where we're going. Go down below and find something to wear."

His hand felt as if it was crushed. About time, thought Derek. "Aye, Aye Captain. Thanks. You're play from here," he said.

"Ready to cast off," Ross commanded.

Scituate, Massachusetts
October 30th
6 a.m.

The seas were flat as they left the mouth of Scituate Harbor. From port side, the lighthouse saluted them farewell; mansions on first cliff with their manicured lawns guarded their approach from starboard. The horizon glowed with the spectrum of sunrise as the Elizabeth Rose carefully followed the wakes of other fishing vessesl. The waves began to pick up the further they moved from the harbor rolling them between the wave crests, sea spray stinging their face between the dips and peaks. They had gone from perfectly flat seas to three-foot waves in a matter of a few minutes. This was freedom, and Derek loved every minute of it. He kept his footing without difficulty. Years of growing up around sailboats helped. At the third buoy marker they turned due east.

"Not bad for a land turtle," Ross teased with a hint of admiration. He half expected his passenger to be begging for mercy with the first roll, puking over the railings.

"We learn to adapt," Derek said, relishing the freedom of the open seas even in his present circumstance. It had been a couple of years since his last sail, shortly before his wife's death. Rose, Elizabeth Rose – the coincidence of the names was not lost on him. He had lost his wife. Then came the miracle of Kelly, but only to lose again. Now he was riding this messenger of the gods, his first wife's namesake, to find closure. He focused on the horizon. A magnificent sunrise was cresting over the morning ocean cloudbank. Behind him a three quarter moon was setting to the west. For a brief moment, he waxed philosophical. Raising his arms he was at the center of an inverted pyramid with the sun to the east and the moon to the west. Derek closed his eyes against the sting of the wind driven sea spray. Over the past few days his known universe had collapsed under the weight of evil and money. The love of his life had been stolen and the men he called brothers lay cold in the ground. Now all he could think about was the sun and the moon and the secrets of the ancients. He wanted so desperately to leave his body behind and soar with the seagulls that trailed the Elizabeth Rose.

An hour later and they were outside the sight of land. Specks of other commercial fishing boats crisscrossed the seas in search of the perfect catch. The whale tours out of the North Shore, Boston, Plymouth or the Cape wouldn't be out for a few more hours. Derek had no idea what, if anything was expected of him. It was only a mild surprise when Ross began to load baitfish into the lobster traps on his deck. The man was really fishing – not quite what he had expected.

Ross used an ice pick to separate the frozen chunks of bait into fist-sized pieces placing them deep in the wire mesh of his traps, a labyrinth the lobsters could navigate only one way. The traps were tethered together in sets of five with hundreds of feet of line in between. Ross placed the traps on the edge of the Elizabeth Rose's stern and released the first trap. The other five traps followed in time as the first trap hit the water and sank two hundred feet to the bottom. Colored buoys with his personal numbered codes marked their location for pick up one week later.

The Elizabeth Rose moved continuously eastward in the hunt for the elusive shellfish delicacy. At their next stop, Ross picked up a buoy with a grappling hook, attaching it to a power winch and hauled a line of traps from the ocean bottom. A hundred feet of line later, a lobster trap emerged from the sea. Inside was a feisty green crustacean. Ross measured it from eye to body and flipped it back into the ocean. "Not a keeper," he said out loud loading the trap with new bait.

No wonder lobsters cost so damn much, thought Derek loosening his jacket. The sun was hitting him full in the face, its warmth entering every fiber of his being. He stood on the bow seeing nothing but the waves that surrounded him. The isolation was perfect, the feeling exhilarating. If life could only be this simple. The sensation of peace was interrupted by a sudden lurch as the Elizabeth Rose abruptly changed it's heading to North by Northeast.

Two hours later Ross put down his hand held GPS unit, idling the engines next to a line of buoys marked with his colors. Swinging the ten-foot grappling hook over his left shoulder he leaned over the side staring at the water. "We're past the three mile limit. I'm picking up the transmission at 37.5 kHz like they told me," he said. "We've got to be right on top of it. Which one in the line is it?" He said looking at Derek impatiently.

Derek recalled Lansky's hand written entry. "Number three," he replied with hopeful certainty. Their lobster trawler was alone in the area, the next closest vessel beyond clear binocular distance.

Ross placed the buoy on the winch harness and engaged the motor. Just before the lobster trap broke the surface, the gruesome form of a half-eaten human being popped to the top of the winch line, the man's leg tied to a lobster trap and weighted down with bricks. Ross took his knife and cut the man free with the same emotional ease he displayed throwing back the undersized lobster earlier in the day. The dead man's body slipped back into the water for eternity. "Not a keeper," he grinned looking back at Derek. He spit a wad of tobacco juice into the water.

Derek watched as the corpse bobbed in the choppy waves and drifted off to sea. He had witnessed so much death that nothing fazed him anymore in the least.

The third trap broke the surface. It was clearly distinguishable from the first two because of it's size, being twice as long as the others in the chain of lobster traps. An electronic marking buoy was tied to the inside. Ross opened up one of the floorboards of the Elizabeth Rose removing two duffel bags. One was apparently custom made for the task of sequestering the retrieved item. The other he used for the black briefcase Derek had brought on board loaded with hundred dollar bills. Using a wire cutter to open the metal mesh of the trap, he placed the rescued piece inside the first duffel bag, effortlessly slinging the weight over his shoulder carrying it to the pilothouse. Ross cut the remainder of the lines. "I guess I can afford to lose some rigging now, right?" he said smiling.

They rode the Elizabeth Rose in silence back to the docks in Scituate. Just inside the harbor, the boat stopped at a lobster pound and delivered its catch for the day. Another stop for refueling and the lobster trawler came along side its slip at the main town dock. Derek helped secure the lines fore and aft. Ross gave Derek the duffel bag with the retrieved package and took the other one with the black briefcase on his own shoulder. "My regards to the Colonel," he said simply.

If only I could, thought Derek. If only I could.

Scituate, Massachusetts
October 30th
5 p.m.

Sitting on the highest point of Third Cliff, Ani's restaurant overlooked the half-mile wide sand spit of the North River. Derek sat alone, his car buffeting the chilly ocean wind, staring at the package retrieved from the Elizabeth Rose. Cricket nested on the front seat oblivious to everything except the soothing rays of sun penetrating the passenger window. If this had been summer, a line of cars would have interrupted Derek's meditation; now it was just the seagulls. The crush of summer folks to the 'Irish Riviera' was over for another season.

Marine activity was surprisingly heavy for this time of year. The final days of fall brought out everyone who owned a boat before winter hibernation. Most of the pleasure crafts were returning from a day sail. Fishermen usually returned en masse at twilight, still a few hours away. The homes around him were empty except for weekenders. A few more weeks and the seasonal homes would all be boarded up.

The duffel bag from the Elizabeth Rose sat empty and crumpled on the passenger floor. He had kept the small trunk unopened - partially from fatigue and no small amount of fear. What could it contain that was worth the lives of so many people? Derek repeatedly touched the box, moving it around, shaking it from side to side. His fingers traced the margins of the two latches that secured the lid. It measured about two feet cubed and weighed about seventy pounds at his best guess. The possibilities were limitless. Radioactive material seemed unlikely. Bagdasarian didn't seem the terrorist type. Besides, the lead casing required would make a trunk this size weigh several hundred pounds. Drugs were remote because this was a lot of work for less then a hundred pounds of cocaine, heroin or even those of the designer kind. High tech equipment, pirated technology, microchips, circuit boards, all impossible. Only a fool would risk sensitive electronics to salt water.

Firm thumb pressure released the latches the trunk springing open spontaneously. Inside was a box the size of a personal computer. The exterior was some kind of metallic alloy, probably titanium, and colored red. The words 'Flight Recorder- do not open' and serial codes were clearly marked on the surface in black on white background. This was an ELT, an emergency locator transmitter, the kind usually first searched for after any aviation crash. Derek's mind raced over the recent news. There had been no military or civilian plane disasters that he could recall. What might this Flight Recorder contain if not data from a crash? Why would anyone go through all this trouble?

Derek searched the exterior for a way to gain entry into the black box. The bolts were hexagonal and recessed. All he had on his key chain was a small pocketknife, hardly up to the task. Making a sharp U-turn in front of a surprised dog walker he drove to downtown Scituate in less then a minute. The town had a first run movie theater, two first class restaurants and four liquor stores lining the main drag. On the water side of the street was a sign for a hardware store. He pulled in, remotely locked his car and went inside. A pimple-faced clerk helpfully directed him to a series of wrenches sized in both US and metric scales. Derek bought both. Returning to his vehicle, he took the short drive to Scituate lighthouse on the north side of the harbor and parked under a streetlight. Cricket began to whine and scratch the inside doorknob. The dog needed to take a piss. He gave the animal a quick whack to the rump dissuading it from destroying his leather upholstery. The dog would wait.

He held the box in his hands repeatedly rotating it looking for the best place to apply the wrench. Twelve bolts stood between him and the end of a mystery. A few quick turns later and the casing of the flight recorder were released. Derek removed the metal exterior dropping it on the floor next to the dog. Inside was a hermetically sealed plastic bag the size of a child's lunch box. The bag resisted only a few seconds against the sharp point of his pocketknife as he slit the plastic open from end to end. Inside the bag his fingers felt the soft texture of velvet. He pulled out the cloth pouch holding it in the palm of his hand. It weighed only about a pound, about as much as a can of beans or tomato sauce. His fingers fumbled with the drawstring for a minute before it opened revealing the two objects inside. Now he understood why so many lives had been lost.

Love is usually once in a lifetime unless, of course, you were lucky enough to have the two jewels he held in each hand. Then you should love twice. Derek was not a history buff, but even he recognized the pieces as very old and probably Egyptian. Two stones, larger then anything he could remember from the Smithsonian museum in Washington, sat in the center of a spectacular gold casing. One stone was red and the other primarily white with a tinge of yellow. His guess was a ruby and a diamond the likes of which had not been seen in a millennium. The workmanship was exquisitely detailed. He could recognize tiny figures of ancient Egyptian mythology pressed into the borders of the gold. A thick gold chain connected the two stones like a broach.

The treasure hunt was over but the victory was hollow. He could visualize the piece woven into Kelly's hair or perhaps slung over her shoulders like a cape. Her lavender scarf would complement the yellow of the gold. It was his, after all. He could do anything in the world he wanted. He could give it to anyone whenever he felt like it. He slung it over Cricket's neck for amusement. The dog clearly was not amused. The stones probably weighed more then she did. If he didn't take her out soon, she'd soil his car.

The cell phone at his waist rang. He pressed send, but the phone was dead. No, the phone kept on ringing. Then Derek remembered he had two phones strapped to his waist. Removing Lansky's phone he pressed the green button. The phone activated and then died, the battery totally drained. Shit, he thought. He took Lansky's cell phone and plugged it into the charger on his cigarette lighter jack. The phone was silent. He'd have to wait until someone called him again.

Braintree, Massachusetts
October 30th
6 p.m.

The line was dead. *Kacknem sichter,* Bagdasarian cursed silently. He pressed redial on his phone but this time all he got was the standard response from the carrier about the customer not being available. No matter. The exchange was going to be in three hours outside a restaurant near Faneuil Hall, downtown Boston. He looked across the parking lot of the Hilltop restaurant grimacing at the line of traffic heading north on Route 3. Post rush hour traffic in Boston meant just half the nightmare of the hideous traffic jams that characterized the city. And a nightmare was still a nightmare. He had three hours to find a suitable hotel and temporarily park Kelly, buy some clothes, shower and shave before he would meet Lansky and George Stadikis, the buyer. The thought of all that money helped to relax his usual white knuckle driving.

A billion dollars. It was a huge sum of money. The price was easy to negotiate; Stadikis was an educated man who knew his history. The world of biotech had made him fabulously wealthy thanks to his genetic splicing innovations. As president and CEO of Mytosis, Inc. he had the resources to buy the world if he chose. His initial deposit of one hundred million dollars for the double crown of Egypt was in the form of diamonds. The remainder would be in bearer bonds and Swiss Accounts due upon delivery. And delivery was only a few hours away.

The Marriott Suites were ideally suited for Bagdasarian's purpose. Semidetached, just off of Route 95, north of Boston, the units were clustered in one of the few densely wooded areas of Stoneham with lots of angles and shadows leading from the parking lot to the front doorway. He made sure he had the most remote unit offered.

"Come with me, *Hokees,*" he ordered stroking her face to nudge her awake.

Kelly's eyes barely opened as she exited the car. Responding to his orders her movements were stiff and awkward. Mumbling a few incoherent words her legs shuffled in the direction she was lead, most of her weight on Bagdasarian's arm.

They negotiated the winding walkway together as two drunken lovers. Bagdasarian opened the door to his suite with one hand and moved Kelly to the king size bed. Her body collapsed on the mattress as soon as he released her. He double locked the door then went to the bathroom to get a glass of water. Three pills were left. "Here, *Hokees,* drink this down." The girl's mouth opened and she swallowed on command. He still had a couple of hours before the meeting. "Let's get those old smelly clothes off," he said unbuttoning her blouse.

"No, Jack, no," Kelly protested unconsciously. Her eyes were still closed, the words came out sticky and garbled. Resistance was futile.

"Excuse me for a moment, *hokis*." Bagdasarian went to the bathroom and turned on the faucets to fill up the tub. He returned and disrobed her slowly, peeling off every piece of clothing like a stripper. There had to be some fun for him in all this after all. He carried her gently into the bathtub and was grateful the water did little to revive her. He used the soap and shampoo to wash her down, paying particular attention to her breasts and pubic area as he let his bare hands rub. Finishing, he drained the tub, picked her up and dried her off. This time he chained both wrists and feet to the bed frame. He still had a couple of hours left. He might as well put them to use.

Boston, Massachusetts
October 30th
8 p.m.

It was Friday night in the Hub. Crowds were packed like sardines, moving in and out of the stalls, booths and kiosks of Faneuil Hall in a chaotic flow of humanity. Derek sat in the marketplace courtyard on a bench next to a statue of 'Red' Auerbach, waiting. He could be waiting for Godot for all he knew. The tiny festive white Christmas lights decorating the trees did little to alter his underlying mood. He wanted to hurt someone. It didn't quite matter who, just someone. The twin jewels lay draped around his neck hidden underneath his jacket. Cricket sat on his lap, her head bobbing up and down and from side to side tracking every new smell that crossed her path. One of Derek's hands stroked her neck, the other hand held a semi automatic gun concealed beneath her body.

Lansky's diary ended with the words 'Bos F.H. Auerbach 9 p.m.'. It didn't take a genius to sort through this last clue. The world famous general manager and coach of the Boston Celtics sat immortalized in bronze in the courtyard of Faneuil Hall market place. Derek sat impatiently waiting to see who might show up. It made no matter who; he had the jewels.

Two blond teenage nymphets muscled him to the far end of the bench draping themselves over Auerbach's lap pressing their breasts against the bronze cigar. Five feet away one of their friends snapped their photograph with a yellow throw- away camera. They laughed and giggled appropriately for their age and moved on. An Oriental couple with five indistinguishable children in tow hovered around the statue taking snapshots with their hi-tech digital camera. The comedy connection on the second floor of the brick market place let out its first show. The crowds swelled to levels impossible for Derek to survey alone. What was he doing here? The question was unanswerable in the context of his training, but he was no longer acting in the capacity of a police officer. It was a mission.

It was nine o'clock. A middle-aged man sat down on the bench next to him, eating a chilidog loaded with mustard and onions. A dribble of yellow dripped down his chin forming an incongruous contrast to his finely trimmed beard. On his lap was a small leather bag with a strap wrapped tightly around his wrist. Dressed in sloppy sweats with a Celtics logo emblazoned on the front, he wore a gold ring on the pinky finger of his left hand - a lion head with two tiny rubies in the place of its eyes. There was something vaguely familiar about his face but Derek couldn't place it.

Derek extended his hand. "Derek Ekizian, how ya' doin'?"

The man looked back and politely feigned a smile. He was clearly caught off guard. "George, ah George Smith," he said limply shaking back. His eyes darted around the flow of people. Clearly he was waiting for someone he knew.

"Like dogs, George?" Derek leaned over bringing Cricket closer. His gun stayed hidden. Violating personal space was always the first rule of interrogation.

The man frowned and stared at the offered Yorkie. "Yeah, sure, sure," he replied. He patted Cricket's head like the butt end of a watermelon. "Nice dog. What's its name?"

"Cricket." Derek watched as the man rocked his foot nervously. For a guy in sweats eating a chilidog, his shoes were hand made. It was now 9:05 p.m.. The fellow moved his head from side to side looking over the throngs of people. Someone was late. Only Derek knew they were going to be permanently late. "Waiting for someone?"

The man turned to Derek narrowing his eyes. "As a matter of fact, yes, I am." The man reached inside his pants and pulled out a roll of bills. "Here," he said handing Derek a twenty. "Why don't you go and buy yourself a sandwich or something. I'd like to keep this seat open, if you don't mind."

Derek's index finger played with the trigger. The safety was still on otherwise the weapon would have discharged in the crowd right then and there. He breathed in deeply locking his eyes on the man's face ignoring the twenty. "Are you looking for this?" he said, reaching his left hand up to his open shirt and exposing a tantalizing peak at the tip of one of the jewels.

The man leaned back in the bench. "Who are you," he asked. His eyes didn't move from Derek's chest.

"I already told you. Derek Ekizian." He was smiling now. The ball was in his park. "And you are…?"

"George Studikis," this time he shook Derek's hand for real. "How did you …?"

Derek interrupted, "Come to acquire the items in question? That's not important right now. What is important is that I have something you want." Studikis. That name he recognized. Someone very well connected to Biotech and big money.

"Permit me to correct you," Studikis said. "I've already made a down payment. What you have belongs to me."

"Only after payment is made in full. "What do you have for me?" Derek asked.

"I've got nothing for you," Studikis said. "I have something for your boss, though." He suddenly smiled and stood up. "Jack!" he said looking over Derek's shoulder.

Cricket began a low growl, which changed into a series of barks. Derek turned his head just enough to see a ghost. Bagdasarian was sauntering towards him, hands in his pocket smiling as if it were just another walk in the park. He looked at Derek without recognition and then suddenly came to a dead stop. Derek stood up dropping the dog unceremoniously on the ground, his gun hand exposed. He clicked off the safety. The weapon was primed. Bagdasarian lurched towards an elderly woman walking towards him and grabbed her, spinning the matron around to use as a human shield while drawing his own gun. In the dark chaotic parade of tourists enjoying an evening out, the sight of two men brandishing guns was enough to set off panic.

"Freeze!" Derek shouted moving his gun around several times unsuccessfully trying to find a clear shot.

Bagdasarian dragged his hostage backwards on her heels slowly withdrawing in between the hordes of screaming men, women, and children. Everyone around him was ducking or falling to the ground. He let loose with a brief series of shots disappearing into the mass of hysterical humanity.

Derek jumped on top of the bench to get a better vantage. There must have been several thousand people in the Faneuil Hall market place. Bagdasarian, the man whose body had been identified as dead in a house explosion in Key West, was gone leaving carnage in his wake. Studikis lay dead, half the man's head missing from a shot that was meant for him. Three others lay moaning or screaming on the cobblestones close by. He put away his weapon and began to render what first aide he could muster.

Bagdasarian was alive. Maybe Kelly was alive as well.

Boston, Massachusetts
October 30th
10:30 p.m.

The Irish cops were caricatures, reeking stale booze breath. They were big, arrogant and insipid in their interviews, violating even the most basic of evidentiary rules. Derek was dismissed from the crime scene as just another material witness despite offering up his name and FRPD badge number. George Stadikis was dead but no one was able to directly connect him to the scene. A thousand people and two thousand pairs of eyes and no one came forward to place him as one of the two men brandishing a gun. No wonder homicides were rarely solved.

A black woman in a green Newport Creamery uniform sat on Red's bench stroking Cricket's neck. This total stranger had remained with his dog for over an hour, patiently waiting for the police interviews to finish. Her tightly knit salt and pepper hair framed a wide smile telegraphing experience through a life of hard knocks. "Heck of a way to spend your evening out," she said handing over the animal.

Cricket made the transition reluctantly. The woman must have had magic in her hands. The dog buried its nose underneath Derek's leather jacket and came to rest. He mumbled an acknowledgement of thanks stuffing Stadikis' twenty-dollar bill into her uniform pocket. What else could he do with the dead man's money? "Thanks very much, ah, Maria, is it?" He said looking at her name tag. "Wasn't quite what I had in mind when I came here tonight," he said grim faced.

"You can call me CBC, cool black chick. Everyone does." Maria folded her hands into her lap and cautiously lowered her voice. "I seen you packin', too," she said simply. "You were waitin' for that dude, weren't you?"

Her frankness took Derek by surprise. How much had she seen? "I'm a cop. A Fall River detective to be exact. I was here on police business."

"That's not what you told those dumb ass white cops," Maria answered flashing a big toothy smile.

Derek sat mute rubbing Cricket's right ear. Awake for over twenty-four hours, his focus was getting sloppy. What did she call herself again, CBC, cool black chick? Was she after more money? He still had a wad of bills he had taken off of Lansky's body. "If you know so much, how come you didn't say anything to the cops when you had the chance?" he replied staring at the cobblestone street.

"Hey, ain't none of my business," Maria said chuckling heartily. "No difference to me if a couple of white folks go and shoot each other. I've got my own problems." She leaned backwards on the bench and stretched both arms out. She turned again towards Derek. "I got somethin' here that might come in handy for you someday." She threw a super 8 videocassette tape on Derek's lap. "Got the whole thing right here."

Derek's eyes opened wide in disbelief. "How...?"

"Let's just say it's a hobby of mine. I walk around here a lot after work and tape whatever I can get. You'd be surprised to see some of the things I catch on camera. Make more money doing that then doin' this." Maria said pointing to her green uniform. She got up to leave. "And don't bother to thank me. I love dogs, too," she said then disappeared into the night.

He sat stunned and grateful at the turn of events. He had lost count at the number of dead bodies falling in his path. At least this time he had some evidence to show he was a victim rather then a perpetrator. Derek leashed the dog and walked back to his car in the Government Center parking garage two blocks away. From the outside the car was just fine, and for Boston that was a big thing. As soon as he opened the door he saw the phone was ringing, Lansky's cell phone. It could only be one man. "Yes," he answered.

"*Parev,* hello, my friend," a familiar voice replied. Pawn to King four. He didn't say anything else.

It was Derek's move. He wasn't in the mood for a gambit. Knight to queen's bishop three. "Lansky's dead," he said simply. "I'm going to hunt you down and kill you." Derek's voice was drained of emotion. He was just stating a fact.

"Oh, yes," Bagdasarian answered. "I'm sure you will, little man. But first things first. We have some important matters to discuss, you and I."

Derek pulled out of the parking garage and headed towards the expressway. "Only after I piss on your grave." His level of agitation was growing exponentially.

"Look, Detective. I've spoken to Ross. He told me that you have something that belongs to me. I have something, no, make that someone who belongs to you. Let's make a deal."

Derek almost caused a chain collision as he jammed on his brakes. Was it possible? "Kelly, is she alive?"

Bagdasarian snorted. "Of course. Do you think I would damage anything that belongs to me?"

Derek's speech became pressured. "Last time I checked your house was missing and the Monroe County Sheriffs and Florida State Police had more bodies on their hands then they knew what to do with." There was no response on the other end. Derek swallowed. "If Kelly is alive, prove it!"

Bagdasarian's voice dripped with satisfaction. He knew he had the other man by the short hairs. "Sure. Say hi, Kelly. Oops, I'm sorry. She's tied up at the moment. But you can take my word for it that she's all right; at least for now."

"Look mother fucker, I need to know that Kelly's alive and well. If she doesn't talk to me in the next ten seconds I'm hanging up and you can kiss your precious little jewels goodbye." Derek had no choice. He had to know.

"Fine, little man. Ask her a question and I'll give you her answer."

Another insult. Derek hesitated for the moment it took him to realize that he was on the wrong end of the rifle barrel. The man knew Kelly well from their previous relationship. For all Derek knew, Kelly was with him voluntarily. It had been a lifetime since their pledge of eternal love. The promise of money might tempt anyone. He had to ask something so private only Kelly would know. "OK. Ask Kelly what my grandmother told me never to do." The phone was silent for a minute. Derek could hear Bagdasarian's voice and then another one, female but slurred just outside the microphone's range. The words 'Kelly' and 'wake up' were repeated over and over then the question was put to her. She was there but something wasn't quite right.

Bagdasarian returned to the phone. "She said something about never kissing a girl who has had too much Raki."

Derek threw his head back against the car's headrest and sighed with relief. Kelly was alive! That's all that mattered. All that time believing she was dead had taken a toll on him. He could not lose the same woman twice in the same week. "Touch one hair on Kelly's head I will hunt you down to hell and back if I have to."

Bagdasarian chuckled sarcastically. "Jesus Christ, no wonder you're such a loser. How else can a guy expect to get laid?" he snorted. "Now let's cut the shit. I guarantee you that your little flower here will be dead unless I get my package back. Oh and yes, by the way, you're a little too late as far as the touching part goes."

Derek didn't answer. He wouldn't give the man the satisfaction.

"Hello, you still there? You'd better answer before I decide to make her a trophy."

"Like you did Lansky's girlfriend, Boerner?"

"Nice touch, don't you think? If it weren't for your intrusions, you two would be safely tucked away in Fall River drinking coffee somewhere and catching a late night movie. Now let's try this again. Make the deal!"

Derek had no choice. "Let's deal, fucker."

"Oh, I'm so afraid," Bagdasarian mocked. "You're playing in the big leagues now, little man. Do what I tell you like a good boy, or Kelly's history."

Derek sat back and listened.

Stoneham, Massachusetts
October 31st
2 a.m.

He needed the jewels back. He was going to squash the Detective like an ant. From Alexander's Macedonian phalanx to Napoleon the theory of military strategy was always the same; take control of the battlefield and keep the enemy off balance. Twenty years of service in the United States intelligence community had given him access to technology and an amoral code of life. That combination had proven deadly to countless numbers of enemies of the United States and those who dared cross his path on any personal level. The plan he had in mind was a favorite of the cold war era. The technology was simple. It was just gathering the components that were going to be an inconvenience.

Stoneham Memorial Hospital was a mile away from his room at the Marriott and at two in the morning it was his only option. Bagdasarian sat next to Kelly's unconscious body sorting through the various passports in his briefcase, finally pulling out an expired one from Syria. All he needed was the photograph. With that he could initiate the cascade of events accessing the necessary electronic components. He tucked a gold police shield into his wallet and then checked the clip from his semiautomatic. There were seven rounds left not counting the two full clips he had in his pocket. It was time to move out.

Centre Street was classic suburban Boston. Large Federal style homes rubbed shoulders with Protestant churches with their long white steeples. He needed at least two victims. Walking along the sidewalk he kept his weapon hidden underneath his left armpit, finally stopping at the only intersection in town with a traffic light. At this hour even the pizza shops and 7-11's were closed.

Several cars passed by the intersection before the light changed. Three laughing teenagers bounced around on the inside in beat to some obnoxious rap music. Their movements were wild enough to engage the car's shock absorbers. His plans were interrupted when two other vehicles came in line directly behind his target. That was two too many. Ten minutes later and the situation was perfect. The car at the light was a big Ford Explorer, it's windows open and belching cigarette smoke. The young couple inside was arguing noisily ignoring his approach until it was too late. Bagdasarian waved his gun in front of the driver's face. "Excuse me, would you mind moving over for a moment." Carjacking was so damn easy when you had a gun pointed at someone.

"Please don't hurt us, mister," the driver said, sliding over towards his wife.

The woman began to cry. "Oh Jesus, mister. I'm pregnant. Don't do anything to hurt the baby," she begged.

"Just do as I say and no one will get hurt," Bagdasarian lied putting the car in drive. The ride towards the hospital took less then a couple of minutes. The two terrified passengers babbled incessantly about kids and babysitters and having mercy. A few blocks away from the hospital he pulled over. Their words slid off him like water on a duck's back. "I'm sorry, folks, it's time to get out now." The grateful but bewildered couple jumped out the passenger door, tumbling to the ground in a pile of arms and legs. Smiling, Bagdasarian reached over across the passenger window, raised his weapon and fired twice. Their bodies fell silent. One might recover, but not both. He drove the remaining distance to Stoneham Memorial pulling up to the emergency room parking lot. It wouldn't take long for the victims to be discovered.

Ten minutes later the wail of an ambulance siren pierced the night air. A fine rain began to fall. Timing his walk perfectly, Bagdasarian appeared at the emergency entrance as the two ambulances pulled up with his gunshot victims. One ambulance was a BLS unit, basic life support. The other was a full paramedic unit. A town this size couldn't afford to have two Paramedic Units at nighttime. Too bad, maybe both victims would have had a chance to survive. He flashed his fake police badge entering the double doors of the ER just as the second victim, the woman, was brought in. She was already intubated and CPR was being performed. He felt the woman's bloodied hand brushed along side his back as the stretcher rushed by. All it took was a couple of shootings to send a typical American ER into total chaos. It was something he counted on tonight.

Hospital security directed him through the labyrinth of corridors just as the words 'code 99' echoed over the hospital intercom. A gold shield could get you in almost anywhere but not from this point on. A male respiratory therapist came towards him at a semi-run, obviously on his way to the code. Bagdasarian stopped him with a flash of his badge, and then pulling his weapon, led him into a nearby room. One muffled gunshot later and he was wearing the man's white lab coat with his magnetic stripped ID security badge, replacing the photo ID with that from his expired passport.

He walked down the hallway, this time with a new identity. A lab tech bumped into him as he turned a corner. "Excuse me, EKG department?" he asked.

She was only too happy to oblige.

Northern New Hampshire
October 31st

Derek's mood was foul. Happy Halloween? Bull crap! Oncoming headlights reflected off his windshield, their diffuse glow spreading bizarre shadows inside the car's cockpit. His mind played tricks from fatigue. Only Bagdasarian's death would satisfy Derek's blood lust. But there was also another kind of lust lurking in his mind. Exhausted from stress, he pushed the VR-4 to 95 miles per hour along 93 north, passing other cars pretending to do the speed limit. The car hardly flinched.

The slimy bastard must have been running scared. Why else did he retreat into Canada? Derek knew Bagdasarian had tentacles that reached across continents. He could be rushing headlong into oblivion for all he knew. The thought of being outflanked physically or mentally was depressing. It was well within the other man's talents to bury him if given half a chance. He would have to be at his best. It was going to be 'mano et mano', promised Bagdasarian. Kelly's life depended on his cooperation.

His next instructions were going to be waiting for him at Marie's café in Magog just across the border. There were still a couple of hours before the rendezvous when he pulled up to a long line of cars snaking towards Canadian customs. The jam soon split into separate lines for commercial and passenger vehicles, moving forward at the pace of molasses flowing uphill. Everything irritated him. His mind flirted between homicidal impulses to romantic desperation. The elderly couple who couldn't decide whether they wanted to return to the US or not suffered the wrath of his car horn. He wished he could shoot the tires off their boat trailer that hogged two lanes a couple of car lengths ahead. The gas gauge flashed red warning he was driving on fumes. The dog whined its whine of having to go pee or take a dump. Too bad, she'd have to wait just like he did. He was tired, his car was tired and the worst was yet to come.

It was his turn. He pulled up to the inspection booth. The young female guard scanned him and mechanically punched in his license plate number, beginning her usual litany of questions. "Citizenship?" she asked. Her accent was Quebec French.

"American," Derek replied, trying to be as polite as possible. Visibly distracted, his thoughts were on Bagdasarian's next scheduled contact at a café a few miles up the road. He checked his watch impatiently. There was still an hour and a half left before the deadline. The customs guard was not unattractive; the way her hair and make up was applied caught his attention as few in the States could do. God bless the French Canadians. He was exhausted, but alert enough to appreciate the beauty of full feminine lips pursed in a French accent.

"Place of birth?" the guard asked.

"Providence, Rhode Island," Derek answered impatiently, drumming his fingers on the leather wrapped steering wheel. Cricket began to bark. Not now, dammit!

"Purpose of visit and length of stay?" the woman inquired craning her neck out of the booth checking the inside of his car.

"Ah, just sight seeing," Derek said. The dog began barking wildly once again. "Quiet!" he barked back at Cricket. The Yorkie was making such a commotion that he was tempted to muzzle the dog's mouth with his hand in order to hear the question. "Probably won't be longer then a couple of days," he added nervously. He watched the Canadian officer mark a piece of paper. Shit! The last thing he needed was to be triaged for inspection at a secondary customs station while the clock ticked in Bagdasarian's favor.

"What's your dog's name?" the inspector inquired, emotionless.

"Cricket. But it's not my dog. She belongs to my fiancé," Derek answered, stroking the dog's head repeatedly. The motion mesmerized the animal into quiet submission.

"Bringing any firearms or alcohol into Canada?" The woman kept looking at the dog.

"Of course not," Derek lied, consciously feeling the weight of the holstered .45 automatic against his left chest. He had forgotten about the weapon and the critical nature the Canadians guarded their sovereignty against American guns. The pressure of the two pieces of clustered antique jewelry that hung around his neck also made him flinch. For all he knew they, too, were contraband and probably stolen from someplace famous. Maybe there even was an APB out for him from Massachusetts. He remembered he wasn't supposed to leave the state after the shootings at his house and that at Kasson's. Maybe there was an international watch out for smuggled antiquities. Hell, if he got caught, at least Canadian jails had a far nicer reputation then their American counterparts. If he got caught, Kelly was toast. He couldn't get caught.

"Any pet brought into Canada must have papers documenting current rabies vaccination status. Those papers must be presented on demand. Are you aware of that law?"

Derek had been mentally prepared for almost any contingency. This wasn't one. He was ready to drag race the local authorities across the Queens Highway if they tried to pull him over. The VR-4 was unmatchable in any pursuit of equals. He was prepared to shootout tires like a scene out of a Steve McQueen movie if they tried to block his way. He was certainly not above shamelessly flashing his badge and begging for forgiveness, calling on the universal brotherhood of police officers. But this, this issue with the dog was not on his agenda. He needed to move the process along. Time was of the essence.

The stupid dumb ass dog had led him to Bagdasarian and Lansky. The dog helped to bring Kelly into his life. He owed the dog big, but now, the animal had suddenly become a liability. Let a Korean family adopt the animal. It could become someone's next meal for all he cared. "Look, officer, this is my fiancé's dog." He lowered his voice and continued. "The truth is, we had a fight not too long ago about the little thing. I'm heading up to see her now to apologize. If I show up without the dog, she'll never talk to me again." He was stroking the custom's inspector with all the die-hard French romantic illusions he could muster.

The woman looked at him professionally and frowned. Derek anticipated a disaster. What else was new? It was only a matter of time before everything would close in around him like a net. Then, out of nowhere, the inspector broke into a smile. "Next time," she said, waving him on with a warning.

Next time for sure, thought Derek. He patted the dog on the head and drove off to his appointment.

Magog, Canada
October 31st
6 p.m.

Marie's Café was little more then a white cinderblock diner at the end of an exit ramp. Ten Formica tables and an equal number of red counter seats stretched cozily opposite a short order grill. No one looked familiar. Derek noted 'Marie' was a man in his late sixties, lumberjack tall, whose sweat stained greasy t-shirt must have been the secret ingredient to the 'world famous meatloaf' sign advertised outside. Sitting down at the far end of the counter away from the door, he ordered a cup of coffee using what little Fall River French he could muster. "*Café, noir.*" The menus were all in French. The little packets of sugar were all in French. This was clearly not a tourist hangout.

"Chloe! O*u est tu?* Damn it girl, where are you?:" the cook bellowed, clearly irritated with waitress' absence and flipping a hamburger on the griddle.

Derek studied the Canuck absentmindedly twirling his spoon, one eye watching the door and the other towards the unisex bathroom. He had no intentions of being surprised from either direction. Even his car was parked behind the restaurant and out of the way. He unzipped his jacket to better access his weapon if necessary. Six-fifteen, then six-thirty came and went with nothing out of the ordinary happening. A steady flow of customers filled the seats, ate quickly then went on their way. Almost all ordered the meatloaf. Derek hated meatloaf, but, when in Rome.... The meatloaf with a pound of mashed potatoes buried under thick brown gravy landed on his plate at seven o'clock. Two bites later and he had to admit that this sweaty Canadian was definitely onto something. If it had to be his last meal, he could have done worse. Too bad he wasn't in the mood to eat. He'd save the rest for the dog.

"*Y a-t-il un person qui s'appele Dereek?* Is there anyone here by the name of Dereek?" the cook yelled, waving the pay phone receiver. "Chloe, what do you want me to do? Run the restaurant by myself? *Merde*!"

The name was butchered but the call was clearly for him. He went to the edge of the counter and cautiously took the call. "Yes?"

"Enjoying the meatloaf?" Bagdasarian asked.

Derek pivoted wildly looking at all the customers, his weapon half drawn. He was the only one in the room with a phone to his ear. Was it a lucky guess? "Let me speak to Kelly," he demanded.

"In due time. All in due time," Bagdasarian answered. "It's seven o'clock. I would like to invite you for dinner in Quebec City at nine. I'll call you and let you know exactly where a few minutes before."

"Not without speaking to Kelly first. I'm not going anywhere." He was fed up being dragged around the Canadian wilderness.

"Oh, all right. Kelly, *hokees,* there's a nice man who wants to talk to you on the telephone. Here, answer the phone, sweetheart."

The delay was agonizing. Finally Derek heard heavy breathing followed by an incoherent mumble, but it was clearly her voice. "Kelly, it's me, Derek." The telephone airways were filled with silence.

"Derek?" she slurred as the name floundered in her brain for recognition. "Derek! Oh, Derek. There's a girl...."

"That's quite enough love chit chat," Bagdasarian interrupted. "Now you'd better hurry. I've left you a little present. In five minutes I'm going to make a call to the local Magog police notifying them there is a problem at Marie's Café. The Mounties always get their man and in about ten minutes you're going to be a wanted man. Good bye."

What did he mean, thought Derek ominously. The phone went dead. Once again he had no choice. He paid his bill with American dollars ignoring the prevailing exchange rate. What the hell, it was Lansky's money anyway. Stepping out into the crisp Canadian night, he pulled his jacket tight against the cold and walked to his car parked behind the restaurant. He needed a map. Montreal was to the west and Quebec City lay somewhere to the east, but that was about it for his knowledge of the trans Canada highway system.

The car was parked against a chain link fence behind the restaurant. Darkness and metal wire separated civilization from the rest of the great northern wilderness. Derek stopped about ten feet away from his vehicle. Someone was sitting in the front seat. Shit! He thought he had locked it before going inside the diner. Removing his .45 automatic from his shoulder holster, he cautiously approached. All he could see was long hair against the driver's headrest. Crouching low he crawled up to the driver's side of the car and yanked the door open. The body of a young girl tumbled out. Blood was caked on her brown hair. She had been shot once in the head. The nametag on her uniform said 'Chloe'. He could almost hear the police sirens in the distance. It was time to play Houdini once more.

Quebec City, Canada
October 31st
9 p.m.

The call came on Lansky's cell phone at exactly 9 o'clock just as he was crossing the St Lawrence, exiting off Autoroute 73 onto the Grande Allee. Bagdasarian spoke only four words, 'Lowe's Hotel Atrium Restaurant', and then hung up. The last time Derek had been to Quebec City was as a reluctant teenager forced to keep company with his parents on a family trip. He was desperate to see Kelly. He was desperate to put a bullet in Bagdasarian's head and end this insanity. The hotel was a vertical landmark in a city of short stubby brownstones. The Atrium was a premier rotating restaurant sitting on its twenty-fourth story like a crown jewel.

Traffic lights were maddeningly against him the whole ride off the bridge. An art show at the University slowed him even further, delaying his mad dash to the hotel but giving him time to think. Hatred had to be tempered with caution, prudence and vigilance. Peterson and Lefevre were 400 miles to the south. There was no one to cover his back this time. Bagdasarian was capable of anything. Derek kept thinking back to the poor Canadian teenager shot dead in the front seat of his car. Was Chloe the daughter of the restaurant's owner? Did it make a difference who's daughter she was? The madman would stop at nothing for the jewels Derek had over his neck.

Heading towards the old city, Lowe's Hotel was on the right hand side of the Grand Allee. A large bronze plaque across from the street said 'Plains of Abraham', commemorating the famous battlefield between the British and French in the 1700's. The streets around the hotel were empty; tourist season had ended a month before. What was he looking for: snipers, uniformed guards, men in three piece suits wearing sunglasses in the middle of the night, Claymore mines? The possibilities were endless. Bagdasarian could have a few of his henchmen anywhere tonight and he'd never know until it was too late. The one thing for sure was that he was alone.

Ignoring the bellboy and doorman, he left the dog in his car at the door, pocketing the car keys and cautiously entering the lobby. Everything from the gift shop to the registration desk appeared quiet. He half expected to see someone reading a newspaper with holes cut out for surveillance sitting in a chair by the main entrance. No one cared he was there. Nothing seemed out of place. Guests and service personnel went about their business in a classic European cadence, everyone adhering to the meticulous French dress code except for him. Between the docks of Scituate, Kasson's cesspool and an uninterrupted four hundred mile ride north, Derek was suddenly aware he smelled like spoiled fish.

The hotel had four elevators, but only one went all the way to the top restaurant level. It wasn't a popular time of year to explore the city; the line to the elevator was empty except for a few hotel guests. A bellboy, closer in age to forty then to twenty, slowly maneuvered an overloaded luggage dolly belonging to a blue haired matron and her white poodle. The dog was better manicured then most humans. Derek followed behind them, avoiding the snapping dog and took the express elevator to the top.

The Atrium was a splendid crown to the Lowe's chain of hotels. A rotating gourmet restaurant in a city of gourmet restaurants enchanted as well as delighted the senses. From its perch high atop the hotel, the St Lawrence Sea Way, the Laurentian Valley and mountains were visible for fifty miles. Derek took his firefighter's elevator key off his key chain locking down the elevator as he exited. It was time to take back some semblance of control. He put the key back in his pants pocket and patted it twice for luck. No one was going to leave the restaurant via the elevator without his permission.

A sultry hostess in a long black evening gown greeted him at the entrance podium. "*Bonjour, monsieur.* A party of one?"

"I'm here to meet a friend," Derek said walking abruptly past the girl ignoring her mild protest. He reached under his jacket and slid his Beretta part way out of the shoulder holster. Within seconds of scouting around, he spotted Bagdasarian and Kelly at a window table. He approached his nemesis cautiously, the memory of the Faneuil Hall shoot-out galvanizing his determination.

The closer Derek came, the more he saw how awful Kelly looked. She sat stone-faced against the window corralled by her captor. Her hair was tossed and unkempt, her clothes wrinkled as if she had slept in them. Still she was alive and that was all that mattered.

Bagdasarian looked up just as he came to the table. "Ah, glad to see you Detective. I had almost given up on you," he said checking his watch. "Please have a seat," he motioned with his hand across the table. "I hear the rack of lamb is a specialty of the house this time of year. I can heartily recommend this Beujoulais, too," he said raising his glass to the light. "Not too sweet and not too dry. A wonderful color and bouquet, don't you think?"

Derek ignored his comments and inane conversation. "Kelly, you OK?" he asked. He stared into her eyes, looking for some sign of allegiance. The night they pledged their love in Florida was so long ago that it sat like a dream in his heart. So much had happened since then. It was just a few days ago that he was convinced of her death. Part of him had died that day as well. Now she sat in front of him, resurrected. Did she still love him?

"She's fine, she's fine," Bagdasarian said answering for her.

Kelly looked back at Derek and, for the first time in days, her eyes focused on reality. "I think so," she slurred. "Things have been foggy. I haven't been thinking straight for days. He's kept me doped up on some kind of drug."

"Ecstasy," Bagdasarian interrupted. "An amazing chemical, really. It helped convince her to be a much more willing travel companion these past few days. Unfortunately I just recently ran out of my supply."

"What have you done to her?" Derek demanded fist clenched towering over the seated figures. The ambience of white linens and tuxedoed waiters stymied the urge to kill.

"Derek, be careful. He's got me wired to something," Kelly said.

Bagdasarian took a bite of a buttered roll and sipped some more wine. "Please keep your voices down. You're beginning to upset the other patrons," he counseled.

"I'm going to cut your heart out, you bastard. You are gonna' die right here and now." This time Derek grabbed Bagdasarian by his exposed hand, locking it vice like firmly against the white linen tablecloth. Pulling his other hand from beneath his jacket he put his gun to Bagdasarian's head aching to squeeze the trigger right there. He could think of nothing better then to see the man's brains splattered on the walls of this fancy restaurant. It was the moment he had been dreaming about for days.

Bagdasarian flinched. For the first time in years, someone was causing him physical pain. He could not remove his hand from the Detective's grasp. "I think not," he said revealing an electronic touch key in his other hand and placed it next to Kelly. "My finger is on the control of Kelly's little electronic surprise, so get your damn hands off me!" he exploded uncharacteristically. He hated losing control in public.

Derek was taken off guard. He looked at the device and hesitated in his mission of death. All he could tell for sure was that several lights were flashing on the unit. Again, it seemed that his vengeance was going to be delayed. He looked at Kelly's frightened face then reluctantly released his grasp on his mortal enemy stepping back from the table. His gun remained pointed at Bagdasarian's head.

"That's a good boy," Bagdasarian said. "You see, if I take my thumb off this little red button here, then poof, we all go up in one big ball of fire."

"Cut the shit," Derek spat. "What do you want?"

"The stones, just give me the stones and I'll be on my way," Bagdasarian answered.

He had a pair of aces. Should he draw for a third? Would he ever get another chance? "Not a chance until I know Kelly is away from you and safe," Derek replied, seething between breaths.

"Now that is a shame," Bagdasarian said. "I really do want those jewels. I'm afraid I can't live without them. Can you say the same thing of this beautiful young lady? I am fully prepared to die. Are you?"

"Then I might as well blow your brains out now," Derek answered, each retort just upping the ante. He placed his .45 automatic at the back of Bagdasarian's head again and pulled back the slide, no thought of hiding the weapon from any passing waiter or roving dinner guests. He could have cared less who saw him pull the trigger.

Bagdasarian hesitated stunned at the audacity of this stupid small town detective. No one had ever threatened him and lived for more then a few seconds. This man had done so twice in less then a minute. "Listen to me very carefully, my stupid Armenian friend. Kelly has a modified Holter monitor wired to her chest; a very lovely chest, I might add. The monitor must see her EKG at all times. She must remain within the range of my transceiver and the assurance signal from my control device here or a tiny package of C4 in the Holter monitor will detonate. And you know that kind of explosion will ruin her beautiful dress. Only I have the code to deactivate this ingenious device. So put your stupid gun away and give me my stones!"

If this were poker, he was about ready to be called. Derek hesitated, the information slowly registering. He was just too tired. He slowly retracted his weapon and holstered it. "Can't do it. I don't have it here with me," Derek answered straight faced.

"*Ashag,* you ass!" Bagdasarian yelled incredulously. "I can't believe you left them out of your sight! Go get it!"

"Only if I can take Kelly with me," Derek said. He had to

have something.

"I'm glad we understand each other. Sure, take her. Won't do you any good. You're just a stupid little man. You can't beat this. It comes from the best minds of the intelligence services. You can't pull it off her chest without detonating the device. You can't leave the range of my transceiver and that's only about a hundred feet. What are you planning on doing, hero?"

"I'd just feel better if she was with me." Derek reached behind Bagdasarian's back and took Kelly by her bound hands, gently rising her up from her chair. Her hesitation evaporated with one look into the eyes of the man she loved.

"OK. I'll tell you what. I'll turn off my transceiver for, shall we say, forty- five minutes. The devise is still armed, so you can't remove it; but it will permit you time to go and retrieve the package. If you are not within a hundred feet of me by eleven o'clock tonight, then I will reset the transceiver and up she goes." Bagdasarian motioned his hands in a dramatic arch to the ceiling. "Now I trust we understand each other. Do we have a deal?"

Derek nodded grim faced.

"Now I hope you have the jewels in a safe place and not too far out of town. Remember, eleven o'clock and no longer. Oh, and by the way, did I mention that the detonator is also attached to a timer? You'd better hurry. You were a tad late for dinner. I think you have only about an hour left before you don't have any more time left...if you know what I mean."

Kelly leaned her weight against his shoulder. "Where?" Derek asked.

"Go to Montmorency Falls. It's just a few miles out of town. Meet you on the cliff walk. I'd hate for something to go wrong and end up hurting any innocent bystanders, so you'd better hurry. I'm going to stay here and finish my dinner, if you don't mind."

"Since when do you give a shit about anyone else besides yourself?" Derek said. He began to walk away from the table with Kelly in hand. Suddenly he turned towards Bagdasarian. "Know this in your fucked up heart. If anything happens to this lady, you can kiss the stones goodbye. And I will kill you with my bare hands," he added for effect.

Bagdasarian frowned. "Yes, yes, yes. I'm sure you will. You're wasting your breath and my time. Now move along like a good boy and bring me my package."

Quebec City, Canada
October 31st
10 p.m.

"Get in, get in!" Derek shouted, rudely pushing Kelly's head down inside the front seat of his car. "We don't have much time." His Eddie Bauer knife severed the restraints on her wrists. Cricket yelped, startled from sleep by Kelly's simultaneous appearance in the car and sitting on her foot. He shoved the knife inside his leg strap and turned on the ignition.

"Where are we going?" Kelly asked, the sudden acceleration of the car knocking her off balance into the seat cushion. "You heard him. We can't go very far. And, besides, we don't have much time left." She saw a sign for Montmorency. It was in the other direction. What was this crazy Armenian doing now?

The lights of downtown Quebec faded as Derek zipped in and out of traffic, ignoring every light and stop sign along the way. "Don't you get it Kelly? He's going to kill us no matter what we do." Checking the mirrors, his head bobbed back and forth in wild swings. "The stones are the only things keeping either one of us alive. As soon as I give them up, we're both dead. I've got to get this thing off you now, otherwise neither one of us has a chance in hell."

Kelly strained to connect the veiled image of the past few days. The drugs were wearing off and her memory still suspect. "He could be bluffing, Derek. I don't really think he'd hurt me." Fleeting image of a gunshot flashed in her memory. "Oh my God, there was this young girl ...," staring out the window her voice faded. "I think he might have hurt her."

So much had happened over the past few days. There was no other way to tell her but to just say it. "Kelly, your pal, Jack, doesn't bluff. Rick, Al and Steve are all dead, and I don't know how many others." Derek revealed the trail of death and destruction from the Keys to Canada that followed in the man's wake. Summarizing the financial transactions discovered on Bagdasarian's computer, he concluded with Kasson's death at Lansky's hands and then Lansky's end as well. There was no love lost between residency classmates at this point.

Kelly moaned quickly mutating into a heart-wrenching sob. The past few days existed only in the form of shadows and the chemical haze of dreams. This reality was horrid. Rocking back and forth in the front seat, tears flowed down her cheeks for the men dead by

Bagdasarian's hands. They had all been her friends, too.

"Come on, now," Derek reassured, patting her on the knee. "Crying now isn't going to help. Save the tears for when this is all over. I've got you covered. We're going to beat him. We really are. I promise."

Somehow it was all her fault. Everything was collapsing around her. If only she had never disobeyed her boss in the medical examiner's office everyone would still be alive. "Leave me alone!" Kelly screamed through her tears. "I can cry if I want to." She turned her head away from him burying her face in her hands. The ligature marks on her wrist glared back. It was all just too insane. Was she still a hostage or just another potential victim? She had once loved Jack, spending two years of her life with the man. Now he was threatening to put an end to her life. How could that be? Her last few minutes on earth were going to be spent with someone she loved but hardly knew. She pushed back her tears. "Derek, all I have is another hour. I don't want anyone else getting hurt because of me." Her mind drifted off to Nunez' face. She couldn't imagine him being dead. "You're not a bomb technician. Even if you knew your way around the electronics, you'd need all kinds of specialized equipment. Just go away and save yourself," she pleaded.

"Sorry, Kelly," Derek said with a reassuring smile. "I'm not going anywhere. You're stuck with me for life."

"I wish you could rephrase that," Kelly said reaching to the floor picking up Cricket. The weight of the dog pushed against the harness strapped onto her chest. "How far out of town do you have the stones hidden?" Kelly asked.

"You're lookin' right at it, babe."

She was in love with a madman. "What! You've had it on you all along?" She said looking at him incredulously. Was he inspired or just plain crazy?

"Listen up, Kelly. I need to know a few things." An ambulance blocked his lane bringing traffic to a full stop. "Is he working alone up here?"

"Yes, no, I think so." Her face collapsed into the babble of stress as she tried to concentrate. "Jeezes, Derek. I really don't know."

"Take your time and think," Derek coached patiently. Traffic was moving again. "I've been chasing him for the past ten hours. I know he hasn't slept during that time because neither have I. I know he called me a couple of times from his cell phone. Did he speak to anyone else?"

She was beginning to remember. "He never left me out of his sight even when I had to go to the bathroom." That image was suddenly very embarrassing. "I don't recall seeing anyone else with him. He did do a lot of talking, but it was all to me. 'My queen this, *hokees* that'. How we were going to begin a new life together and get a second chance. Just too weird," her voice faded off.

Derek cringed. Could it be Bagdasarian was still in love with her? Insane! "Well, at least I know that he's working up here alone. That may not put the odds in our favor but at least it evens them up a bit. I hate to be shot in the back while I'm trying to save both our rear ends."

"So, now what?"

"I've been thinking about an idea that should work," Derek said calmly. "Sometimes these government types forget the simplest rules. Remember the acronym K.I.S.S.?"

Kelly shook her head to the negative.

"It stands for 'Keep it simple stupid,'" Derek said. "Just remember, the guys who built and designed this device are the same ones who would buy a $500 ashtray. There's a hospital right up the road from here on the Grande Allee. All you doctors follow the same set of rules and guidelines, don't you? You all read the same books, right? An EKG is an EKG whether it's in English or in French, right?"

"Most always," Kelly answered, nervously tracing the box at her waist with the tips of her fingers. "Sometimes our medicines are a little different but for the most part everything is pretty much homogenized. A McDonalds' is a McDonalds whether you're in Fall River or in Quebec."

"Good. That's what I wanted to hear. Tell me everything you know about Holter monitors."

"Jeeze, Derek, I don't know," Kelly replied searching her memory. "I order them for my patients in the ER when I'm worried about arrhythmias. They operate at a range of 450-470 megahertz. All they do is record electrical signals of the heart to a continuous tape. The recorder lasts from 24 hours to a couple of weeks depending on the sophistication of the unit. Then the tape is removed and read by a computer or cardiologist." She looked at his face. "Derek, I love you, honey, but you ain't no cardiologist."

"Don't have to be, don't wanna be," he said smiling at her. "Look, I want you to start loosening your blouse so I can get access to those wires."

"Why? Jack's already told you that the unit would detonate

with C5 if we attempt to remove the wires. If the monitor misses just one heartbeat, I'm toast! Just give him what he wants and maybe he'll let us go."

"C4," Derek corrected. "And he has no intentions on letting either one of us live."

"C4, C5... who cares! I can't believe all this is just about money." Kelly began to cry again despite her best efforts to put up a brave front.

"Look, Kelly, what Bagdasarian wants, the jewels he's already killed for, is beyond anything you can imagine. If I were smart, I'd dump you now and live happily forever after on the fortune they'd bring. He can't afford not to kill us, no matter what we do. We both know too much. If we turn around now and show up at Montmorency Falls with the detonator intact, he will kill both of us as soon as the exchange is made. We have to get it off you now and then deal with him once and for all."

Kelly brushed away her tears and starred ahead in silence. She knew the truth as well.

Laval Hospital, Quebec City
October 31st
10:15 p.m.

Laval Hospital looked just the same as its American counterparts except the signs were all in French. Derek pulled Kelly inside the ER, the sweat and intensity on his face conveyed his urgency to anyone who tried to block his path. "English! Does anyone here speak English?" he asked the triage nurse flashing his police shield. Based on the woman's bored look, he was probably perceived as just another rude intrusive American who was going to have to wait his turn like everyone else. Derek glanced nervously at his watch opening his jacket just enough to expose his weapon and glared at the nurse. She quickly rose from her station retreating into the patient care area.

A moment later a young female physician approached them. Tall, thirtyish, with striking straight long black hair and an attitude projecting French superiority in all manners, she introduced herself as Dr Broulee. "What is dees with you Americans and guns? What is zee problem that makes you so obnoxious in my Emergency Department?" she demanded, her eyes flashing angrily.

The lady had balls. He liked her. Derek outlined the urgency of his needs, opening Kelly's blouse to expose the wires while she stood mute. At first the French ER physician just stood and stared. This was one emergency for which she had never been trained. Then the woman smiled, relishing the idea of adventure and drama they were about to share. Apparently adrenaline junkies existed on both sides of the border.

"My first name is Lily. Please call me Lil, everyone else does," she offered, her voice now sultry instead of a pissed-off French. "Ohh, dees sounds so much like zee James Bond, doesn't it?" she added with a childlike squeal. She yelled some commands in French to her waiting staff. "Outside. Outside. We cannot stay here. Go and I will bring za equipment personally." She motioned for Kelly to get on the nearest gurney and out the automatic doors of the ambulance bay.

"Go, Go Go!" she commanded.

Derek rolled with Kelly and the hospital stretcher past the emergency entrance, past the ambulance turn-around circle, parking himself in the middle of a large red cross painted on the concrete of a helicopter landing-pad. The night air was cold. It was Canada. Somewhere the stars saturated the sky but he couldn't see squat underneath the glare of the high intensity lights

A moment later the French ER doc appeared outside the ambulance entrance riding a stretcher loaded with two large boxes. She dismissed the two orderlies accompanying her outside. "What can I do to help?" she offered.

"Just hold your light here," Derek ordered guiding her hand to the front of Kelly's chest. The thin beam of light shimmered along the multicolored wires of Kelly's Holter monitor. Pivoting he opened the first box on the stretcher. It was an ACLS rhythm simulator. He turned on the unit and listened to the comforting beep of the electronics as a green EKG pattern appeared on the black screen.

"We give these ACLS courses all the time. Just like in America. Probably even better," Lily said proudly.

"How much time we got?" he asked.

Kelly looked at her watch anxiously. "About forty minutes, give or take. And if you don't take this off me real soon, I'm going to scream," she added.

Derek looked at her in the eyes. "Might as well assume the royal position," he said motioning his hand in a horizontal sweep. "It's now or never."

Kelly obeyed. She opened her blouse, revealing the series of multicolored wires that spread across her chest like tentacles. She was there only as a passive participant; her brain had not yet engaged in assisting the detective with any plan. "What are you going to do?" she asked. Her eyes were distant and averted.

She still didn't get it. "Kelly, remember in Fall River awhile back, I met you at St Chris' while you were giving an ACLS course?" He watched her head nod in recognition. "The rhythms simulator, how does it work? Think!" he commanded.

The vacant glare in Kelly's eyes slowly lifted. A smile slowly crested on her lips. "Sure. It's a modified Zoll unit. The smaller box controls the rhythms and the machine reads the patterns, displaying them on the monitor to your right, there," she pointed. "I use it all the time for our ACLS courses. That thing can mimic every kind of cardiac rhythm known to man and God. Hey, I'm beginning to catch on. Do you think it can work?" Her attitude flipping a complete 180.

"Just like a Holter monitor, right?" Derek said with a smile.

"You're a genius if this works," Kelly said, smiling for the first time that night.

"If it doesn't you're going to spend eternity telling me 'I told you so'," Derek quipped.

Lily interrupted their love fest. "Enough of this congratulations. I think you'd better hurry."

The French woman was right. Derek removed his Eddie Bauer knife from his leg strap. With deliberate short swipes of his blade, he stripped the three wires leading to the Zoll defibrillator and did the same to the Holter monitor. Then he froze. The package of C4 or what might be C4 was clearly visible. Would Bagdasarian really have killed Kelly over money? In front of him lay the woman of his dreams, half naked, vulnerable and helpless. A bizarre concoction of wires and explosives threatened to end the lives of everyone present literally in a heartbeat. So far, this had not been a traditional courtship. Then the faces of Rick, Al, and Steve flashed in his mind. He saw their bodies sprawled out on the floor of his own home. He saw Kasson' bulging neck veins popping over his stupid bow tie and his mind replaying Lansky's spiral dance of death into the Fall River mud. A mistake now would end time. When you die the whole world dies.

"Derek?" Kelly prodded. The man had suddenly become lost in thought.

He refocused and looked into her eyes. He was all she had. "I'm here, babe," he reassured. He reached over and took the flashlight out of the doctor's hand and put it in his own mouth. "Out," he instructed through his teeth. He waved the Canadian away. Surprised, she looked at him, nodded in assent and withdrew to a safe distance back to the ER entrance. "Where do they go?" he mumbled again. The words came out garbled.

"What?" Kelly asked.

Derek removed the flashlight from his mouth. "I said, where do they go?"

"Just follow the color codes. RA is right arm. LA is left arm and so on."

He did as instructed, splicing each wire to the appropriate terminal in the Zoll unit. Meanwhile the simulator kept the rate at a steady sixty beats per minute on the teaching unit. So far, so good. He was ready for the next step. "Here goes," he warned.

"Wait, wait. A kiss for luck," Kelly demanded. She reached over and pulled him towards her face. Their lips met and their mouths separated. Time stood still for them once again, violating every known law of the physical universe.

Derek had to force himself away. "Wow! We should try wiring

you with bombs more often," he teased. One by one he removed the Holter leads and replaced them with the dummy ones from the simulator. They held their breaths. Nothing happened. The ACLS rhythm simulator fed the electronic currents uninterrupted, the same ones the Holter monitor recognized, preventing the bomb's detonation. He undid the harness from Kelly's body and helped her re-button her blouse, reluctantly watching her breasts disappear from sight.

Tears of relief flowed down Kelly's cheeks as she buried Derek in an avalanche of kisses. "Let's get out of here," she begged. "Let the police take care of this."

He held her tightly by both shoulders and looked at her. "Can't do that."

"Why, Derek? Why?" she beseeched.

"'Cause he's going to keep on coming until he gets both the jewels and us. We can't just keep running away." She just didn't get it. The real world didn't work nice and polite.

"Derek, what if I talk to him...," her words fading uncomfortably.

It was a question that shouldn't have been asked and they both knew it. "How much time do we have?" he said putting the knife back into his leg strap. While Kelly looked at her watch he bundled the Holter monitor and ACLS rhythm simulator with some duck tape.

"About thirty minutes," Kelly said back on his team. She looked at Derek incredulously as he carried both boxes in his arms back towards his car. "You're not seriously considering making me ride with that thing again, are you?" she asked.

"Workin' on a plan," Derek said simply.

Montmorency Falls, Quebec
October 31st
10:45 p.m.

The Falls lay about six miles outside the famed walled city of Quebec. Although higher then Niagara, they were not as wide or as spectacular. As with everything else this time of year in Canada, the park was closed after dusk. The Canadians assumed that everyone would simply be on their honor and obey the law. No guards, no gates it was a perfect set up for an ambush or an exchange of Egyptian artifacts.

Derek tapped his bulletproof vest once for security looking uneasily at the walk up to the bottom of the Falls. The body armor sat unused for years in the trunk of his VR-4 despite departmental regulations. Nothing ever mattered that much before. This time he had someone to live for. It was his insurance policy. The simulator and booby-trapped Holter monitor slung over his shoulder emitted a continuous electrical current to Bagdasarian's sensor. As far as the electronics were concerned, Kelly was still wired.

Kelly tapped him on the shoulder to get his attention. "Ah, Derek. There's something I may have forgotten to tell you about the simulator," she said.

"Like what?" Derek asked distracted. Using the car's trunk as a screen, Derek surveyed the top of the cliffs. They were being watched, he was sure of it.

"Did I mention that the rhythm simulator has a battery life of about one hour, max? We don't even know if this unit was fully charged when we made the switch. When that battery dies, the Holter monitor will detect an end to my EKG pattern and detonate." She looked about them nervously. "I still think he's bluffing."

"Great. Now you tell me. Just one more nail in our coffin," he joked exasperated. "Your friend doesn't know how to play poker. I can tell." He brushed her hair into an annoying tussle to distract her. The look on Kelly's face exuded love mixed with fear. What did she read in his eyes? He needed the package as a decoy. "Do me a favor and double check the tape. I'm going for a hike." There was one more thing left to do. Derek reached down to his right leg and removed his back up piece from his leg holster. "Do you know how to use this?" he asked handing the weapon to Kelly.

It was the first time she had ever held a gun before, fumbling with it like a hot potato. "Aim and pull the trigger?" Kelly whispered.

"It's 'squeeze' the trigger. And don't forget to release the safety," Derek directed, pointing out the release mechanism on the handle.

Kelly held the gun like a fragile piece of Limoges glass, surprised at her own timidity. "Derek, I've never hurt anyone in my life; at least, not deliberately. Here, take this back. I hate the bastard. I wish he were dead; but I don't think I could shoot him. I don't think I could shoot anyone," she said, handing the gun back to Derek.

"Hey, careful which way you point that thing!" Derek warned, redirecting her outstretched hand away from his general direction. "Just do me a favor and hold on to it, in case." She was so fragile. All he wanted to do was wrap his arms around her and take her away from all this. Instead, he was leading her into the Valley of Death. He removed his bulletproof vest strapping it on Kelly's jacket.

"In case what?" Kelly asked fumbling with a Velcro clasp.

"In case he finds you instead of me. In case he sees me first and I don't come back to you." The implications were clear.

He left her with no choice in the matter. "Fine. Have it your way," Kelly said reluctantly. She reached up and held Derek's face in both hands. Despite his words, he exuded confidence and determination. "Which way are we going?"

Derek stood up to his full height. "There is no 'we'. You're going to park your cute little behind somewhere out of sight. Whatever happens I don't want you to come out. Use this gun only if he comes after you. Don't show yourself. I'm going to have enough trouble worrying about Bagdasarian. I don't need to have a second front."

Kelly shook her head, no. "I'm not leaving. Just think of me as your new partner; sort of like a rookie cop."

"That's what I'm afraid of. Like Sherman always said, 'always stepping on their cocks.'" The thought of his dead friend hardened Derek's resolve.

"With all due respect to Al, I don't have a cock. If you go, then I go."

Derek smiled sadly, thinking about his nail biting friend. She stated her position as a fact. It would be useless to try and argue the point. "Whatever. If you insist on coming, just stay low and out of sight." He picked up several large stones from the trailhead and placed them in his jacket pocket.

They began the ascent together, hand in hand. The Falls above them cascaded violently down the 180 meters into the basin along side their path, a full moon adding to the ambience. The Canadians had artfully enhanced nature by strategically placing a series of colored spotlights around the ledges and rock outcrops that formed the dome of the cliff. If not for their life and death predicament, it would have made a romantic backdrop to a beautiful night out.

Derek had Kelly. He had the jewels. How easy it would have been to just head to the nearest police station or American consulate. But then what? He was a few ounces shy of being classified as a cocaine trafficker. Three men were dead in his home. The blood of a teenager from Magog was splattered on the front seat of his car. It was his gun that Lansky used to kill Kasson. He couldn't run and hide from Bagdasarian for the rest of his life. He wanted a life with Kelly, not a living death. What mischief the man had planned for him up the cliff was a small price to pay just to get close enough to nail the fucker forever. It was probably going to be his only chance.

A few more yards up the trail and the tourist walkway took a sharp turn to the right. Motioning silence with his hands, he deposited Kelly behind an outcrop of rocks within seeing and hearing range of the unfolding drama. Derek spotted his nemesis standing on the cliff walk on the opposite side of the falls, the figure acknowledging him with a wave. The darkness made it impossible to tell whether the bastard was alone. Both men were clearly outlined against the night. They faced each other no more then thirty feet apart at the entrance to the cave beneath the falls. Bagdasarian had a backpack strapped to his shoulders and looked edgy. Never play poker, man, thought Derek; you'd lose.

"That's far enough," Bagdasarian said. "Let me see your hands."

"Let me see yours!" Derek demanded.

Both men simultaneously but cautiously held their arms out to the other. Neither had a weapon exposed. Bagdasarian held a remote in his left hand. How long would it take for either of them to draw a gun and fire? He noticed Bagdasarian wasn't wearing any ear communication device. Maybe he was alone after all.

"Where's the girl?" Bagdasarian demanded.

Good. At least Bagdasarian hadn't seen Kelly being dropped off yards away. "A safe distance from you," Derek answered, rolling his weight imperceptibly from foot to foot. If he had to jump, he was ready.

"Not too smart, little man. I'm the only one that can deactivate the bomb. And you're running out of time, too. No matter. Where are the stones?"

Derek stepped a few feet closer out into the light. "In fact,

I've got both right here. I'm wearing the jewels," he said, slowly reaching up to the top of his leather jacket. He unzipped the top lifting out one of the twin jewels for Bagdasarian to see. "And I think this belongs to you, too." He dropped the bundled Holter monitor with the rhythm simulator at his feet.

Bagdasarian was clearly surprised by the turn of events. "Not bad, little man. I don't know how you pulled that off but I've got to give you credit for your ingenuity. No matter. Now hand over the stones before I activate the detonator. I have an appointment in the morning and I'm going to need my beauty sleep."

"What, and risk scratching your precious little jewels? I don't think so." Removing the gold chain connecting the pieces from his neck, he teased Bagdasarian with brief glimpses of the treasure. Bagdasarian had to be salivating by now. Still, he wasn't getting an opening to draw his gun. He moved closer only to see Bagdasarian had both the transponder and a .45 automatic in his hands. Derek was beaten again. He began to withdraw back into the shadows but was stopped by the wave of Bagdasarian's gun.

"Drop the monitor over the side, now and step away from it!" Bagdasarian commanded, pointing to the foaming whirlpool at the base of the Falls just behind them.

"You sure?" Derek asked.

"Do it!"

Derek smiled. The pendulum was just going to swing in his favor. "Look, Jack, just put the gun away and let Kelly go. I just want to make sure she's safe from you," he said, his mind racing for whatever limited options were still available. On command he picked up the bundle and threw it into the water below.

The moment the electronic pakage hit the water, the unit shorted and then exploded. Derek had anticipated the avalanche of noise and spray of water. Jumping in the opposite direction into the shadows, he disappeared from Bagdasarian's sight.

Suddenly Kelly's voice erupted behind Derek. "You bastard! I can't believe you actually tried to kill me!" she screamed at Bagdasarian, rushing out of her hiding place.

Derek cringed at the sound of Kelly's voice. At some primal level he was pleased that she was witness to this final betrayal; but now he had to worry about her vulnerability as well as his own.

Bagdasarian responded by firing once towards her as she ran.

Kelly went down somewhere in the shadows. Derek's heart bottomed out at her silence. He couldn't tell whether she had been hit or not. Instinctively he could feel Bagdasarian approach. He was in a piss poor position to defend. He had to move. With a flick of his wrist, Derek threw one of the stones he had pocketed earlier into the air in a gentle arch. The psychology books were right again. Bagdasarian followed the rock as it flew above his head splashing into the pool of water below, distracting him just long enough for Derek to dive in the opposite direction underneath the railings into the caves behind the Falls.

Bagdasarian followed him with two wild shots into the curtain of water. "*Kacknem, sichteer,* fuckin' son of a bitch!" he screamed, cursing in Turkish, English and Arabic.

Montmorency Falls, Quebec

Derek removed his service piece from his shoulder holster and checked the clip. The only missing bullet lay somewhere in the marble floor of Kasson's house. Pulling back on the slide, he held the gun in a death grip, the weapon ready to fire. Kelly had his back up revolver. At least she had one last chance to defend herself – if she were still alive. He felt the handle of his Eddie Bauer knife inside his right boot, then put a few more large rocks in his pocket just in case.

Bagdasarian had to come to him. How far did the caves extend beneath the cliffs? Several times he slipped and fell into small side pools or puddles that leaked from the main falls above, slicing and chaffing his hands along the way. He made small sloshing noises with every step. The icy cold of the Canadian water saturated his shirt, pants and jacket cutting his breath into short bursts. Not only were his knuckles bleeding, but, he was having a hard time keeping his fingers mobile and flexible. Still, the only finger that had to work was his right index, his trigger finger.

"Come out and play," Bagdasarian called, yelling over the sound of the falls.

"Come and get me, you prick," Derek answered. Bagdasarian was capable of making mistakes. The move with the Holter monitor was stupid. Guys like Bagdasarian never did their own dirty work unless they had to. Bagdasarian was alone.

"Don't be afraid, little man. I'll make this quick. You know who I am. You know you can't win. Your kind always comes in second. Sort of like sloppy seconds, if you know what I mean," Bagdasarian taunted.

"Son of a bitch!" Derek screamed rolling away from Bagdasarian's voice. He had to stay low. "Why? Why did you have to kill so many people?" The longer he kept the man talking, the easier it would be to find him in the dark recesses of the caves. The memory of years of training in the military came back in short staccato bursts. Unfortunately, it was easier to roll on the ground when you were twenty than when you were pushing forty. Would he ever live to see that birthday?

"Nothing personal, my friend," Bagdasarian answered. He had moved about twenty feet to the left. "Strictly business. Everyone was just getting in my way. You know how troublesome that can be, don't you?" He fired another series of shots at Derek's head.

A bullet zipped past his ear. That was pretty good shooting for the dark; or did the man have a technological advantage? He rolled away crawling on all fours along the cave rim, parking behind a series of boulders. "They're just big fuckin' jewels. There are plenty of big jewels in the world. What makes these so special?" Derek fired blindly towards Bagdasarian's position and heard a curse. Had the man been hit?

"Ah, the squeaky mouse has a bite. Ever hear of the crown jewels of England? Well, the two pieces you carry represent a piece of my people's history as well. They are called the Eyes of Horus. They are the final pieces of the puzzle from my lifelong quest. When I am done with you, I will sell the completed crown and live happily ever after." Bagdasarian sent another barrage of bullets at Derek.

This time one round ricocheted off the cave wall and struck Derek in the right leg just below the knee. Derek stifled a moan and felt his calf. Something had torn through the muscle, in and out. Already lightheaded, he would have to staunch the flow of blood if he was going to have a chance. Was it the pain or was he losing more blood then he expected? He slid out his pants belt and tied it on his thigh to act as a tourniquet. It certainly looked easier in the movies, he thought fumbling with the belt buckle.

"Ah, I hear a little pain," Bagdasarian said. "Come out now, and I will end this quickly. If you don't I guarantee you that I will enjoy making you suffer. Perhaps a gut shot and then I'll leave you here to slowly die. The shit in your bowels will leak into your peritoneum. You'll get septic and die very, very painfully. Or maybe I'll just shoot you in the chest and watch you drown in your own blood. It will fill your fragile alveolar tissues and prevent air from coming in. Every breath you take will just force the blood into your lung tissues faster. You ever see a man drown in his own blood before? Quite entertaining, really."

Derek held his breath and froze motionless on the wet ground as Bagdasarian approached from his right, the exterior spotlights outlining his shadow as he came closer. Seizing the opportunity he fired twice. Bagdasarian fell backwards hitting the ground, twisting violently then stopped moving. It was over. Derek slowly got up and approached the body, dragging his bad leg stiffly behind him. The pain from the gunshot to his leg was almost unbearable, but the satisfaction of seeing Bagdasarian dead served as a powerful analgesic.

He stood over Bagdasarian's body barely making out the man's face in the darkness of the cave. Bagdasarian had a set of infrared night goggles strapped to his head. No wonder his firing was so accurate. Derek began his pivot to leave the cave complex, thinking just about Kelly. Suddenly the 'dead man' sat up and fired. The bullet struck Derek in the left shoulder, smashing the bone and spinning his whole body around, the force throwing him into the rocks. The pain was incredible. The gun dropped from his hands. He collapsed on his knees falling backwards against a bolder, his head bouncing off the basalt like a basketball. Full consciousness was only a few moments from ending. Derek's breaths came in short painful bursts. He remembered enough from his days in the service to know something had probably ricocheted into his lung as well.

Bagdasarian stood up and brushed the dirt and mud from his clothes. "Kevlar is an amazing substance, don't you think?" he asked, slowly wrapping a handkerchief on his blood soaked left hand while cradling his gun in his left armpit.

His vision came in and out of focus. Shit! A fuckin' bulletproof vest. Who would have thought? Time was running out. No Peterson or Lefevre to back him up this time. "You're under arrest," he forced out painfully. "Do you want me to read you your rights?" he wheezed.

"I'm going to enjoy this," Bagdasarian said towering over him.

"You wouldn't hurt a fellow Armenian, would you?" Derek asked. He used his one good leg to push himself upright against the cave wall. He couldn't move any further. It was all he could do not to pass out. "Besides, it's a federal offense to shoot an officer of the law, particularly when it involves transportation of a kidnapped victim over state lines."

"Do you really think I give a shit?" Bagdasarian smiled malevolently. "Besides, we're in Canada. You've got no legal authority here. And as far as being a fellow Armenian, guess what? I think of myself as ninety-nine percent Egyptian. I'm Moselm. You're just a fucking infidel, you know," Bagdasarian laughed. "I'm going to heaven for killing you."

Derek saw another figure move in silently behind Bagdasarian. It was Kelly. Her hair was matted from falls' spray. Her clothes were disheveled and torn. Her face, furrowed and caked with mud, had a ferocity imprinted on it that made her almost unrecognizable. She had the blind purpose of a cruise missile. He had never seen anything so beautiful before.

"He's got a vest on, Kelly. Aim at his head," Derek grunted

gasping for breath.

"I'm disappointed in you," Bagdasarian said. "I thought your last words would be a bit more creative. What am I supposed to do, turn away from you and look to see who's behind me?"

Kelly moved in closer. She raised Derek's back up weapon head high. "Don't move," she spit, clicking off the safety.

Bagdasarian froze. Was it the sound of her voice or the click of the guns mechanism? "Ah, *Hokees*, so good of you to join us. What do you plan to do, make a citizen's arrest?"

"Don't move, Jack. I mean it," she said screaming the words above the sound of the falls. "I'll shoot you if I have to."

Bagdasarian put both hands on his weapon and began his move.

"He's turning, Kelly," Derek yelled with his last good breath. "Fire! Fire!" he begged.

Bagdasarian pivoted.

Closing her eyes Kelly squeezed the trigger once. The recoil of the handgun took her by surprise while the echo of the discharge pounded her unprepared ears. The man still stood. The shot had grazed Bagdasarian's head, nothing more.

Bagdasarian hesitated for a second as he wiped a dribble of blood from his forehead. Starring at the blood in his hand, he looked back at Kelly's face, pissed. He raised his gun above her and struck Kelly once along the side of her head with the full weight of the weapon. Kelly crumpled lifeless to the ground. He returned his focus back to Derek straddling his prostrate body. "My jewels, please," he said, reaching down to Derek's neck to relieve him of the Egyptian artifacts.

Derek prayed for one last opportunity. He lunged once with his good arm. With a single motion he brought up his Eddie Bauer knife into Bagdasarian's exposed crotch, the one place unprotected by the Kevlar body vest. The serrated blade caught something fleshy. Then he twisted the blade.

Bagdasarian screamed dropping to the ground, writhing in pain, rolling and cursing with every breath. Clutching his groin blood spread between his fingers, saturating his pants.

Derek leaned forward picking up the automatic weapon dropped at his feet. He aimed it at the pathetic figure squirming and moaning on the ground. Somewhere behind him he could hear Kelly moan. Thank God, at least she was alive. He coughed up a mouth full of blood. How much longer did he have?

"Fuck you! Fuck you!" Bagdasarian squealed like a wounded pig. "I give up. See, I'm unarmed. You win. You are my arresting officer. I demand my constitutional rights. Get me to a doctor! Get me to a hospital, now," he babbled incessantly.

"I don't think I'm in any shape to help you," Derek answered. The weight in his gun hand was too much. He put the weapon down in is lap resting in between breaths.

Bagdasarian pushed himself upright against a rock five feet opposite Derek. His moans barely diminished. "Fine pair we are, huh?" he muttered. "Speaking of jewels, look what you did to mine," he laughed. He separated the cloth around his crotch and revealed a partially severed penis and testicle.

The man was insane, thought Derek. He looked at his enemy with surprising compassion. It had only been a few days ago that he fired his weapon in anger and struck another human being. That wound was only in a foot. The worst injury he had ever previously inflicted was a bloody nose on some hoodlum from the Flint district years ago as a beat cop. He had never stabbed anyone before. There was something very personal about violating a human body with a cold piece of steel. Something very satisfying as well, he thought. Conflicting emotions oozed and seeped like the wounds Bagdasarian had inflicted on his own body, his own psyche.

"I hope you and Kelly live a long and happy life together," Bagdasarian said in between a deep groan. "By the way, if she has a baby within the next nine months, it's going to be mine!" He was still taking pleasure in mentally torturing his captor.

The implication was not lost on Derek even in his impaired state of mind. The colors inside the cave danced surreally within his brain. The shadows on the walls assumed the shape of faces. For a moment he was convinced he could see and hear his dead friends calling him. Was he about to die? Derek looked into Bagdasarian's eyes. All he saw was cocky self-confidence and hatred against an inferior. He thought of what pain Kelly suffered at the man's hands. Derek's hesitation was replaced with resolve. Elevating the gun, he squeezed the trigger of Bagdasarian's weapon once. The single round struck Bagdasarian in the head. He stopped moving forever.

"Now you're under arrest."

Fall River, Massachusetts
November 7th

"Take a deep breath in and hold it." The female x-ray tech stepped behind the portable machine to the full length of the control cord. A lead apron protected another white-coated student at the bedside helping to lift the patient's left arm out of the way. A high-pitched beep signaled the x-ray was taken. "Thank you, sir. You can breathe now. Just lean forward a bit so we can get the cassette out, please." Derek felt several pairs of hands giving him an extra boost. He maneuvered his one good arm against the back of the hospital bed off the metal frame of the x-ray cassette. "Mom, you're embarrassing me. You're almost seventy years old. Don't try to lift me. I can do it by myself."

Alice Ekizian glared at her son. "If you were all right, you wouldn't be here. Besides, where does it say a mother stops being a mother when she turns seventy? George, tell him he should be more grateful," she appealed to her husband.

The elder Ekizian sat quietly in the corner staring at the World Federation Wrestling grudge match on TV. "Yes, Alice. Derek, be more respectful to your mother," he said without taking his eyes off the screen. "We may be old, but we're not dead. Remember, once we were like you. Someday, you are definitely going to be like us, unless of course you decide to get shot again."

The appearance of the attending physician and his entourage of students interrupted the editorializing. "Mrs. Ekizian, Mr. Ekizian," acknowledged the impeccably groomed John Brady with a smile. He turned towards the patient. "How are we doing today?" he asked Derek.

"We are doing just fine. Can you take out this damn chest tube and Foley?"

Alice spoke up again. "Derek! Where did you learn to talk like that! We never brought you up that way. It's those police characters you hang around with. Now if you became a doctor like Dr. Brady, here, you wouldn't have been shot in the first place."

"Yes, mom." If there were a hole he could crawl in, he would have. "What's the verdict, doc?"

"Actually, I do have good news for you," Brady said. "We're going to take both of them out right now; unless of course you give your parents, here, a hard time. Then maybe I'll leave them in a few more days for punishment."

Derek was surrounded. Well-intentioned but less then gentle

hands pushed, poked and prodded him as they maneuvered various tubes and catheters out of his body. Then others strapped, taped and stitched any residual leaks from the offending orifices or artificial violations of his flesh. "Hey folks, are we done yet?" he asked impatiently.

The foley catheter came out last. "This won't hurt a bit," Brady said taking a particularly evil satisfaction in removing the catheter himself.

That was the last straw. Derek pulled the sheets around his waist. "Jesus Christ! Doesn't anyone have anything else better to do then stare at my pecker! Out! Everyone out!" he commanded. He watched the students and even his parents leave in grumpy single file.

"We'll be back tomorrow," the elder Ekizian said.

Brady interrupted their farewell. "If you do, it's going to be as volunteers in the gift shop. I'm discharging your son today." He scribbled a few instructions handing them to the charge nurse.

Kelly entered the room just as everyone was leaving. "Hi, Mom and Dad Ekizian." She leaned over and gave Derek's parents a kiss on the cheeks.

"See, our almost-daughter-in-law can give us a kiss but you're too much of a big shot to kiss your own mother," Alice complained. "I knew there was a reason I liked you so much, honey. Just be careful of him today. He has quite a bite."

"Alice, *ga paveh,* enough!" the Ekizian patriarch bellowed.

"Oh, George...." their voices disappearing down the hallway together in constant squabble.

They were alone at last. Entering the room Kelly closed the door behind her. She walked to the window and placed a large box on the windowsill, then sat on the hospital bed on Derek's good side, leaned over and gave him a kiss on the lips. "Yucka. You'd better get some mouthwash. You've got maggot breath."

"Please, please don't use that word around me ever again," Derek begged stroking her fingers. "What do we have this time?" he asked looking at the box on the window ledge. "Chocolates? Sushi?"

"I brought this back from Canada just for you. Here open it," Kelly said, using a small pocketknife from her key chain to help him split the tape. Reaching inside the box she removed a blue Lands End backpack and placed it on Derek's lap.

He recognized it instantly. "You're kidding!"

Kelly stared into Derek's eyes. They were bonded forever.

"No joke. I've sat on this a whole week waiting for you to get well enough so we can open this together. There are certain perks you get as a doctor, you know. Sort of like the cops getting a free cup of coffee at Dunkin' Donuts. By the time the Royal Canadian police arrived at your drama in the caves, I had you half patched up. I think I may have actually saved your life this time. There was so much blood everywhere that all they were interested in was what I could tell them. They never paid attention to what I had slung over my shoulders."

"You're a better man then I, Gunga Din," Derek teased. "If the rolls were reversed, I wouldn't have given you a second thought. I'd be sitting somewhere in Tahiti just about now."

"Hardly. You had your chance before Montmorency and you didn't take it. You're stuck with me forever, buddy," Kelly laughed. She was about to give him a jab in the ribs but wisely thought better of it.

Slowly they opened the zipper of the backpack hand in hand. Peeling away layers of bubble wrap, a large object slowly emerged - a spectacular golden crown. Ancient Egyptian motifs came to life as he rotated the treasure in his hands. The Uraeus, the royal cobra oriented the front from the back. The face of a falcon blended underneath, two sockets empty of life. No wonder men would kill for this, thought Derek staring at it in awe.

Kelly reached her hands back up around her neck. Unbuttoning the top of her blouse, she removed the two jewels Derek carried with him in his hunt for the madman. Slowly she slid them into place on either side of the crown. They were a perfect fit. The crown was now whole.

"You are truly amazing," Derek said. "I'm not sure which one of you is more beautiful."

"Thanks, I needed that," Kelly replied. "Come on. We're getting out of here. I'm going to take care of you from now on."

"Great! What's for dinner? I'm starving. This hospital food is awful."

"I've got some shish kebob and pilaf cooking on the grill. You're mother has been teaching me a few things. She says I'm not bad for an *odar*, a non-Armenian. Even your long lost grandmother, Amelia, would be proud of me. What do you want for dessert?"

Derek held her hand tightly in his own. Their fingers interlocked as one. They were a perfect match. "Breakfast," he said without missing a beat.